THE BLACK WIFE EFFECT BOOK 3

The 7-Day Hitch

T.L. MARTIN

CONTENT WARNINGS

Well, here we are, friend. The final chapter of *The Black Wife Effect* series. You've laughed, gasped, side-eyed, and maybe even yelled "WHAT?!" at the pages—probably more than once. And through it all, you've stuck with me, and with the unforgettable trio that is *The Cockpit Chix*.

First, thank you. Seriously. This wild, witty, emotionally tangled ride wouldn't be what it is without readers like you who embraced the chaos and leaned into the love (and the morally gray decisions). What started as a cheeky intro to my dark romance world turned into a story—and a book club—that took on a life of its own.

Now, before we dive into Charlie and Xavier's final chapter, here's your heads-up: this story includes **mentions** of sensitive topics. They are not front and center, and they don't define the story—but they are there, tucked quietly into the corners of these characters' lives.

Mentions include:

- Grief and Loss

- Miscarriage

- Classism and Racial Reckoning

These themes are handled with care and minimal detail, and are ultimately overshadowed by the core of this book: Charlie and Xavier's messy, magnetic, and deeply human journey toward love, healing, and trust.

So if you need a moment, take it. Your well-being always comes first. But if you're ready—grab a drink, channel your inner Cockpit Chix, and buckle up. Because love, like a book club meeting with these three, rarely goes according to plan... and that's half the fun.

With gratitude and mischief,

T.L. Martin

Author, Chaos Curator, and Dark Romance Devotee

CONTENTS

PROLOGUE

Charlie

Fifteen Years Old

"Shh! Be quiet before he hears you!"

Geneva and I crouch behind the old school building, whispering and giggling like two criminals staking out a crime scene.

We should be home getting ready, but snooping on our English teacher, Mr. Gary, takes priority. Nobody knows anything about him. He barely speaks in class, hands out endless reading assignments, and when our class gets out of hand, he doesn't yell—he just plays the *Peanuts* theme on repeat until we quiet down. It's weird. He's weird. And nobody knows anything about him.

So naturally, Neva and I had the genius idea to peek into his backyard and see what he does when he's not torturing us with piles of homework.

Okay, fine. It was my idea. But Neva was just as eager.

Which is why we're out here now, binoculars in hand, watching his little brick house behind the school like two detectives on the brink of cracking a case.

"You think you're gonna kiss him?" Geneva asks out of nowhere, yanking me out of my very serious surveillance mode.

I gag dramatically. "Ew! No! Why would I do that?"

Geneva shrugs. "I don't know! I thought that's what you're supposed to do. I see your brother kissing Jenny Morris all the time... with *tongue*."

I make a face. "Well, you don't have to worry about that with me and Lucas. He barely looks at me, and I could care less about him."

Geneva flashes me a knowing smile. "Mmm-hmm. That's what you *say* now. Just wait. There's gotta be something special about kissing with tongue, 'cause it seems to make Jenny Morris crazy!"

We both collapse into laughter, our shoulders shaking as we try not to be too loud in case Mr. Gary hears us and calls the cops—or worse, gives us extra homework.

"Well, Miles said he's gonna rub my booty tonight at the ball and I told him he could. Maybe we might kiss, too!"

"Neva!" I gasp. "You are so fast!"

She shrugs. "I'm just mature. Don't hate!"

I roll my eyes, and we both collapse into laughter again. "You are so nasty!" I say, smacking her playfully.

After a minute, Geneva straightens, brushing dirt off her dress. "We better head home before our mothers send a search party."

I wave her off. "I can't wait for this to be over. I'm just gonna throw my hair in a bun and slap on that monstrosity of a tiara."

"Don't even remind me!" Geneva groans. "I love my dress, but my mama will not let me get out of wearing Mother Dear's big ass crown."

I snort. "I'm sure it won't be *that* bad."

Geneva levels me with a look. "Well, my butt-whoopin' will be if I don't get home."

With that, she hops onto her bike and speeds off.

"I'll see you in a little while!" I call after her.

I should follow her lead. Should get up and go home, too. But Mr. Gary still hasn't made an appearance, and I need to see what this man does when he thinks no one's watching. So I stay put a little longer, eyes locked on his front door, waiting for the mystery to unfold.

The sun must have been stronger than I thought because I passed out. But as it starts to set, a jolt of panic rips through me, snapping me upright—realization slamming into me like a freight train.

"*Shit!* I'm gonna be *so* late!"

I take off running, already bracing for the wrath of my mother when I walk through the door.

"Charlesetta Anastasia Sinclair!"

And here we go.

"What on earth is wrong with your hair!?" my mother yells, her southern twang shrill enough to cut through the thick, muggy air. I'm *very* late. And I'm certain this lady is going to murder me.

I barely make it into the foyer before she's already throwing a fit, her manicured hand flailing in my direction like I'm some kind of disaster. I glance down at myself and—okay, maybe she has a point.

My once-crisp white tank is now smudged with streaks of dirt, and my cut up jean shorts have seen better days–especially since they probably haven't been washed in a week. My boots? Scuffed and splattered in mud from taking a shortcut through the river out back from Neva's house. But I don't let any of it stop me from standing tall and accepting whatever punishment I have coming. Daddy always says it's best to face your consequences head on with your chin up.

"Hey, Mama!" I say sheepishly, trying to flash my best innocent smile.

"Don't you 'Hey, Mama' me!" she snaps, storming over. "The ball is supposed to start in fifteen minutes, and you look like a field rat!"

"Cynthia," Big Daddy chides in his soft but commanding tone, stepping between us like a human buffer. "The child is here now. No use in getting all worked up."

She ignores him. "Where have you been?"

"Me and Neva were—"

She doesn't give me a chance to finish. "Do I look like I'm Geneva's mother to you?"

"No, Mama! But–"

She doesn't even stop to breathe. "If you want to go live with them and give up the life you have with us here, you go right ahead! Plenty of starvin' children in Ethiopia *wish* they had it as good as you, young lady!"

"They haven't had to eat your cookin'," I mumble under my breath. "They'd choose starvation."

Big Daddy clears his throat and jumps in before Mama has a chance to knock me into the middle of next week.

"Okay, ladies," he cautions, turning to me and wiping a stray smear of dirt from my cheek. I hear Mama huff behind my back and I roll my eyes. "Can you be ready in ten minutes, Charlie Chaplin?"

I grin, the warmth of the nickname settling in my chest like an old familiar song. He gave it to me when I was little, back when I thought I'd be the next great pianist, banging on the ivory keys with reckless enthusiasm. My mother hated it then, and she hates it now—hates that I shortened my name into something "boyish," something that refuses to conform to her vision of what a debutante should be.

"Yes, Big Daddy," I nod enthusiastically. Sometimes, I feel like he's the only one who really gets me. "I'm gonna take a quick shower, throw my hair in a bun, and put on my first outfit."

He leans down and kisses the top of my head. "Then you'd better get to it."

As I hurry toward the stairs, I hear my mother mutter under her breath, "I don't know why you coddle her like that. Never holding her accountable."

"She's just a child, Cynthia."

My mother sucks her teeth. "She's a menace in combat boots and cut-off 'Daisy Duke' shorts, Joseph."

I hear him chuckle under his breath. "Well, she's *our* menace, and I refuse to make her follow a path she refuses."

The Sinclair family is as uptight as the name suggests. Descendants of slaves, my great-granddaddy bought this very land that once held our ancestors captive and turned it into something new. He spent the first thirty days as the owner of that plantation tearing down every structure that bore the memories and cries of slavery. Then, he began building something for his family—for **legacy**.

During Prohibition, he made and sold the best moonshine on this side of the Mississippi, landing himself in jail a few times for transporting it across state lines. But that never stopped him—he just got smarter.

Daddy used to tell me stories of how my great-granddaddy would joke that white folks were going to need all the alcohol they could get because they had no clue how to function without slaves to beat or do their housework. So, instead of risking more jail time, my great-granddaddy started experimenting with different spirits, thinking maybe he'd open a saloon one day after Prohibition was lifted. My great-grandmother had a different idea in mind.

One afternoon, as they walked through town, my great-grandmother's sharp eyes caught sight of a towering sign—a well-known European wine brand, its name dripping with prestige. No one remembers exactly what it said, only that the moment she saw it, everything shifted. She stopped in her tracks, tilting her head as realization struck.

In that instant, she saw beyond the small dreams of a saloon or a restaurant. She envisioned something far greater. A **dynasty**.

"You could do that," she said to him, her voice steady, her conviction unshakable. "Not just sell drinks. Build a name." She was a visionary before most folks really knew what that meant.

She didn't just offer him a vision—she breathed life into it, planting the seed of ambition deep in his soul. She spent nights sitting beside him, mapping out dreams by candlelight, whispering affirmations in his ear when doubt threatened to creep in. Because that's what a good Black woman does—she sees the greatness in her man before the world ever catches on.

She worked with him, pushed him, stood beside him through every late night and failed batch, every setback that could've broken a lesser man. She didn't let him settle for "good enough." They weren't just making liquor; they were making history.

Just like my great granddaddy predicted, Prohibition was nothing more than a temporary roadblock—a mere pause in what was destined to be a **dynasty**. The moment the restrictions were lifted, he wasted no time. He threw open the doors to his land, inviting the curious and the connoisseurs alike to taste something different, something bold. His signature bourbon. A spirit so rich, so masterfully crafted, it didn't just warm the throat—it commanded attention.

Word spread like wildfire, whispers turning into demand, and before long, Sinclair Spirits was born. The first Black-owned liquor brand of its kind—not just a business, but a statement. A symbol of resilience, brilliance, and the kind of legacy that doesn't just last generations—it redefines them.

Today, our family is filthy rich, but I've never wanted any part of it. Wealth, in our world, isn't just about comfort—it's about appearances. About keeping up with rich white folks who sip imported champagne and pretend they invented class, while my mother grooms my brother and me like prized ponies for society's grand stage. *Or pigs for slaughter.* Sometimes I can't tell the difference.

I hear a sharp bang on the door. "Charlesetta? Are you about done in there? We have five minutes to get you to the event stage!"

Today is the day my mother introduces me to society in the time-old tradition of the Debutante Ball. A tradition that runs deep in Black culture, especially in the South. It started as a way to uplift and showcase Black excellence in a world that constantly tried to diminish it. Generations of Black families used these balls to introduce young women to society, setting them on paths of prestige, education, and legacy-building.

It was meant to be a symbol of grace and class. But to me, it's just another way my mother tries to shape me into something I'm not.

I hate it. The suffocating expectations. The carefully curated performances. My mother insists I be the perfect debutante—the kind of girl who smiles on cue, marries a doctor, and quietly fades into the background as some man's ornamental wife. No matter how much I fight her on it, she insists I'm just going through a phase.

Then there's my father. He's not as controlling, but he's just as blind in his own way. He assumes I'll follow *his* script, get a business degree, and seamlessly step into the empire that is Sinclair Spirits.

But I don't want that either. I don't want any of what they've *prepared* for me. I want my own path—one they don't choose, but one they respect when I choose it for myself.

"Charlesetta!" Mama yells, banging again with more force. "We *cannot* have Lucas Ballentine waiting! It's a big deal he agreed to escort you!"

I roll my eyes at my mother's barely contained excitement over the fact that a *Ballentine* is escorting me to the ball.

"I'm almost done, Mama!" I call over my shoulder, forcing as much humility into my voice as I can manage as I pull my white slip over my head.

Lucas Ballentine is the man my mother *designed* for me—the one she prayed for, schemed for, all but *manifested* into existence.

He was practically bred for greatness—the flawless son of Dr. and Mrs. Andrew Ballentine. Polished. Poised. The heir to an empire built on power, wealth, and carefully crafted expectations.

He's had a crush on me since the third grade, always trailing behind me like a devoted little shadow, waiting for the day I might finally give him a chance. But I've never wanted to. Not really. And for a long time, I couldn't quite put into words why.

It's not that he isn't attractive—because he is. Tall, caramel-skinned, effortlessly refined, always perfectly put together. But he's boring. Predictable. The human equivalent of a well-executed game plan—strategic, calculated, safe.

I don't even like football, but even *I* can tell he never strays from the plays on the field. Never spontaneous. My brother always jokes that Lucas looks like he was born in a blazer and his first words were probably accompanied by a firm handshake and a perfectly practiced, "Pleasure to meet you."

And that's exactly why he could never be for me.

Because a man like Lucas Ballentine would spend his whole life trying to give me a future most women would die for—without realizing it would suffocate me in the process.

I brush my hair into a bun and slick it back with gel and hair grease before applying this obnoxious crystal crown. I take a step back from the mirror, letting my eyes drag over the walking contradiction staring back at me. And I almost smile.

The gown is a masterpiece, I'll give them that. Ivory tulle and beaded lace, stitched together to create something straight out of a royal fairytale. The bodice hugs my torso like a second skin, the sheer sleeves dotted with delicate crystals that catch the light every time I move. High at the neckline, a cascade of fabric roses bloom across my chest—soft, feminine, and just ostentatious enough to remind everyone in the room exactly who I'm supposed to be tonight.

My best friend Geneva has been counting down the days to tonight since we were seven years old, and the mere thought of her brings a full-fledged smile to my face. We're best friends, but we couldn't be more opposite. Where I roll my eyes at the pomp and tradition, Neva lives for it—she's dreamed of this moment, of gliding across the ballroom in the perfect gown, tiara sparkling under the chandeliers, basking in the attention like she was born for it.

I even let her pick out the fabric for my dress because she cared about it way more than I did. And as I grab the heavy, glittering tiara that both my mother and aunt wore to their debuts, a grin tugs at my lips. Neva got stuck with her grandmother's tiara, and that thing is a monstrosity—bigger, shinier, and somehow more obnoxious than mine. I can already hear her dramatic sighs about trying to balance it on her head all night.

And just like that, the thought of my best friend makes this whole ridiculous evening a little more bearable.

I hear another tap on the door. Lighter. "Charlie, I'm quite certain your mother is gonna bust a blood vessel any moment now. You 'bout done?"

My perfect bun makes my cheekbones look sharper, my posture impossibly straighter, like I'm molded into a version of myself that almost fits. Almost.

I press my fingers into the bodice, smoothing it down as I let out a breath.

"Yes, Big Daddy," I say.

I look beautiful. There's no denying that.

But I still don't look like *me.*

CHAPTER ONE

Charlie

Present Day

    "What it is, ho? What's up? Every good girl needs a little thug."

We belt out *Doechii* at the top of our lungs, pretending we're about to settle into our next smutty book for book club—but really, we're too deep in our shenanigans to care.

With Tika and Timantha still glowing from their newlywed highs, the conversation has been less about books and more about Timantha's borderline obsession with Meghan *Duchess of Sussex* Markle as she settles into the massive new house she and Will just bought.

Meanwhile, Autika is on a mission to get pregnant before summer so she can rock a baby bump all winter long.

"I refuse to be hot and fat during spring or summer," she declared, flipping her braids over her shoulder. "Besides, winter fashion is way better for pregnant Black women. Cozy, chic, and no one has to see my swollen ankles."

We're at Timantha's place this time, which means fewer rules and way more freedom. And drinks. A lot more drinks.

"Can I just say *Doechii* is basically a version of all of us from college and through our reckless twenties?" Autika announces, spinning in the middle of Will and Timantha's cigar room, where we're dancing like we don't have to work in the morning.

"Yes!" Timantha shouts, throwing her hands up. "She is *all* of us!"

"Who is *us*?" I ask, raising a brow in mock offense.

Autika sucks her teeth, hands on her hips. "Okay, fine. Me and Timmy had fun in college. I don't know what the hell *you* were doing."

"Murder," Timantha deadpans.

Laughter explodes between us.

They never miss an opportunity to tease me about my super secret past life or hint at my *body count.*

"Shut up!" I gasp between breaths. "I was just studying my ass off to make sure I never had to end up back home, living with my parents."

"You mean in the *big house in the sky*?" Autika teases. "I swear, you're the only rich kid I know who actively runs away from millions and a life of luxury."

I exhale sharply. "You just don't get it."

"You're right, I don't," she says, shrugging. "But feel free to trade places with me anytime. I'd be happy to get a bird's-eye view of the situation. *Especially* with that fine-ass brother of yours."

"Eww!" I groan. "Please *never* bring up my brother and his attractiveness in front of me again."

Timantha gives Autika a *you're out of your damn mind* look. "Especially with how crazy Justice is about you. You better be quiet before he picks up on some subliminal signal that you're talking about another man and shows up here like a Black Avenger to snatch your ass up."

We all cackle, the visual way too easy to imagine.

"Speaking of snatching asses," I say, stretching my arms overhead, "since we are at book club, are we actually gonna talk about this book? Some of us have work in the morning."

Autika groans dramatically. "Uggh! All you *do* is work these days! I thought going into the private sector meant you'd finally have *more* time for us. Now we barely get you—just scraps before you run back to whatever client drama has you locked down."

"What? I *love* my job," I say, a little too defensively.

Autika narrows her eyes. "Yeah, but it seems like you're working to avoid something, not because you're actually enjoying it."

"Whatever. That's not true."

My phone buzzes before they can dig deeper, and I grab it like a lifeline. Because if I'm honest? I *am* working more these days. Burying myself in my clients' problems so I don't have to deal with my own.

Ms. Lorraine and Will stroll in with a tray of freshly baked cookies, but I barely register it. I'm too caught up in my screen, my thumb hovering over a notification.

"That smells *so* good," Autika moans, already reaching for one.

"White chocolate chip and macadamia nut," Ms. Lorraine announces proudly. "Special recipe I got from Kiyah at Anastasia's office."

"What were you doing at Stasi's job, Ms. Lorraine?" Autika asks, lifting a perfectly arched brow.

My friends don't know *everything* about my life, but they do know no one just *pops in* to my office. If you're walking through the doors of the Fury Alliance, you're either neck-deep in drama... or dragging someone else into it.

There's no in-between.

Ms. Lorraine glances around like she's checking for wiretaps. "Messing around with these YN's, baby. This little boy came into my house, ate up all my Whole Foods groceries, then had the nerve to ask why I don't keep grape soda in stock like I run a corner store."

"Girl!" I cut in, barely holding back my rage. "And then he tried to steal her identity—so he could buy his main girl a diamond necklace!"

The ladies gasp.

Timantha lifts a brow and silently mouths, YN?

I sigh and nod toward her. "Young Ninjas, Tim. Emphasis on ninjas."

She's the one who banned us from saying the N-word—even as a reclaimed term—so we've started swapping in alternatives to keep from disappointing our resident queen of Black consciousness.

"Oh!" Timantha says, eyes wide. "It's crazy the stuff people come up with these days. Why can't we just call Mama a cougar like we used to?"

"Because times have changed, Tim—and that term's not even new," I reply, giving her a look.

The only reason I even know the term is because of my nephew. He texts me all the cool new sayings and trends. When I worked in the field, he actually helped me stay modern and relevant.

Autika groans and tosses her hands up. "Why can't we just say what the N stands for? I only keep it cute out of respect for Will's house. But y'all ninjas are doing *too much*. I'm not letting anyone take another thing Black folks have claimed and flipped into power."

Respectability politics have never been Autika's ministry.

"I *would* feel more stupid," Ms. Lorraine continues, "but the boy was hung. Had me hollerin' all over that house Tim and Will bought me."

Timantha shrieks. "*Mama!* Ew!"

Me and Autika lock eyes, then double over in laughter.

When Ms. Lorraine came to me for help, she swore Timantha couldn't know. She was embarrassed. Ashamed she'd been finessed by a boy who still used "lol" in actual conversation and insisted on calling Ms. Lorraine "bro."

I told her the truth: even the smartest women get caught up in situations like this. What matters is the comeback—and having someone like me in your corner to make sure it never happens again. Once she let me loop in Timantha, the girl went full Scorched Earth. Ready to roll up on his place with a baseball bat and a hoodie.

I went for something a little more... creative.

I hacked his phone, transferred every last cent back to Ms. Lorraine, then deepfaked a full apology video where he tearfully confessed to being a "clout-chasing man-child with the emotional depth of a teaspoon." I *airdropped it to every iPhone within 200 feet of his workplace*—Starbucks, bus stop, nail salon. It was glorious.

Then I did what any mildly unhinged woman with a Wi-Fi connection and a moral compass set to "petty" would do—I made him famous. Uploaded that same apology video to Timantha's dating app under a profile with *his* name, *his* face, and a bio that just said, *"Ask me about the necklace."*

Could he get mad? Sure. Try to sue? Maybe. But every upload traced right back to his own IP address.

Oops.

Now, we all reach for a still-warm cookie Ms. Lorraine and Will have just brought in.

Timantha narrows her eyes at Will. "Husband? By 'special recipe,' does my mama mean *mean and green?*"

I bite down a smirk. She definitely means weed.

Will takes a cautious bite of a cookie, chews, and shrugs. "Would I be eating it if it had weed in it?"

The way he smirks tells us absolutely nothing.

Timantha bursts out laughing. "Okay, ladies, it's safe. Will vowed never to touch my mama's weed pastries again after last time. We ended up calling the team doctor because Will swore he was having a heart attack—while doing laps back and forth in the pool!"

"I also recall him having a serious case of the runs!" Ms. Lorraine adds, completely unbothered.

"Mama!"

"Ms. Lorraine!"

Will and Timantha shout at the same time.

I finally glance up from my phone, unable to hold back a laugh at the madness unfolding around me. But just as I start to enjoy the moment, my phone buzzes again. And again. I sigh, already annoyed.

It's my brother blowing up my messages.

Elijah: You have your read receipts on, buster. Answer your fucking phone.

Me: I'm busy right now, ass breath! I'll call you later.

Elijah: Yo mama.

I snort.

Me: I'm telling her as soon as I see her.

Elijah: Which will be sooner rather than later. Grandmommy isn't so good.

My stomach drops.

Me: How long does she have?

Elijah: Maybe two weeks?

Me: Ok. I'll make arrangements to come.

Elijah: You better.

Me: *Middle finger emoji.*

"Everything okay, Stasi?" Autika asks, pulling me back into the present.

I clear my throat. "Yeah. Just my brother giving me the latest update on Grandmommy."

Will, ever the gentleman, passes a drink to his wife before turning to me. "If you need the jet to fly home, we've got you, Stasi."

Why couldn't Xavier have been more like him?

"Thanks, Will. But that won't be necessary. My brother says she's got at least two weeks, so I have plenty of time to make plans." I force a smile, trying to shake off the weight settling in my chest.

Plus, if my mama found out I flew private, she'd insist I try to take Timantha down and steal her man.

"Well, I'll leave you ladies to your book club or whatever," Will says, leaning down to press an affectionate kiss to Timantha's forehead.

We watch him walk away, collectively swooning over the way he adores her.

"Must be nice," Ms. Lorraine says with a sigh.

"And *is!*" Timantha shouts, making us all laugh.

I remember when Timantha and Will first got together—how he stayed out of sight, barely showed up, and always seemed more standoffish than anything else. For a while, we thought he just didn't like her friends. But once Tim explained he had social anxiety and needed time to warm up to us, we gave him grace.

Now, he's *one of us*. He jumps into our debates, makes sure we eat when we've had more cabernet than carbs, and offers up his private jet anytime we need to go see about family.

I love what they've built, what they've become. And I can't help but wonder what a love like *that* could feel like for me.

Ms. Lorraine hands me a cookie, shaking her head. "They don't make 'em like that anymore. Especially these Black men."

"Speak for yourself," Autika fires back. "Justice is a *good* Black man. Just because the older generations couldn't see past Frederick Douglass' triflin' ass doesn't mean all Black men are bad."

Ms. Lorraine falls out laughing. "Touche, baby! Touche! Fred Douglass was the first fuck boy to ever walk this planet and be praised for it by other Blacks."

"See, that's why these men out here still defending the deplorable!" Timantha adds. "Once a Black hero has a pedestal, it's hard to make him pay for his sins."

"That's true and all but, I'm with Tika." I say, pointing at her. "I refuse to believe there are no more good Black men just because the very worst of them happen to be of the variety seems to keep getting exposed. I just hope there's at least *one* more Black man with an island and a boat."

Autika and Timantha exchange a look. A very *pointed* look.

"What?" I shriek.

Autika shrugs. "It just sounds like you're trying to Black-face Xavier Darcy."

"I'm sorry, *what* now?"

"Like you're trying to transplant a Black man into the spot that's already occupied by a *white* one," Timantha clarifies, arching a brow.

"One that is absolutely *bonkers* about you, boo," Autika adds.

I suck my teeth. "Whatever! Xavier is *nice* and all, but we've already established he's not for me. Does he have certain amenities I enjoy? *Yes.* And I've just decided I'd like those same amenities... *in someone else.*"

I take another sip of my drink. "Besides! Are we forgetting I never wanted a relationship to begin with? I enjoy escaping into these smut stories with ya'll but ya'll know I've never been the settling down type! Any talks of Xavier Darcy are pointless."

"Mmm-hmm." Timantha folds her arms. "You're going against the natural flow of your fantasies, Stasi."

I frown. "What's that supposed to mean?"

Timantha exhales, as if she's preparing to drop something *heavy*. "Look, all of us have a story—how we met our person, how we got engaged. And *every* single one of those stories started here, in the book club."

I tilt my head. "I don't follow."

"Over the past year, whenever we've met and talked about our fantasies, something... *happened*. Some kind of magic unlocked, and we ended up meeting the exact men we dreamed of and talked about among each other." She pauses, giving me a knowing look. "And I *can't* help but point out the fact that, right before my bachelorette party, *you* spoke Xavier Darcy into existence."

"Yeah, and now you're avoiding him like he *isn't* possibly the best thing for you," Autika suggests.

I scoff. "How do you figure he's the *best* thing for me? Did you forget that the man is *screwed up*? That he pulls me in just to push me away the second I get too close? That I don't want a man?"

Timantha's voice softens. "No. But tell me—who *hasn't* had to work through something to get to their happily ever after? Who hasn't ended up entangled in something they never saw coming, only to end up on an adventure of a lifetime?"

"Not you," I say pointedly, narrowing my eyes at her. "You and Will didn't have to work out anything other than which bank account he'd add your name to!"

"Well, *I* did have some shit to work through!" Autika yells, and we all crack up, recalling the very humiliating way her ex left her...for a man. He was fine, though.

Timantha rolls her eyes. "Nobody's comparing traumas or difficulties. All I'm saying is—don't shut your heart off to Xavier so fast. Not without *being sure*.Not without really examining *why* you're avoiding him so much. Why you're avoiding *wanting* him."

I take a bite of Ms. Lorraine's cookie, letting the buttery sweetness melt on my tongue while Timantha's words loop in my head like a cursed TikTok sound.

No. I'm not doing this.

Just because she and Tika are out here being disgustingly happy and in love doesn't mean it's supposed to happen for me and Xavier.

Some people get fireworks and soulmates.

Others get exciting escapades and situationships.

Guess which one I am?

I'm halfway to launching into a full protest when a ringtone cuts through the moment—*Drake*.

Not my phone. Tika and Timantha look equally confused at the sound.

I freeze. "Ms. Lorraine..." I gasp. "Did you unblock that little boy? All that work I did to get your money back!"

She snatches up her phone like it's on fire and bolts for the door.

"I just wanna see something!" she yells over her shoulder. "I *think* he's got my phone charger!"

And just as she hits the hallway—

"...and a big ole dick!"

The door slams. Silence.

I blink.

Timantha gags.

Autika drops her cookie.

And I swear I can hear the ancestors judging us all.

CHAPTER TWO

Xavier

I sink into the leather seat of my jet, stretching my legs as the faint hum of the engines fills the cabin. Across from me, Juliette, my publicist, and Nathan, my business manager, sit with their laptops open, their faces tight with concern.

"I need to know how bad this is," I say, exhaling slowly.

Juliette adjusts her glasses and glances at Nathan before flipping her screen around to face me. "It's bad, Xavier. And it's getting worse."

I lean forward, scanning the images on her screen. They're crisp, high-quality—whoever did this knew what they were doing.

Days away. That's all I have before SecureTomorrow goes public—before I change the game in an industry that's been robbing hardworking people blind for *years*.

I developed a fintech app that allows people to round up their change at participating stores and funnel those cents into community-driven life insurance plans. It's a simple idea with *massive* potential—giving families an opportunity to *finally* start building generational wealth. And, of course, financial institutions are pissed.

So now, they're playing dirty.

Cooked-up images. Manufactured scandals. Exes coming out of the woodwork with *heinous* accusations. All to derail *me*. To make me look like a fraud.

And now that I've given them something *real* to grab on to, their tactics have gotten worse.

"They aren't simply orchestrating a smear campaign," Juliette continues, scrolling through the first batch of photos. "They've launched a full-scale nuclear takedown. Deepfake videos, fake receipts, bullshit accusations. They're painting you as reckless, unethical—practically a sex addict."

"The type of sex addict women hate. Not the ones they send you to rehab for where you get fan mail," Nathan offers.

I grunt, unamused. "That's ironic."

Nathan lifts a brow. "How so?"

Juliette smirks, leaning back in her chair. "Ironic because he's being taken down for being a sex addict when the man avoids sex like the plague."

"Juliette!" I snap, practically embarrassed.

"It's Nathan! He's not going to tell anyone. Speaking of, I need to know exactly *how long* it's been, X?"

I drag my gaze to her. "That's none of your business."

Juliette arches a brow, arms crossing like she's preparing for battle. "My job is to keep your business in the black and this IPO on track.

That means *everything* that's hitting the media right now *is* my business. And we have two weeks to get ahead of this mess."

I grind my teeth. "Seven years. More or less."

Less if you count that one stupid night, but I don't volunteer that just yet. There's no need.

Nathan chokes so hard I half expect him to need the Heimlich. "Talk about them *dry* bones," he mutters under his breath.

Juliette clears her throat, visibly trying to suppress a reaction. "Okay. That's... um... excessive. Don't you think?"

"Yeah, why so long?" Nathan adds, his expression somewhere between amused and horrified.

I shift uncomfortably in my seat. "It's personal."

Juliette gives me a flat look. "It *was* personal. Now it's public, and we need to spin it before someone decides to turn your dry spell into a *headline*."

Nathan snickers. "Emphasis on the *head*."

Juliette ignores him, swiping through images on the screen. "Have there been any women who were offended that you wouldn't sleep with them?"

I frown. "Plenty, why?"

"Because. We need to show this whole takedown attempt is outdated and doesn't work on you because of your squeaky-clean *good guy* image. Even if you do carry the perception of being a bit of an asshole," she adds.

"I'm not an asshole. I'm introverted!"

Nathan hums. "I believe the last paper called you the *philanthropic brood in a Brooks Brothers tux*?"

"Thanks, Nathan," I say dryly, taking a sip of my scotch. "Memory like an elephant, that one."

Juliette keeps scrolling through the recent batch of leaked content, pausing at each photo or video for me to confirm, while Nathan mutters under his breath, "Seven years, man. I just feel like maybe you need to see someone about how *okay* you are without *fun* in your life. Seriously, how long are your showers?"

I exhale sharply. "Cool it or I'll banish you to commercial flights for a month."

That shuts him up. Nathan hates mixing and mingling with *commoners*.

The first photo Juliette shows me is a grainy shot of me in what looks like a dimly lit club, a woman pressed up against my side, her lips near my ear, my hand up her dress. The caption running with it makes it sound like I'm doing something scandalous, but I don't even recognize the place or the woman.

"Fake."

She swipes again.

This time, it's a video clip—grainy but clear enough. Me, supposedly stepping out of some luxury penthouse with a woman draped in a floor-length fur coat like she's auditioning to play the wife of Tony Soprano.

The caption practically screams *exclusive* and the context? Obvious. They're trying to paint me as the kind of man who drops cash on high-class escorts and calls it "business."

I scoff.

If they knew anything about me—anything real—they'd know a woman like that couldn't stoke my fire if she were dipped in gasoline.

"Fake."

Another swipe.

A series of intimate photos. Me, in bed, sheets pooled at my waist, the side of a woman's face visible as she sleeps against my chest. My jaw tightens. The lighting is dim and the angle is believable, but it's not me. It's some AI-generated version of me, crafted for the sole purpose of destruction.

"Fake."

It's a pattern. Each image, each video, carefully designed to fabricate a man who doesn't exist. A reckless, indulgent playboy with no control.

I don't even flinch—until Juliette stops at the last set of images.

My entire body stiffens.

These aren't fake.

They're very real.

I lean closer, my pulse kicking up as I take in the screen. The angle, the detail—whoever took these had *access*. Real proximity. And that's what makes it worse. Was I bugged? Who would give someone this level of access to me? To us?

One image shows me standing in a dimly lit hotel room, shirtless, a drink in my hand. The lighting is moody, casting long shadows, but the real problem isn't me—it's *her*.

She's in the background, sprawled across the bed, her back to the camera. The soft curves of her body are unmistakable. But what makes this a disaster is the tattoo.

Bold cursive, inked down the length of her spine.

The next image? My hands on her hips, pulling her against me. Her face isn't visible, but the unmistakable bob haircut that frames her face...Charlie.

My breath nearly stills as I scroll to the video, my chest tightening as I hit play. It's short—just a few seconds—but it's enough. The way I plunge into her, the way her body arches into me. It's *undeniable*. It's *us*.

My mind races. How the hell did someone get this close? How did they get *me* like this?

I grab my phone and dial the one man who can handle this.

Hayven Sally. The greatest hacker the world's never heard of, despite the fame of his family. Hayven is a man who can disappear you from the digital landscape or, just as easily, make you look like the devil himself.

He's also part owner of *The Fury Alliance*, an elite reputation management and private security firm that operates in the gray areas—cleaning up messes, burying scandals, and handling problems the traditional legal system is too slow or too corrupt to fix.

The call connects in seconds.

"X," Hayven answers, his voice laced with curiosity mixed with suspicion. "What's going on?"

"Just sent you an email. I need you to look into this for me."

There's a pause, just long enough for me to know he's already working the problem in his head.

"Does this have anything to do with why you're all over the news right now?"

I rub my temple and let out a loud breath. "You guessed it. Someone is trying to tank my IPO. They're coming after me with a smear campaign—deepfake videos, falsified reports, the works. But some of these?" I glance at the screen again, my stomach twisting. "They're real. And I have no idea how they got them."

There's silence on the other end as Hayven scrolls through everything I just sent him. Then his voice drops, low and wary.

"I don't understand," he says slowly and I can tell it's becoming apparent who else is in the photos. "Has *she* seen these?"

I stiffen, part of me wondering how he can tell it's Charlie since her face doesn't show up. But there's no time for my jealousy. I'll deal with that, her, later. "No. At least, I don't think so. Can you help?"

"I *think* we need to take this to *her* first," he mutters. "I don't want to move without her giving me the go-ahead. If I have to go deep, this will get *personal.*"

I let out a sharp breath. "I tried going to her first, but she won't take my calls, won't answer me on social media. I can't get a hold of her."

There's a long pause before Hayven chuckles, low and knowing.

"Oh, fuck. What did you do?"

I shake my head, jaw tight. "Not the time, brother. Seriously. *Not* the time."

Hayven exhales, tone shifting. "Alright. I'll handle it. I'll get Anastasia on board."

There's a pause. I can hear him clicking something in the background—probably pulling files. Then—"But while I've got you... does the name Lincoln Smith mean anything to you?"

I shake my head instinctively, even though he can't see me. "Not beyond what's public. News articles, business roundups. I know he's from the same town as me, operates in some of the same markets. But we've never crossed paths, not directly. Why?"

Hayven lets out a measured breath. The kind that says *things are getting weird.*

"I'm not sure. He was at a business summit I attended last week. Seemed smooth, polished—but I didn't like the whispers I heard. Now that your name's floating through the press, his keeps popping up in adjacent conversations. The timing feels... off."

I lean back, tension crawling up my spine. "Well, if anyone can get to the bottom of this—*all* of this—it's you. You and the team at The Fury."

"Yeah," he says slowly. "But now that Stasi's involved, we need to tread carefully."

That grabs my attention.

"I had to pull a lot of strings to get her in here without raising red flags," he continues. "If someone is dragging her into this mess, it has to be intentional and we need to move. Fast, but clean. No slipups."

I nod, already mapping out next steps in my head.

"Then let's pull her in. Whatever you need to do to get her onboard."

Because if anyone can help, if anyone *needs* to help me out of this, it's *her.*

I just hope she forgives me—for what I've already done.

And for what I'm *about* to do.

I look at Nathan and gesture toward the front of the plane. "Let the pilot know we're about to make a detour."

CHAPTER THREE

Charlie

The intercom on my desk crackles, cutting through the quiet in my office and I'm already irritated at the intrusion.

I wasn't supposed to be here today, but there were accounts I needed to hand over, instructions to leave before I headed home. Loose ends to tie up so no one needed me while I was gone.

Grandmommy has always been fashionably late, so she can wait a few more days for me to get back home.

Not that I'm actually excited to go home or anything. Because going home means splitting myself in two again. It means stepping back into the double life I've been living for the past fifteen years—one part super secret operative, the other part daughter, sister, girl who left and never fully came back.

I haven't even been home in a decade. And every time I do go back, I feel the same thing: distance. Like there's a pane of glass between me and the people who used to know me best.

To my family, I've always been the jet-setting business consultant—gliding through airports like they were second homes, advising corporate giants on how to scale, streamline, and dominate. It's not exactly the version of me they pictured, but it's the version I knew they could understand. The polished, successful woman they raised me to be.

Mostly.

My mother would've preferred I married a doctor and popped out a boatload of babies. My father's convinced I'll take over the family business someday. And somewhere in between their expectations is *me*. The real me. The version I'm still learning how to be.

Because the truth? It's a little more complicated.

Before I even walked across the stage at North Kensington University, I was recruited into an elite government agency—someone flagged my test scores, and the next thing I knew, I was sitting in a briefing room instead of a job interview. I couldn't explain it, but as soon as the opportunity was presented to me, it felt like it was meant for me.

I started as an analyst. But quickly proved myself and became something else. Something fierce.

A field operative. The kind who handled high-risk rescues, deep-cover infiltrations, and black ops that never made the news. The kind of missions where knowing too much could get you killed—and my job was to make sure it didn't get that far. And let's just say, I'm good at my job.

My life was classified. My real job? A ghost. And my family? *Completely* in the dark.

Every time I go home, it's an Olympic-level performance—dodging questions, spinning lies, crafting elaborate client stories that don't exist. *Client confidentiality,* I always say when they push too hard.

My father eats it up, convinced I'm some corporate powerhouse, making connections that will eventually bring me back to Sinclair Spirits. According to him, all this supposed business experience was just me biding my time before coming home and falling in line with the family empire. I let him believe it because it's easier than the alternative. If he, or my mother, ever found out the truth—what I've really done, who I've really been—it would kill them. Then my mother would return from the grave to kill me.

Now, I've traded government secrets for private-sector chaos, working at The Fury Alliance. A few months in, and I'm still adjusting. I don't take orders well, and I'm not used to working with people who actually want to know my real name. *Or the real me.*

"Anastasia, I have Xavier Darcy on the line for you?" Grace's voice comes through, smooth but hesitant, like she's bracing for impact.

I frown. Grace is Logan Fury's assistant. "Why is he calling Logan's line?"

"Because he says he couldn't get through on yours, ma'am." There's a waver in her tone, like she understands exactly what's happening here but doesn't want to be caught in the crossfire.

My grip tightens on my pen. *That arrogant asshole.* He knows I won't want to jeopardize his relationship with any of my bosses, so he made sure to call Logan's line. Even if I don't report to Logan directly. *Slick bastard.*

I inhale sharply, forcing down the irritation creeping into my voice. "Put him through, please."

"Will do, Anastasia."

I can't seem to escape him.

A little over a month ago, Xavier and I were best man and maid of honor to my best friend Autika and Justice for their impromptu Las Vegas wedding. The rest of the details of that weekend are pretty fuzzy from all the drinking and partying, but what I do remember clearly is that Xavier is not the man for me. But he hasn't wanted to take no for an answer.

Xavier Darcy has been relentless—calling, texting, refusing to take the hint. I thought I was rid of him, thought he'd finally given up, but just when I started to breathe easy, his messages picked back up. He's even resorted to reaching out on social media, as if sliding into my DMs might change my mind.

But it won't.

I want nothing to do with him.

I glance down at my phone, watching as the call gets transferred. The red button blinks, demanding my attention. With a sigh, I press it.

"You have thirty seconds, Xavier."

Silence. Then a breath—deep, slow, like he's relieved just to hear my voice. And I might be happy to hear his too.

Fuck you, nipples.

"No *Mr. Darcy* today, Charlie?"

I suck my teeth. "It's Anastasia and I'm extremely busy, Xavier. What is it that I can do for you?"

"I'm guessing you haven't seen the news?"

"I haven't had time. I'm preparing to head home to Louisiana to see about my family and I'm only at the office to wrap some things up."

"Charlie," he sounds tortured. "There's something I need to tell you. Show you. Can I see you? I promise it's not what you think."

"You have no idea what I'm thinking, Xavier."

He lets out a soft chuckle. "Well, I have several million pennies for a couple of those thoughts, Charlie Sinclair."

I grit my teeth. "Call me Anastasia, Xavier. And no, I'm not in a position to meet you."

"I don't trust myself when I'm near you," I admit—silently, to myself. A truth I refuse to let slip past my lips.

"Just five minutes, Peach. It's important."

Peach. The nickname slides from his lips like he knows exactly what it does to me. He's calling me everything that pulls at the memories I've tried to lock away—our night on the plane, the villa in Greece, the way he looked at me like I was something he'd already claimed. He's tugging at every damn string, trying to make me unravel.

And I can't let him in.

He's reckless with his emotions, unpredictable, and every time I let myself get too close, I end up burned—left to deal with the fallout of his ever-changing whims.

"Call me *Anastasia*, Xavier." I whisper, so he can't hear the desperation in my voice. The need.

"I wish you'd call me *Mr. Darcy*," he rasps, that damn Southern drawl making my pulse spike.

"And I wish you'd kiss my natural Black ass!"

And with that, I hang up.

Because I need to be done with him.

I need to *not* be aware of him.

I need him out of my head, out of my chest, out of the space he somehow always manages to occupy—even when he's nowhere near me.

Before I can exhale from the distraction that is Xavier Darcy, there's a knock at my door.

It's *him*. My boss. Hayven *fucking* Sally.

I swear God must be playing some elaborate joke on me, suddenly surrounding me with an army of fine-ass white men. It's almost cruel at this point.

With his low-cut sandy blond hair, piercing blue eyes, and the kind of rugged handsomeness that should belong to a *mafia boss*, Hayven is every bit as dangerous as he looks. Not that you'd be able to tell if you saw him on paper. He's also the privileged son of some of the scariest political powerhouses in the world. *No, not Clarence and Virginia Thomas.*

"I thought we weren't meeting until ten," I say, flicking my gaze to my phone to confirm. Still thirty minutes until our staff meeting.

"Something's come up," he says, shifting his weight like the words taste bad coming out of his mouth.

I arch a brow. "Okay?"

"A friend of mine, mutual friend of ours, is being targeted with deepfake videos and images—someone's trying to tank his company and ruin his IPO."

I squint at him. "Hayven, you could hack your way to the bottom of this in your sleep."

He exhales through his nose, reluctant. "I could, but... this case is different." He pauses and suddenly sounds *off*. And I can't put my finger on why.

"Uhh, Hayven? You're not making any sense."

"I know. I just think it would be easier if you saw what was in the file first and then we can talk more."

I'm about to press him for more, but my office phone rings, cutting through the moment.

"Stasi?" The receptionist calls. "I have your brother on the line. He says it's urgent."

I glance at Hayven, debating.

He nods toward the file then looks at me. "Just check what's in the file and see me when you're done?"

I sigh. "Fine."

Hayven disappears out of my office, and I shake my head as I reach for my phone. "White people can be so weird," I mutter to myself.

Then, I pick up my phone with a grin already forming. "What's up, apple-head-ass buster?"

"Shut up, you old Milky-Way-shaped-head-ass gorilla," my brother fires back, and just like that, we dissolve into laughter.

God, I've missed this. Him.

"What do you want, boy?" I tease, settling back into my chair.

He lets out a sharp breath, his tone sobering. "I thought you said you were coming home this past weekend."

I roll my eyes. "You said she still had another week, at least. How many times do I really need to say goodbye to Grandmommy? I feel like she's just taking advantage at this point."

He *laughs*, deep and genuine. "You're going to hell for that. You know that, right?"

I suck my teeth. "Shut up. Is she really going down this time?"

His pause is heavy. "Yes, Charlie," he drawls. "It's for real this time."

His voice carries a weight that makes my stomach knot. My brother is a doctor. He would know.

I press my lips together, suddenly feeling that familiar urge to retreat. To run.

"Ok, Elijah. I'll get there as soon as I can. It's just that I just got a big case put on my desk and—"

"Charlie." His voice slices through mine, sharp, no-nonsense. He *knows* me. Knows how I work, how I avoid things when it comes to going back home. "It's time. You've gotta come home."

I swallow hard, already knowing he's right.

Already knowing I don't have a choice.

"Okay," I whisper. "I'll be there in the morning."

"And me and Prince will be there to pick you up."

I smile at the thought of seeing my brother and my nephew—it's been way too long.

Without a word, I scoop up the files Hayven left on my desk, shut my laptop, and head straight for my car. I'm halfway down the hall before I realize I forgot to stop by Hayven's office.

Too late. I make a mental note to catch up with him once I'm settled.

It's time to go home.

CHAPTER FOUR

Charlie

"Would you like a glass of champagne before takeoff, miss?" I look up at the flight attendant just as I'm getting to my row.

I turn to give her a bright smile. "Yes, please."

I'm putting my bag under my first-class seat, preparing to adjust my seatbelt just as a shadow falls over me.

"Excuse me?" A breathy, high-pitched voice cuts through my pre-flight peace. *Where is a sexy billionaire with a private jet when you need one?*

I glance up to find a woman who looks like she time-traveled straight from a 90s paparazzi shot of Paris Hilton—blonde, perfect, and wearing oversized sunglasses indoors. Behind her, a man with floppy hair and an apologetic smile shifts awkwardly. They smell like fruit loops and ThC.

"Would you mind switching seats so my boyfriend and I can sit together?" She blinks at me like I'm supposed to find her *adorable*.

I don't.

I flash a tight-lipped smile. "Yes, I mind."

Her perfectly glossed lips part in shock. "Oh, um... may I ask *why*?"

I tilt my head, offering a fake but polite smile "In the event of a plane crash and my untimely death, I want to make sure I'm in my assigned seat so authorities can properly identify my likely disfigured body."

Her mouth opens, then closes. Her boyfriend clears his throat.

I slide my eye mask over my face and lean back in my seat, effectively ending the conversation.

A moment later, she settles into the seat next to me, all smiles—while her boyfriend? He starts making his way back to coach.

Oh, she must have lost her damn mind if she thought I was about to switch seats and downgrade to *coach*.

The privilege of it all.

One hour. Just sixty minutes before I'm back in Louisiana, back home to say goodbye to Grandmommy and I need as much time to settle my nerves as possible.

I let my mind drift just enough to slip under. If I hadn't taken one of Ms. Lorraine's gummies before boarding, my thoughts would be spiraling out of control by now. Instead, I sink into the delicious haze of sleep.

...

Xavier's lips are *everywhere*.

My legs wrap around his waist as we ascend in what looks like a glass elevator, the city lights flashing beneath us in a dizzying blur. He's pressing me against the cool glass, his mouth searing a path along my throat, his hands gripping my thighs like he owns them.

Then he pauses and brings his eyes to mine. And, my goodness, the look in his gaze. "Tell me you're mine, Charlesetta," he murmurs, his hazel eyes burning into me.

My breath catches. My thighs clench tighter around his waist as he *smacks* my ass from beneath my dress. A sharp gasp escapes me.

"You're taking too long to answer me, Sweet Peach," he warns. "I know you like to hear me beg, but I won't ask you again."

My body betrays me, arching into him, chasing the heat of his touch. His command. "I'm...yes...I'm yours, X," I breathe out.

A wicked smirk spreads across his face before he leans in and *bites* my neck.

"Shit!" I yelp, my fingers twisting in his shirt.

His grip tightens, and my skin is so hot it feels like it will melt the cold glass of the elevator. The sensation steals my breath, but it's his voice—low, dark, *possessive*—that sends chills through my body.

"Call me..." He says, as his tongue drags a slow, torturous path from the valley of my cleavage, up the column of my throat, until his mouth is just a breath away from mine.

His eyes burn into me, daring me to disobey as he finishes his command. "*Mr. Darcy.*"

And fuck if I don't obey.

I crash my mouth against his just as he slides the thin string of my thong aside.

"I'm all yours."

Then, just as he plunges two fingers deep inside me, I whisper against his ear, my fingers tangled in his hair— "*Mr. fucking Darcy.*"

...

"Miss?"

I gasp.

A voice jolts me back to reality, and I flinch so hard I might as well have been caught stealing from the collection plate. In my startled state, I accidentally knock the glass of champagne the flight attendant is holding—straight onto the lap of my blonde seatmate.

"Are you *freaking kidding me*?!" she screeches, jumping up like she's been set on fire.

My eyes go wide with horror. "Oh shhii—oh girl. I am *so* sorry," I say, mortified, hands hovering uselessly in the air like I'm trying to Jedi-mind-trick the liquid away.

The flight attendant gasps, then bolts. "I'll go grab a towel!" she yells over her shoulder.

"Flight attendants, please lock the cabin doors," I hear the pilot call over the intercom.

Meanwhile, my seatmate is standing now, wringing her hands dramatically as remnants of the champagne *mysteriously* keep splashing in my direction and into my hair. Oh, she wants to fight. This is a *silk press*, bitch. My hair is staying put!

"So," I say, forcing a fake smile, "would you still maybe want to change seats? You know, find that handsome boyfriend of yours?"

She glares. If looks could kill, I'd be an entire crime scene.

Just then, the flight attendant returns with a towel, and my unfortunate neighbor snatches it before storming off to the bathroom, still muttering under her breath. *Bet you won't say it to my face.*

I sigh and turn to the attendant, trying to salvage what's left of my dignity. "I *really* am sorry about that."

The attendant just shrugs, dabbing at the mess. "Honestly? Happens all the time. She'll be fine," she says, before walking away with a wink.

She comes back with a fresh glass of champagne and I flash her a grateful smile. "Thank you," I say. Then the PA system crackles to life.

"Good morning, folks, and welcome aboard Excelsior Air's flight from Atlanta to New Orleans. Our estimated flight time is just over an hour, and we should be landing by 11 AM. Sit back, relax, and enjoy the ride."

I slump back in my seat, adjusting my eye mask. *Yeah, sure. Relax. Great idea.*

If my skin were any lighter, I'd be bright red. I shift, clearing my throat and willing my body to shake off the *very real* heat still lingering from my dream. What the hell was that? .

I exhale slowly, running a hand over my face.

I can't stop dreaming about Xavier. I can't stop *wanting* the man.

Ever since Greece, ever since that night on the plane, he's unlocked something in me no one else ever has. And I hate it. Despise it. Because I *can't* go there with him again.

At the rate my dating life has been going, I might as well buy a cat while I'm ahead. Staying single has been the safer bet—no complications, no drama, just me, myself, and the occasional entanglement when necessary.

Autika calls me "the man" in our friendship because for as long as they've known me, I've kept love at arm's length, and I've loved every minute of it.

But as the plane begins its descent into New Orleans, my stomach twists with an unsettling realization—Lucas is still here. And he's probably still waiting for me.

What can I say? Your girl is a pimp.

A little over an hour later, the plane touches down with a smooth jolt, and within minutes, I'm stepping off into the thick, humid air of New Orleans—where the scent of spice lingers, wrapping around me like an old memory.

It's familiar. It's nostalgic. It's home.

It's New Orleans. Where everything moves slower, hits deeper, and somehow even the air feels flirtatious.

And yet, none of it distracts from the joy settling in my chest. Because I already know who's waiting for me when I step off the escalator.

Elijah and Prince. My heart clenches in the best way, and when I spot them near baggage claim, I don't even try to hide my grin.

"Aunt Charlie!" Prince's deep voice booms through the terminal as he *lifts me off the ground* in a bone-crushing hug.

I gasp dramatically when he finally sets me down, forcing myself to look *up* at him. "Prince Elijah, do my eyes deceive me?" I don't know why I suddenly sound like my mother, but the Southern Auntie in me just slips out whenever I see him. "You're eleven years old and you're actually taller than me!" I slap his chest in mock outrage.

Elijah steps up behind us, arms crossed, pretending to be offended. "Now don't act like you forgot who the big boss is around here."

I snort. "Oh, hush, you *big Shrek-ass lookin' fool!*"

"Ooooh!" Prince claps a hand over his mouth. "Aunt Charlie *cussed*, Dad!"

I lean in, whispering conspiratorially, "You're supposed to have my back!"

He laughs, his dimples deep and familiar. "*Always*, Aunt Charlie." And he means it.

I don't get to see my brother and my nephew as often as I'd like. Elijah usually brings Prince to Atlanta when they're in town for college tours or work trips. When that happens, I make it a point to spoil him—take him to a ball game, stuff him with sugar, and bully Elijah into going out and enjoying himself for once.

But no matter how many texts we exchange or video calls we squeeze in between schedules, every time I see them in person, I'm reminded of one simple truth: it's never enough.

Prince's mom was obsessed with the singer—that's how he got his name. But she never got the chance to say it out loud. She died giving birth to him, another Black woman whose pain was brushed off until it was too late.

My brother, Elijah, was one of her doctors. A nephrologist. She'd called him herself when no one else would listen—when she knew something wasn't right. By the time he got to her, she'd been ignored for hours. Her body was already failing. The damage had been done.

She had Lupus. Her complications weren't routine. She needed to be heard. She wasn't.

Her husband had already been taken from her—killed in action overseas. Prince was their last embryo. Their final shot at building the family they dreamed of.

She died bringing him into the world, leaving behind nothing but the son they fought so hard to have.

But before she passed, she made one final request: give her baby the middle name *Elijah*—to honor the only doctor who took her seriously in a place that was supposed to protect her.

My brother did exactly that.

And now, every time someone says Prince Elijah's name, they speak her strength... and his promise to never let her be forgotten.

You saw the message? That Grandmommy passed?" Elijah asks, his voice lower than usual.

I nod, squeezing his hand. "Yeah. I'm sorry I didn't make it back in time."

"I'm sure she knew how much you loved her."

"Of course she did. She was my ace growing up."

"And you were an ass—always dragging her into your battles with Mama."

I smirk and shrug. "Favor ain't fair."

"So... who's already at the Big House?" I ask.

Elijah lets out a *deep* laugh, shaking his head. "Better question is, *who ain't* at the house already?"

The *Big House*—the Sinclair family compound—stands on the very land that once held my ancestors as slaves. Now, it's where we gather for every holiday, every special occasion, every moment that calls for family.

In addition to my parents' monstrosity of a mansion, the land also holds four small houses and four duplexes, built for family to come and stay—a weekend, a season, or forever. My great-grand-daddy believed that no matter how far we wandered, family should always have a place to lay their heads. My great-grandmother just wanted everyone close. So over the years, The Big House has been expanded, added onto, reimagined—all to fulfill those wishes. To keep us rooted in something bigger than just blood. The Big House is our bright star, our compass.

"So, what you're saying is, everyone is there?"

He laughs, grabbing my carry-on suitcase with ease, then he hands my shoulder bag to Prince before wrapping a solid arm around my shoulders. His grip is warm, steady.

"You're in for a real family reunion, Charlie Chaplin. The one you've been avoiding all these years."

I groan. This is going to be *hell*.

CHAPTER FIVE

Charlie

Seventeen Years Old

"You clean up nice, Charlie Sinclair."

I blush, tucking a loose strand of hair behind my ear. "You don't look too bad yourself, Lucas Ballentine."

It's how we've greeted each other since the night he escorted me to the Debutante Ball. The night everything changed for us.

I never thought I'd be excited about going to prom—let alone going with *him*. But ever since Neva and I tried on dresses over winter break, I haven't been able to stop thinking about it. Or about Lucas, if I'm honest.

After the debutante ball, Lucas and I grew close. We talked—*really talked*—and let each other in, in a way that made us instant friends. And that friendship slowly turned into something *more* when we realized just how much we had in common—how we were both suffocating under the weight of our parents' legacies, trapped in futures that had been decided for us long before we had a say.

At the end of freshman year of high school, he asked me to be his girlfriend. I wasn't even into boys enough yet to fully understand what that meant, but I still said yes.

Our relationship has always been *polite*. Structured. A checklist of the things our parents expected from us—movie dates in a group (*Mama's orders*), attending church functions together, the occasional school dance when she *doubled* my allowance just to see me in a dress.

We were an awkward pair, always toeing the line between best friends and whatever else we were supposed to be. But mostly? Lucas was just *my person*. Him and Neva.

By senior year, the awkward boy with braces had transformed into the star quarterback every girl wanted. But he only wanted me. And I sort of liked that.

"On Bended Knee" by Boyz II Men plays as we sway together, his hands firm but gentle on my waist. Then, Lucas leans down, his breath warm against my ear.

"I like this song," he murmurs.

His smile is easy, his dimples deep, and for the first time *ever*, I feel things when a boy is close to me. It's unfamiliar in the most exhilarating way.

Goosebumps rise along my arms. "Me too," I say. "It's kind of sad, though, don't you think?"

He pulls back slightly, frowning. "Why do you say that?" he twangs, his drawl thick and lazy.

Oh, how I love a man who breathes the Bayou through his lungs.

I let out a soft laugh. *"'Can we go back to the day our love was strong? How does a perfect love go wrong?'"* I quote, tilting my head. "Sounds like they're anything *but* in love."

Lucas shrugs. "I guess you have a point. I guess I just like it because it's slow." His voice reminds me of my daddy's. As much as I've wanted to escape the South, I can't deny how much I love the sound of it. It feels like home, even when home hasn't always felt welcoming.

"The melody is nice," I concede.

"You smell nice," he murmurs, and I grin at his attempt to be smooth.

We've never kissed, and tonight was supposed to be the big night—the one where we finally went all the way... with *tongue.*

I glance over at Neva and her boyfriend Tommy dancing, and it's clear they've got *big* plans for tonight. The way he's gripping her waist, the way her body is practically molded to his—I'm honestly shocked none of the chaperones have stepped in.

Then, as if she wasn't already pushing it, Neva lifts her leg and wraps it around Tommy's waist. Mrs. Penny, our science teacher, lets out a sharp gasp, clutching her pearls like she just witnessed a full-blown scandal.

I shake my head, smiling to myself as I turn my attention back to Lucas. Neva has *always* been a little more advanced than me. But tonight, everything changes. Prom night. Mama always said it was special.

I glance up at him, my heart hammering, wondering if this is it. If this is *the* moment. But then I hesitate—because, really, did I want my first kiss to be to a *breakup song*?

"Thank you," I say, my voice softer than I intended. "It's... my mama got this perfume for me. It's by Milana, you know, the super-model?"

Lucas smirks, his eyes darkening just a little as his eyes sweep over my petite frame in my floor-length red satin dress. "She's a model. But she's still not as pretty as you."

"Boy, stop!" I laugh, smacking him on the chest. "I know I'm cute, but you don't have to—"

His lips press against mine, stealing my breath, my words, stealing my every thought. The kiss is soft—hesitant at first—but then, as if something inside him snaps, it deepens.

Just as I start to remember that the song playing is about heart-break, it shifts. "*Weak*" by SWV hums through the speakers, and it feels like fate. Because my knees absolutely go weak in that instant.

"*I get so weak in the knees, I can hardly speak...*"

Lucas' tongue brushes against mine, slow and teasing, and I melt against him. His hands grip my waist firmer. *Tighter.* Like he's at war with himself—*to be or not to be* a gentleman? To let his hands trail lower, past the safe zone, down to where mama says scandal and sin live? That is the question.

Then, a *different* war begins to wage. A more... *physical* one.

Because just as sure as I feel his hands gripping my waist, I feel *something else* pressing against my stomach.

I freeze, halting our kiss abruptly before jumping and glancing down.

Oh.

My eyes flick back up to his. "Umm. Is that—"

Lucas immediately steps back, but to my horror—*he's not even embarrassed*. If anything, he looks *pleased*.

"It is," he says, shrugging with *zero* shame. "I guess we've never been this close before. I liked it more than I thought I would." He *grins*.

Oh, sweet Lord.

Neva and I talk about sex all the time—it's kind of our thing. Mostly because we're the only two girls in our class who *haven't* done it yet. But while everyone else has been sneaking around in backseats and breaking curfews, I've been buried in my studies, *strategizing* my escape from Louisiana before my parents even catch wind.

Neva, on the other hand, has been desperate to throw her virginity away. The problem? Her boyfriend is a preacher's kid who's convinced he'll be damned the second he has unmarried sex. Last time they made it to third base, she said he started speaking in tongues.

My daddy always says, *boys aren't going anywhere.* And so far? He hasn't been wrong.

My brother Elijah warned me about the things boys would say to get me into bed, made it sound like some dirty trick I needed to avoid. So I've never felt like I was missing out on anything. But kissing me with *SWV* playing, touching me like he's unashamed, like his body is telling me I'm special? That doesn't seem so bad to me.

But right now, standing here, watching Lucas *beam* as something resembling a *Nissan 350Z* aims directly at me from his groin... I'm thinking maybe I should've asked a *few more* questions.

Maybe cracked open one of those *scandalous* books Mama keeps under her bed. Because right now? I am *utterly* unprepared.

Then—because she has the worst timing in the history of the world—Geneva rushes over. "You guys! The limo is leaving in five minutes to take us to the hotel!" Then she rushes back off to another group of our friends to alert them.

I pull back, breathless, my eyes locked on Lucas.

"Did you still want to go?" he asks, his voice lower, rougher.

The hotel after prom. The tradition. The unspoken expectations that lingered in the air. Our parents had all pitched in to rent a suite for us to celebrate in—as long as we had one adult chaperone. That *adult*? My big brother. He's five years older than me so, thankfully, he's always been the stand-in adult in my life.

I hadn't really thought about it much. It was just another thing we were *supposed* to do—a rite of passage into adulthood.

There was nothing else for me to consider.

Not until now.

Not until *he* kissed me like *that*.

Not until I realized just how much I wanted *more*.

I nod. "I still want to go... if you do."

"I do," he says. Then, after a beat, "But before we go, promise me something."

My brows knit together. "Okay?"

He grabs my hand in his. "Promise me that no matter what happens tonight, we don't let our parents dictate our futures. Whatever we do—whatever we choose—it's for us. No one else."

My heart clenches.

We've talked about sex. About how we wanted our first time to be—what it should feel like, what it should *mean*. But Lucas has never pressured me, never pushed for more than conversation.

Another reason I fell in love with this boy. Another reason he's always been too good for me.

He wants me to know if we take this next step—if I give him my virginity—it won't be a chain binding us together forever. It'll be a *choice*. One that won't define the rest of our lives unless *we* decide it does.

And I love him a little bit more for that.

"I promise," I whisper, hooking my pinky around his. A vow. A covenant. A choice.

A choice that belongs to us alone.

And that night, after we make love for the first time, I keep that promise...for a little while.

CHAPTER SIX

Charlie

Present Day

The Sinclair compound hasn't changed.

The long, winding driveway stretches ahead, flanked by sprawling oak trees draped in Spanish moss, their gnarled branches like outstretched arms welcoming me back. The greenery is thick, humid, *alive*, the unmistakable scent of the Bayou weaving through the air, clinging to my skin like a memory I can't shake.

Prince grabs the bags as soon as the car rolls to a stop, his long legs carrying him toward the house before I even step out. "Aunt Charlie's home!" he bellows, his voice echoing through the yard like a siren call to the entire family. The entire town, really.

My stomach twists.

The last time I was here—Christmas, ten years ago—it was *hell*. The relentless questions about why I wasn't married yet, the disappointed glances when my answers weren't good enough. And then there was *him*.

Lucas Ballentine.

The boy I once planned a life with. The man who, once I got a taste of life outside of Louisiana, spent months pleading for me to come back. I've left him in tears more times than I care to admit, and I don't think I can stomach breaking his heart again. It's one of the many reasons I stayed away so long.

Because with where I am now, I'm not sure I could say no to him again. And something about being back here, being *home*, makes me wonder if I would even *want* to.

The *Big House* looms ahead, grand yet familiar.

Inside, it's madness in the best way. Laughter, loud conversations, the smell of home-cooked food thick in the air. As soon as I step through the doors, I'm *ambushed*.

"Look at you, girl! That little bob haircut is *too* cute!"

"Lord, Charlie, you ever gon' put some meat on them bones? Is corporate America even feeding you?"

I'm pulled into hugs, kissed on the cheek, my face squeezed between hands that smell like cocoa butter and cornbread. Then, the crowd *parts*, and the only man in this house who can make me feel like a little girl again *booms* through the room.

"Is that my Charlie Chaplin?!"

A grin breaks across my face. "Hey, *Big Daddy!*"

I run straight into my daddy's arms, burying my face in his chest, inhaling the scent of home—cedarwood and fresh linen. His arms wrap around me, squeezing *just right*. My favorite place in the world has always been in my daddy's arms.

He's still tall—just like I remember. Time has only made him look more seasoned, more dignified. His deep, rich chocolate brown skin looks like it was poured straight from a Godiva mold, and his white hair, neatly trimmed into a goatee and mustache, adds to the kind of presence that makes people sit up a little straighter when he enters a room.

Joe Sinclair. Man of the people.

But to me? I'm just his little girl.

He steps back, eyes shining. "My baby girl finally came home to visit. Guess you're too busy for us these days."

I hang my head, sheepish. "I'm sorry it took so long." I glance around at the smiling faces of my family. "And I'm sorry *this* was the reason why."

Before he can respond, another voice I know *too well* cuts through the moment.

"Charlesetta. Is that you?"

I turn to face her. "Hey, Mama." The words come out soft, unsure—like I'm sixteen again, waiting for approval I'll never get.

She eyes me up and down, then sighs. "I see you're still wearing your hair like a boy."

I barely get the chance to roll my eyes before Daddy jumps in. "I *like* her hair like that. Makes her look sophisticated."

I flash him a grin. "Thank you, Big Daddy." And just like when I was a kid, I have to fight the urge to stick my tongue out at Mama just to piss her off.

After what feels like hours, the greetings fade, the crowd disperses, and I take a deep breath before making my way to the room where Grandmommy rests.

In the South, tradition runs deep, especially among wealthy families. When someone passes, their body doesn't have to sit at a funeral home for a viewing. Sometimes, they stay in the family home for viewing and visiting—giving loved ones time to sit with them, speak to them, *grieve them.*

It's a practice rooted in history, one our ancestors carried from Africa, one that white wealth tried to claim as its own. But *we* never forgot. And in the Sinclair family home, we still do it the way *we* always have.

The formal living room, usually reserved for Mama's guests, has been transformed. Candles flicker softly, floral arrangements surround the room, and Grandmommy sits peacefully, her hands folded over her lap, as regal in death as she was in life.

I sit beside her, exhaling a breath I didn't realize I was holding.

"You were always so damn stubborn," I whisper, my voice shaking.

"Probably why we got along so well." I huff out a soft laugh. "Probably why Mama and I *don't.*"

I let my fingers graze over hers, cold but still unmistakably hers. "Thank you for keeping my secret." My throat tightens, and I close my eyes. "And please... look in on my baby."

No one else knew. No one else *would* know. But Grandmommy did. She was the only one who ever could have. When I was eighteen, when I lost the baby I made with Lucas on prom night, she took me away. Told the family she was rewarding me for good grades, when really, she was saving me from drowning in grief I didn't understand.

Morocco, a beautiful tapestry of culture surrounded me, even though the colors were muted to me. But that time, that place, wasn't just about leisure. It was about letting go.

Morocco was where Grandmommy let me cry, let me *feel*, let me rage against the betrayal of my own body. She told me the truth—*that nothing prepares you for that kind of loss, no matter what you thought you wanted.* It was a bond women shared, but so few talked about. A bond that me and Grandmommy shared.

And now she's gone.

I sit with her for twenty more minutes before I press a kiss to her hand and let the grief wash over me. Then I finally pull myself away.

"I love you, Grandmommy," I whisper. "I'll see you both soon."

CHAPTER SEVEN

Charlie

The kitchen is exactly as I expected.

Aunt Beth is at the counter, cutting collard greens—fresh from Mama's garden. Aunt Janie-Mae is at the sink, rinsing black-eyed peas, and Mama is at the island, chopping up neckbones.

We may be bougie, but Mama never let us forget our roots. *White people stole our language, erased our names, tried to strip us of our heritage,* she always said. *But we'll never let them take what we built here.* That's why Sunday dinners still happen. Why, no matter what, we comfort each other with food.

Everything on display here is the very definition of comfort—the kind only Southern food can give. It's warmth and history, pride and love, all served up on a plate.

But the peace doesn't last.

"So, Charlie," Aunt Janie-Mae starts, her voice *way* too innocent. "You still *single*?"

I freeze mid-step. *And here we go.*

Aunt Beth shakes her head. "Girl, with all the traveling she does, she probably *ain't got time* for a man."

Mama sniffs. "Well, she better *make* time before it's too late."

"She could at least get one of them boob jobs!" Janie-Mae *offers,* like I'm not even standing in the room.

I instinctively grab my breasts. *I thought men liked bite-sized boobies.*

Lord *help me,* these women better be glad I respect my elders—at least *this* version of me does. The *docile* Charlesetta that comes home. Because the defiant operative who enjoys *snapping necks* and doesn't mind hurting feelings, would have this lady in tears before I drop-kicked her bow-legged ass. Talking about my titties.

I don't understand why women are so obsessed with marriage anyway! Why being *married off* is still the ultimate goal.

Since I can remember, my momma has been planting ideas in my head about finding a *good* husband, settling down, and making a *proper* home. But I am my own woman. I don't *settle* for anybody. And my luxury apartment—fully paid for by The Fury Alliance—is as good a home as any.

But they won't leave me alone. And if I don't shut these women up soon, they'll start parading church boys in front of me *during the funeral.*

The heat rises in my face, and before I can stop myself, I blurt out the first thing that comes to mind.

"I *do* have a man, actually."

Silence.

Then, *chaos.*

"What?"

"Who?"

"Why haven't we heard about him?"

"Is it Lucas? You're coming back to be with Lucas Ballentine, finally? Oh, thank you Lord!"

I wave a hand, like I'm swatting away their questions. "No. It's not Lucas," I say quickly. "It's just, he's in the public eye. We have to keep it quiet." *I lie.*

And because he has the *worst* timing in the world, Elijah walks in.

"You are *such* a liar."

I shoot him a glare. "Mind your business, with that ugly ass Sherman Clump haircut on your head!"

He smirks. "Oh no, *this* is my business now."

Elijah can always tell when I'm lying, which means he doesn't *let up.*

The smug look on his face is enough to make me want to throw something at him, but instead, I do the next best thing—I *knee him* in the shin while fending off the aunties.

He hisses, stumbling back. "Payback is coming, *Cruella!*"

I flash him a sickly sweet smile. "Bite me, *dick face*," I mutter under my breath, my teeth clenched as I dodge another nosy question.

They all start pressing for details, but I hold my ground. I've worked for the government. I've handled interrogations that would make their questions look friendly.

I can handle the aunties.

I just have to avoid talking about my *very real, totally not made up* boyfriend for the rest of this visit.

Easy.

Right?

CHAPTER EIGHT

Charlie

I wake up to the familiar scent of home—the mix of old wood, jasmine from Mama's garden, and the faintest hint of Big Daddy's cologne lingering in the air.

But when I blink my eyes open, I feel like I've stepped straight into a time machine.

My old bedroom looks exactly like I left it. The same pale yellow walls, the same floral curtains Mama picked out, and the same damn posters of *Immature* and *N Sync* plastered on every inch of available space. I stare up at a young Marques Houston, his eyes staring back like he's personally offended that I left him here to collect dust for over a decade. *I'm too old for you anyway.*

I groan, dragging a hand down my face.

I need to get out of this room before my teenage self tries to drag me back into the era of low-rise jeans and rhinestone-encrusted Nokia phones.

After a long shower and a fresh change of clothes, I make my way downstairs, following the smell of something sweet and buttery floating through the house.

Elijah stands at the stove, flipping blueberry pancakes with the ease of a man who knows he's *that guy* when it comes to breakfast.

"Well, well," I say, pulling out a chair at the kitchen island. "Dr. Sinclair himself, gracing us with his presence."

He smirks, not bothering to turn around. "I live here, dumbass."

"In the *cottage*," I correct. "You got your own house, yet you're in here stealing the good syrup."

"Whatever. You know you couldn't wait to get you some of these," he says, sliding a perfectly golden pancake onto a plate and setting it in front of me. "And since Mama and Big Daddy are at the church meeting with the pastor about the funeral, I figured I'd feed your bony ass."

I smirk before taking a bite, the warm burst of blueberries making me hum in satisfaction.

"Where's Prince?" I ask between bites.

"Outside playing with Neva's kid."

I pause, glancing at him. "How is Geneva doing these days?"

He shrugs, but I catch the way the corner of his mouth quirks up just *slightly*.

"She's good. Ms. G's Jazz & Jambalaya Café is killing it. Live music most nights. Best jambalaya in town."

I narrow my eyes, setting my fork down. "You seem to know a lot about my best friend."

He shrugs again, keeping his face neutral. "It's a small town. Everybody knows everything about everybody."

I don't push it, but I file that information away for later.

Elijah shifts gears quickly, a devilish grin spreading across his face. "By the way, how's that *man* of yours doing?"

I groan, already regretting that lie. "Elijah, I swear—"

He leans against the counter, arms crossed. "Uh-huh. The mystery boyfriend. What's his name again?"

I roll my eyes. "Mind your business."

"See, I *would*," he says, flipping another pancake, "but I don't like being lied to."

"I'm *not* lying."

Elijah stares at me. He knows me too well.

I stuff another bite of pancake in my mouth to avoid further questioning.

"Anyway! What's up with that grin of yours every time you bring up Neva?"

Later that morning, I decide to surprise Geneva at her restaurant. It's been too long since I've seen her. We used to talk every day, spend every weekend together, and sleep over at each other's houses like it was our second home. But once I left for Atlanta, everything changed. When you live a life of secrecy, it keeps you from the people you love most. Guilt creeps in because you can't share your whole self with them. So eventually, it just becomes easier to stay away.

But the second I step through the doors of Ms. G's Jazz & Jambalaya Café, I feel her presence in every inch of the space she's built.

It's like stepping into a 1920s French speakeasy—velvet drapes, dark mahogany, dim golden lighting that flickers off the ornate chandeliers. Vintage photos line the walls, showcasing Black musicians who shaped history. The bar is sleek, polished, lined with top-shelf whiskey and bourbon. The stage at the far end of the room is set for tonight's live performance, and a jazz record plays softly in the background.

And then I see it—a wall of fame, filled with pictures of celebrities who have visited. PJ Morton. Charmaine Neville. Tyler Perry. Trombone Shorty. Dawn Richard. Some of New Orleans' finest sons and daughters, all captured in time, having once stood where I stand now.

A wide grin spreads across my face.

Before I can turn around, a loud voice booms from behind me.

"Hell has truly frozen over because I could swear I see Charlie Sinclair standing in *my* establishment! But that can't be right since Charlie ain't been home in years!"

I spin around, already beaming. "*Neva!*"

I run into her arms, burying my face in her shoulder. "I've missed you so much," I say, my voice muffled against her. She's taller than me, and I *always* have to dodge her boobs when I go in for a hug.

She pulls back, holding me at arm's length. "Your brother said you were coming home, but I told him I'd believe it when I *see* it! Why didn't you call me? I would've come to get you from the airport!"

"I didn't want to bother you," I say. "I know you're busy running the most popular joint in town."

"Please," she waves me off. "I'd drop everything for you, Charlie. You're family."

I missed her.

She pulls me toward the bar. "Now sit your skinny ass down and tell me all about your fabulous life in Atlanta. Did I *see* you in pictures on a *private jet*, honey?"

I laugh and launch into the story of Will and Timantha's wedding. And because I *can't* help myself, I tell her about Xavier too.

She gasps, slapping my knee like I just told her the juiciest secret. I sort of just did. "You mean to tell me the same man who designs apps and services for needy people, the one we *never* see in public, is a bonafide freak?"

I nod with *way* too much enthusiasm. "Girl, the *freakiest*. Do you hear me?"

Neva throws her head back, laughing. "You'd never guess that someone as polished and quiet as Mr. Darcy himself is so damn kinky!"

I didn't realize it until now, but Xavier is well known around here. And Neva knows about him like she's memorized his entire Wikipedia page.

Growing up in this city gave him a deep, abiding love for its people. And even though he's rarely in New Orleans these days, his wealth never took his heart far—he keeps it rooted here, pouring money into the opportunities he wished he'd had as a kid.

And Damn it!

I hate she's telling me things that make me like him even more. Not now, nipples!

"Well," I say, forcing a shrug, "it was fun while it lasted. But he's not someone I can have a future with."

Neva frowns. "Why not? If what you're telling me is any indication, y'all seem like you've got something electric."

I exhale, struggling to find the right words. "That's how it seems but..." I trail off, shaking my head.

How do I explain it? The pull between us is too strong and too volatile at the same time. We're like two live wires—every time we come together, we spark, we *ignite*, and it always feels like we're on the edge of an inferno. One that could consume us both.

I don't know how to explain that staying away from him isn't just easier. It's necessary. Safer.

Before I can finish, the door swings open.

I glance over and freeze.

Lucas Ballentine.

The blast from my past looking entirely too good for my peace of mind.

I turn back to Neva, narrowing my eyes. "What is *he* doing here?"

She shrugs, grinning. "I may have texted him while you were in the restroom and told him to come down. Come on, when was the last time the three of us were together?"

I shove her shoulder playfully before getting up and heading straight for Lucas.

The brotha has filled out.

Like...*Damn.*

He smirks. "Good to see you again, Charlie."

I inhale as my head is buried into his chest. And *damn it*, he smells good too.

I school my face, silently cursing my whoremones. Emphasis on the *whore* in me.

"You too," I say, and it comes out breathier than I expect.

His expression softens. "Sorry to hear about your Grandmommy. I know you two were close."

He has no idea how close. I never told Lucas about the baby.

"Thanks," I say, stepping back because this man is *too much*.

We all sit, talk, reminisce, and it feels like no time has passed at all. Like we've picked up right where the three of us left off in high school. And, as always, as the conversations are wrapping up, we pledge not to let this much time pass before we see each other again.

Before I leave, Lucas glances at me, his voice smooth and low. "Come back tonight," he drawls.

Louisiana men have a way of saying things—it's never really a question when they want you. It's a command wrapped in suggestion, a statement dressed up as an invitation.

"Come hang with me. It's New Orleans Night. It'll be like old times with New Orleans native music."

I hesitate.

Then I nod. "Okay."

Neva claps her hands. "The gang is back together at last!"

As I step outside, the cool Louisiana air wraps around me, thick with the scent of magnolias and something that feels a lot like nostalgia. My heart beats a little faster than I'd like to admit.

I didn't expect to feel this way about seeing Lucas again. The easy warmth between us, the way his voice still carries that familiar pull. Being back here, standing in the middle of my past, I wonder if time and distance were exactly what I needed—to step away long enough to see things clearly, to return with fresh eyes and a heart that isn't weighed down by what-ifs.

Maybe Grandmommy is orchestrating something else from the other side. A different kind of reunion. One I never saw coming.

CHAPTER NINE

Charlie

I smooth my hands over my dress, eyeing myself in the full-length mirror. It's been a long time since I got dressed up for a night out in *this* town, and for some reason, it feels heavier than it should. Maybe it's because I know what's waiting for me outside this bedroom door—a past that refuses to stay buried.

Right on cue, my mother appears in the doorway, her knock light but unnecessary. She was coming in whether I answered or not.

"Where are you off to?" She asks, leaning against the doorframe, arms folded.

I keep my focus on my reflection as I reply. "Geneva's restaurant. Going to see Neva, have a drink, listen to some music."

She nods, and for a brief moment, there's no tension between us. "How's Geneva doing?"

I glance at her through the mirror, caught off guard by the softness in her voice. "She's doing really well. The restaurant is thriving." I pause to add a bit of gloss to my lips. "I've missed her."

Mama hums in approval, then after a beat, she adds, "I heard you tell your brother you were seeing Lucas tonight."

I roll my eyes before I can stop myself. *And here we go.*

"I'm not *seeing* Lucas, Mama. We're catching up. That's it."

I brace for the speech—some variation of *don't mess things up this time* or *he's the best thing that ever happened to you.* But instead, she surprises me.

"I see now that Lucas was never right for you."

That catches my attention. I turn fully, frowning. "Why do you say that?"

She exhales, crossing the room, running her fingers along my dresser like she's inspecting for dust.

"He's a nice, sweet boy, Charlesetta—"

"And what? I'm not good enough for him?"

She shakes her head. "That's not what I said. Now if you would just let me finish—"

"It's fine, Mama," I say, waving her off. "I need to get ready."

I turn back to the mirror, hoping she'll take the hint.

She lingers, just for a moment, and I catch her reflection watching me. Studying me. But she doesn't say anything else. Just stands there, like she wants to, like she *almost* has something more to say.

I can't recall the last time we stood in the same room without it turning into some kind of battle. We've never really gotten along, never seen eye to eye. If it weren't for Big Daddy constantly stepping in, I'm not even sure how often I'd speak to her at all. It's a strange thing—how women born of the same blood can be so opposite, so fundamentally incapable of understanding each other.

She hesitates a second longer, then turns and walks out the door.

...

On my way out, Big Daddy is waiting in the foyer, sitting in his usual chair by the door, watching me with the same knowing eyes he always has.

"Where you headed, Charlie Chaplin?" he asks, smiling.

"New Orleans Night at Neva's," I say, leaning down to kiss his cheek.

He tilts his head, looking me over before pressing a kiss to my forehead. "You look pretty, baby girl."

I grin and do a little twirl. "Thanks, Big Daddy."

His expression shifts slightly, more serious now. "You know you need to be at The Big House tomorrow by one o'clock, right? That's when the formal viewing starts."

I nod. "I'll be here."

His eyes narrow slightly. "Wearing a dress?"

I smirk, rolling my eyes playfully. "Yes, Big Daddy. I'll be wearing a dress."

Little does everyone know, I have filled out quite nicely and I don't mind seeing my ass in a dress these days.

Daddy grins, satisfied. He knows I'd do anything for him.

"You mind if I take the Maserati?" I ask, keeping my voice as casual as possible. Like it's *just* a car. Like I'm not asking for the one thing he refuses to let *anybody* drive—not even Mama.

Big Daddy lets out a huff, already seeing through me. "The Mercedes drives just fine, Charlesetta."

I groan dramatically. "But it's parked funny, Big Daddy, and you know I can't back out of the driveway when you park like that! The Maserati is just so conveniently parked, so I can just drive right on out!"

"You mean so you can *speed* right on out," he corrects, side-eyeing me.

I stomp my foot like a child. It's not my proudest moment. "Big Daddy, *please*?"

He sighs, shaking his head. "Fine. But if I see one scratch on my—"

I don't even let him finish before I *lunge* into a hug, cutting him off mid-sentence.

He chuckles, patting my back. "And don't tell your brother," he warns. "I won't hear the end of it if he finds out I let you drive it and he hasn't."

"Mum's the word," I promise, already halfway to the garage, excitement thrumming in my veins.

Big Daddy isn't much of a car collector, but when he sets his sights on something, he *only* gets the best. The Maserati was his treat to himself for his sixtieth birthday—a symbol of years of hard work, of everything he built.

And now?

It's mine for the night.

A grin spreads across my face as I slide into the driver's seat, the rich leather molding to my body like it *knows* it belongs to me. The engine purrs as I rev it, the deep, throaty growl sending a thrill straight through me.

And then—The tires screech against the pavement as I gun it out of the driveway, laughter bubbling up in my chest.

Big Daddy's gonna kill me.

CHAPTER TEN

Charlie

W hen I pull up to *Ms. G's Jazz & Jambalaya*, the energy is *electric*. The line stretches around the building, music spilling out from the open doors, blending with the rich, smoky scent of spices that cling to the humid night air. Laughter rings out from clusters of people waiting in line, conversations flowing as effortlessly as the drinks being poured inside.

Black joy is everywhere—vibrant, unapologetic, alive.

I take a moment to soak it all in, my chest swelling with pride. Geneva didn't just open a restaurant; she built a home for the people of this city. A place where food, music, and culture collide. A space that feels like home, no matter where you've been.

I shoot Lucas a quick text to let him know I've arrived. A minute later, the doors open, and there he is, stepping out to meet me.

He moves through the crowd easily, people shifting without question to let him through. There's a quiet authority to him now, something that makes people pay attention.

Lucas is different than I remember.

Confident. Sure of himself. Like a man who knows exactly what he wants but doesn't *need* to have it. Like he's over me. And for some damn reason, that makes me want him a little more.

He's wearing a baby blue V-neck sweater with dark jeans, and he smells like cedar oil and shea butter.

"Come on," he says, placing a hand at the small of my back as he leads me inside.

We move through the restaurant, past tables full of diners, past the bar where drinks are being poured, until we reach our seats right at the front.

And that's when I see him. Jon Batiste.

A New Orleans legend, a Grammy-winning musician who blends jazz, blues, and soul like it's second nature. The man can make a piano sing, and his voice carries the kind of warmth that makes you feel like you're home, even if you've never been there before.

I'm floored.

"You good?" Lucas asks, smirking.

I turn to him, still grinning. "You didn't tell me *Jon Batiste* was playing tonight."

"You wouldn't have believed me," he says, signaling the waitress.

She comes over, smiling warmly. Lucas looks at me. "You still like a Vieux Carré?"

I blink, surprised he remembers. A smile spreads across my lips. "Yes. That's perfect, actually."

It only takes a second before a memory of Xavier flashes across my mind—uninvited, vivid. But I have no interest in replaying that reel, not right now. I steady myself, take a breath, and bring my focus back to the present. Back to Lucas.

Lucas takes a few moments to look at me, really *look* at me, before tilting his head slightly. "You're different."

I feel my cheeks warm under his gaze. "I could say the same thing about you!"

He nods, slow and measured. "Yeah, I know I've changed. Matured." He takes a sip of his drink, his eyes never leaving mine. "But you... you seem to turn into a new version of yourself whenever I see you."

I raise a brow. "I haven't been home in forever. How would you even know the difference?"

He lets out a soft chuckle. "You forget who you're talking to. I'm the one who held your hair back when you were throwing up after we snuck into Big Daddy's bourbon stash after homecoming. I've seen you at your worst—and your realest. I remember everything."

The memory makes me smile despite myself, shaking my head as it washes over me.

"I always knew you'd change," he says. "Knew you'd outgrow this place. Especially after grad school. But looking at you now?" He pauses. "I'm not sure I know this version of you at all."

I straighten in my seat. "I don't think that's such a bad thing. I'm evolving."

He huffs out a quiet laugh, swirling the liquid in his glass. "I've just come to know it as *the Charlie thing*," he says wryly.

My brow arches. "And what's *that* supposed to mean?"

He levels me with a look, and I hold my ground, refusing to look away.

"You have a tendency to change up every time someone lays out any expectations for you or asks anything of you that you don't necessarily like."

I blink, caught off guard. "I don't *change*," I say, incredulous.

"Fine," he says, setting his glass down. "You *run*."

Something inside me bristles. I don't like the way his truth settles over me, how it sticks to my skin like humidity in the dead of summer. I don't like how easily he lays it all at my feet, like he's been holding onto this for *years*, waiting for the moment to throw it in my face.

I need a way out of this conversation. Fast.

"You seeing anybody?" I ask abruptly, reaching for my own drink.

Lucas smirks, like he knows exactly what I'm doing, but lets it slide. "Nah. Too busy at the clinic with your brother these days."

I frown. "My *brother*? You two work together?"

He looks genuinely surprised. "He didn't tell you we opened a practice together? That we're partners?"

"Uh, *no*!"

I always thought my brother couldn't stand Lucas. They never seemed to have much in common—Elijah always rolled his eyes whenever Lucas came around, calling him a square and complaining that he was too straight-laced.

So the fact that they not only get along but actually opened a practice together? And nobody thought to tell me?

It feels like I'm being locked out of my own life, watching from the outside while everyone else moves forward without me.

Lucas leans back in his chair, shaking his head. "Going on five years now. I can't believe you didn't know."

I scoff, my irritation shifting targets. "I can't believe Eli didn't tell me."

Lucas watches me for a beat before he speaks again, his voice quieter now. "I can't believe it's taken you this long to come home."

Before I can respond, he reaches across the table and takes my hand in his, his thumb gliding gently over my skin. The simple touch sends a strange, unwelcome warmth curling in my stomach.

"You might learn a lot more if you came home more often," he says softly. "Saw what was here *waiting* for you."

That word. *Waiting.*

Every time I come home, I feel it—pressing down on me like a weight I can't shake. The expectation. The guilt. The unspoken *why don't you stay?* hanging in the air.

Lucas has always been here. Waiting.

And while some might call that romantic, to me, it's always felt a little tragic. Because as handsome and charming as he is, he could have any woman he wants—but he doesn't. He just waits. For me. For life to happen to him.

But I don't want a man who waits.

I want a man who hunts.

Who needs *me*. Wants me so badly he'd tear down walls and burn bridges just to get to me.

Maybe that's why Lucas only makes sense here—home. The one place where everything, and everyone, seems to stand still.

Of course, I'd never say that out loud. To him.

The drinks flow, the music fills the space, and for a moment, everything feels *easy*.

Neva has stopped by to check on us a few times, but we waved her off, telling her we understood if she couldn't stay long. She has a business to run, and watching her in her element—moving through the restaurant with effortless command, making sure everything runs smoothly—fills me with pride. My best friend built this.

She did that.

Then Jon Batiste shifts into a bluesy tune, something easy and rich, the kind of song that's soaked in soul and sensuality. The melody weaves through the air like smoke, curling around me, wrapping tight.

And then—

Lucas stands, reaching for my hand.

"Dance with me."

I hesitate, but he tilts his head, waiting. And maybe it's the music, maybe it's the nostalgia, but I take his hand as I stand to my feet.

He pulls me onto the dance floor, his hands settling at the small of my back, just far enough to be respectful, but close enough I feel the heat of him.

We sway to the rhythm, moving effortlessly together, his breath warm against my neck.

"I like this song," he whispers. And just like that, I'm back at prom. The night we first kissed with tongue.

The night we made love.

The night we created a life.

The baby no one ever knew about.

My breath catches, and I *jump* back, startled by the rush of emotions that slam into me.

"Charlie?" Lucas looks at me, concern etched into his face. "You good?"

Tears sting my eyes, and I swallow hard, forcing a nod. "Yeah... yes. I'm fine. I just—" I step back, needing space, needing air. After so long, there's still so much between us.

"It's just a lot happening right now," I say. "And I think I should be home with my family. For my daddy, you know?"

I don't know what else to say. I don't have another excuse.

It's just the easiest thing to blurt out in this moment. The one thing he *won't* question.

My grief.

His brows knit together, but after a second, he nods. "Okay. Sure. Can I drive you home?"

"No," I say quickly. "I'm fine getting home by myself."

Because I don't like the way he makes me feel. I don't like how being around him makes me question everything. I don't like how easily I slip back into wallflower Charlie whenever he turns on that charm.

Before I can leave, his voice stops me.

"Can I see you tomorrow?"

I pause, keeping my back to him.

"Out by the bayou?" he adds.

I take a deep breath, prepared to say no, but then he continues.

"No expectations, Charlie. I just wanna talk to you. I miss my best friend."

And *that* is what gets me.

I turn slightly, meeting his gaze. "Okay," I say softly. "Tomorrow at seven."

CHAPTER ELEVEN

Xavier

I roll my suitcase through the private airfield, the Louisiana humidity already wrapping around me like a damn wet blanket. It doesn't matter that it's the end of March—it's still muggy as hell. The kind of thick, sticky air that clings to your skin, makes your shirt stick to your back, and reminds you exactly where you are the second you step outside.

I left Louisiana when I was twenty-five. Mama was gone by then, and after that, it never really felt like home again.

It's familiar, sure. People still know my name, still call me *X* when I walk the streets. But familiarity isn't the same as belonging. There's nothing tying me here anymore. No roots, no anchor pulling me back.

"You sure about this, boss?" Nathan asks, rushing behind me as I head to my SUV, his tone somewhere between cautious and deeply concerned.

"Positive," I say, not breaking my stride.

"Because from what I've overheard Hayven saying..." Nathan trails off, clearly trying to find a diplomatic way to phrase it. "It sounds like Anastasia might be *dangerous*."

I huff out a laugh. "She's feisty, no doubt. But I know how to get *my* Charlie to soften to me." I flash him a confident grin before rolling my suitcase out of the airport lobby.

Behind me, Juliette calls out, "I really hope you know what you're doing, Xavier. I can't stress enough that you need to keep a low profile."

I wave her off. "You and Nathan work on damage control at my house. I'll handle Charlie."

Even though I haven't lived in Louisiana in nearly twenty years, I still keep a place here. A residence I visit just enough to justify keeping the lights on but not enough to call it home.

Nathan and Juliette will be there, handling the mess brewing around me while I try to smooth things over with Charlie.

I hope.

...

I pull up to Charlie's childhood home—or, rather, the *estate*.

The place is massive. Sprawling. A compound would be more accurate. Rows of pristine white columns, towering oak trees draped in Spanish moss, and land that stretches far beyond what I can see from where I'm parked.

My jaw tenses.

I knew Charlie had money, but I wasn't expecting *this*.

Where I grew up in a one-bedroom apartment with my mother, scraping by on whatever she could make as a housekeeper, Charlie was raised with this. Old money. Wealth that looks like it was passed down through generations.

For the first time in a long time, I feel something foreign settle in my chest.

Intimidation.

Just because I have money now doesn't mean the scars of poverty have faded. Wealth doesn't erase the memories of struggle—it just buries them under tailored suits and polished appearances.

I'm not ashamed of where I come from, but there's a difference—a *glaring* one—between those born into privilege and those who had to claw their way out of nothing to find some semblance of it. It's in the way they carry themselves, effortless and unbothered, never questioning whether they belong. And it's in the way *I* hesitate, always aware that no matter how much success I have, I'll never quite move the same way they do.

That's why I stay out of the limelight. Because no matter how refined I appear, I know that part of me—the part shaped by struggle, by *survival*—is always there, lurking beneath the surface, waiting for a moment to show itself.

I check my watch. Noon.

Probably not the best time to show up unannounced, but Hayven wouldn't give me the address, so I had to go through my own channels to find her. I wasn't sure how long she'd stay in one place, so I didn't wait.

But after a few moments of sitting and staring at the massive home, something clicks.

I know this place.

This house. This family.

You don't grow up around here without knowing who the Sinclairs are. Their name isn't just respected—it's woven into the fabric of the community. And Joe Sinclair? He's not just some wealthy man with a legacy. *He's* the legacy.

Joe Sinclair is a name you don't forget and...*holy shit*. Charlie?

I've served the poor alongside him at food kitchens. I've donated to his foundation—the one working to restore the sugarcane industry in Haiti so they can become a self-sustaining nation again. The man is a legend in philanthropy, a force for good.

And Charlie is *his* daughter.

This just got a whole lot heavier. But I still need to see her. Need to *talk* to her. If anyone can help me out of this mess—*our* mess—it's her.

I step out of the car and take in the flurry of activity. Caterers, florists, cars coming and going. It looks like an entire operation is happening here.

What the hell is going on?

I probably should have had Juliette look into things—make sure there weren't any events happening that would draw press or make my unannounced visit even more complicated. But nothing about this day, this *week*, is going according to plan.

I hesitate for a moment, my gut telling me I'm walking into something important. But I've already come this far and I really don't have the luxury of time on my side right now.

I ring the doorbell and wait, my pulse picking up as I hear footsteps approaching.

And then the door swings open.

Charlie.

My breath stalls at the sight of her.

The plump lips I've spent too many nights thinking about. Those big brown eyes that could read me like an open book. And that damn bob haircut—sharp, sleek, *deadly*.

She's wearing a black leather pencil skirt and a fitted black turtleneck, the kind of effortless elegance that makes it impossible to look away. Her makeup is soft, subtle—just enough to highlight the sharpness of her cheekbones and the fullness of her lips.

I've missed her. And I have to put my hands in my pockets to keep them from grabbing her.

But Charlie? She just narrows her gaze, her expression shifting from shock to something else.

"Hey, Peach," I finally say, my voice soft. My smile wide.

She steps toward me, eyes locked on mine, her expression unreadable.

She's coming in for a hug.

Relief floods through me as I open my arms, ready to welcome her back into them.

Then—

Pain. *Blinding, soul-crushing pain.*

Charlie's knee collides with my groin so hard I see God, and before I can even process the betrayal, she stomps on my foot for good measure.

A strangled wheeze escapes me as I double over, hands clutching my very existence, vision spotting like I've just taken a damn bullet.

Somewhere in the distance—past the ringing in my ears, past the sheer agony swallowing me whole—I faintly hear her yell:

"What the fuck are you doing here?!"

CHAPTER TWELVE

Charlie

The morning of Grandmommy's wake starts the way any proper Sinclair family gathering does—with the *absolute symphony of mayhem*.

Mama's voice bellows from downstairs, barking orders at the kitchen staff like she's leading an army into battle. The clatter of dishes, the rush of footsteps, and the unmistakable scent of something buttery and fried fill the air.

I groan, rolling over in bed, and check my phone. *Two hours.*

Plenty of time to make myself presentable. But first—pancakes.

I shuffle downstairs to find Elijah at the stove, flipping pancakes. Prince sits at the kitchen island, eyes glued to his phone.

"Good morning!" I chirp, sliding into my usual seat.

Both Elijah and Prince glance up, giving me the same unenthusiastic greeting in unison. "Morning."

Before I can even ask, Elijah sets a plate of fresh blueberry pancakes in front of me.

"Thank you, favorite brother," I tease, picking up my fork.

"Your *only* brother, ape lips."

"Forget you, monkey nuts."

Prince lets out a laugh. "You guys are *so* mean to each other!"

I lean in, nudging him playfully. "It's just because he loves me *so much*. If he were nice to me, he'd have to admit he can't live without me."

"And we can't be having people believe that *bullshit*!" Elijah shouts from the stove.

"Language!" Mama's voice cuts through the kitchen like a whip. She steps inside, arms crossed. "Now, you two hurry up and get out of my kitchen so Lucille can clean up!"

Lucille is technically the housekeeper, though Mama flat-out refuses to call her that. Says it makes her feel like she owns slaves. So instead, she just calls her by her first name and pays her a six-figure salary.

If there were ever such a thing as Black guilt—guilt for having wealth—Mama oozed it when it came to paying for help.

"Okay, Mama!" we all say in unison, Prince included.

Mama softens immediately, leaning in to kiss Prince's cheek and tickle his ribs. "Not *you*, Big Mama's baby. You can sit here as long as you want."

I roll my eyes. Mamas really do turn into *Glenda the Good Witch* when grandkids are involved.

Then, I remember I'm still mad at Elijah. I turn to him with a frown. "How come you never told me you run your practice with Lucas? I thought you couldn't stand him."

He shrugs. "He grew on me. We did our residency together, and we realized we shared a lot of the same values around patient care."

I narrow my eyes. "I see. I *still* don't understand why you wouldn't tell me you were so close with my ex. *So* close that you opened a whole damn business with him!"

Elijah sighs, setting his spatula down. "Don't get mad at me because you left and went into hiding like you were in the damn witness protection program! Call more. Come home more. You'd know more, Charlie."

Mama, never one to let an argument go unpunctuated, scoffs. "Come home more, and you might have a *husband*, too, *Charleset-ta*."

I throw my fork down. "Mama, I *swear* to Black Baby Jesus, *today is not the day!*"

She gasps, her hand flying to her chest. "I *beg* your finest *pardon*."

Elijah, always the peacekeeper when Big Daddy isn't around, steps in. "Alright! Let's all go get ready for the wake, shall we? We're expecting a lot of people today."

Mama sniffs, adjusting her robe. "Elijah, make me one of them grocery order things, would you? I need some mustard greens."

We have an entire staff that could handle this for her, but Mama *insists* on ordering from local food delivery services once a week. Says it keeps people working, gives them something to do.

Her way of keeping money in our community, I guess.

It's admirable. *Or whatever.*

Elijah turns, exasperated. "Mama, we're *having today catered*! Why do you need *mustard greens*?"

Mama simply *stares* at him. She doesn't need to say anything else. Elijah sighs in defeat and pulls out his phone to place the order.

"Guess she told you!" I cackle, as I head upstairs to get dressed.

...

By the time I come back downstairs, the house has been transformed into a *proper* Southern wake.

Flowers are arranged, chairs set up for the viewing, the scent of fresh magnolias lingering in the air. The whole town is going to come through today, and Mama has made sure Grandmommy is honored with the kind of elegance she deserves. I admire that about her. She did this for her own mother, and now she's doing it for Daddy's Mama.

I exhale and walk toward the foyer, just as the doorbell rings.

One of the staff members looks at me, waiting for instruction. "I'll get it," I say, figuring it's my turn to start greeting guests.

I swing the door open and—

The blood drains from my face.

No. No, no, no.

"What the fuck is he doing here?!"

Xavier fucking Darcy.

Tall. Broad. Neatly trimmed reddish-brown hair. Those devastatingly handsome hazel eyes. And currently standing on my family's front porch.

If I wasn't pissed and completely caught off guard, I might actually be happy to see him.

"Charlesetta?" Mama's voice calls from behind me. "Who is it? Is it my mustard greens?"

I don't answer. I step outside and *slam* the door behind me before anyone else can get a look at him.

"Charlie?" Big Daddy's voice booms. "Mrs. Ballentine was sending over a cake, too! Make sure it goes to the catering entrance!"

Mercy me.

I'm *panicking*. My heart is hammering. But most of all—I'm *furious*.

I march toward him and do the first thing that comes to mind.

I *nut-kick* him. *Hard.*

He doubles over instantly, a strangled sound escaping his throat as he re-evaluates his entire existence. Then, for good measure, I stomp on his foot.

"What the fuck are you doing here?!"

He doesn't answer. He's... "Are you crying?"

"Are you crazy?!" he wheezes, clutching himself.

"Answer the question! Who told you where I lived? Who told you who I was?!"

"Who you are?!?" he chokes. "Who you are is a fucking lunatic!"

"Charlie?" I hear from behind me.

I whip around.

Xavier leans against the front column, trying to stand upright. *Hot Prince Harry is stronger than I gave him credit for.*

"Charlie," he pants. "I need to talk to you. It's urgent. Please."

I glare. "Are you fucking kidding me?"

Xavier, still hunched over in pain, wheezes, "Hayven said—"

I start bouncing on the balls of my feet like I'm gearing up for a boxing match, cracking my knuckles.

"Oh! Hayven told you where I was? I swear to God, I'm gonna kill that motherfucker too!"

"No! Charlie, I—"

"Charlesetta!" Mama's voice cuts through the air. "Is that my collard greens?!"

"You said mustard greens, Mama!"

The entire family is closing in.

I hear their footsteps, their chatter, the sudden eagerness of people who never answer their own door, now acting like they do this all the time.

I cannot let them see Xavier. Not like this.

I whirl back toward him. "Get on your knees."

Xavier blinks. "What?"

"Get on your knees, Xavier!"

"Charlie?" Big Daddy calls.

"Charlie," Xavier groans, his eyes widening as he gestures towards his groin area. "My balls. It's gonna hurt."

I have no time for this.

Without hesitation, I pull the gun holstered between my thighs and point it straight at his beautiful face.

"Get on your fucking knees, right now. Or I'll shoot."

His eyes go wide, but he drops.

Just as the front door swings open.

"Charlie!"

"Charlesetta?!"

I do the only thing I can think of.

I drop to my knees, throw my arms around Xavier's neck in a death grip, and yell—

"Yes, I *will* marry you!"

CHAPTER THIRTEEN

Charlie

Mama is the first to break the stunned silence. "I'm confused. You just got engaged to the *Uber delivery driver*?"

From the kitchen, Aunt Janie-Mae yells out, "We can't be picky about how God answers prayers!"

More silence. More stunned faces.

I force a tight smile. "No, Mama, Xavier isn't the Uber delivery driver."

Mama's face looks as if recognition begins to register. Like she's seen Xavier somewhere before.

Before I can say more, Big Daddy *bulldozes* through the crowd of aunties, gently moving Mama to the side like she weighs nothing. His deep voice booms through the foyer. "This can't be Xavier Darcy. Man of my city. Coming to propose to my baby girl—my *only* girl—without so much as a courtesy call?"

Xavier is speechless. I don't know if it's because he's still in pain or because I've just publicly forced him into betrothal at gunpoint.

"Uh. Ummm." Xavier opens his mouth, then closes it again. Poor man can't form words.

And just as he looks like he's about to recover enough to say something, the *actual* Uber delivery driver pulls up with Mama's mustard greens.

I clap my hands together, my voice too bright. "Hey, everyone! This is all so sudden, and Xavier doesn't really like crowds or attention, so I'm just gonna take him inside to get settled."

Without waiting for a response, I grab Xavier, yank him off his knees, and drag him into the house like a damn hostage. I guess now, he technically is.

As soon as we round the corner, out of earshot, I spin on my heels and level him with a glare.

"I'm going to ask you *one more time*, Xavier. What are you doing here?"

He just stares at me. Motionless. I have rendered the man deaf and dumb. He looks like he's experiencing an out-of-body event.

"Blink twice if you can hear me."

He blinks. Okay, good, so there's still some brain function left.

I wave a hand impatiently. "Xavier, I really need to *speed things along*. If you haven't noticed, people are arriving at my parents house any minute now. What the hell is going on?"

His voice is hoarse when he finally manages, "You are a *fucking lunatic*."

I stare at him, deadpan. "You said that already."

He groans, adjusting himself in his pants, and I stifle a grin.

"I came here because there is an important matter that needs your attention," he says through clenched teeth. "And due to your particular background and skill set, I thought you'd want to get ahead of it as quickly as possible. But instead, I have been assaulted and humiliated in front of a man I respect."

I frown. "Respect, The Uber delivery driver?"

"Mr. Sinclair! Your *father*!"

I blink. "Yeah...How *do* you know my father?"

Xavier throws his hands in the air. "How do you *not* mention that Joe Sinclair is *your* father?"

"Because it's nobody's business. Because of what I do, because of who I am outside of Louisiana, nobody can know who my father is!"

"Well, all you had to do was say that! You didn't have to launch an all-out attack on my dick!"

"Shhh!" I whisper-yell, covering his mouth with my hand. "Do you *want* to wake the dead?!"

Xavier pulls my hand away, suddenly looking around. His eyes flicker with realization as he takes in our surroundings.

With a straight face, he says, "Charlesetta?"

"Mmm hmm?" My lips press into a thin line.

"Why am I standing in a room with a *dead body*?"

"Because your stupid ass decided to show up on the day we are mourning my grandmother, you fucking prick!"

His expression turns serious. "Watch your mouth! Show some *respect*!" He gestures toward Grandmommy's body at the front of the room.

I throw my hands up. "Well, good thing Grandmommy was always hard of hearin'!"

Xavier rubs his temples. "Can we please go somewhere else to talk? Preferably somewhere where I don't feel like I'm violating a corpse's ears?"

"Fine." I grab his arm and yank him toward the back of the house.

As we walk, I glance over my shoulder. "And since you're here as my fiancé now—"

"Yeah, we really need to talk about that."

"Later." I wave him off. "For now, since you're here as my *fiancé*, you need to address my father like family."

Xavier looks at me warily. "What does that mean?"

"You call him *Big Daddy* instead of Mr. Sinclair. He prefers it."

Xavier stops walking. "I am *not* calling another grown man Big Daddy."

"Oh, yes you *will*."

"I most certainly am not and you are *out* of your fucking mind if you think I will."

I turn to him and lean in, my voice a whisper. "I love how you think you can win this, considering you showed up at my doorstep needing me."

Before he can respond, Big Daddy's voice booms from the other side of the room. "Charlie Chaplin!"

I flash Xavier a smug look before turning around. "Hey, Big Daddy!" I plaster on my best innocent-daughter smile. "I was just taking Xavier to one of the cottages. He's gonna stay there while we wrap things up with the wake, if that's alright with you?"

"Of course, baby girl."

Big Daddy's eyes flick to Xavier. He folds his arms, studying him. "Xavier Darcy, you and I still have a conversation to have."

Xavier steps forward, clearing his throat and extending his hand.

I *quickly* step in front of him. Strategically. Covering his groin...blocking his dick.

Big Daddy grabs his hand to shake. Xavier hesitates, then forces a pained smile. "Sure thing, Mr.—"

His voice *cracks* and strains as he corrects himself. Because I'm squeezing his *dick*. "Big... Daddy, sir."

Big Daddy chuckles. "Big Daddy is just fine. No need to add *mister* or *sir* to it."

Xavier lets out a pained laugh. "Ha. Right. Sure thing, Big...Big Daddy."

I grin as I lead Xavier out the back door.

"I fucking hate you," I hear him mutter.

...

The family cottages sit near the lake, draped in Spanish moss, framed by the towering trees that make the whole place feel untouched by time.

The walk seems longer than usual, probably because I'm painfully aware of Xavier walking beside me. As is my body. It's been a long time since we've been alone together. Not terribly long, but long enough.

I flash back to the dreams I keep having. The ones I refuse to acknowledge. The ones where Xavier does things to me that make me wake up flushed and frustrated.

I shake it off as we reach the cottage door. Entering the code—my birthday—I push the door open and step inside.

Xavier follows me, and I can't help but take in how effortlessly put together he looks. Blue jeans, white polo shirt, and a navy blue sports coat—clean, simple, but expensive in that *quiet money* way.

The preppy look suits him. Too well.

The cottage is the perfect mix of old and new—like someone took a piece of history and gave it a facelift without stripping away its soul.

The oak flooring stretches through the entire space, rich and warm, the kind of wood that creaks just a little underfoot, like it has something to say. The walls are painted a soft cream, and the marble finishes in the kitchen and bathrooms give it a polished, modern feel. But somehow, despite all the upgrades, it still feels *homey*.

Once we're both inside, I turn to face him, arms crossed. "Now," I say, leveling him with a stare. "What do I need to do to get you the *hell* out of here, Mr. Darcy?"

CHAPTER FOURTEEN

Xavier

I rake a hand through my hair, trying to steady my nerves. This is already going worse than I anticipated, and I haven't even told her the full truth yet.

Charlie watches me, arms crossed, expression unreadable. She's waiting, and I know better than to keep her waiting too long. I walk over to my bag, pull out a file, and set it on the coffee table between us.

"Sit down," I say.

She stays put, arching a brow. "Why?"

I don't bother answering. No need to fight with her on this. I just slide the file toward her and gesture to it.

She sighs, drops onto the couch, and flips it open. I watch as she casually flips through the images, her expression unimpressed. "These are colorful, I'll give you that. But what do these have to do with me? Why couldn't Hayven handle this himself?"

I motion toward the file. "Keep going. There's more."

She rolls her eyes but does as I say, her fingers flipping through the pages—until she stops cold.

Her entire body goes still.

The images in front of her aren't just deepfakes or manipulated scandals. I can tell she's reached the ones that look real. That *are* real.

One, in particular, catches her attention. A profile shot. Her naked body, the unmistakable curve of her side, and the tattoo I remember tracing with my fingers.

I step up behind her and bend down, bringing my mouth to her ear and lowering my voice. "I remember every inch of that tattoo," I breathe.

Her breath hitches. She jumps up, putting space between us, but there's only so far she can go. The cottage isn't that big.

I follow, gently, watching as she backs toward the wall that separates the living room from the rest of the space. She's cornering herself, probably without realizing it. My favorite position to have her in.

I stop just short, giving her enough room to breathe, but not enough to escape. "Charlie," I murmur, voice low.

Her eyes dart to mine—wide, uncertain.

She's flustered.

I love that. Love knowing I can rattle her cool exterior with nothing more than a glance.

But what I hate?

How fast it flips the switch in me.

How just being near her turns me from composed and respectable to desperate and starving.

Like a man who's forgotten every ounce of discipline the second she enters the room.

Calm down, X.

"Xavier, I don't understand. How? When did this happen?"

A sharp pang hits my chest. She really doesn't remember. Not even *a little bit.*

"You seriously don't remember?" My voice is more firm now. "Any of it?"

Charlie shakes her head, eyes darting back to the photos. "No. Xavier, what is this? What's going on? Why does someone have *naked photos* of me?" She's no longer flustered, she's confused and panicked.

I take a breath. "When we were in Las Vegas, after Justice and Autika's wedding—"

"After clubbing, I remember going to the buffet, eating my life away, and then going to bed."

I nod. "And then, for some reason, you ended up back at the hotel club later that night."

She frowns. "That doesn't sound right..." Her voice trails off.

"I was there, having a drink after a business meeting, when *you* walked in."

Her expression hardens. "And what, you picked me up?" She asked, trying to piece together the night but still coming up blank.

"Not right away." I smirk. "At first, I just *watched* you."

Charlie tenses.

"You seemed to function well by yourself. In your element," I continue. "Didn't mind turning men down, people-watching, swaying back and forth in your seat to the music."

She rolls her eyes. "*That* sounds about right."

"Then a man slid into the booth with you. And *that's* when you stopped saying no."

She crosses her arms. "And that's when you came to rescue me? When a handsome man caught my eye?"

I shake my head. "No. I watched you."

Her eyes narrow. "How long?"

I hesitate. "A while."

Her lips press together.

"He touched your hand. Brushed a strand of your hair behind your ear—"

"Oh, I bet you hated that," she teases.

I clench my jaw. "I may have bit off a piece of skin inside my mouth."

"Tasted blood?"

I nod, almost grinning. "Tasted blood."

Her expression softens for a second before she shakes it off. "Then what?"

"You tried to get up—probably to go to the restroom—but you stumbled and fell back into your seat."

Her brows furrow. "Okay... I was drinking."

I nod. "Then I thought back to that moment. When he touched your hair. And how he *slightly* touched your drink."

Charlie's face pales. "I *wouldn't* have missed that. I'm trained to *not* miss things like that."

"Like you said," I remind her, "you were drinking."

Her hands go to her temples. "Shit."

"That's when I went over to get you."

Her gaze snaps to mine. "And *him*? Did you kill the asshole?"

I exhale. "We won't speak of him."

She lets out a humorless laugh. "Xavier, I have *quite* the body count. You can tell me."

"He's not dead."

Her eyes narrow.

"At least I don't *think he is*." I shrug. "I've come to learn it's best that my men don't let me in on the details."

She takes a beat, then nods, deadpan. "Okay. My prince. My knight in shining Armani. How exactly does this story end with me naked? In your bed?"

I should tell her everything. But not yet. Not while she's working to solve my case. I don't want anything distracting her from that.

She's still standing near the wall, arms crossed, jaw tight, trying to act unaffected. But I see it—the way her chest rises just a little too sharply, the way her fingers twitch like she doesn't know whether to push me away or pull me closer.

I shove my hands deep into my pockets, *forcing* myself to stay put. If I touch her now, I won't stop. I won't be able to. *Focus, X.*

I take a breath, steadying myself. And then I finish the story, telling her everything—the moments that led up to it, the sheer rage that nearly drove me to murder a man with my bare hands.

Until the moment she murdered my self-control and passionately assaulted my dick.

"It turns out he drugged you, *Peach*," I say, testing the name on my tongue like I always do. "And... well..."

Her eyes narrow. "Well?"

I clear my throat. "You... *sort of* peer-pressured me for sex."

Charlie blinks. Once. Twice. Then tilts her head like she *must* have misheard me.

"I'm sorry. I *what*?"

I cross my arms, meeting her glare. "I tried to say no. Tried to keep you away from my—"

"Dick?"

"Yes! But you wouldn't let me!"

"You mean to tell me that God-knows who has naked pictures of me because I *seduced* you? Like...I took advantage of you?"

I gesture wildly, then point at her facial expression she's making as if the idea is absurd. "*That*! That exact look you're making right now—like the idea is *absurd*! You think because you're small and petite and I'm tall and muscular that this couldn't happen, but—" I shake my head. "You are deceptively strong and alarmingly convincing!"

She bursts out laughing.

I scowl. "It's *not* funny, Charlie. You were *relentless*. You were on me like a damn heat-seeking missile, and no matter how many times I tried to slow you down, you—" I pause, shaking my head like I *still* can't believe it. "You were a *feral* little thing. A *determined, highly skilled, deceptively strong* little thing."

It's the truth. And I'm not proud that I caved so easily. Then again, standing this close to her now, feeling that same gravitational pull, I'm shocked I hadn't caved *harder*—much *sooner*. She's *irresistible*.

Her grin stretches wider as she walks around me.

"I was *on drugs*, remember?" Charlie fires back, hands on her hips like that somehow absolves her of the *actual crimes* committed against my self-control.

I scoff. "I felt like I was being attacked by a Vought Supe!"

Her mouth drops open. "*Shut up!* And *how dare* you compare me to one of those psychos from *The Boys*? I am much better suited for Marvel."

I cross my arms. "I said what I said, Peach. Not my fault you turned into a *sex gremlin* the moment you got a taste of me."

She gasps, snatching up a throw pillow from the couch and *whipping* it at my face. I catch it easily, smirking.

"I believe your exact words were, 'I've been *waiting* to fuck you for a *week*.'"

Charlie's amusement vanishes. Her eyes narrow into slits. "You *liar*."

I shrug. "Want me to call the hotel? Get the security footage?"

Her glare sharpens, but I don't miss the way her jaw tightens—just the slightest hesitation, the flicker of doubt that maybe, just *maybe*, I'm telling the truth.

"So I got you to break your celibacy streak? Little old me?" She says with a southern twang.

"It's rather disappointing you don't remember."

She shrugs. "So you're saying sex with you wasn't a memorable event?"

"I'm saying you were on drugs and the moment you remember, you'll be begging for more."

And that's why I'm grateful that, at least for the time being, there is no footage of that night. Because she won't just see the proof of what I'm saying. She'll see *everything else*—things I'm not ready to let her in on yet. Things I don't even know how to explain.

She huffs. "So what? These people, the ones who want to bring your company down, are they blackmailing you?"

"In a way. They're leaking images daily to tank my IPO. If I back down, shutter my business, they'll back off."

"And if you don't?"

"I won't have much left anyway."

Charlie inhales sharply. "Xavier, images of me, my identifying marks, you showing up here with my family? Did you even consider how this could ruin me? How this could put my family in jeopardy?"

"I was thinking that telling you, getting ahead of it as quickly as possible, would help both of us. I didn't think it would put you in danger. Or anyone else for that matter."

She shakes her head. "Nobody ever means to put someone in danger, Xavier. But when you don't think things through, this is what happens."

I sigh. "So what now?"

She scoffs. "What do you mean, what now?"

I widen my eyes. "How do we stop this?"

"I *love* how you keep involving *me* in this. *I* didn't ask for this."

"No," I smirk. "You *took* it from me. In an *elevator*, no less."

Charlie stops, a flicker of something crossing her face and her entire demeanor shifts in an instant.

"Charlie? You good, Peach?"

She shakes it off. "I'm fine. And stop calling me Peach."

We both sink onto the sofa.

"Fine. How do you suggest *I* handle this?" I ask. "I'll follow your lead. I just know I *can't* do this without you."

She exhales. "Because I'm in the pictures?"

"Because you're *the best*. Anything less is unacceptable to me."

After a long silence, she nods. "Fine. I'll help you."

Relief washes over me, but before I can fully exhale, she lifts a finger. "Under one condition."

Here we go.

She tilts her head, eyes sharp with mischief. "While we're here, you play along as my fiancé."

I blink as the panic settles deep in my stomach. "And face Joe Sinclair? You heard the man! He's already pissed I didn't ask for your *fake fucking hand* first!"

Charlie shrugs, completely unbothered. "You should've thought about that before you just showed up like this." She tilts her head, grinning. "Now you're stuck. We go together now!"

I gape at her. "*Go together*? Charlie, this isn't some high school relationship where you claim me at lunch in front of your friends—"

"Oh, but it *is*, fiancé," Charlie teases, dragging out the word just to make me suffer. "And now that you've put them all in jeopardy, you *have* to help me keep their suspicions at bay when it comes to the life I *really* lead."

I frown. "Really lead? What does that even *mean*?"

She inhales deeply, hesitating for just a second before meeting my gaze. "Can I trust you?"

I smirk. "Charlie, you have a *distinct* advantage over me."

Her brow lifts. "And what's that?"

I gesture vaguely toward her thigh—the one I *know* she's hiding another weapon in. "A gun. Several, actually." I tilt my head. "So, if you're asking if you can trust me? The answer is *yes*. If you're asking if the *only* reason you can trust me is because you're currently *armed to the teeth*? Also *yes*."

She grins. "Guess if we're gonna be *fake engaged*, there are some things you should know about me."

She sits on the edge of the couch, her expression unreadable as she starts talking. About her family. The expectations she's spent her life trying to outrun. About the boy she left behind—the boy her family thought she'd *eventually* marry.

And for some reason, I feel a flicker of appreciation. A rare kind of *privilege* in the way she trusts me with all of this.

"So," I say after a moment, piecing it all together, "your family has *no clue* that you've been *practically* a spy for the last fifteen years and instead think you're just some big-shot *business consultant*?"

She shrugs. "Yep. It was my official cover for years, so they even sent me to business school to make it believable. Now I look the part. Talk the part. And my family has no idea what I really do. *Used to do.*"

I shake my head. "Fascinating."

And I *mean it*. She is, without a doubt, one of the most *fascinating* people I've ever met.

She leans forward, her voice lower now. "So you understand why they can't find out about me, right? It would be just as dangerous if they started snooping around, asking questions."

I groan, rubbing my temples. "I swear to God, you're going to be the *death* of me."

She winks. "Don't threaten me with a *good* time, *Mr. Darcy*."

I run a hand down my face. "Charlie, this is *serious*—"

"So is my family. And if you want me to keep your life, your company and your penis intact long enough to fix your problem, you better get comfortable being my loving, devoted, soon-to-be husband."

It won't be hard. I just hate that I'm being forced to do it under duress.

I stare at her, incredulous. "You do realize pretending to be engaged is an actual commitment, right? We're talking PDA. Family questioning how we met. Possibly even—" I swallow. "Matching outfits."

She grins, wicked. "You scared, Mr. Darcy?"

"Of you? Yes. Very." I say, adjusting myself in my pants.

I narrow my eyes. "We should draft a contract. Lay out the terms."

Charlie snorts. "A *contract*? That's adorable. And when it comes to PDA, we can play it by ear. I'm a professional at faking it, remember?"

I cross my arms. "If we're doing this, we need *boundaries*, don't you think?"

"I have a gun. That's a boundary."

"I think we need something more concrete. Something binding, don't you?"

She stands and begins pacing before she turns to me and raises a brow. "Such as?"

I don't like how *defiant* she is. It's like talking to a brick wall wrapped in sarcasm and a smart mouth. It's impossible to get through to her when she *thinks* she's in control.

So, I change my approach.

I inch forward, watching closely. Her breath hitches—just slightly. It's almost imperceptible, but I *catch it*. She's trying to play it cool, but I know her better than that. She's fighting it. Fighting *me*.

And *losing*.

"A contract that addresses things like touching?" I ask, my voice dropping just enough to make it a challenge.

She squares her shoulders, steadying herself.

"No touching. Not unless *absolutely* necessary."

"See, how was I supposed to know what you wanted if you didn't *tell* me?" I ask, my grin sinful. "It should be put into writing."

I step closer, letting my fingers trail along the inside of her wrist, tracing deliberate circles against her skin. Her pulse flutters beneath my touch, betraying her calm facade.

"What about this?" I murmur. "Hand holding? Like when we step into a crowded room full of your family and closest friends. It has to *look* real, right?"

Her breath slows, but she doesn't pull away. "That's fine, I guess," she finally says, voice just a touch softer than before.

This new approach seems to be working just fine.

I step even closer, my body nearly pressing into hers. "And this?" My hand moves up, grazing her cheek with the lightest touch. "Do you mind my hands touching you like this, Peach?"

Her lips part slightly, her eyes flickering with something I *definitely* recognize.

"Depends on where you touch me." she says, her voice the faintest breath.

I smirk. "Your back..." My fingers ghost down the line of her spine before coming back up to cup her jaw. "Or maybe even something as gentle as this."

Charlie sways, just a fraction of an inch, before catching herself.

"If the time calls for it," she manages.

"And kissing, *Peach*?" I murmur, my thumb brushing along the edge of her mouth. "Can I put my mouth on you?"

I move to close the space, my hand sliding to the back of her neck, tilting her chin up to mine. I can *feel* her breath against my lips, warm and unsteady.

But just before our mouths touch, she *turns her head*.

Her voice is sharper now. "Only when I *say* and only when *I* make the first move."

I grin, not the least bit deterred. "With tongue?"

She narrows her eyes. "Only if *I* lead."

I chuckle, tilting my head. "You're going to have to get it out of your mind that you have *any* power here, *Peach*. You only win because I *let* you. You'd do well to remember that."

She rolls her eyes, folding her arms. "Okay, *Darkwing Duck Dynasty*. Take it easy."

I blink. She's instantly killed the mood. "Did you just call me a duck-hunting superhero?"

She smirks, folding her arms and effectively shielding her nipples. "If the swamp people accent fits!"

I step even closer, my voice dipping low. "Don't act like you don't *love* the way my voice *sings* your name, *Charlesetta*."

Yeah. She *likes* it.

And I love that she *likes* it.

"So again," I continue. "Do you think we need a contract for this? So we remain on the same page and all."

She shakes her head, muttering under her breath as she walks over to the coffee table. Not wanting to allow her to put too much distance between us, I follow her.

Then—without warning—she hikes her leg up onto the coffee table and I jump back, my hands instinctively fly to my crotch. "Charlie, no!"

She smirks. "Relax. I'm not about to neuter you."

Slowly, she reaches down to her ankle and pulls out—Jesus Christ—a knife.

I exhale. Not sure if I should be relieved or more concerned.

She twirls the blade between her fingers, then extends a hand toward me. "Give me your palm."

I eye her warily. "For what?"

She sighs. "Just give me your hand."

I hesitate. "Couldn't we just—I don't know—sign something? I'm really good at signing things."

She steps close with a seductive smile. "Don't you trust me, Mr. Darcy?"

"With a knife in your hand? Absolutely not." I snap back.

Charlie pulls her bottom lip into her mouth. "Paper can be destroyed. *This?*" She flips the knife effortlessly. "This is forever."

Something about the way she says it makes my throat tighten.

I grumble but I remain still.

She takes the knife, pressing the blade gently against my palm. With one smooth motion, she makes a small, precise cut. It stings, but barely. Before I can say anything, she slices her own palm in the same way.

Then, she clasps my hand in hers and squeezes.

I stare at our joined hands, the warmth of her skin, the slow mingling of our blood.

"Blood brothers?" I murmur.

Charlie smirks. "Something like that."

We have *nine days* to fix this before my IPO goes up in flames.

Nine days to outmaneuver the bastards trying to take me down.

And somehow, in the middle of all this madness, I've ended up *engaged*—to the most dangerous, unpredictable, *exasperating* woman I've ever met.

God help me.

CHAPTER FIFTEEN

Charlie

Twenty Years Old

Geneva stands off to the side by her truck, arms crossed, watching quietly as Lucas makes his *last-ditch effort*.

"We're supposed to go to grad school here," he says, his voice tight, desperate. "*Together*. In Louisiana."

Lucas' grip on my waist is just a little firmer than usual—like he thinks he can hold me here, keep me from slipping away.

We've done everything together—me, Lucas, and Neva. We were a unit, inseparable since freshman year.

I was supposed to study law at Xavier University. Lucas was going to med school there. Geneva had always dreamed of opening her own restaurant and lounge, and she was well on her way. She even put herself through hospitality management school, because her parents wouldn't dare pay for her to go to school to own a juke joint when they expected her to go to law school. We had a plan. A future. A promise to stay close, to build our lives together here in Louisiana.

But then North Kensington University in Atlanta came calling, and saying no was never an option.

It was still the South, but not *our* South. It was *new money, skyscrapers, and progress*—a world away from the slow drawl and small-town expectations we grew up in.

It's always been my dream.

I didn't even tell anyone I'd applied. I knew my parents would refuse, that they'd shut the idea down before I could even explain why I wanted to go—why I *needed* to go. And maybe that was exactly why I had to. Why I had to break Lucas' heart like this.

I lift my hand to his cheek, my thumb brushing over the sharp line of his jaw. "I know, Luke. And I'm sorry. But how often does someone who looks like us get offered a full-ride scholarship to North Kensington University?"

I say it like I *needed* the scholarship to go, like it was my only option—but the truth is, I couldn't risk my parents cutting me off. If I didn't go where they wanted, they likely wouldn't have paid a cent.

And I wasn't about to give them the power to control my future. Not anymore.

His jaw clenches. "It's all the way in Atlanta, Charlesetta. When will we even see each other?"

My chest tightens. Every time he says my name like that, it cracks something deep inside me. It's not just the pain in his voice—it's the way he's reaching for a version of me that doesn't exist anymore. The girl I used to be. The one who never would've thought about leaving him behind.

Charlesetta.

For a while, I convinced myself I could settle into the life my mother was carving out for me. That I could be the daughter she wanted, the woman she expected. The wife of a doctor.

Loving Lucas for the rest of my life would be easy—he's the kind of man every woman dreams of. And for a while, the deeper I fell in love with this man, I started to believe loving him would be enough.

But I could see it happening. *Feel* it happening.

Lucas was settling into the idea of me becoming his high-end wallflower. His perfect, poised wife. And a piece of me started to wither at the thought.

So I have to go.

I *need* to.

"This is my dream, Lucas," I whisper, my voice raw. "You, of all people, should understand that."

His throat bobs. "I do," he says. "But you are *my* dream, Charlesetta."

Tears burn the back of my eyes, and I step closer, pressing my forehead against his. "I'll come back for you." The promise falls from my lips before I can stop it.

Lucas exhales sharply, his hands gripping my arms like I might vanish right in front of him. "Promise me," he murmurs.

I slide my pinky against his, just like I did on prom night, sealing my fate with a touch so small it shouldn't feel this big.

"I swear."

And then I leave.

I leave Louisiana.

I leave Lucas.

I leave the promise behind, too.

CHAPTER SIXTEEN

Charlie

The air is thick with the scent of fresh flowers and polished wood, the familiar hum of hushed voices and quiet sobs filling the space.

Grandmommy's wake is *exactly* how Mama planned it—elegant, dignified, a celebration of life rather than an expression of grief. But grief is still here, lingering beneath the surface, clinging to every word of condolence, every hand squeeze, every long, drawn-out hug.

I keep moving through the space, nodding, smiling where appropriate, exchanging pleasantries with people I barely remember but who *clearly* remember me.

Xavier stayed behind at the cottage, checking in with his team, doing whatever it is billionaires do when they're not busy making life infinitely more complicated for the rest of us.

I don't know what to do with the way he affects me. Every time he gets close, it's like my body betrays me, pulled to him in ways I can't explain. I *hate* that I let my guard slip with him. That he gets under my skin, past my defenses, into my head.

I've infiltrated armies. Interrogated terrorists. *Been* interrogated by some of the best in the world.

And yet *this man*? He shatters every layer of defense I've been trained to keep intact.

It's some real enemies-to-lovers shit, the kind I read about, but none of my smutty romance novels ever included a fake engagement sealed with a blood oath and a looming international scandal.

I have no idea how to fight it.

Or if I even *want* to.

"Shut up, Charlie. You can't have him."

I never understood the need for something that felt a lot like two funerals. We won't bury Grandmommy for another 2-days, and yet here we are, dressed in black, shaking hands, nodding politely as people murmur the same condolences.

I've been hiding out in the kitchen, keeping busy, pretending I'm here for a reason other than avoiding eye contact with people who think they knew my grandmother better than I did. I'll go back in once I hear the minister make the announcement for prayer.

I take a deep breath, reaching for a piece of ham off the counter, letting the salty bite distract me from the heaviness of the day.

"Saw that," Big Daddy's deep voice rumbles from behind me.

I don't even flinch, just chew and shrug. "Figured somebody would." I turn to face him, offering a small smile. "Mama sure did a good job today."

Big Daddy steps closer and presses a kiss to my forehead, his way of saying he sees me, even when I try to disappear. "Make sure you tell your mother that."

"She already knows. She's a perfectionist."

Big Daddy gives me *that* look. The one that says *you think you know everything, but you don't know shit.* "Your mother is more sensitive than you think, Charlie. Tell her what you just told me."

He's always trying to get me and Mama to understand each other better. Says we're too much alike, too damn stubborn for our own good.

It usually takes a few attempts—mostly because neither of us likes to admit when the other has a point—but if anyone can get through to us both, it's Joe Sinclair.

Big Daddy has a way of making people listen. Even when they don't want to. *Especially* when they don't want to.

Before I can argue, Mama walks in, heels clicking against the floor, still carrying herself like the most composed woman in the room. "Tell me what?"

Big Daddy nudges me, and I feel my stomach tighten.

I clear my throat, my voice stiff. "I said you really did Grandmommy proud. Everything is beautiful. Just like you always make it, Mama."

It feels like *choking down glass*, but there—I said it. I paid her a compliment.

Mama stills for a moment, as if she's making sure she heard me right. Then she nods, her voice softer than usual. "Thank you, Charlesetta. That... that means a lot."

I can tell she *needed* to hear that. And I guess, in some way, it feels good to make her feel good.

I wish I knew where our relationship fell apart. When things shifted from easy to strained, when simple conversations turned into landmines, and compliments started feeling like obligations instead of natural moments between a mother and daughter.

Because despite everything, despite the years of tension and the stubborn walls we've both built, I do *wish* we had more of this—whatever *this* is. Not saying that I want us to be like Timantha and her mom, they're borderline unhealthy with how close they are. But I do wish we had *some* sort of relationship.

Before I have time to think about it too much, the minister rings a bell, signaling for everyone to take their seats. The ceremony Mama planned is about to begin, where friends and family will stand and share memories about Grandmommy.

"I guess we'd better get out there," Mama says, smoothing the fabric of her dress before walking ahead.

Big Daddy walks behind us both, placing a firm, warm hand on my shoulder.

"You did good, *Charlie Chaplin*," he whispers.

...

I glance at my watch, relief washing over me as I realize the most exhausting part is finally over. Without hesitation, I make a beeline for the kitchen.

I had just endured an endless loop of long, drawn-out speeches about Grandmommy—how she sang soprano in the choir for thirty years, how she was the *only* deaconess trusted to count the money after the last pastor got caught using church funds to pay off his *mistresses*, and, of course, how she made the *best* chitterlings on this side of the Mississippi.

"And they never stanked!" someone had yelled from the back during that particular speech.

I smile as I remember some of the ridiculous speeches, but now, as I enter the lobby area where people are gathered with plates of food, I stop short.

Because standing there, front and center, is Lucas' family. And staring directly at me, her expression unreadable but *already* on the offensive, is Mrs. Ballentine.

I can already feel my patience wearing thin. We've never liked each other, but she really started hating me after I left Lucas pining for me—twice.

Her eyes sweep over me, and I *know* she's about to come at me sideways before she even opens her mouth.

"You always did clean up well, Charlesetta," she says, lips pressed tight in that way that's meant to look polite but feels like a slap. Her eyes skim over me, then stall on my hair. Her nose wrinkles like she's just smelled low-income. "Good to see you're no longer running around in the mud with frogs. Though I suppose you're still in that... *phase* with your hair."

I smile sweetly, tilting my head just enough to be condescending. "You mean the phase where I wear my hair how I damn well please? You know, that un-stuck-up, sophisticated, bad-ass kind of way?"

Heffa.

Her jaw tightens like she just bit into a lemon.

Point for me.

"And your career," she continues, voice dripping with condescension. "Still off doing God-knows-what for that elusive business of yours?"

I tilt my head. "You mean the *very successful* business that allows me to travel the world and live life on my own terms?"

She purses her lips, clearly unimpressed. "You could have had a great life with Lucas. A family. Stability."

Mmmm. Hmmm.

"But I guess," she sighs dramatically, "you were always too good for this town. Too good for my Lucas."

I don't even think before I respond.

"Oh, I don't know, Mrs. Ballentine. I'm seeing Lucas tonight, actually." I smile, slow and sweet, watching as her face pinches.

"He would have told me."

I tilt my head sarcastically. "Would he, though?"

She lets out a huff, turning on her heel and marching off, clearly fuming. *Old wench.*

Unfortunately, my victory is short-lived.

"I *thought* I heard you were engaged to a white ass billionaire?"

I whip around to find Elijah, grinning.

I shush him immediately. "Keep your voice down!"

His eyes narrow. "So, what's all that about?"

I shrug, brushing imaginary lint off my dress. "I just said it to piss off Lucas' mom. I'm only seeing him as a *friend*."

Elijah folds his arms. "And what does your billionaire fiancé think about that?"

I lift my chin. "He has no opinion one way or the other."

Because I haven't told him.

"So," Elijah says, cautious, his eyes scanning the room like he's checking for bugs. "I got the weirdest alert on my phone."

That gets my attention. I narrow my eyes, already bracing myself.

"Geneva sent me a screenshot of an article," he continues. "It's you. At least it looks like you. In a pretty compromising position."

I groan. "Shit. Where was it posted?"

"Some Atlanta tabloid site. But it's already making waves down here in NOLA. Your skin tone, your haircut—unmistakable. The only thing keeping people guessing, is the fact that they're calling you Anastasia in the article. But now that you've rolled up here all engaged or whatever, it's only a matter of time before Mama and Big Daddy catch wind."

I slap my hand over his mouth. "You cannot let them find out! They will be scandalized, and I'll never hear the end of it."

He pulls my hand away, arrogant. "So what's it worth to you? How much you gonna pay me to keep quiet?"

I smack him in the chest. "I'll pay you in silence. By not telling Big Daddy you scratched his Maserati while he was out of the country—and used my people to get it fixed before he noticed."

His mouth drops. "You traitorous cow."

"Ya mama."

Even though Elijah always knows how to keep me grounded—teasing, joking, pushing my buttons like only a big brother can—I'm not immune to the way my heart's pounding right now.

The thought of those photos spreading, making it this close to home? It's a gut punch.

I make a silent note to pull away soon and call Hayven. I need to know what he's found, what kind of digital fire we're walking into. And what's being done to contain it.

Guilt twists in my stomach. I brushed him off when he tried to warn me—when he brought it up back at the office, soft and careful like he was trying not to spook me. But I was too busy trying to outrun Xavier, too focused on putting distance between us instead of paying attention to the threat staring me in the face.

Now it's here.

Loud. Messy. And dangerously close.

And Lord have mercy, if my mama gets wind of this—if she so much as sees a *thumbnail* of one of those photos—she won't just be mad. She'll be convinced I've signed my name in hell's guestbook, front and center, in permanent ink, with the devil himself as my witness.

Elijah shakes his head, narrowing his eyes as he shifts topics a bit. "And what exactly are you doing with Xavier Darcy anyway? The man always gave 'emotionally constipated mogul' energy. He's got that whole 'I donate millions to look good but secretly hate people' vibe."

I scoff, ready to fire back, but my words never make it out.

Because my mind drifts.

To the endearing way Xavier stumbles over his words when he's around me, how his confidence—so effortless with everyone else—seems to falter in my presence. To the way he watches me, like

I'm something he doesn't know what to do with. Like he wants me, but doesn't know how to want me. Like I unnerve him in a way he's not used to.

And damn it, I like it. *Love* it, actually.

The control it gives me over him. It's intoxicating. The power struggle between us, the relentless push and pull, the electricity that fuels both our passion and our rage—it's the kind of addiction that ruins people. It's ruining me and I've barely touched him.

Part of me—a big part—wishes I remembered that night. *The* night. The one from the photos.

At least then I'd have something real to hold onto. Some memory I could tuck away and keep just for me.

A moment that was *ours,* not captured through a lens or pieced together from secondhand stories.

Just him.

Just me.

And whatever magic happened in between.

Because I *can't* have him. Not now. Especially not when I'm working with him to fix this mess. Things are already complicated enough. And with Xavier Darcy, complications are guaranteed and disaster just as imminent.

"Charlie?" Elijah snaps his fingers in front of my face, dragging me back to earth.

I blink. "What? Sorry. Zoned out. What did you say?"

"I asked how you even met Xavier."

"Oh. He and Timantha's husband are best friends. Business partners, too. I've seen him at a few events over the years." I shrug, reaching for my drink. "One thing led to another. We hit it off."

Elijah leans back, arms crossed. "Yeah, well... he's not like anyone you've ever been with."

I roll my eyes. "Lucas is the only man you've ever seen me with for longer than five minutes."

He doesn't laugh. Doesn't say a word. Just watches me like he's trying to read between lines I haven't written yet.

And it makes me nervous.

Because he's not wrong.

"Still, he seems like an ass. Nothing like I'd expect for you."

I clear my throat, shifting under his stare. "Xavier was like that at first with me. But I got to know him, and he got used to me. We have an *understanding* now."

Elijah raises a brow. "I'm a *doctor*, and even *I* think that sounded clinical as hell. Like your engagement is some sort of an *arrangement*."

A flicker of panic sparks in my chest.

I let out a *too loud*, nervous laugh. "*Ha!* What? Boy! That's *crazy!*" I wave a hand dramatically. "*An arrangement?* Who even says that? Just because Xavier is a billionaire, you think he participates in arranged marriages or something?"

Elijah crosses his arms. "What's going on with you?"

Damn it. I wipe a hand down the back of my neck. "Hmm? What do you mean?"

"Charlie—I always thought the day my baby sister came home with a man on her arm, you'd be...I don't know... happier. Planning the big day with Mama or something—"

"Elijah, when have you *ever* known me to be all giddy and girly about a man? Or planning *anything* with Mama, for that matter?" I blurt, desperate to shift the focus. "Or *anything* ever?"

He smirks. "I guess you were always running around beating up on boys instead of kissing on them."

"Exactly! Just the fact that I allowed a man to come home with me—"

"Sounded like he ambushed you."

I groan. "Fine. Whatever! The point is, the fact that I let a man be here at all, around your *illiterate* ass, should say a lot more than the words I use to describe my relationship with him!"

Elijah narrows his eyes, clearly not convinced.

I glance around, debating if I can knock over a candle. Because if he keeps asking real questions, I might have to set something on fire to create a diversion.

"Anyway, I need to take some food to my man, my man, my man!"

"Eww."

I gather up a plate of food for Xavier, grabbing an extra serving of cornbread just to be nice.

As I head toward the door, Elijah calls after me.

"Try to keep it down if you two plan on *pre-maritally sinning* in that cottage tonight."

I don't even turn around. I just flip him off over my shoulder and head out the door.

CHAPTER SEVENTEEN

Charlie

The walk back to the cottage feels like the green mile—each step heavier than the last—as I make my way toward the man who lights everything in me on fire.

Xavier. That man will be the death of me. And the worst part is, I think I might die smiling.

I find myself adjusting my dress, smoothing my hair, while simultaneously scolding myself for even caring how I look before stepping inside.

I push open the door, holding up the plate. "I come bearing food."

Xavier looks up from his laptop, his hazel eyes sweeping over me before settling on the plate. "That's the best thing you've said all day."

I head to the kitchen to set the food down on the kitchen table, eyeing him with mock disapproval. "You *really* need to work on your flattery, X."

He closes the laptop in his lap and leans back against the couch, watching me with that unreadable expression that always makes me nervous. "I said it's the best thing you've said to me all day," he murmurs. Then, his voice drops just slightly, smooth and soulful. "But seeing you walk through that door? *By far* the best thing I've seen in my entire life."

My stomach does that annoying little flip—the one that betrays me every damn time he's near me. It won't let me deny it or lie to myself...

I want him.

"Whatever," I mutter, waving him off as I *try* to ignore the heat creeping up my neck. I busy myself adjusting the containers of food, pretending like his words didn't just burrow under my skin. "Anything happen while I was away?"

"I met with my team. They're working on tracing the leak. Something about the photographer's angles—it wasn't random. Someone was *trailing* me. And the only way they'd know exactly where I'd be is if someone *inside* tipped them off."

I nod, processing. "Okay. *Progress*," I say, grabbing two wine glasses from the cupboard. "I've got my tools but we'll need every lead we can get."

I don't turn around immediately, letting the weight of what he's saying settle. This isn't just a smear campaign—it's *calculated*. Someone is playing a long game, and whoever it is, they know exactly how to hit him where it hurts. And more importantly, they know me.

Xavier steps up behind me and grabs the wine bottle and the corkscrew. Then he opens the bottle of wine with practiced ease, pouring us each a glass before settling into the chair at the small kitchen table. It looks like a child's table with him sitting at it.

I glance around the cottage, taking in the modest surroundings. This must be *so* uncomfortable for him. A man who flies private, lives in a *ridiculously* luxurious but secluded home (yes, I may have internet-stalked him), and—oh yeah—*owns a freaking island.*

I lean against the kitchen sink, watching as he prepares to dig into his food, fully expecting him to eat in silence.

But then he looks up at me, his hazel eyes locked onto mine.

"Share a meal with me, *Peach.*"

That thing with these Louisiana men again. The way Xavier doesn't ask. The way he never really has to with me.

"I know you are sort of working with me on this case but, you don't have to guard me like I'm some asset. Come sit with me."

I'm not used to this.

I'm not used to environments like *this*.

I enjoy my time with men, and then I leave them where they're at. They don't follow me home. They don't sit at my family's estate, acting like they belong. They don't invite me to share a meal with them like we're something more than temporary. And they sure as hell don't call me Peach.

I don't know how to be with him. How to *act* around him. So, I do what I've been trained to do. I treat this like an assignment. *A job.* The only way I *know* how to be. Unattached.

Because everything about this situation feels foreign. Everything except him. And that's the part I can't explain. Every instinct I've honed, every move I've mastered—fades the second he's near. Like he rewrites the rules just by existing.

I exhale, shaking my head as I pull out a chair. "Fine. I'll eat with you."

Xavier smirks like he just won something. Maybe he did. But I'm too hungry to examine it.

I lift the lids off the containers one by one, rattling off each dish as I go. "Mac and cheese, collard greens, cornbread, red beans and rice, smothered pork chops, candied yams, baked chicken—" I pause, sniffing the last container. "And, of course, sweet potato pie."

Xavier's eyes widen, his fork already halfway to his mouth. "Damn. I haven't had food like this in ages."

I raise a brow. "Where the hell did you ever eat like this?"

He gives me a pointed look. "This is Louisiana, honey. *Everyone* has someone in their life with enough soul in them to throw down in the kitchen."

I burst out laughing. "And who was it in *your* family?"

Xavier winks. "Me."

"Whatever! I'll believe that when I see it."

"You just might, Peach. You just might."

We spend the first few moments digging into our food. Xavier is humming in approval before looking at me thoughtfully. "Why do you lie to your family about who you really are?"

His question catches me off guard.

I sit back, stalling. "What do you mean?"

Xavier's gaze is steady, sharp "You heard me, Charlie. Why do they only get *pieces* of you?"

I push my food around on my plate, avoiding his eyes. "Because I never wanted the life they painted for me, but it's easier to pretend. What my family expects of me is suffocating. Stuffy. *Predictable.*"

His frown deepens. "What's wrong with predictability?"

I snort. "That's like asking what's wrong with *only* fucking missionary."

Xavier chokes on his drink, coughing into his fist before quickly composing himself. His eyes narrow, sharp and assessing. "Do you always use humor and crass language to avoid your truth, *Charlesetta?*"

My shoulders tense. It's not lost on me that he's switched to my *full name.*

But more importantly—*who the hell does he think he is?*

I scoff. "I'm not—" I stop, my mouth snapping shut. Because I don't actually *know* how to finish that sentence. And by the way Xavier's watching me, all smug and knowing, he *knows* it too.

"Not what?" he presses. "Not hiding who you really are? Not siphoning pieces of yourself off so you're deemed acceptable to the people *you think* are most important? So their opinions of you are favorable?"

I shake my head, trying to shake him off. "You don't get it. My family—"

Xavier leans forward, resting his elbows on the table, eyes locked onto mine. "I've spent time with your father—volunteering, speaking at community events. He doesn't seem as unreasonable as you make him out to be."

I snap my head up, my amusement *gone*. "Don't," I warn. "Remember why you're here, Xavier. You're playing a part and I'm helping you. You don't know me *or* my family."

Before he can say anything else, I check my phone and jump up.

"Where are you going?" Xavier asks, his tone clipped.

"I have to get ready."

"For *what*? You haven't even finished your food."

I casually shrug. "I'm going for a walk with Lucas."

Xavier drops his fork with a sharp clatter. His jaw tightens, his fingers flexing like he's trying to resist the urge to strangle something. Or someone. Probably Lucas.

"You mean *Lucas*, your *ex*?"

"Yes, *my ex*," I reply, dragging out the words just to see the vein in his neck pop. "But we're *just friends*."

His eyes darken, his expression full of disbelief. "Okay then. Tell your *fucking friend* to sit his ass on this couch so the *three* of us can have a chat. Hell, I'd like to take a walk. I could use the exercise."

I roll my eyes. "Don't be ridiculous, Xavier. I'll be back before you know it. *Finish your food.*"

But he's already out of his chair, *stalking* after me as I head into the bedroom where the staff has brought my bags.

"You *finish* your food," he mutters through gritted teeth.

I glance over my shoulder, arching a brow. "This demanding side of you? The one where you *think* you can control me? *Cute.* Really *cute*," I say, dripping in sarcasm as I pull a red sweater dress from my suitcase.

Xavier folds his arms, standing in the doorway, brooding. "Charlie, you are *not* leaving this house in that."

I flash him a slow, defiant grin. Then, keeping *perfect* eye contact, I grab the hem of my black funeral skirt and shimmy out of it, leaving me in nothing but my black lace bra and panties.

Xavier freezes. "Peach…" He groans.

I watch his throat bob as he swallows hard. His hands clench into fists, like he's trying to figure out what to do with them.

I take my time slipping into the dress, smoothing it down over my hips before turning to face the mirror. I make a show of checking myself out, adjusting the hem, and then—just for fun—I do an extra little turn, paying special attention to my behind..

"I'm not wearing what *where*, Xavier?" I ask, feigning innocence before strutting into the bathroom to freshen up my makeup.

Xavier is *fuming*.

"If he's just a *friend*, why do you need to put on makeup?"

I sigh dramatically, dabbing on some lip gloss. "I'm a *grown-ass woman*, Xavier. I wear makeup for *me*. Never a man."

He lets out a humorless laugh, his frustration simmering just beneath the surface.

"Look, if this has anything to do with what I said about your father—"

I whip around, holding up a hand. "Let me stop you *right* there. You were *not* a part of this equation, or even my life, until *twelve hours ago*, okay? I already made these plans *before* you got here, and I'm *not* canceling them just because your *feelings* are hurt."

His nostrils flare. "My *feelings* are *not* hurt."

I raise a brow. "Really? Because you *sound* hurt."

"We were *having a conversation*, Charlie, and you're just *up and leaving*—"

"I'll be back *soon*."

Xavier lets out a sharp laugh. "Back *soon*? Ha. Yeah. What the *hell* does that even mean?"

I grab my jacket, slipping it on as I brush past him into the living room. "I just need a few minutes to catch up with him, that's all."

"A few *minutes*?" His voice drips with sarcasm as he follows me. "You *just need* a few *minutes* with *him*?"

I throw my hands up. "Stop *mocking* me like a toddler."

His eyes narrow. "You *stop*—" His sentence trails off as realization dawns.

I smirk. "Yeah. You hear it now, don't you?"

I grab my purse and head for the door. "I'll be back in an *hour*."

He rubs a hand over his face. "Why the *hell* do you need to take a *walk* anyway? What is this, junior high school?"

I smirk. "What are you, *jealous*?"

His jaw tightens. "You're supposed to be my *fiancée*. I'm definitely not okay with it *even looking* like you're entertaining someone else."

I scoff. "This is not the *eighteen hundreds*, X. I am *more than capable* of defending my own honor to the nosy people of NOLA."

His voice drops. "I'm not capable of controlling my temper when it comes to another man putting his hands on you."

I take a breath, suddenly *way* too aware of how close we are. "This is *fake*, Xavier. Stop acting like—"

Before I can finish, he's in front of me, *towering* over me, closing the space between us in an instant.

I'm pinned between him and the door and this sudden shift feels like something I've never felt from him before, yet it's familiar.

"*Say it again.*" His voice is low, rough. *Dangerous.* "Look me in my eyes and say it isn't real, Charlesetta."

I swallow hard, his hazel eyes burning into mine, daring me to finish my sentence.

I don't.

Xavier steps closer. "Do you want me to show you how real it is?"

I hold my ground, forcing steel into my spine. "I want you to stop playing these games with me, Xavier."

His head tilts slightly, assessing me like I'm some kind of puzzle he needs to solve. "What is that supposed to mean?"

I exhale sharply. "Exactly what I said! Stop trying to seduce me. Stop trying to make me *feel* things for you."

His brows knit together, his gaze burning into mine. "Why?"

I pause. The real answer is sitting right there, hovering between us, waiting to be spoken.

But I *won't* give it to him.

Because my work has taught me *one* thing above all else—you *never* trust anyone with your weaknesses.

So I deflect. "Because."

He waits.

"Because I don't do serious relationships. I'm used to quick encounters and leaving things there."

His jaw ticks. "And that's what you want with me?"

"No, Xavier." I square my shoulders, my voice firm. "I don't want anything with you."

His expression darkens, but I push forward before he can interrupt.

"For right now, you are my client, and I am responsible for solving this case for you. As payment, you are pretending to be my fiancé so my family doesn't get put into any more danger now that you've shown up here. Is that understood?"

"And then, when this is all over, we just go our separate ways?"

"Exactly."

A muscle ticks in his jaw. His expression is unreadable, his eyes stormy.

"I don't believe that's what you want, Peach."

"Believe it, Xavier."

I expect him to argue. To push. To press his advantage like he always does.

But he doesn't.

Instead, his voice drops, quiet and raw. "Charlie," he whispers.

And damn it, there's something in his tone—something wrecked, something pleading that makes me want to step closer when I should be stepping away.

"It's almost dark outside," he murmurs.

It almost sounds like a *plea*.

I bend slightly and lift the hem of my dress, just enough to remind him of what's beneath... just inside my thigh.

His eyes *immediately* drop, and he sucks in a sharp breath as he takes in the sight of the holster strapped around my leg.

"Once again—gun." I tap my thigh for emphasis, smirking when his gaze lingers longer than necessary. "I can take care of myself."

Xavier exhales, dragging a frustrated hand through his hair. "That's not the point."

"Then what is the point?"

His fists clench. And for a second—just a *second*—I think he might actually *say* something. Something that would make me want to stay.

Because Lord *knows*, it wouldn't take much.

A word. A look. A *reason*.

He steps closer to me and I feel my breath hitch. But his expression has shifted to one of resolve. Like he's settled something inside himself.

"Fine." His voice is tight, controlled—like a predator playing with its prey. "Strictly business. Unless you *beg* otherwise."

He leans in, his breath hot against my ear, making my pulse slam into overdrive. "But that won't stop my name from slipping past your lips when you mean to say his. It won't stop the way you'll think of me when his hands touch you—when his eyes linger, trying to see what I've already claimed."

He steps back, smirking as if he already knows he's won. "But sure, Peach. Go take your little walk. Pretend like I'm not already under your skin."

CHAPTER EIGHTEEN

Xavier

I rub a hand down my face, exhaling hard. I should've stopped her.

The entire day has been a goddamn whirlwind, one insane thing after another, and now she's gone. Walking around in the dark with Lucas fucking Ballentine, while I sit here with a plate of food guaranteed to make anyone's back fat and a growing headache.

And the worst part? She was right. I didn't think this all the way through. I was so focused on getting to her before her pictures hit the news, so damn desperate to get ahead of this mess that I never stopped to consider what walking into her world—unannounced, uninvited—would mean.

And maybe I also wanted to see her.

I needed to see her. Been dying to see her since Vegas.

I glance at my watch. Just after 7 PM.

I pull out my phone and dial. The phone rings twice before I hear the familiar baritone of an old friend.

"X! What's good? You tell her yet?"

I shake my head, already dreading this call. "You just get right to it, don't you?"

"Have you known me to be any other way all your life?"

"I've known you to be a dick all my life."

"That's Pastor Dick to you, Mr. Darcy."

I laugh. "I'll still kick your ass on the basketball court, Lucky."

"Hey. You know I go by my given name now—Jonah."

Jonah Steele—AKA Lucky when he was running the streets—is my oldest friend. We grew up together, two latchkey kids with working parents, bonding on the streets in ways that a Black kid and a white kid ordinarily wouldn't. He taught me how to play Spades, I taught him how to properly eat crab legs and crawfish. He helped me master Algebra, and I helped him figure out how to talk to girls. Somewhere along the way, we became more than friends—we became brothers. Brothers who chose slightly different paths.

I went to business school after college and Jonah went to Bible school. He's the main person who has kept me grounded since my mother passed away. Jonah's got a way with words. With wisdom. And even though I refuse to show up at his church, I still send my tithes.

"Sorry, Pastor Jonah—"

"Yeah, yeah. Save it." His voice dips, all humor gone. "Why haven't you told her yet?"

Apart from Will and Grant, Jonah knows more about me than anyone and I tell him everything. Including the story about Charlie and me.

The *whole* story. And Jonah—being who he is—doesn't judge. But he sure as hell doesn't let me off the hook either.

I sigh, rubbing the bridge of my nose. "Well…" I laugh nervously. "It started when she kicked me in the balls."

Jonah chokes. "Wait, what?"

"Then she stomped on my foot."

"X, you're lying to me."

"Nope. Then, the maniac held me at gunpoint and forced me to pretend to propose."

There's a long stretch of silence before Jonah bursts out laughing. Hard.

"So much for just laying it all out there and doing the right thing."

"Which you still haven't done, if I'm hearing you correctly!" Jonah chuckles.

"I'm sorry," I say, dripping in sarcasm. "I can't hear you over the throbbing blood vessels in my dick!"

Jonah sighs. "Calm down, brother."

"Don't calm down, brother me! What the hell am I supposed to do now?"

"Well, what was the last thing that happened?"

I tell him—emphasizing the fact that Charlie wants nothing serious and nothing physical with me.

Jonah hums. "Which is smart."

I scowl. "Shut up, Pastor Dick," I snap, knowing full well he's talking about the fact that Charlie and I shouldn't be sleeping together. "But if she won't even let me in, how the hell am I supposed to get her to listen to me?"

Jonah lets out a deep sigh. "So what—you think the only way she'll have a real conversation with you is if you seduce her?"

Yes.

"No!"

Jonah chuckles. "You sure about that?"

I grumble, shifting in my seat. "I just like my odds better when I can... *bend* her to my will."

"You're a sick bastard."

"I'm a practical man who knows his strengths."

Jonah snorts. "How about you just talk to her? Leave X-Man out of it."

"Fu—forget you," I grumble, catching myself before I curse at the good pastor.

Jonah cackles. He lives for moments like this. When we were in high school, I had an alter-ego—X-Man, the persona I put on whenever I was chasing after women. I'm not proud of it, and Jonah knows it, which is why he brings it up every chance he gets.

His voice softens. "Seriously though. Have you prayed about it?"

I sigh. "Jonah..."

"Xavier," he counters, firmly.

He's been trying to pull me back into my faith for years. But I can't recall the last time I prayed. I haven't even been able to say amen without bitterness curling around my throat. I've had a beef with God for a long time now. I'm not ready to square up with Him just yet.

But I love that my friend keeps trying to save me.

"I haven't gotten around to it yet," I say. "But I will."

Jonah sighs but lets it go. "Let me know when you tell her. And quit cursing so much. It's unbecoming."

"Your face is unbecoming," I snap back. But I promise to try to do better because Mama would have said the same thing.

We hang up, and I sit there, staring at the wall for a moment, forcing myself to think instead of acting on impulse.

But then I remember the way she looked when she talked about Lucas. All happy and whimsical and whatever. And suddenly, sitting still isn't an option.

If I let Lucas get his hands on her, if I let him win without even trying, I might not ever have a chance again. And Charlie and I—whatever we are, whatever we could be—will be over before anything even has the chance to start.

I push back from the table, storming toward the door, ready to find her, ready to tell her everything, ready to drag her back here if I have to.

But the moment I yank open the door, I stop short.

A small figure stands in front of me, looking up expectantly.

I blink. Look around for an adult. There isn't one in sight.

"Uh... hey, Prince." I clear my throat, adjusting the collar of my shirt as I glance around. "Where's your daddy?"

He crosses his arms and lifts an eyebrow. Still no adult in sight.

"You need something, little fella?"

He scoffs. "I ain't little. And nobody says 'fella' anymore. You sound old."

"Alright, *young man*. Can I help you with something?"

"Where's Aunt Charlie?"

Ugh. With that asshole Lucas.

"She's out," I say, slowly. "Taking a walk with her friend, Lucas."

"You mean her ex-boyfriend?"

Who asked you, kid?

"Yes. Her ex."

Prince nods, thoughtful. "My daddy says she was Lucas' first love. And he was hers."

My jaw ticks as I lean against the door frame, my hand in one pocket. "Oh yeah? What else does your daddy say?"

He shrugs. "Just that they need to stop actin' like idiots and get married, have lots of sex and have some babies."

My eyebrows shoot up. "Your daddy said that?"

"I added the babies part."

"Right."

"And the sex part."

"Yeah, I figured," I mutter.

"I like the word."

"Sex?"

He giggles. "Yeah. I've been practicing my bad words since Aunt Charlie came around. Her and daddy make it look fun."

I shake my head at the precocious little shit. "Well, as long as you're not *doing* it, I won't tell."

He smirks. "Why you let Aunt Charlie go on a date with Lucas if you love her?"

"It's not a date."

"So you *do* love her," he says, grinning now like he just cracked a code.

As much as I love kids—and as much as I care about giving back to the communities where underprivileged kids Prince's age need it most—I've never pictured myself as a parent. I've never thought I could slow down long enough to find a wife, let alone start a family. But being around Charlie's family... feeling the bigness of their love, the warmth I've quietly craved for years, it does something to me.

I'm not proud of it—but I've been watching Charlie from a distance for a long time.

After the first time I saw her, I had my team dig around, try to find out more. Came up with almost nothing. No trail. No past. Like she didn't exist until the moment I laid eyes on her. Which only made me more obsessed. More curious. So I did the only thing I could—I started showing up. Events I knew she'd be at. Places I figured she might pass through. Always casual. Always careful. Close enough to see her, far enough not to be seen.

And I catch myself doing it again. Today. She left the cottage to be with her family, to handle her part in the tradition of this place. Said she'd be back to check on me later. And instead of waiting like a normal man, I wandered. Slipped out and roamed the grounds like a ghost. Not looking for trouble—just for her. Watching. Observing.

Watching her slip so easily into the role of a daughter, a niece, a cousin—it's like watching a part of her I didn't know existed unfold in real time. And now, sitting here, talking to Prince, seeing how sharp he is, how funny and honest... it makes the idea of fatherhood feel a little less impossible. Even adoption doesn't seem so far-fetched anymore. Not with her in the picture.

If only I could get her to see me differently. Not as the man who barged into her life uninvited, dragged secrets into her family home, or turned her world upside down without asking. But as someone who *sees* her—really sees her. I want to be the person she lets in, not the one she keeps at arm's length out of fear or habit.

Standing here in this doorway while she's out with another man, I'm afraid I've already screwed things up too royally for any sort of future with her. Maybe I moved too fast. Maybe I pushed too hard. Or maybe she was never going to let me close in the first place.

I exhale. "Why the fuck are you so smart, kid?"

"Why the *fuck* do all you grown-ups say bad words?" he fires back.

I blink. "Does your daddy know you say fuck?"

"Does yours?"

"Don't know. Don't know where my daddy is. Or who he is, for that matter."

When I was younger, my mother rarely mentioned my father. Not in passing, not in anger, not at all.

She never gave me the dramatic story or bitter speeches you'd expect from a woman left to raise a child on her own.

Instead, she'd say, *"Focus on your blessings, baby. Any man who can't see how amazing you are isn't worth a single thought."*

So I didn't waste any.

I never built up fantasies about who he might've been. Never clung to some ideal or daydream of him showing up to make things right.

I knew the truth, even if she never said it.

He left us.

Let us suffer.

And while she chose grace, I chose rage.

I've hated a man I've never met for my entire life.

Prince softens. "I don't either. Know who my daddy is, I mean. Elijah adopted me when I was a baby. My grandma is like my mama. She's the best."

"And what about your aunt Charlie?"

"I wish she was around more. My daddy always takes me to visit historical places, Black colleges and museums. So, whenever we are in Atlanta, we meet up with Aunt Charlie. But she doesn't come here much."

"You miss her?"

He nods. "Yeah. A lot. She's funny."

"She is," I echo.

I've heard whispers about Charlie's absence while settling into the cottage today. Conversations at the wake, murmurs in the kitchen—little breadcrumbs of surprise that she actually came home this time. It's clear people didn't expect her to show, and even clearer they've been quietly hurting in her absence.

She walks around like she's untouchable, like no one really sees her or understands her. Like she's alone, even in a room full of people who adore her. But I wonder if she realizes what a void she's left behind. How many people miss her; especially Prince. The way he lights up when he talks about her, the way he watches the door like she might disappear again any second. That kind of love doesn't happen by accident. And I don't think she realizes what she has here. That she has something so many others only wish they had.

He pauses, then tilts his head. "So why you lettin' her go on walks with other dudes like a bitch?"

"Aye," I hold up a hand. "Watch your mouth, kid. I draw the line at *bitch*."

"Sorry," he mumbles, then quickly follows up. "Still. You're being one."

"I'm trying to be respectful. Respecting her space. Women like it when you don't try to force yourself on them."

He rolls his eyes. "That's dumb. If you love her, you *tell* her. You definitely don't let some light-skinned, soft-spoken, Dr. Do-Too-Much take her on walks."

I squint. "You think he looks better than me?"

"I think he's got home-field advantage."

"How old *are* you?"

"Almost twelve." He says it so matter of factly like twelve is the equivalent of twenty.

I shake my head. "You're smart as shit. You know that?"

"Yeah. And you're dumb as shit if you don't go get Aunt Charlie before Lucas takes your girl."

He turns and starts walking back toward the Big House, like he didn't just drop a bomb on me.

I run a hand down my face, staring after him.

Damn kid might be right. *"If you love her, you tell her."*

But I don't love Charlie. I mean, I like her—more than I should. I can't go a damn minute without thinking about her. She's in my head, constantly, like a song I can't get out of my system. And yeah,

I'd burn the whole world to the ground if it meant keeping her safe.
No question.

But love? No. Definitely not.

Right?

CHAPTER NINETEEN

Charlie

By the time I make it back to the cottage, the moon is high and Xavier is exactly where I expect him to be—sitting on the front porch like some Southern noir daydream, cigar in one hand, drink in the other, and brooding.

But he's so pretty. This Louisiana light fits him.

On the way to meet Lucas, I got a text—he'd been called into the hospital and couldn't make it.

Honestly, it was probably for the best.

Seeing him at Geneva's stirred up old feelings, memories coated in nostalgia more than anything real. Familiarity can be a dangerous kind of comfort, especially when you're standing in the ruins of your own confusion. And I don't need confusion right now.

Not when Xavier is here.

Not when I'm still trying to make sense of a night I barely remember...And a man I can't seem to forget.

"I didn't realize you smoked cigars," I say softly.

He doesn't look at me right away. Just takes a slow drag of his cigar and blows the smoke out into the thick air like he's got all the time in the world. "There is a lot you don't know, Charlie. How was the walk?" he asks, voice low but sharp.

I step onto the porch and lean against the railing. "Didn't happen. Lucas got called into the hospital, so I walked along Bayou alone."

He turns his head toward me, eyes narrowing just slightly. "That safe?"

"Safer than staying here with you," I say with a smirk.

He grins, but it's tight. Reserved. Like he's holding something back. He always is.

"I guess that's probably true. I seem to get pretty predatory whenever I'm near you."

Which I absolutely adore. But I don't say.

I sit down on the step, not too close, but close enough to smell the cedar and smoke clinging to his skin. I stare out into the darkness, into the silhouettes of moss-covered trees swaying like ghosts and the lake out back.

Reminiscent of the night on their team plane, I take the drink from his hand and take a sip.

"I'm sorry about earlier," I whisper.

Xavier tilts his head, eyes narrowing. "Which part, exactly? It's been a pretty eventful day, Peach."

A small smile tugs at my lips. "All of it. The knee to the nuts, the gun—"

He cuts in, lips twitching. "The part where you made me call Joe Sinclair *Big Daddy*?"

I grin, shaking my head. "Nope. Not sorry about that at all. And if you know what's good for you at the funeral tomorrow, you'll make sure to put some extra *D* in Daddy."

He laughs, and so do I—because that will never get old.

"You really expect me to show up to the funeral, too?" he asks, still chuckling but watching me carefully.

"Yes," I nod. "As part of our deal. I'll be up all night hacking through your digital disaster, and tomorrow you'll play your part—smile for the crowd, stand by my side, kiss my forehead if necessary."

"Touching you is always necessary, Peach," he says, his voice so sure.

My cheeks flush instantly, the warmth betraying me. Damn him. He's comfortable now—settled in. I can see it in the way his body leans back, relaxed, like he's got all night to play this game. And he's winning—because once again, he's taken me completely off mine.

His smile fades just a little. "And Lucas?" The way he says it—almost cautious—makes it sound like the name tastes sour in his mouth.

I exhale. "Don't worry about Lucas." I look away, my thoughts drifting to the people in this town and how none of them seem to mind their own damn business when it comes to me and him.

"My mother always imagined I'd end up with Lucas," I say softly. "Hell, the whole town probably did. I was the smart girl with the sharp tongue, he was the golden boy with the polite smile. It was a Hallmark movie waiting to happen."

Xavier listens quietly, not interrupting.

"But I never felt like it fit," I continue. "Like I was trying on a dress two sizes too small. Tight in all the wrong places, never mine. My whole life here has felt like that. Like I never quite measured up to what everyone expected of me. Not "shark" enough for my father, not soft enough for my mother, not obedient enough for Lucas' family. So I left. Maybe ran," I admit softly, thinking about something Lucas said to me.

"I get that," Xavier says after a beat, his voice rougher now. "After my mom passed, I stopped coming home. Couldn't see the point. Without her, it didn't feel like my town anymore. Nothing here fit. Just a place I used to know."

We sit in quiet stillness, the hum of cicadas and the distant rustle of trees filling the air like a lullaby. It's the kind of silence that doesn't beg to be broken—warm, easy, unforced.

I can feel him next to me, not just in proximity, but in energy. Xavier is thinking. I can tell by the way his thumb brushes over the rim of his glass, slow and distracted. He takes a drag of his cigar like he's turning something over in his mind, weighing whether to say it aloud. And I already know what it is. Or I think I do.

But I don't let him say it. I already drew the line between us, even if it was a lie.

Still... I miss him. God help me, I miss him in a way that makes no damn sense. Maybe it was Vegas. Maybe it's something older, deeper. But ever since that night—even with the blank spaces in my memory—he's lived in me. Like he found an opening and wedged himself in.

And after all these years of dodging anything that looked remotely like attachment—because of the job, because of the risks, because of *me*—I finally meet someone who bypasses all my defenses like he's got the cheat code. And for once, at the worst possible moment, I don't want to let him go.

But I need him to. For my safety. For his. For whatever's left of the life I've spent years trying to control.

He turns to me with a resolve in his voice. "Peach, I—"

"How did she die? Your mother?" I cut him off just as he was about to say something that felt too heavy for me right now. So I caught him off guard with a personal question.

That's when he puts his cigar out and stands. Slow, like he's carrying something heavy he doesn't want to give to me. He holds out his hand to help me up, but the expression on his face is...Expressionless.

"No need in gettin' into all that," he says, brushing off the question with a crooked smile. "Since this thing between us isn't real, right?"

My hand stays in his, warm and grounding. But before I can say anything, he drops it gently and heads inside.

"Goodnight, Charlie Sinclair," he says without turning around. "I'll see you in the morning."

And just like that, he disappears behind the screen door, leaving me alone with the sound of cicadas, a half-burned cigar, and a whole lot of questions.

Xavier

1:17 a.m.

I stare at the ceiling. Again. I've counted every groove in the wood, memorized every creak this damn bed makes, and still—sleep won't come. My body's heavy with exhaustion, but my mind? It's a live wire, sparking and restless. Because of her. Only a few hundred feet away, and somehow still taking up all the space in my head.

I reach over to the nightstand and grab my phone. I hesitate for half a second, thumb hovering over her contact. But then I hear it—again—the soft shuffle of her footsteps in the hallway. The creak of the floorboards. The faint click of the kitchen faucet. She's been up and down all night, getting water, pacing.

I don't just feel it anymore. I know she's awake. Something's troubling her and I hate that she won't trust me. Won't let me shoulder any of it for her.

I decide to send her a text.

Xavier: *Peach.*

I watch the screen like I've just launched a missile and I'm waiting for the impact. For a second, there's nothing, and I think maybe I've read it all wrong. That maybe I'm just the lovesick idiot I swore I'd never be.

But then—

Those three dots appear and I exhale.

Charlie: *Yes?*

A smirk tugs at my mouth. I stretch out on the bed, one arm behind my head, the other typing.

Xavier: *What's on your mind?*

Charlie: *What makes you think something's on my mind?*

Xavier: *Isn't there?*

Charlie: *What do you want, Xavier?*

Straight to it. That's her. Sharp, impatient, always pushing past the pretense. But I'm not biting. Not yet.

Xavier: *I want to know you, Charlie. Really know you.*

There's a pause, just long enough for me to regret it. But then—

Charlie: *You scare me.*

My heart tightens. I stare at the words like they're a trap, like saying the wrong thing will detonate her trust completely.

And this is exactly why I needed more time. More time to reveal everything the right way. To win her over. To show her a side of me she wouldn't bolt from—the part of me that's steady, safe, hers.

Xavier: *I'm sorry. I know I'm not the easiest man to get close to. But I can do better. For you.*

Another pause.

Charlie: *It's more than that. It's complicated.*

Xavier: *Then let's start simple. What's your favorite color?*

Charlie: *Black. Yours?*

Xavier: *Blue.*

Xavier: *Favorite song?*

Charlie: *Steady Love, India Arie.*

I smile. That one was unexpected.

Xavier: *U2. Still Haven't Found What I'm Looking For.*

Charlie: *LOL. That tracks.*

Xavier: *Why do you say that?*

Charlie: *Because of how long you went without sex. I think that was proof you hadn't found what you were looking for.*

I laugh out loud.

Xavier: *What does it mean that all my effort was shot to hell after being enticed by you? After one look at you...*

No answer. Just silence. And now I've gone too far. So I back up a bit.

Xavier: *Favorite book?*

Charlie: *Pride and Prejudice.*

I nearly drop the phone from how hard I grin.

Xavier: *Hey Charlie?*

Charlie: *Yes?*

I wait a beat, just to draw it out, just because I know she's holding her breath.

Xavier: *You have bewitched me, body and soul.*

There's a long, long pause.

Then—

Charlie: *Goodnight, Mr. Darcy.*

I set the phone down on my chest and close my eyes. And for the first time in days, I actually think sleep might come easy.

CHAPTER TWENTY

Xavier

I can't remember the last time I woke up in Louisiana. It's not my house, not my childhood bed, but something about waking up here makes me wonder why the hell it's taken me so long to come back.

I roll over, groaning as I reach for my phone, expecting spam or more leaked photos. Instead, I find three text messages from Nathan, each one more frantic than the last.

I really need this man to lay off of coffee.

Nathan: *We need to talk. NOW!*

Nathan: *Seriously. You cannot be ignoring me right now when your fucking world is on fire, X!*

Nathan: *Your biometric data has been compromised.*

My blood runs cold. I call him immediately, and he picks up on the first ring like he's been waiting by the phone all night.

"About time!" he barks. "You can't ignore something like this, X."

I rub the sleep from my eyes. "Calm down. It's six in the morning and I'm just now waking up."

"Huh? You never sleep past four."

I yawn, dragging myself to a stand and stretching. "I know. It's the oddest thing. I was out cold for the first time in forever."

"Well, wake the hell up. Because shit just got real."

I move toward the window, cracking it open for some air. "What do you mean someone has access to my biometric data?"

"You know how The Fury Alliance rebuilt all your security protocols—blood drops, retina scans, fingerprints, the whole Men In Black package?"

"Yeah. What about it?"

"Well, someone's hacked into the vault. Your entire biometric profile has been stolen."

I freeze. "That's not possible. You need *my* biometric data just to get into that part of the system."

"Exactly," he says. "Which means someone's either gotten to *you*, or gotten dangerously close."

I rake a hand through my hair, trying to stay calm. "No one's been near my house. Ever. You know that."

"Well, I dunno. Maybe they disguised themselves as a lost Amazon driver, or something. Either way, your shit's been accessed. I'm sending over everything I've got."

"Send a copy to Hayven, too. I'll run it by Charlie. You take care of that other thing I requested?"

There's a pause. "She still got you all twisted up, huh?"

"Just answer the question, Nate."

"All set. I'll text you when it's arrived."

"Thank you, as always."

"Also, Juliette warned that the news has mostly remained local to the financial news outlets, however, it's spreading. It's only a matter of time before the national news picks up the story. All of the stories."

"Damn it!" I groan. "I'll have Charlie look into that too."

"Since you're staying in such close proximity to her, have you rekindled what you started in those photos? You know, in Vegas?"

I don't dignify that with a response. "Talk soon."

I've done everything I can not to dwell on the fact that Charlie was the one who shattered my celibacy streak. After years of dodging temptation, years of beautiful women trying to wear me down just to say they cracked the code, it wasn't lust or seduction that broke me. It was her. Her, and whatever the hell she was on that night. I should be angry with myself. Maybe I am. Because I had a plan for her.

I wanted to court her. Show her that I wasn't just some reclusive billionaire with a haunted past or a man reduced to the craving he feels every time she walks into a room. I wanted to earn her trust, not tear through it in one night of heat and hazy memory.

But Charlie... she tests every boundary I've ever drawn. She pokes at every soft spot until it splits open. And the truth is, I never stood a damn chance. Not me. Not my plan. That train derailed the second she said my name like a prayer and called me *Mr. Darcy*.

Now all I've got left is one move. The only one that might give me a shot at something real with her. Tell her the truth. All of it. Every messy, complicated part. And then brace for whatever happens next. Whether she slams the door in my face or pulls me through it—I have to know.

But not today. Not on the day she says goodbye to her grandmother. Later.

After I hang up with Nathan, I walk into the living room, heart still pounding. I need to think—but then I spot her.

Charlie. At the sink. Singing to some R&B track I don't recognize. She's wearing pink pajama shorts and a white tank top. A silk scarf is wrapped around her head and tied like a cone on top, and she's barefoot, swaying her hips like she's the only person in the world. She's laughing at herself, pouring water into a glass, completely unguarded.

I've seen her in action from a distance. Seen her corner men twice her size and tear their egos apart without breaking a sweat. But this? This is different. This is the Charlie I don't think she lets anyone else see. The real her. And I wish she didn't feel like she had to hide it.

I meant what I said—that I'd keep things strictly professional if that's what she wanted. But God help me, every time I see her like this, all soft and wild and completely unaware of how goddamn beautiful she is...I want to grab her. Kiss her. Remind her she's mine, even if she doesn't know it. Even if she's too stubborn to admit it.

She spins, eyes wide, and screams loud enough to wake every ancestor buried within a five-mile radius. Before I can blink, she lunges for the nearest knife like she's about to reenact a scene from *Kill Bill*.

"Shit! Charlie!" I throw my hands up, stumbling back. "Do you *always* have to respond to everything with violence?"

"Yes!" she snaps, still panting, one hand clutching the counter and the other wrapped firmly around the knife handle. "It's what I've been *trained* to do!"

"Well, it's *deeply* unnerving, Charlie. You should really talk to someone about your homicidal reflexes."

She glares, then shrugs like I'm the one being dramatic. "You should announce yourself when you enter a room."

I lower my hands slowly, feeling confident she won't murder me. "Well, I didn't want to interrupt."

She lowers her head a little, muttering under her breath. "I dance when I'm str—" she stops herself from saying the word stressed. "I dance when I need to focus."

A dull ache settles in my chest—sharp, unexpected. I hate that she still doesn't know. That she doesn't realize she can bring her stress to me. That I *want* her to. That she can lean on me, curse the world, break down if she needs to—and I'd take it all. Gladly.

And despite the fact that she just tried to shank me like we're in a prison yard, a laugh escapes before I can stop it. Because apparently, being threatened at knife-point doesn't stop my body from responding to the sight of her.

The blood rushes exactly where it shouldn't, and there's not a damn thing I can do about it.

Charlie narrows her eyes. "Um, Darcy?"

"Yes, Peach?" I answer, trying to sound casual.

"Your penis is pointing at me."

I look down, then right back at her with zero shame. "You were dancing."

"That's all it takes for you?"

"*You're* all it takes for me. How many times are you gonna make me say that?"

She rolls her eyes. "Enough. Now."

"And it's morning," I say with a shrug. "Our members have a schedule. It's science."

"Well, your member better remember it has a job to do, and it better stay in its goddamn holster."

I laugh softly, then shift gears, ready to bring up what I actually came in here to talk about. "I spoke with Nathan on my team."

Charlie lifts her water and takes a sip. I catch the quick flash of her knocking back a pill. Probably a vitamin, but I clock it anyway.

"Oh yeah?" she says, not missing a beat. "What did he say?"

"You're not gonna believe this," I tell her, leaning forward slightly, "but someone's accessed the biometric data your boss put in place."

She freezes, eyebrows pulling together. "Seriously? That security system is insane. Next to impossible to breach. Hell, the government doesn't even go that far."

I nod. "Yeah. And yet... someone did."

She exhales sharply, setting her glass down a little harder than necessary. "What the hell are you into, Darcy?"

I meet her gaze, steady. "You make a lot of enemies when you're trying to change the world. Give people security where no one else would."

"I guess so," she mutters, eyes distant now, like she's already running calculations in her head.

I glance at my phone. "What time is the funeral today?"

"Eleven," she replies, still eyeing me like I might pounce.

"I'll go get myself together. Luckily, I travel with a black suit."

"You mean *the* black suit. It's the only one I've ever seen you in."

"At least you know what to expect from me."

She raises a brow. "And what's that?"

"The same old me. Plain and simple."

I turn toward the hallway, but something in me won't let me leave without saying it. I pause, turn back, and catch her watching me.

"Hey, Peach?"

"Yeah?"

"I like the way you move."

She shakes her head, blushing. "Whatever, Mr. Darcy."

Charlie

I twist, strain, and practically dislocate my shoulder trying to catch the zipper with my fingertips. No luck. The damn thing won't budge, and now I'm sweating out the edges of my hair.

I take a deep breath, trying to steady the mayhem inside me. I'm a ball of nerves, and I hate that I can't pinpoint why.

It's not the funeral—grief and ceremony don't shake me. At least that's what I've come to believe about myself. I've seen far worse in far more dangerous places. At this moment, this convergence of lives—the secret past I've buried, the fake present I'm pretending to live, and the future I'm barely holding together with duct tape and denial—it's enough to make me question every choice I've ever made.

As complicated as things are with my mother, I don't want her disappointed in me. I don't want to see that look in her eyes. And for all my tough talk, for all the times I've claimed not to care—I do. I want my family to accept me. To see me. The real me, not the curated version I've fed them for years.

I'd thought about telling them the truth. Some of it, anyway. But if they find out like this? Through scandal. Through whispers. Through tabloid headlines and backdoor shame?

That'll be so much worse.

I groan, glaring at myself in the mirror as a text comes through from Elijah.

Elijah: *Limos are twenty minutes out. You decent or should I send Mama to come make you hurry up?*

Charlie: *I'm ready. If you send Mama back here I'll tell her you fingered Stacey Lattimore in the back of her car in the twelfth grade.*

Elijah: *There's a special place in hell for snitches, you old bat.*

I laugh, throwing my phone down and heading to Xavier's room, calling after him. "Darcy? My brother texted and said the cars would be at the Big House in twenty minutes."

No response.

I push his door open, only to find him in the mirror, adjusting his cufflinks. His eyes meet mine, and I swear I forget my own name for a second.

"Hey, Peach."

I'll never get tired of the way he says that.

"Did you hear what I said?" I repeat, a little breathless. "The umm. The cars'll be here in twenty."

He smiles. It's soft but edged with something reserved. "Then I guess we'd better get a move on, huh?"

I nod, glancing down at the back of my dress. "Can I get you to zip me up?"

I've worn black a thousand times before—comes with the territory in my line of work. But this one? This one's for Grandmommy. A simple, elegant Betsy & Adam cape-sleeve dress that fits like it was sewn onto my body. Classic. Tasteful. Just enough curveage to be noticed. Not enough to be judged.

Xavier's face shifts the second I turn around.

"You sure do know how to drive a man mad, Peach," he mutters, walking over to me with a grin that's more tortured than teasing.

I smile to myself and offer him my back, glancing at him in the mirror. I don't say anything. I don't have to. The air between us is already loaded.

His fingers brush my spine as he grabs the zipper, and his breath—warm and intentional—fans across the nape of my neck.

"How are you feeling about today?" he asks.

I shrug. "I've said my goodbyes a few times now. My grandmother and I had something special. Today's just... formality." I pause, then lower my voice. "Can I tell you something?"

"Go on."

"I've never been to a family member's funeral before."

He stills behind me.

"How is that possible?"

"I was out of the country when my mother's mom passed. Traveling for work. That was the excuse, anyway. Everyone else in my family has been lucky enough to stay alive."

The zipper's long done, but he doesn't move. He's still standing behind me like a wall—solid, unmoving, mine.

"Can I tell *you* a secret?"

I nod, swallowing hard.

"I haven't stepped foot inside a church since my mother's funeral."

I turn to face him. "Really? Why?"

He raises an eyebrow. "My mother's dead. Do I need another reason?"

His voice is calm, but his eyes aren't.

"It's been that hard for you?"

"Among other things."

"And you're going today with me, just to make good on your word?" I ask, the guilt creeping in. "Xavier, if this is going to hurt you, if it's going to crack something open, please don't—"

He cuts me off with a kiss. No warning. No build-up. Just a hot, devastating press of his mouth against mine that silences every doubt and burns through every breath I've got.

When he pulls back, his eyes stay fixed on mine, unwavering. There's no smirk this time. No charm, no game. Just truth, thick and heavy in the space between us.

"Xavier. We—"

He presses a gentle hand to my lips. "I'd do anything for you, Peach."

The words settle into my chest, heavy. My voice comes before I can stop it, soft and uncertain. "Why?"

Because I really don't get it. I've had men want me. Lust after me. Try to possess me. But no one's ever looked at me like I was the answer to a question they've been asking their whole life. No one's ever followed through. Until now. Until him. And I don't know what to do with a man like Xavier Darcy—intent on making me his obsession... and somehow becoming mine at the same time.

"You still don't remember?"

My stomach flips. "Remember what? You mean...Vegas?"

He gives me a look. "A bit reductive, but yes."

"I..." My mind searches for something, anything.

Then he almost whispers, "*À bientôt, alors, mon amour.*"

My breath catches.

I've heard that before. But *where?*

"What does that mean?" I ask.

He leans in, presses a kiss to my forehead. "I'll tell you soon enough."

And then he lets go. Just like that. Steps back like he didn't just reformulate the oxygen in the room.

I want more.

Then he turns me back toward the mirror, positioning me between him and our reflection. I look so small in front of him, his large frame curved around mine like a shadow.

Then he pulls me flush against him, his lips brushing my collarbone.

"I can tell you're uneasy about today. I recognize the patterns of your breath like they're my own."

He dips lower, tongue sliding along the back of my neck. My knees damn near buckle.

"What do you mean?"

"I see you, Charlie. You can pretend all you want, play the professional, hide behind your sharp tongue and tailored dresses—but I see you."

He tightens his grip on my waist. His hardness is achingly pressing into my back.

"Not your family. Not your boss. Not your friends. *Me.* And I don't think anyone has ever seen you the way I do."

His voice drops to something dark, laced with something dangerous.

"I see the real you, Charlesetta Sinclair."

My pulse stutters. "And what exactly do you see?" I murmur, barely breathing.

He leans in, his mouth brushing the curve of my neck. The heat of his breath dances over my skin, searing straight through to my core. Then his teeth graze that tender spot just below my ear.

He bites. Not hard. Not soft. Just enough to make my knees threaten betrayal.

"Vulnerability is a curse word to you. Sex is a shield. And love is poison. But I..."

The words trail off, replaced by a groan as his hand slips beneath my dress, dragging it up with intention.

"Peach," he says, voice low and rough, "Fuck, Peach. I'm afraid I'm gonna have to break a promise to you. That 'strictly professional' business? It's not working for me."

"Xavier—" I start, warning in my tone, but it's half-hearted. He knows it. I know it.

"Not when I can tell your nerves are shot. Not when I know exactly how to ease the weight off your shoulders. Just the way you like it."

His fingers find my entrance—hot, soaked, desperate—and he exhales like he *knew* I'd be ready for him.

One finger enters me while another circles my sensitive bud.

"X—"

His other hand finds my breast, thumb brushing over my nipple through the thin fabric. I arch into him, my body already betraying everything my mouth said hours ago.

"Strictly professional, right?" he mocks, his breath hot against my ear. "Then allow me to professionally please this pretty pussy..."

"Xavier..."

"Fuck you, Charlie."

"What?" My eyes instantly go wide at his coarse language towards me.

"Fuck you for pretending you didn't want this. For walking past me all damn day with that look in your eyes."

I reach behind me, fingers wrapping around his length, stroking him slow—greedily—because it's the only part of me that can speak right now. My mouth won't work. Not when he's got me this breathless, this undone.

He grabs my neck, firm but not cruel.

"Fuck you for aching, needing a release just feet away and not coming to me. Not letting me take care of you."

His hands work me and wreck me with sweet abandon.

"Xavier, I...I'm—"

His grip tightens around my throat, just enough to silence me. "And fuck you for lying. To yourself and to me...for saying you don't want me."

Two fingers are inside me now and I can't hold it in.

"Ah!" I cry out, body trembling, heat crashing into me like a wave.

"Say you're sorry, Charlie," he demands. "Say you're sorry for not letting me take care of you."

"I..." The words won't come.

"Go on now, Peach," he murmurs, mouth brushing my jaw, eyes glaring into me through our reflection. "You can do it."

"I'm sorry," I breathe, a tear escaping my eye and down my cheek.

His hand relaxes slightly from around my neck.

"Sorry what?"

His stare in the mirror pins me in place—filthy, full of heat, like a promise and a punishment all at once. His fingers are still buried inside me, drawing slow, torturous circles that steal every breath I try to catch.

My body trembles, my mouth parts, and his name clings to the edge of my lips like a secret I'm too far gone to keep.

"I'm sorry, *Mr. Darcy*," I whisper, not sure what I'm apologizing for—only knowing I'd say it again if it means he won't stop.

I shatter. Completely. My body trembling in his arms, held up only by the strength of him around me. The kind of release that steals your thoughts, your name, your sense of space and time.

Somewhere in the haze, I hear his phone ping.

He doesn't move at first. He holds me until the last tremble fades, his hand slipping from beneath my dress as he lets the fabric fall back into place.

"Feel better?" he asks, voice maddeningly calm.

I nod, barely able to stand. "Yes..."

"Good," he says, bringing his hand to my lips. "Open, Peach."

I do and this man takes his fingers and begins to coat my lips with my pleasure, again, reminding me of the night on the plane.

"From now on," he murmurs, voice heavy and unshakable, "this is how it goes. This is how *we* go."

I narrow my eyes, trying to hold my ground—trying to read him and ignore the wild thump of my heart.

"I don't think I like it when you talk to me like that...the way you just did."

He sticks his middle finger into my mouth and I instinctively wrap my mouth and tongue around it.

I moan.

"You love it and that's why it makes you so damn furious. It's why you've tried so hard to remain in control of this situation."

He brings his fingers to his mouth, licking them slowly like he's savoring the last bite of something forbidden. My teeth sink into my bottom lip as I watch him, heat flooding my chest at the sight of him sharing in my unraveling.

"But I don't care that you don't like losing control, Charlie," he says, his voice low and steady. "I'm not a case for you to crack, some mission you complete and file away when you're done. I'm yours. And from now on, when you need something—when you need me—you come to me. You can hide from the rest of this damn family, from the world even. But not from me. Don't you ever pretend you don't need me again."

He presses a kiss to my cheek then holds my gaze, warm and possessive. "With me, you're not allowed to pretend you're steel when you're breaking. Understood?"

I nod, mute, still breathless from everything he's just said—and done.

"Good. Now go get yourself cleaned up and meet me out front. I've got a surprise for you."

I narrow my eyes. "You bought me a gift... for my grandmother's funeral?"

He smirks, all sexy and sated. "Something like that."

His ability to unnerve me and unburden me in the same breath is something I've never experienced before. Not even with Lucas, and we practically grew up as extensions of each other. He was safe. Familiar. But even at our closest, Lucas never had this kind of effect on me—the way Xavier does.

Maybe that's why it was always so easy to leave Lucas behind. And why I never looked back.

CHAPTER TWENTY ONE

Charlie

We step out of the cottage and head toward the Big House, the morning sun casting long shadows over the yard. Xavier walks beside me, his steps easy and unhurried, like a man who belongs here. With me.

But he doesn't know this place. These people. My world. Still, he moves through it like he's been rehearsing for the role of my fiancé all his life.

I feel the back of his hand graze against mine—once, twice—before he finally laces our fingers together.

"Must you always find a reason to touch me, Xavier Darcy?" I ask, Southern sass dripping in my tone.

He smirks without turning his head. "Well, you *are* supposed to be my fiancée. Shouldn't it look like I can't keep my hands off you, Peach?"

I roll my eyes, but I don't let go. "This is public domain. Aren't you afraid of being seen by the cameras?"

"I'm not afraid of cameras," he says, voice easy. "The only thing about the pictures that scared me was the thought of you seeing those *other* photos before I had a chance to explain. That, and someone else seeing you without me and thinking they had a chance with you."

"There you go acting like you own me again."

"And there you go acting like you don't love it."

I don't respond. Because I don't have a good enough lie this morning.

What he did to me at the cottage—the way he touched me, the way he spoke to me like I was his, like he had every right to claim me—was a filthy, beautiful fantasy I never expected. And worse, I wanted it. I wanted *him*. I'm used to being in control, the one with the upper hand, the one calling the shots. But with Xavier, I soften.

I fucking hate it.

As we reach the gravel path that leads to the front of the house, I spot two familiar faces that make me stop cold. One of them is buried beneath an obnoxiously wide hat and the other is wrapped in a beautifully tailored dress like she's stepping off a runway.

My throat tightens.

"Tika? Tim?" I say, blinking fast, wondering if my grief is finally starting to play tricks on me.

Xavier squeezes my hand. "I told you. I felt your anxiety. I just thought you could use some friends today."

I don't say a word. I just let go of Xavier's hand and take off toward them, like I've been holding my breath and they're the only ones who can fill my lungs again. I fall into their arms and they catch me, no hesitation, no questions—just love. The kind that doesn't need an invitation. The kind that shows up whether you ask or not.

I didn't tell them I needed them. I never do. And I'm taken aback by the fact that Xavier knew I needed them, too. Maybe he saw the crack I refused to show anyone else and decided to patch it the only way he could—with the people who remind me who I really am.

There are hundreds of people here today—family by blood, by name, by neighborhood ties—but *these* women? These two are *my* people. My sisters in every way that counts. And leave it to Xavier fucking Darcy to know that. To *feel* that.

Autika looks over at me and smirks. "That man might be cocky as hell, but I'll give it to him—the jet was first-class."

Timantha nods. "The breakfast was top notch, too! Your man did alright."

"He's not my man," I say under my breath.

"I mean," Tika shrugs, "Will Huntley would've had a sexy, man-masseuse on board, but hey. Xavier Darcy can't win at *everything*."

Xavier, hanging back a few feet, just grins at their antics, his hands in his pockets.

We walk together like the ladies on Sex and the City—Timantha on one side, Autika on the other, both of them anchoring me as we make our way to where the limos are lining up.

Timantha gives my hand a gentle squeeze. "You ready for this?"

I shake my head. "No," I whisper. "Not even a little."

And for once, I don't feel like I have to be.

Autika pauses mid-step, eyes narrowing as Xavier walks up to the car.

"You ever been to a Black funeral before?" she asks, like it's a loaded question.

Xavier frowns. "I've been to funerals where Black people were in the casket... yes, Autika."

He looks genuinely confused, like he's not sure what she's getting at.

Oh, but he's about to find out.

CHAPTER TWENTY TWO

Xavier

Two hours. I've been in this church for two entire hours, and apparently Grandmommy was everybody's best friend, prayer partner, babysitter, bootleg Avon lady, and what the hell is a spiritual midwife?! I am holding in so much urine that my kidneys are about to give out.

Charlie sits next to me, completely unbothered, like she's immune to this anarchy. Autika had a purse full of candy—Now and Laters, Skittles, bite-sized Snickers—that kept us entertained for a while, but she's long since run out.

Timantha's practically folded in half, shoulders shaking with silent laughter as yet another person approaches the podium with a Bible in hand and a story that starts way too far back. Every single one of them has blown past the two-minute time limit the funeral director warned us would be strictly enforced.

Spoiler alert: it has not.

At this point, the pastor will be dead and gone by the time this thing wraps up.

Meanwhile, I'm just trying not to cry.

I lean over to Charlie and whisper, "How long is this supposed to last?"

She doesn't even look at me. Just shrugs and mutters, "It's a Black funeral. What do you think?"

"Hell is that supposed to mean? I heard the usher whispering to your father that we missed the cemetery appointment *an hour ago!*"

Autika leans in and says loud enough for several pews to hear, "That's just white folks' way of keeping Black folks' on time."

"Clearly, they need new tactics," I whisper.

"What are they gonna do, X? Turn the body away once we get there?" Autika whisper-yells.

That sends our entire row into a fit of quiet snickers. An usher gives us the mother of all shushes, complete with that little pursed-lip head tilt like we're about to get thrown out of church.

"I have to pee!" I hiss into Charlie's ear.

She glances at me like I'm being dramatic. "Can you hold it five more minutes?"

"You said that an hour ago when that woman gave a TED Talk on how your grandmother taught her to clean chitlin's!"

Timantha nods solemnly. "It *is* a lost art form to cook them and they don't smell."

Someone behind us shushes us again, and I don't even turn around.

"I'm going," I whisper. "I'm getting up and going now before my bladder explodes in this sanctuary!"

But just as I start to move, the organ fires up and the choir launches into another song.

I freeze mid-stand. "What's happening now?"

Charlie whispers, "A musical selection."

"*Another one?!* How many songs does Grandmommy need to be escorted to glory? Is God himself coming down in a chariot to collect her personally?"

Autika howls. Her head falls forward, full cackle in her lap.

An usher stomps over to shush us again but is quickly distracted by the choir, which has now begun to sing... oh, you've got to be kidding me.

"I Believe I Can Fly."

I lean toward Charlie. "Is this... is this an R. Kelly song? In a church?"

She nods. "They swap out the lyrics. If you say 'Jesus' enough, it becomes gospel."

I shake my head, stunned, as a group of people dressed in flowing white robes, faces painted ghostly white, begin flooding the front of the church like a scene from a holy Cirque du Soleil.

"What's happening now?" I whisper, eyes wide.

Timantha leans over, grinning. "Praise dancers."

There are three women and one man, moving with surprising grace to the swelling music. It's elegant, emotional—actually kind of beautiful.

Then the man lifts one of the "women" right on the word *fly*, and the crowd erupts in cheers.

Only... that woman has a goatee.

"That's a man in a wig!" I hiss. "Charlie, why does that man have on a wig to match his mustache?"

Charlie doesn't even flinch. "Because Chauncey Battle loves a good lace front, honey."

I blink. "What does that even mean?!"

"You've never seen a praise and worship leader at a Black church?"

I turn slowly to her, deadpan. "Charlie, when this is all over, you're going to sit me down and explain *everything* I clearly don't know about Black people...and church."

Perhaps I should have gone to church with Jonah a few times. Clearly I have not been properly prepared for this.

The soloist, a woman in her seventies, belts out *"I believe I can soooaaaarrr—"* and then, quite literally, *her teeth go soaring*—across the choir stand, past the podium, and land directly in the offering basket.

I. Am. Stunned.

Timantha's eyes are wide. Charlie's hand slaps over her mouth. Autika is on the verge of passing out from laughter.

AND THE CHOIR JUST KEEPS SINGING.

As the woman hobbles down to *retrieve her teeth* like it's *nothing*, I feel something break inside me. Like... medically.

My bladder has officially issued a cry for help.

I watch as the woman bends over to hug Charlie's mama—her teeth still in her hand—and casually takes her seat.

Then I notice Charlie's auntie. She's shaking.

"Charlie," I nudge her. "I think something's wrong with your aunt."

"She's fine."

"She's *jumping around*! She's...Charlie, I think she's having a seizure because she's mouthing something unintelligible. She could bite off her tongue!"

Her aunt lets out what I can only describe as a war cry and hits the floor like she's gone down in battle. I jump out of my seat. "SOMEBODY CALL 911!"

Autika swats me. "Boy, that's the *Holy Ghost!* Sit your white ass down!"

"There is nothing holy about any of this!" *The ghost makes sense, though.*

The girls are crying-laughing. I'm about to cry for real. If one more thing happens, if one more person hits a high note or starts interpretive praise dancing, I'm going to need a new prostate.

I wait until the ushers turn to sing along, then I make a break for it—bolting out of the sanctuary like I'm being chased by all of Charlie's ancestors.

And if anyone tries to stop me, I will absolutely take an old lady usher down.

CHAPTER TWENTY THREE

Xavier

A fter the four-hour marathon that was Grandmommy's funeral, we finally wrapped up at the family mausoleum. But the day wasn't over yet. Before heading back to the Big House, I got to experience a New Orleans tradition that defies the typical somber funeral norms—a jazz funeral procession.

As we stepped out onto the street, a brass band awaited us, instruments gleaming in the sunlight. The air buzzed with anticipation. The band began with a slow, soulful dirge, leading us through the streets. Mourners walked in rhythm, some holding umbrellas, others waving handkerchiefs. This was the "first line," composed of family and close friends.

I'm no Will Huntley—dancing has never been on my bingo card. I'm a two-step kind of guy, the type who knows how to stay in the pocket for exactly three songs and then gracefully bow out before embarrassing himself. So yeah, I was awkward—noticeably so—as we walked down the street, the band playing at full volume while I tried to fake my way into rhythm.

I remember looking around and, sure enough, half of Charlie's family had their eyes glued to me like I was the damn halftime show. Aunties, cousins, exes—they were all watching, probably waiting for me to either break out some hidden talent or trip over my own feet.

But I didn't watch them long. My eyes found Charlie, and that was it. The way she moves like she was born with the beat in her bones. She was glowing, laughing, dancing through the street with her girls like she didn't have a single care in the world. And in that moment, I realized I'd never wanted to be part of someone's world more than I wanted to be in hers.

As we progressed, the music shifted. The tempo picked up, transitioning into upbeat jazz melodies. Onlookers and community members—the "second line"—joined in, dancing with infectious energy. It was a celebration of life, a communal send-off that felt both intimate and grand. And I was honored to take part in such a tradition.

I'd seen these types of celebrations all my life—second lines, music in the streets, hands clapping while tears fall—but I'd never actually been a part of one. And when my own mother passed, we didn't have anything close to this. A small ceremony, a few soft goodbyes, and then everyone just... left.

But what I am currently in the midst of is something else entirely.

Being surrounded by Black joy in the midst of mourning—dancing and wailing, laughing and praying, people passing around plates of food while gospel and brass collide in the background—it's not just a celebration. It's spiritual. It's a release. And somehow, it feels like the only way you'd want to send a family member *home*.

Back at the Big House, I'm stunned to find even more food than what I saw at yesterday's wake. Tables are packed—overflowing with dishes like someone catered for an army.

I weave through the crowd, scanning for Charlie, but before I find her, her father intercepts me and leads me into what looks like his formal study.

This is going to be interesting.

I'd been meaning to talk to Mr. Sinclair since the moment I became *engaged* to his daughter, but somehow, the right moment had always managed to slip through my fingers. Either he was surrounded by people, locked in deep conversation with extended family, or I'd chickened out at the last second like a teenager about to meet his girlfriend's dad for the first time.

And now, here we are. No buffer. No crowd. Just me, standing face to face with Joe Sinclair—with his sharp eyes, measured calm, and the kind of presence that makes a man sit up straighter whether he wants to or not.

"You want a drink?" he offers, already reaching for something behind the bar.

"I'm good for now, thank you," I reply, straightening my posture.

"So," he starts, leaning back with his glass. "You and my baby girl, huh?"

The words catch me off guard. I scramble for something half-coherent. "I've been meaning to apologize. For how... *sudden* all of this is."

He lets out a low exhale, something between a laugh and a sigh. "Sudden is the understatement of the century."

I scan the room, eyes landing on the curated collection of memories lining the walls and shelves of Joe Sinclair's office. Awards, plaques, and framed photos—all meticulously arranged, each one humming with history. It's clear none of it is for show. This isn't a man flexing status. It's a man archiving impact. Every piece, every frame, is a brick in the foundation of a legacy built by grit, conviction, and an unshakable love for his family. And his people.

Then one picture stops me cold.

Front and center on the bookshelf, in a frame that looks recently dusted, is Charlie. Dressed in white. A gown that hugs her curves and floats like it belongs in a bridal magazine. She's glowing. Radiant. Only she looks to be about sixteen years old.

And right beside her, grinning like he owns the damn world, is a man I recognize immediately—Lucas *fucking* Ballentine.

I lean in for a closer look, jaw tight.

"That's from her Debutante Ball." Big Daddy offers. "Lucas was her date."

I look up at him with a confused expression. "I didn't realize..." I stutter, looking for the right words. "I didn't know—"

He chuckles. "That Black people had such traditions?"

"Well, yes. My mother always talked about girls coming out in society like it was a high society white woman thing."

"It's a little more complicated than that. But I'll spare you the Black history lesson today. How the hell did you convince my daughter to settle down?"

I laugh nervously. "I'm not sure if you've met your daughter, sir, but she doesn't exactly do anything she needs to be convinced of."

Joe studies me with a thoughtful nod. "You've got a point there."

My family and the Sinclair family never would've crossed paths growing up. Not really. Their family name was carved into marble and magnolias, passed down with land deeds and family crests. Mine was etched into late rent notices and secondhand shoes. We may have lived only a few streets apart, but it might as well have been galaxies.

Still, as my name grew—my net worth, my reach, my influence—I found myself thinking more about men like Joe Sinclair. About what kind of man it took to build something that lasted. To carry not just a name, but history on his shoulders. That kind of strength is intimidating. But it's also magnetic. Because deep down, I wanted to know what kind of man it takes to be that for someone else. To be that for her.

"I've seen your name floated around a lot, Xavier," Big Daddy says, his voice steady but edged. "Big checks to my foundations. Generous contributions. So I know either you've got a good heart—or one hell of a PR team."

He lets the implication sit between us like a loaded gun on the table.

Never in a million years did I think I'd be standing in this man's house—let alone sitting across from him, trying like hell to pretend I'm not completely, irreversibly in love with his daughter.

Not as the kid who used to walk past this estate on my way to school, wondering what kind of lives people lived behind iron gates and wraparound porches. Not as the young man who left Louisiana trying to outrun every piece of who he was. And definitely not as the man who now finds himself entangled in something that started as a lie—but feels more real with every damn breath.

Joe takes another sip of his drink. "You've never seemed all that interested in making a life," he continues. "Not here. Family, legacy... that's never looked like a priority for you."

"You mean the way the media paints me as a quiet recluse?" I ask, keeping my tone respectful but not apologetic.

"No," he snaps, not missing a beat. "I mean the way you avoid putting down roots. The way you treat this town like a memory you've already boxed up and put away."

I pause, my jaw tightening. "I have roots here, sir."

He nods slowly, studying me. "I heard about your mother. I am sorry to hear about her passing. But what about your father? Siblings? Any other family?"

"No father to speak of," I answer, steady but sharp. "And my mother never married or had more children. She was an only child."

"So when I speak of roots—"

"Like I said, sir," I cut in gently, "I have roots. They just aren't as long or as rich as yours."

I don't flinch when I say it. I won't be made to feel small about where I came from. I respect this man, but I won't wear shame that doesn't belong to me. We all carry our history—some of us are contending with it, some running from it, and some doing our best to protect what little we had. None of it looks the same. But it's still ours.

He tilts his head, eyes narrowing. "Wealth had nothing to do with it. My people survived slavery with nothing but their names and each other. But we held tight to family. To community. That's what makes a man, Xavier. Not the money. Not the press. Not the business deals. But who he's building all it for."

And God help me, I want Charlie to be who I build for. I want her to be my home.

He pauses. "So what is it about my Charlie Chaplin that makes you think you can be the man she needs?"

It's not the usual *what are your intentions with my daughter* conversation—but then again, this is far from a usual situation. As far as he knows, we're already engaged. My intentions are basically on public record.

I shift forward in my seat, careful with my words. "Sir... Big Daddy... I won't pretend I'm sitting here full of confidence. I've got more zeros behind my name than most, but none of that means a damn thing when I'm sitting across from a man like you. And if I'm being honest, I'm not sure I *can* be everything Charlie needs. But I'd like to try. Since I met her, I haven't wanted to do or be anything but hers."

He leans back slightly, a slow grin tugging at his mouth. "Is that right? So what did it? What made you fall for my girl?"

"Her beauty catches you off guard," I say slowly, trying to put it into words, "but it disarms you at the same time. She doesn't smile often, but when she does, you know you've earned it. She hates being vulnerable, hates losing control... but she's drawn to places that feel like home. Like family. Where she's able to be unguarded."

I glance toward the door, where laughter and clinking plates echo down the hallway. "I can see where she gets that from. Her love of family."

Big Daddy smiles, wider now. "Sounds like someone's been hit with the love bug."

I grin. "Something like that. And if I'm lucky, there's no cure."

I don't know how she thinks this can still be fake.

How Charlie can honestly believe that when this is all over, we'll just walk away—no strings, no questions, just another chapter closed.

Because sitting here, talking to her father, laying it all bare—why I'm here, what's got me so twisted up over his daughter—it's the most honest I've ever been about a woman in my life.

And the most certain.

"How old are you, Darcy?"

"Forty-two, sir."

He shifts in his seat, and the look he gives me could cut through stone. It's subtle, but it's all Sinclair—measured, disappointed, a little amused.

I clear my throat and sit up straighter. "Forty-two, *Big Daddy*," I correct myself.

The corner of his mouth twitches, but he doesn't let me off the hook just yet.

"So, six years older than my Charlie."

"Correct."

His expression, suddenly serious. "Have you defiled my baby's delicate flower?"

I nearly choke, coughing on the moisture in my mouth. "I—excuse me?"

He raises an eyebrow, clearly enjoying himself.

I clear my throat and manage, "I beg your pardon, Big Daddy?"

Joe bursts out laughing. "Relax, son. I'm messing with you. Charlesetta would strangle me if she knew I asked. Back in the day, I used to interrogate every guy Charlie brought home—told one I'd check the backseat for condom wrappers."

I laugh, tension bleeding from my shoulders. "Appreciate you not taking it that far with me."

His voice softens a little. "Truth is, it feels good that it's you. We've always wanted Charlie to be happy. Watching her here—with you, with her friends—I see something I never saw when she was with Lucas."

"Oh yeah?"

"Yeah. Something about her and that boy never did quite fit."

I nod, wondering if he's ever told her that. "I think she'd love to hear that from you."

He tilts his head. "Why do you say that?"

Carefully, I say, "I just get the sense she feels like she's letting you down if she doesn't live the life you imagined for her."

Big Daddy's expression shifts—thoughtful now. Quiet. Like I've nudged something he didn't know was waiting to be acknowledged.

"I'll have to sit with that," he murmurs. "Pray on it. Thank you for saying something."

I nod once, respectfully. "Anytime, Big Daddy."

I clear my throat and shift in my seat again. "Well, Big Daddy. I know it's a little late and most certainly out of order, but I'd like to ask your permission to love your daughter for the rest of my life?"

I am never going to get used to calling this man *Big Daddy*.

The whole notion feels... odd.

But then again, I didn't grow up with the kind of family that had traditions like this—nicknames that carry weight, history, affection.

So maybe it's not about understanding it.

Maybe I'm just supposed to sit back, take notes, and soak in what it actually *feels* like...

To belong.

To be part of something.

To *have* a family.

He nods with a glint of appreciation in his eye. "I appreciate the gesture. And the sentiment. But if my Charlie Chaplin said yes, that's all the permission you need."

There's a loud crash from the kitchen—something metallic and aggressive, like a pan taking its final breath.

Both Big Daddy and I jolt, turning toward the sound.

A beat later, Elijah barrels in from down the hall, breathless and wide-eyed. "There y'all are! Mama and Charlie had me tearing this whole house apart lookin' for you."

He pauses, eyes narrowing slightly as he takes in the room—the awkward posture, the lingering tension, the half-full glass in Big Daddy's hand.

"Unless I'm interrupting something?" he asks, eyebrows raised.

"Not at all," Big Daddy replies, as smooth as ever.

Elijah eyes him sideways. "Lemme guess... Big Daddy hit you with the ol' *'have you defiled my baby girl's flowers* speech?"

I raise a brow. "Flowers, with an *s*?"

"Best you learn now," Elijah says with a shrug. "Charlie's got both. Y'know... on account of her bein' one of them hermaphrodite women."

I blink. Then slowly turn to Big Daddy, silently begging for confirmation that this is a joke.

Also, I've only been with Charlie once and...I would have *remembered*.

When Big Daddy explodes into full-on, belly-shaking laughter, I know it's safe to follow.

I let out a deep laugh, shaking my head. Elijah's got the same mischievous streak as my best friend Jonah—equal parts foolish and charming. And somehow, it makes me feel even more at home in this family.

"Come on, bro," Elijah says, already turning toward the door. "Charlie's in the kitchen *helping*, and I figured you should know now, your fiancée can't cook worth a damn."

CHAPTER TWENTY FOUR

Xavier

We step out of Big Daddy's study, and I'm just starting to breathe again when Elijah and I nearly collide with a man standing in the hallway.

Tall. White. And dressed like money—tailored suit, silver cuf-flinks, watch worth more than my first apartment.

His smile is smooth, easy, practiced. But the second Big Daddy sees him, the energy shifts. So does mine.

Lincoln Smith.

"Lincoln," Big Daddy says, flat and cold.

The man extends a hand with a practiced charm. "Joe Sinclair."

Big Daddy doesn't take it. Just stares.

"Oh, don't be like that, Joe," the man drawls, Southern as sweet tea. "I'm just here to pay my respects."

But that voice, that smooth, syrupy accent— it doesn't match the look in his eyes.

There's a cold sharpness there. Calculated. Watching.

And then, it clicks.

His name. The headlines. The timing.

The sudden appearance at my Charlie's parents' house, of all places.

This isn't a coincidence.

This is a message.

I'm just not sure what that message is.

There's something in the way Big Daddy watches him, too. In the tension in Elijah's spine. In the way you can tell this man says one thing but *means* something else entirely.

"Thank you, Linc," Big Daddy replies stiffly. "Now if you'll excuse me."

It's the kind of tone that sounds polite if you're not paying attention—measured, composed.

But I'm paying attention.

And it's clear as day.

Joe Sinclair is *too dignified* to tell this man to go to hell, but it's exactly what he wants to do. What he communicates without saying a word.

Every line of his posture, every sharp look, screams it.

Get the hell off my property.

He moves past, brushing the man's shoulder with the kind of energy that says *you're not welcome here,* and doesn't look back.

The man's gaze shifts to me.

"Lincoln Smith," he says, offering his hand with the confidence of a man used to being obeyed. "And you are?"

I pause, my instincts bristling before I can place why. He knows who the hell I am.

"Xavier Darcy," I say, gripping his hand.

For a split second, his face goes still. But then the smile returns—too fast. Too polished. Slick.

Before I can ask anything, Elijah steps in, hand firm on my shoulder. "Come on, man. Let's get to the kitchen and see what the ladies are up to."

We walk away, but I glance back once. Lincoln is still standing there, watching me.

When I ask Elijah what that was all about—why that man looked at Big Daddy like they had unfinished business—his whole body shifts. His jaw tightens, his voice low and even when he finally speaks.

"That's Lincoln Smith," Elijah says flatly.

"I'm aware of the name," I reply, keeping my voice even. "But what does he have to do with your family?"

I'm careful with my tone—too careful—because what I'm really asking is *why the hell does this man keep showing up in my life*, and I don't want to tip my hand just yet. Not until I know what Elijah knows or what we can trust him with.

He pauses. Eyes scanning mine like he suspects I already know more than I'm letting on. Then he leans in slightly, voice low.

"His family's history in this town is... complicated. They owned slaves here in Louisiana, like a lot of powerful white families did. But when slavery ended? They didn't fold. They pivoted."

Elijah shakes his head, jaw clenched.

"They turned their old plantations into resorts—rebranded our pain as "southern charm." They held weddings where whips once cracked. Served brunch on blood-soaked soil. Turned trauma into a backdrop. Into a business.

And the fact that the Sinclair family actually they've kept their land and told the truth about it? That burns him up. In Lincoln's mind, Black people don't have the right to claim that part of history. To own it. To honor it. Not even when it's their own. He believes—like the slaves his family once owned—that history belongs to him, too. To shape. To rewrite. To sell."

I say nothing. Just listen.

Elijah looks me dead in the eye. "And Lincoln? He's always hated that our family wouldn't sell to him.

Hated that we took what they tried to erase and turned it into something they couldn't touch. It burns him up."

He looks away for a second, like he's trying to collect himself.

"He's been trying to get this land for decades. First with offers. Then with pressure. Now? I don't even think it's about business anymore. I think it's about revenge."

Lincoln Smith has haunted this city for decades.

After Katrina, while families were wading through mold and ruin, he was placing bets—banking on poor communities to fail so he could swoop in and turn them into playgrounds for the white elite. Resorts. Townhomes. That grotesque antebellum aesthetic dressed up as progress.

Bad real estate deals. Unsafe conditions. A trail of broken promises to the most vulnerable. The man is ruthless. Vile. And I hate that his name is surfacing anywhere near mine.

Not all wealthy men are cut from the same cloth. I've spent my entire career trying to prove that. But with my name in scandal and his name in headlines, the overlap is too loud to ignore.

And now he's here—at my supposed fiancée's house.

Which means I need to cut this tie before it knots around my neck.

I exhale slowly, finally understanding just how deep this all runs.

And just how personal all of this really is...to all of us.

"And Big Daddy?" I ask, still trying to process the weight of it all.

Elijah looks at me, his eyes steady.

"Big Daddy would never sell to them. Not for any price," he says, voice firm with pride and something deeper—legacy. "These folks refused to give us our forty acres/ So my family went and *took* it."

Their family's history isn't just something they tell—it *walks* with them. Woven into every word, every glance, every silence heavy with what's been endured.

They don't just carry legacy.

They *are* legacy.

And being near them makes me want to rise.

I glance over my shoulder again.

Lincoln Smith is gone.

But something in the air—thick, unsettled—tells me this isn't over. Not even close.

Whatever war we were preparing for before, this just got personal. And bigger than I ever imagined.

CHAPTER TWENTY FIVE

Charlie

It's been quite the day—long, eventful, and full of the kind of Black joy that fills your chest and settles in your bones.

And it was nice...having Xavier around for it all. Not just to witness the drama, but to carry a little bit of the emotional weight without me ever having to ask. Just by being there.

Still, I kept catching Lucas watching us. Not subtle either. Like he was trying to solve some puzzle he didn't even have all the pieces to. Was it jealousy? Suspicion? Did he know Xavier and I were faking this?

He's been weaving in and out of the kitchen all afternoon, hovering, looking for a moment to pull me aside. But I don't have the space for Lucas right now—not for his questions, his nostalgia, or the old story he keeps trying to write us into.

Because, honestly, no matter how hard I try to imagine anything between me and Lucas, the future just looks...blurry.

Forced.

And I'm starting to think that story—the one where Lucas and I end up together at the end—wrapped itself up a long time ago.

We just never had the courage to close the book.

I'm in the kitchen at the Big House, surrounded by the people who know me best—Timantha, Autika, and Geneva—each of them holding a wine glass and holding court like we're back in undergrad talking shit in someone's dorm room.

"Now, Neva," Autika says, narrowing her eyes with mock suspicion, "you're gonna have to spill the beans on all the dirt Stasi has been hiding from us about her upbringing. I swear our good sis is a locked vault."

Geneva leans against the counter with a slow smile. "I'm afraid your Stasi and *my* Charlie are two completely different women, honey."

I pause mid-pour, setting the wine bottle down. "What's that supposed to mean?" I ask.

Neva shrugs. "Exactly what I said. The Charlie who used to chase frogs with me and spy on our middle school English teacher is not the same Anastasia who flies private and gets molested by billionaires mid-flight."

Autika nearly spits her wine. "Did you just say molested?"

Timantha's nose wrinkles. "I'm sorry—did you say *hunt frogs*?"

I laugh, but it sticks in my throat. Because here's the truth: I *have* become someone else.

There was a time when I couldn't wait to outgrow that little girl. Charlie with the scraped knees, wild ideas, and a heart way too soft for the world. I spent my whole adult life building Anastasia. Rebranding. Reinventing. Erasing anything that felt too small, too soft, too *me*.

But Charlie never really left. She just got quieter.

Anastasia is polished, composed, calculated—She flies solo, keeps secrets, saves lives behind closed doors.

But Charlie? Charlie misses home. She misses laughing until her stomach hurts and sitting on the porch with people who knew her *before*.

And maybe I'm tired of being split in two.

"I love how y'all pretend like we don't all have parts of ourselves we keep tucked away," I say, lifting my glass. "Or how women act like we're not allowed to change when the armor we used to wear doesn't fit anymore."

I glance around at the women who know both versions of me.

"Yes, Charlie chased frogs. But Anastasia isn't so different. She's just... armored."

Autika sucks her teeth. "Except your armor's made of vibranium, sis. You keep your shit so locked down, we don't even know what's real."

I smile, but it's soft. Earnest. "And I'm working on that... letting my guard down more. Bit by bit."

I look around at the women who've held space for every version of me—loud, quiet, broken, and bold.

"But I promise," I say, my voice steady, "you already know the best parts of me. And the parts I'm still becoming? You know those too. Because you ladies have helped shape them."

"Whatever," Geneva cuts in, raising her glass with a smirk. "Enough with all that soft shit! Here's to Black women becoming whoever and *whatever* the fuck they want."

We clink glasses and say it together like a sacred promise.

"To Black women becoming whoever and whatever the fuck we want!"

And right on cue, my mother walks in like a well-timed twist.

"Here's hoping *becoming pregnant* is on the agenda," she says, all Southern grace and pointed daggers.

I take a long sip of wine and sigh. "I don't want kids, Mama. Xavier got a vasectomy."

Her gasp is loud enough to silence the blender in the background. "What on earth? Why not?"

"I've never wanted kids," I say simply.

"Nonsense. We've *always* talked about you raising a family—"

"No, Mama. *You* talked. I listened. Because your wishes always seemed to matter more than my voice."

Her spine stiffens. "Now Charlesetta, I will *not* have you raising your voice and talking sass in my house."

"Fine, Mama! I won't talk sass—or shit—or *anything else* in your house."

"Charlie," Elijah warns softly behind me.

"No, Eli!" I snap, my voice rising. "I'm tired of her acting like my life is up for debate."

"Because your choices never made any damn sense, Charlesetta!"

"To *you*, Mama! They didn't make sense *to you*! You never even tried to understand me!"

Timantha reaches out, trying to gently guide me away. "Charlie, maybe we take a walk—"

I shrug her off. "Mama, do you even *know* who I am?"

My mother frowns. "What are you talking about?"

"I've run operations that would make your head spin. I've protected diplomats. I've saved lives you'll never even know about!"

"You're not making sense, Charlesetta."

"I've killed—"

And from behind me, I hear Xavier's voice cut in. Calm. Even. Careful. "Charlie, maybe consider what you're sharing. The implications."

I turn to Mama, my voice cracking under the weight of years of silence. "Why can't you just see me for who I *am*, Mama? Why isn't that ever enough?"

People have stopped moving. The noise in the kitchen is gone. I realize I'm spiraling. Unraveling. Making a scene.

A spectacle. Something Cynthia Sinclair raised me to never do.

I head for the back door, heels clicking against the tile like punctuation—sharp, final, desperate. My girls are right behind me, their presence warm and heavy with concern.

But I stop, hand in the air, voice low. "Just leave me, y'all. I need a minute." Asking them to stay behind.

The moment I step halfway out, the night air kisses my skin—and so does his voice.

"Peach..."

I freeze. Close my eyes as a tear escapes down my face.

"Peach, do you need me?"

He said it this morning. *Don't pretend you don't need me. Don't pretend you're steel when you're breaking.*

And right now I'm breaking.

I nod, barely. My throat tightens around the word, but I force it out anyway.

"Yes," I whisper.

And like he's been waiting for this moment all day, Xavier is there—strong and steady, hand in mine, pulling me close.

He doesn't ask anything else. Doesn't speak. He just moves.

Rushes me out the door like freedom's on the other side—and he's not about to let me miss it.

CHAPTER TWENTY SIX

Xavier

I t's nearly six in the evening, and the Big House is finally starting to thin out. Guests are filtering out, saying their long Southern goodbyes that happen in clusters at the front door and somehow take thirty minutes.

But Charlie's already halfway across the back lawn—barefoot, heels dangling from her fingers like an afterthought—and I just follow.

No questions. No comments. No need to lead.

I just go.

Because sometimes the loudest, most undeniable form of love isn't grand gestures or flowery words. Sometimes it's just the quiet commitment of walking behind someone who doesn't know how to ask for company... but needs it all the same.

I catch up to her just as the grass thins out, and I realize where she's leading me.

A creek.

There's a little rowboat anchored at the edge, old and hand-made—weathered, but sturdy.

"I haven't seen one of these since I was a kid," I say, stepping closer.

She doesn't answer at first. A tear slips down her cheek, and she swipes it away like it, along with her vulnerability, betrayed her.

"Me and Elijah built it when we were kids."

I glance at her. "You and your brother built a rowboat?"

She nods. "We weren't allowed to watch TV during summer break because we refused to go to Vacation Bible School."

I bark out a laugh. So does she—through the sniffles.

"Does it still work?"

"Like a charm," she says softly.

I crouch down, start untying the rope. "Then, let me take you for a ride, Peach."

She chuckles. "It's no Xavier Darcy yacht."

I step into the boat, barefoot now, and reach up for her hand with a grin. "It'll do. Give me your hand. Let me take you away from here for a little while."

She tosses her shoes beside mine on the grass, and lets me pull her in.

The boat creaks under our weight, but it holds steady as I begin rowing us out into the middle of the creek. The light is golden, dancing over the water, and for a moment, we just sit in the hush.

"You know," I say, breaking the silence, "me and my best friend Jonah once tried to steal a rowboat and escape New Orleans."

Her head snaps to me. "What?"

I nod, smiling. "Dead serious. We were fourteen. Had fifty bucks between us, thought we could live off McDonald's for a week 'til we got jobs in Houston or wherever the hell we thought freedom was."

"What happened?"

"We found out the body of water we were escaping through was manmade. Didn't lead anywhere. Just looped around the damn neighborhood."

She snorts. "Y'all tried to jailbreak through a glorified puddle?"

"Pretty much. That's when I knew I needed a real plan. A real way out."

She falls quiet, her gaze flicking out over the water.

"I guess we were both trying to escape this place," she says eventually. "Only difference is... I don't think I ever really had a reason."

I glance over at her. "You sure about that?"

She shrugs. "I blamed my mom for a long time. The way she talked, the way she expected me to fit into this little mold of the 'ideal Black daughter.' You know, respectable. Polished. Presentable."

I nod. I know what she means but don't pretend to understand the way someone in her skin would.

"She wanted us to be the good kind of Black. The kind white people invited to brunch and say things like *you're so well-spoken*."

That makes me laugh out loud.

She rolls her eyes. "I always wonder who I'd be if my mama wasn't trying to raise a version of me for white folks."

I ask her gently, "Have you tried talking to her? Just... laying it out?"

She snorts. "You don't *talk* to a Black mama, Xavier. You listen. You nod. You do what she says, even when she doesn't."

"That doesn't seem fair."

"Fair ain't ever had anything to do with it."

I smile, running a hand through her soft hair. "Your Southern twang sure does sing when you're at home, Peach," I say, watching the way her lips curl around the words, lazy and honeyed.

She smiles, soft and a little shy. "Especially when I'm around you," she admits. Her voice like warm molasses sliding over my skin.

And damn if that doesn't do something to me.

We float in silence again for a moment. The only sound is the soft lapping of the water against the boat and the occasional cicada screaming from the trees.

She tries to pivot, deflecting like she always does. Her eyes flick to mine. "Have you heard anything from your team? About your case?"

Instead of answering, I reach down and wrap my hand around her foot, drawing it into my lap. My fingers find the arch, and I start working slow, punctuated circles into her skin.

She gasps—soft, involuntary—and her head falls back for just a second, lashes fluttering shut. "Oh my God..."

The sound she makes is quiet, but it hits me like a sucker punch to the chest. It's so real, so raw, it curls around my ribs and doesn't let go.

"Thank you," I murmur "For letting me take care of you."

Her eyes snap open, and she scowls like I just insulted her. "Yeah," she mutters with mock-annoyance. "I fucking hate it."

I can't help the low chuckle that rumbles from my chest. I press a little deeper into the pressure point that makes her toes twitch and her jaw clench.

"I know," I say, grinning. "That's what makes it so much fun. I like knowing you wouldn't allow anyone else this close to do this for you."

The sunlight hits her just right—soft and golden, spilling across her skin like some divine spotlight. The bayou behind her ripples gently, catching the light the same way her eyes do when she's deep in thought. And for the first time in days, she's still. Quiet. Not ready to kill me. Not mid-eye roll or mid-insult. Just... here.

I know this is the moment. The one I've been waiting for. The one that feels safe enough to tell her everything.

Because if there's ever going to be a window of time where she won't react by kicking me in the nuts, slapping the taste out of my mouth, or drawing a weapon from a body part I didn't know could holster one—it's now.

She looks at peace. And that makes me nervous as hell. Because I'd do anything not to be the reason that peace disappears.

I've seen her when she's sharp-edged and spitting fire—when her voice cuts through a room like it's wired to detonate. I've seen her when she's wounded and hiding it, covering the cracks with sarcasm and attitude. But this version? The quiet, soft one, barefoot by the water and glowing like she doesn't even know she's doing it?

This is the version I'd kill to protect.

Which is exactly why I hesitate. Because what I'm holding—the truth I haven't said yet—it's a grenade.

And I know the second I hand it to her, I'll be watching the pin hit the ground.

"Tomorrow, Xavier. You'll tell her tomorrow."

CHAPTER TWENTY SEVEN

Charlie

The sun's barely up when I swing my legs off the couch and plant my feet on the cool hardwood floor of the cottage. Xavier's still asleep—sprawled out, his long frame curled slightly, one arm slung over the edge of the couch where I'd passed out last night.

After the funeral... after the repast... after what felt like an endless parade of people sharing memories and casseroles and unsolicited hugs—I needed quiet. I needed space. But more than anything, I needed stillness. And I got it with Xavier. He gave me a stillness that only comes when someone else is carrying the weight for a while.

So when we got back from the boat ride—where the water had calmed my nerves and his silence had soothed my soul—I let my guard down. Just for a minute.

I sat next to him on the couch with the full intention of getting up to work. But then he lifted his arm, and for whatever reason, I sank into him without a second thought. My head on his lap, the steady rise and fall of his chest grounding me. His fingers, gentle in my hair, lulled me faster than any lullaby could.

And somehow, somewhere between breathing him in and trying not to think about how safe I felt... I fell asleep. Right there. Wrapped in his warmth. Vulnerable. Exposed. Unafraid.

Now he's still there, peacefully knocked out like nothing in the world could bother him.

And I'm left staring at him, wondering how the hell I got here—and how I'll ever convince myself to walk away.

But I push thoughts of happily ever afters and whirlwind romances to the back of my mind. I have work to do.

I shake off the warmth of Xavier's lap, the ghost of his fingers in my hair, and move toward my laptop like it's a weapon. Because today, it is.

While Xavier's been doing his part in this fake engagement—charming the hell out of everyone from my nosy aunties to the old men on Big Daddy's porch sipping moonshine, men who usually hate outsiders—it's my turn to make good on the real job: figuring out who's trying to ruin his life, and mine by association.

I make myself a cup of coffee, fire up my laptop, and get to work. Most people wouldn't expect this from me. Hell, I didn't expect it from me either. I wasn't raised with gadgets in my hand—I was outside, climbing trees, skinning knees, breaking bones and rules. But government work has a way of rewiring you. Teaches you how to disappear in plain sight. How to crack systems built to be uncrackable. How to find people tucked so deep into the digital shadows, they've all but vanished.

And when I say I can dig? Your girl can dig.

I start sifting through encrypted files, bypassing firewalls, and cross-referencing IP logs like it's second nature. Whoever got into Xavier's biometric data, however they did it, it wasn't a fluke. It had to be someone with high-level clearance. An inside job.

Coworker. Former employee. Maybe even someone who built the damn system. I rule out family because, well, Xavier talks like he doesn't have one. So it has to be someone else just as close. Someone who has access to his DNA.

Just as I'm narrowing in on something suspicious—an IP address with weird routing patterns—my phone buzzes with a text.

Elijah: *Pancakes. Now. I made blueberry.*

I roll my eyes, but my stomach makes the decision for me. It growls loud enough to remind me I haven't eaten since yesterday. I shoot off a quick text to Hayven, attaching the flagged name I've uncovered and asking him to run it through his database ASAP. Then I toss on a hoodie and stand there for a beat, staring at the door.

Because going up to the Big House means more than just pancakes. It means facing Mama.

And after the argument we had—the yelling, the tension, the heat behind my words—I'm not exactly dying to walk into her kitchen like nothing happened. But I can't dodge her forever. And I sure as hell can't do it on an empty stomach. So I square my shoulders, tell myself I'll deal with whatever's waiting for me, just like Big Daddy always taught me to.

...

It smells like heaven when I walk in the back door. Syrup. Butter. Childhood.

Elijah's plating a stack of three blueberry pancakes just as I walk in. He slides them onto my regular seat at the kitchen island without looking up.

"Morning, ugly," he calls. "Lookin' like Mad Dog done snatched your soul."

I smirk. "Good to know you woke up feelin' like yourself, considering you still look like *that*," I say, gesturing towards his overall annoying brother appearance.

He shakes his head, grinning. "These extra pancakes are for your raggedy friends who are upstairs nursing the hangovers of their lives."

"Oh no," I groan. "Was it bad?"

After Xavier and I got back to the cottage last night, I saw a flurry of texts from Timantha. She and Tika were headed to Geneva's spot for food and drinks, trying to make the most of their time in town. She asked me to come, but I just didn't have it in me. I was drained—emotionally, physically, spiritually. The funeral, the family, Xavier... it was all too much.

I told them to go have fun without me, and I'm glad they did. Though, it sounds like they had way more fun than any of them bargained for. I'm just grateful someone was around to keep them entertained.

Elijah gives me a look. "Autika tried to fight a lamp."

I laugh. "We've been meaning to talk to her about how violent she gets with tequila."

"Timantha danced on the table. Kept asking the other people in the crowd if she was the winner of 'Amenteur Night.'"

"You're lying."

"I swear to God." He widens his eyes, punctuating his words. "White. Girl. Wasted."

Then, from behind me, I hear a sleepy yawn. "They were just blowing off steam. No big deal."

I turn to see Geneva stretching in the doorway.

"Neva. You slept over too?" I ask.

She shrugs. "Elijah insisted we stay so he could play doctor and keep us all from dying from alcohol poisoning."

"How chivalrous," I say suspiciously, clocking the look Elijah gives Neva as he hands her a plate of pancakes.

"Mmm hmm," Neva hums, closing her eyes like the pancakes just gave her a spiritual awakening. She's taken another bite, and I notice the way Elijah lights up watching her chew.

Ew!

Then he reaches over, grabs a napkin, and gently wipes a spot of syrup off her chin.

"Oh, okay." I drop my fork and point it at both of them like I'm holding court. "What is going on between you two?" I say slowly. "Spill it. Right now."

"I don't know what you're talkin' about, Cruella."

"You know damn-well what I'm talkin' about, Shrek and I demand to know! Are ya'll screwing?"

"Language," Mama says from the archway like some kind of Southern ninja. We all freeze.

"Morning, Mama," Elijah sings, and I roll my eyes so hard I almost fall over. He's such a kiss ass.

Neva grins. "Mrs. Sinclair, would you like some pancakes?"

"No, baby. Just a banana and my coffee."

She walks over to the espresso machine like she doesn't see me at all. But then her eyes land on me.

"Charlesetta."

I sigh, offering her a strained smile. "Morning, Mama."

She studies me. "Did you sleep well?"

"I... did," I say carefully. Why is she being nice?

The room goes quiet, the tension thick enough to pour over waffles, and Neva picks up on it instantly.

"Hey Eli, let's go eat on the porch."

"Best idea you've had all year," he jumps, grabbing his plate as they both rush out of the kitchen.

Real subtle.

Once they're gone, it's just me and Mama.

She walks over, leans against the counter.

"Mama," I begin, not wanting to make her do the heavy lifting. "I'm sorry about making a spectacle yesterday."

She waves me off, calm as a breeze. "Honey, when there's a Black funeral, when *isn't* there a spectacle?"

I'm thrown. Caught completely off guard by how... pleasant she is. No lecture. No guilt trip. No dramatic sigh followed by a monologue about family reputation or "what people might think." Just... grace.

It almost makes me uncomfortable. Like I'm waiting for the other shoe to drop.

"I know you feel like I've always been hard on you," she says, surprising the hell out of me.

I don't answer. Because I have no idea where she's going.

"As a mother, a Black mother...I just always wanted you to be okay. Safe."

I shake my head. "Mama, I don't understand."

"Growing up as a Black woman in the South, our options were... limited. And sometimes, all we had was who we married. The right man meant security. A future. And maybe it's old school, but I want to die knowing you'll be taken care of."

She pauses, placing a gentle hand on my wrist.

"It was never that I didn't want you to be yourself, Charlesetta. I just didn't want you to be alone in a world that keeps turning its back on women like us."

Her voice cracks just a little. And then, so does something inside me.

"I don't know much about him beyond what you see in the media, but if that Xavier Darcy makes you feel safe," she says, "then he's already done more than I could have ever imagined for you and Lucas Ballentine."

"Mama, why didn't you ever tell me any of this?"

She exhales slowly, not looking at me right away. "Because it's hard to get you to understand a fear that started long before you were even born. It's hard to translate that kind of awareness—of what safety meant, what security meant—when you aren't living in the same times I was."

Her voice softens. "And maybe that was my mistake. Trying to make you afraid of something that was never yours to carry."

She finally meets my gaze, and in her eyes I see it—not disappointment, not judgment—but a lifetime of worry she never knew how to unload.

"Mama, I'm sorry." That's all I manage. No justifications. No explanations. Just the truth.

I step down from the bar stool that I'm in and into her arms. She wraps me up without hesitation.

We stay like that—tangled in an embrace that feels more like a treaty than a hug. It's fragile. Unspoken. Held together by the kind of silence that comes from years of barely understanding each other—only to find ourselves here, suddenly holding on, both terrified this small bit of progress might slip through our fingers.

"Now," Mama says, her voice muffled against my neck, "what's this I hear about you murderin' people?"

I freeze. She says it like she's asking about vacation plans. My throat tightens as I try to remember how to breathe, let alone form words. I open my mouth—probably to lie—and then close it again because I don't know where to begin. How much to tell. What version of myself she's even ready to meet.

But before I can settle on anything remotely coherent, the back door creaks open behind us.

And in strolls Lucas Balentine.

CHAPTER TWENTY EIGHT

Xavier

I wake up to silence. That's the first clue something's wrong. The second? The empty indentation on my chest where Charlie's head should be.

I sit up, rubbing the sleep from my eyes, still reeling from the emotional whiplash that is being fake-engaged to a woman I might be genuinely obsessed with. And just as I swing my legs off the couch—

Knock knock.

Jesus. Who the hell is knocking at this hour?

I shuffle to the door and swing it open to find Prince Elijah standing there with that same smug look that says he knows more than he should.

"Lucas is back making a move on your girl. Thought you might want to know!"

I blink. Hard. "Good morning to you, too."

"Good morning, old man."

"You and these damn nicknames—"

"Are you hard of hearing? I just said Lucas is at the Big House making a move! I think I heard him say something about Charlie being the love of his life and not letting her get away this time."

My brain is still booting up, but one word registers like a slap to the face.

Lucas.

"The fuck he did."

Prince shrugs. "I could be wrong. But pretty sure that's what I heard."

The little shit smirks. He's playing me, but I can't even risk that he's telling the truth.

My phone buzzes in my pocket. Juliette.

"Juliette, everything okay?"

"No. Absolutely NOT OK."

Her voice is sheer panic.

"What is it?"

Buzz. Another text.

"Check the screenshot I just sent you."

I do.

"Oh. My. Goodness."

"Oh *fuck* is more like it, Xavier! Is this real? Because if so, the board now has everything they need to vote a vote of no confidence in you. You broke protocol!"

"Calm down, I didn't say it was real."

"Is it?"

I pause. Then sigh. "Yes. It's real."

"Fucking fuck, fuck shit, Xavier *fucking* Darcy! What the hell!"

I wipe sweat off my forehead and glance down at Prince. "Yo! You're just gonna let Mr. Steal Your Girl swoop in like that?" He yells.

Then it hits me. "Shit. I need to get to her before she sees this."

Before I hang up I shoot Juliette sharp instructions. "Juliette, call and have my pilot prep the jet. In case I'm not dead in a few hours, I have a feeling we're going to need to make a quick exit."

I rush out the door of the cottage towards the Big House, Prince jogging to keep up.

I've never thought about having kids. Not seriously. Not in the sleepless-nights, sticky-fingers, permanent-goldfish-crackers-in-the-car kind of way. The idea of raising a whole person always felt like something other people did—people with stable lives and childhood photo albums and matching holiday pajamas. Not me.

But every time I'm around Prince, I feel something shift. That kid's got a way of wedging himself into my chest like he's always belonged there. I don't know if I could ever handle diaper duty or midnight feedings or the kind of emotional vulnerability that comes with watching a tiny human call you Dad.

But adopting? Giving a kid who needs someone an extra hand, a place to land? That doesn't feel so far-fetched.

Still... Charlie would never go for it. I heard her say she didn't want kids. I don't know why, but it was like twisting a knife in my gut. And what the hell is wrong with me that I even let it bother me? I'm not building a future with a woman who carries a gun strapped to her thigh and keeps me at arm's length unless she's dragging me into her bed. So why the hell am I sitting here wondering what it'd be like to build a life with her? Kids? A family?

I need to get away from this family before they plant any more crazy ideas in my damn head. First, it's Charlie crawling under my skin, then Prince hitting me with his pint-sized wisdom, now Big Daddy's got me out here soul-searching for family after our little chat. I swear, one more heartfelt moment and I'll be in the backyard carving my initials into a tree.

This place...these people...are messing with my wiring.

As we approach the Big House, I spot her on the wraparound porch. And I freeze.

Because Lucas—*Lucas*—has the audacity to brush a strand of hair behind Charlie's ear like he's in a Nicholas Sparks movie and she's about to say yes to his cornball proposal.

I see red.

Not a hint of red. Full-on, hellfire, four-alarm rage.

I charge forward like I'm storming Normandy, but the grass decides it's Team Lucas today, slick as ice and just as cruel. My foot slips, gravity wins, and I fall flat on my ass.

Prince? That tiny traitor? Laughs so hard I'm pretty sure he snorts. "Man down!" he hollers like this is a damn video game.

I push myself up, soaked, stained, and pissed. And still very much in love with a woman who's currently standing on a porch with a man who needs to be launched into the Bayou.

Charlie spots me and stands abruptly, eyes wide. Lucas just grins like the light skinned son of a bitch he is.

Those were Prince's words. Not mine.

"Charlie!" I yell. "I need to talk to you!"

She yanks Lucas into the house like I'm a rabid dog.

"No the fuck she didn't," I mutter.

"The fuck she did," Prince confirms.

"Fuck off, kid."

I barge into the house like I'm on a mission, startling her mother in the kitchen.

"Xavier," Mrs. Sinclair says. "I've been meaning to talk to you. Come sit, have some coffee—"

"I would love nothing more, ma'am. But I need your daughter for just a minute."

"Yeah, Grandmommy. He's gonna go beat up Lucas Ballentine," Prince pipes in.

"I beg your pardon?"

"Nothing like that," I lie through my teeth.

I glare at Prince. "Little traitor," I whisper.

"Pretty sure they're in Big Daddy's study," he says, entirely too pleased with himself.

I kiss Mrs. Sinclair on the cheek and sprint down the hall. I pause at the door, hearing voices. Lucas is definitely in there confessing his undying love.

I kick the door open. I'm not proud, especially at how loud it is.

"Xavier! What the hell?!"

"Charlie! You cannot be moved by this man. You cannot be the love of his life. And you absolutely cannot marry him."

"Xavier, what are you talking about?"

"And why couldn't she marry me if she wanted to?" Lucas snaps, puffed up like a damn peacock.

"Because." I swallow, panting. "It's a really funny story. One I'm sure we'll all laugh about in the very near future."

"Xavier?" Charlie's voice is warning. "What are you rambling on about?"

I take a deep breath, still trying to recover from running and falling. "You see, Peach... we're already married."

CHAPTER TWENTY NINE

Xavier

Four Weeks Ago

It's Vegas. Loud, electric, spinning with lights and sin. And somehow, despite the energy of the place, all I can focus on is her.

Charlie Sinclair.

I should have been home by now.

That cryptic message I got after Justice and Autika's wedding had me rushing to get back to Atlanta. But when my pilot called to tell me the plane needed maintenance, I made the only smart choice—put safety first and decided to stay put for the night.

Which is how I end up here.

Standing in the corner of a hotel nightclub. Watching some asshole get dangerously close to what's mine.

I spot the man long before he makes his move. There's something off—eyes too wide, smile too controlled. I see him slide into the booth beside her, and for a moment, I do what I've been trained to do best. I watch. I study. I wait.

Growing up the son of a housekeeper, I learned early how to navigate spaces I didn't belong in. Learned how to blend in, how to read a room, how to predict a move before it happens. People in those spaces made damn sure I knew where I stood, where I belonged. And so I made damn sure I always stayed ten steps ahead of them.

That instinct kicks in now. I sit back, calculating, tracking every movement. Every glance. Every shift. Until his hand brushes against her drink. Without a moment's hesitation, I'm up and moving, the decision already made before my body even catches up.

One second, I'm nursing a drink and minding my damn business, and the next, I'm across the room like a heat-seeking missile, alerting my security detail to follow me.

Because it's not just the hand on the glass that does it—it's the way his body crowds hers, the way she stiffens for half a second before forcing a smile. It's the way predators operate when they think no one's watching.

But I am. I'm always watching when it comes to Charlie.

By the time we reach them, she's already swaying slightly. He tries to play it off by holding her up, looking around to see if anyone notices. But he's a dead man walking and doesn't know it yet.

I slide up next to Charlie without so much as a nod of acknowledgment to him. My arm drops casually along the nape of her neck, staking a silent claim.

"Hey, Peach," I say smoothly, ignoring the confusion on her face and the scowl blooming across his. "You ready to go?"

Her eyes widen—drugged, a little confused, but some part of her instincts still firing because she nods, her fingers already fumbling for her bag.

The man tries to protest, something about her not being ready to leave, but the look I give him shuts that shit down immediately.

I nod once to my head of security—Clive—and that's all it takes. The guy disappears from the booth and won't be seen again until his teeth meet a sewer grate.

Now, Charlie is the problem.

Because whatever was in that drink is hitting, and she's wrapped around me like a vine with a vendetta.

"You smell like expensive sex," she purrs into my chest as I half-carry, half-drag her to my suite.

It's probably a terrible idea to bring her to my room. I know that. Every headline I've avoided, every ounce of effort I've poured into maintaining my damn celibacy is screaming: *Don't do it.*

But leaving her out there—stumbling, glassy-eyed, giggling at shadows—isn't an option.

So I do what I've been doing more often than I should lately, especially where she's concerned.

I choose her. I choose Charlie.

The decision is an easy one because the alternative is worse. One wrong assumption and suddenly I'm the guy who drugged her, not the one pulling her out of danger. And after that message I've already received, the last thing I need is a scandal.

So yeah, it's probably reckless. But if the last few weeks have proven anything, it's that I'm completely incapable of doing anything that makes sense when it comes to this woman.

"And *you* smell like a lawsuit waiting to happen."

She giggles. GIGGLES. And I swear, I'm the one who's drugged. She's adorable.

Once we get into my suite, I have Clive call a physician from my private network—something my team set up years ago. I don't trust insurance. I don't trust hospitals. I pay a retainer to a network of elite doctors, and any time I need one, they show up. No questions asked.

She's a woman in my care tonight, and I'm not letting anything else happen to her without someone I trust giving the all-clear.

Dr. Elias shows up in fifteen minutes flat—bless the retainer system and its magic bat signal for concierge medicine. He's cool and professional, the way you'd expect a man who's seen it all to be. He checks her pupils, draws blood, runs a few quick tests with a handheld scanner that looks suspiciously like something from *Star Trek*.

"Small dose," he says finally with a European accent I can't place, snapping off his gloves. "She'll be fine. Sleep it off. Maybe get something in her stomach."

Charlie giggles beside me, then turns her glossy eyes my way and practically purrs, "I'd like *you* in my stomach."

I freeze.

She doesn't stop there.

"In. My. Guts," she whispers, like it's a national security secret. Each word enunciated. Her eyes wide. Dead serious.

Dr. Elias, bless his heart, pauses like his soul has just exited his body. "I'll let you two..." He gestures vaguely towards Charlie and makes a beeline for the door like the room's about to explode.

"Leave some Plan B, Doc!" Charlie calls out as he's fleeing. "I'm tryna get Hot Prince Harry *pregnant* tonight!"

I pinch the bridge of my nose, fighting the laughter bubbling up from the deepest corner of my chest.

"Charlie, please stop talking."

"Why?" She whines.

"Because that's not how any of that works."

I manage to thank Dr. Elias and tell him where to send the invoice, but I'm pretty sure he's already halfway down the hallway in a full sprint.

Then I turn back to Charlie.

She's sprawled out on the couch, dress riding high, cleavage practically offering up a prayer to heaven, and all I can think is—*Nope. Absolutely not.*

So I do the only thing I *can* do to keep from destroying every ounce of willpower I've got left: I help her to her feet, straighten her dress, and get her upstairs to the rooftop restaurant. My Peach needs carbs.

Because there is no version of this night where I survive being alone in a hotel suite with a very feral Charlie Sinclair.

...

Once we get to the rooftop, I find a quiet corner tucked away where no one will bother us. Las Vegas glows like a damn movie set below, neon flashing, sirens wailing somewhere off in the distance—but up here, above all the noise, it's almost peaceful. Almost.

I glance down at the menu and spot the price on the steak: four hundred dollars.

For that price, I better also receive peace that surpasses all understanding with my plate.

I laugh at myself whenever one of the scriptures Jonah sends me pops up in my memory.

The waitress approaches and before she even finishes the sentence—

"Hennessy," Charlie says, pointing a perfectly manicured finger.

"Water," I snap at the same time.

She scowls. "He'll take water. I'll take the brown juice of my ancestors."

I cover her mouth with my hand and flash the waitress a tight smile. "We'll both have Pellegrino. And do me a favor—no one else up here. Once that couple leaves"—I nod toward the corner—"no more guests."

I slide her five crisp hundred dollar bills. She nods and scurries off.

Charlie yanks my hand off her mouth and glares at me. "You're bossy."

"You're high," I counter.

She tilts her head, grinning like I just told her a joke. "You're hot. Hot Prince Harry, indeed!"

Then—because God clearly enjoys torturing me—she takes my index finger and slides it into her mouth. Slow. Wet. Eyes locked on mine like she knows exactly what she's doing. Like it's a damn challenge.

"Christ."

It slips out, gravelly and broken, more to myself than to her. I drag a hand down my face, trying to hold on to whatever shred of control I have left.

I lean back in the chair, muscles tight, jaw clenched so hard it feels like it might snap. I'm one second, one heartbeat away from clearing the rooftop and replacing that finger in her mouth with something far more deserving. Something aching for her.

But I don't.

As brutal as it is—I hold back.

Because I don't want to just fuck her.

I want her to remember it.

Every word I breathe against her skin. Every kiss that steals the air from her lungs. Every second I spend worshipping the woman who's haunted me since the moment I first saw her—months ago, across a crowded room. The moment *nothing* was enough for me—not the money, not the accolades, not the women, not the power—was the moment I realized I couldn't breathe right without her.

If I give in to her now, it won't be just sex.

It'll be everything.

And if she wakes up tomorrow and can't remember the way I came apart for her—if she forgets even a second of it?

It'll fucking destroy me.

Her skin glows under the rooftop lights, her eyes glassy but sparkling. She's lost in her own world and somehow completely glued to mine.

And this—this is the beginning of the end. I already know it. I'm fucked. And not even because I want to be.

Because I'm already hers.

After I force-feed Charlie water, the waitress comes back to the table. Not that Charlie notices—or cares. She slides her hand under the table and strokes my penis with absolutely no finesse, like it's her God-given mission.

It's not even subtle. The hand movements are obvious enough that a blind man two blocks over could probably file a sexual harassment complaint.

The waitress tries her best to act like she doesn't see what's happening, keeping her eyes trained somewhere above my head while I sit there pretending my dick isn't currently being forged into a steel beam in Charlie's hand.

I slap her hand away. It does no good. She brings it right back.

"We'll have an order of steak fries, please," I manage to grit out.

"Catchup too!" Charlie chirps, beaming up at the poor woman.

The waitress nods like her life depends on it and nearly trips over her own feet trying to get the hell away from us.

I reach under the table, grab Charlie's wrist, and still her hand before I embarrass myself...in my pants.

"Peach," I say under my breath, locking eyes with her, "you're gonna have to restrain yourself. Let me get some carbs in you."

"Is this because of the no sex until marriage thing, Darcy?"

I raise a brow. "It's because of the 'we're in a public place and I don't want to go to jail' thing!"

"Ok well what about in a private place?"

"What, Charlie?"

"Fuck me in a private place, Xavier."

She's testing me. Even under the influence of a tranquilizer the woman knows how to get to me. Yes I want to wait until I'm married to have sex again. Yes this woman makes me want to break every vow I've made to myself. Yes this woman makes me want to—

"Marry me," she literally burps out.

Would you look at that, I'm hard again. Stiff as a nail.

"Here are your fries, sir."

Thank heavens. I needed a moment of reprieve. To shake myself out of even considering the idea.

"Thank you, Alisha," I say, noticing the name on her nametag. I'm usually more polite and would have addressed her by her name sooner. If only there wasn't a petite temptress with her hand down my pants, asking me to marry her.

The couple that was eating on the rooftop gets up and leaves and I don't miss the waitress rushing to lock the doors from the outside, putting up the closed sign. We're alone. And Charlie has put her hand back on my engorged penis.

"Charlie. Eat," I order, my voice strained and rough. She ignores me, pouting stubbornly, eyes locked onto mine and she squeezes me through my pants.

"Tell me you'll marry me, and I'll eat a fry."

I exhale sharply, trying to keep a lid on the chaos swirling in my chest.

"I will do no such thing," I growl. "You're intoxicated. You're not thinking clearly—"

She leans in, her voice a whisper of wicked temptation.

"I've been waiting to fuck you for a week. Longer than that. I *want* you, Xavier. And if I need a damn ring to get more of what you lit on fire on that fucking plane... then say yes."

A muscle ticks in my jaw.

I shove back from the table and stand, yanking the heavy curtain closed around our rooftop villa, cutting us off from everything but this—whatever the hell *this* is.

Behind me, she doesn't stop.

"You're horny, Peach. Plain and simple."

"It's not just the sex, Xavier," she says, her voice low, almost hesitant. "I like being near you. I like how the conversation just flows, like we've been doing this forever. How slow the kisses are. How you make everything feel... different.

Safe.

Safe in a way I never imagined anyone but me could give myself."

I grip the edge of the curtain, jaw clenched, eyes shut tight.

Her words hit hard—no warning, no armor. Just raw truth.

And I can't tell if it's the remnants of whatever drugs she was fed, or if she's finally letting me see the version of her no one else gets.

But I shake off whatever wild ideas are flying through my head right now. I need to be sure. I need her sober. Clear.

Because if she meant it—even a fraction of it— I wouldn't hesitate. I'd marry her, no questions asked. And I couldn't tell you why.

When I sit back down beside her, I take the plate of fries in my hand, my eyes never leaving hers.

I pick one up slowly, patiently. "Let me feed you, Peach."

She parts her lips without hesitation, her tongue darting out to brush the tip of my fingers as she takes the fry.

Heat surges through my veins. "Whatever it takes," I say with a grin.

I feed her another, grazing her lower lip with my thumb afterward, savoring the way her mouth closes around the food, the way her lashes flutter like I'm feeding her something forbidden.

Another fry.

I brush my fingers over her lips, and this time, she captures the tip of my thumb in her mouth, licking the salt from my skin.

Each bite more intimate than the last. She moans low in her throat, barely audible, but I catch it—and I stiffen painfully against my pants.

By the time half the plate is gone, it isn't about food anymore.

It's about control.

It's about her surrendering, one slow, sensual bite at a time.

I hand her another water and give her a look that says *no arguments*. She pouts but drinks it, and only when she finishes do I feel like I can breathe.

Now that she's had her fill, it's time to get mine.

I clear the table with quick, practiced movements, stacking empty plates and containers onto the dining cart tucked in the corner of the villa. Then I straighten, turn to her, and hold out my hand.

"Come here, Peach."

She places her hand in mine, and I guide her around to the front of the table. I grip her by the hips and lift her on top of the table, setting her down like she weighs nothing at all.

I'm damn grateful she's so petite—the table barely creaks.

Dropping to my knees, I push her dress up to her thighs, my hands smoothing over her soft, warm skin. I lick my lips, savoring the view, savoring her, as I prepare to feast.

Charlie tilts her head and smirks down at me. "Does this mean you're gonna marry me and then fuck me?"

I chuckle, shaking my head slowly as I nudge her panties aside with my tongue, making her shiver in my hands.

"Bien au contraire, mon amour," I murmur against her skin. *Quite the contrary.* "It means I'm giving you something that'll have to satisfy us both... until I can get my grip on reality again. And maybe... one day..." I press a kiss to her inner thigh, feeling her tremble, "Faire de toi ma femme, véritablement." *To make you my wife truly.*

I press my mouth against her, slow at first, savoring the taste of her like it's the first meal I've ever earned.

Her thighs tremble against my shoulders as I drag my tongue through her folds, teasing, tasting, claiming.

I hate that I've been brought to this.

She's been drugged. And I don't know what's real and what's not with her right now. I can't tell if it was the drug talking or the truth cracking her wide open.

I don't know if she meant the things she said, or if her body's just desperate for relief.

And still, I can't stop.

I can't stop myself from sinking into her wetness, from devouring every begging piece she's willing to give me.

Even if it's wrong.

Even if it ruins us both.

She gasps, her hands flying to my hair, gripping hard, anchoring herself as I work her over with a rhythm that's all hunger and no mercy.

"You taste so good, Peach. Just like I remember."

She thrusts herself into my face, desperate, and I suck her clit hard enough to make her cry out.

"Shit!" she whimpers, her body jerking against my mouth.

I lift my eyes to hers, a warning wrapped in a smile. "Sshhh. We don't want them calling the authorities, do we?"

"I don't care," she whimpers, wrecked and reckless. And I smile into her wetness, into the taste of the woman who will ruin me completely.

I slide my hands up her thighs, forcing them wider as I bring her sensitive bud into my mouth, licking and flicking with just enough pressure to make her curse.

Her hips roll against my face, desperate, mindless, her need pouring off her in waves.

I groan into her, the sound vibrating against her skin, and she whines, tipping her head back, giving me everything.

She's soaking, wrecked, pleading in broken whispers I can barely make out.

I flatten my tongue against her and drag it slow and firm, feeling her tighten, feeling her body coil tighter and tighter until—

She shatters.

Hard.

Loud.

Her body jerks against mine, her cries echoing off the stone walls of the villa.

But I don't stop. I don't let her come down easy.

I keep licking, keep sucking, dragging every last tremor from her until she's a filthy, panting mess on top of the table.

Finally, when her hands go limp in my hair and she tries to pull away, too sensitive to take more, I ease up and press a kiss against her swollen, spent center. I stand, wiping my mouth with the back of my hand, my dick throbbing against my zipper, ready to tear myself open just to get to her.

Charlie's eyes flutter open, hazy, dazed.

But then she smirks—a wicked, knowing smile that slices straight through me.

She grabs the front of my shirt and yanks me down, our mouths barely a breath apart.

"That was cute, Xavier," she whispers, her voice wrecked, raspy, dripping with the aftershocks I just ripped from her body. "But it's not enough."

And fuck me—she's right.

The blood that should be fueling rational thought is long gone, fed straight to my dick, leaving nothing behind but raw need and a dangerous kind of desperation.

I'm not thinking anymore.

I'm running on pure, reckless instinct.

Because I've awakened something in her.

Something wild.

Something insatiable.

Something mine.

And there's no chance in hell it's going back to sleep.

Before I can even breathe, Charlie leans in and drags her tongue slowly across my lips, licking the taste of herself from my mouth like she's branding me.

Claiming me.

Fuck. I love how filthy my Peach is.

I'm not walking away from this.

From her.

Dammit. Xavier.

I think I'm going to have to marry her.

CHAPTER TWENTY
THIRTY

Charlie

Four Weeks Ago

I can't stop giggling.

Everything feels floaty, like I'm underwater and the whole world's one big, colorful cartoon.

This is *so* funny!

They're dressed like a pimp and a prostitute! Satin, feathers, and rhinestones sparkling like a disco ball.

Their mouths move but their words sound like they're coming through a long tunnel.

"It's your turn, baby." The pimp says.

"Oh! Sorry!" I hiccup through my laughter. "I, Anastasia, take you, Hot Prince Harry, to be my groovily wedded husband! I know—hiccup—I'm a bitch sometimes and I don't let anyone get close to me. But you, Xavier Darcy, are the first man I want to let in and give my whole heart to. Let's make a baby."

Wow. I'm marrying Hot Prince Harry.

The crowd—that is a crowd, right?—cheers and claps.

Somewhere, floating on the air like a weird kind of magic, I hear the opening chords of a song...

"I Choose You." From *The Mack.*

Yes! That's the song. I know this song!

"I like this song!" I swoon, spinning a little where I stand.

I feel so warm.

I feel so happy.

I feel so—

"I think I'm gonna be sick."

And then the world tilts sideways, the lights smear into one long, colorful streak...

And everything goes black.

CHAPTER THIRTY ONE

Xavier

F our Weeks Ago

I can't believe this.

I can't believe we did this.

We're married.

The words feel unreal in my head, like they belong to someone else. But they're ours now. Stamped, sealed, and spoken in front of strangers and God. And the way she looked at me—what she said at that altar—it felt real. Like she knew. Like she meant every word.

Right?

Maybe I should pause. Let my guilt catch up. Sit with the weight of what just happened. But I can't. Not when she's standing next to me in that dress.

Because the second the elevator doors slide closed, all I can think about is peeling that dress off her. Getting her on the nearest bed.

And making her mine so completely, neither of us remembers our own names by morning.

Seven years.

Seven years of discipline, of restraint. Seven years without a woman, not because it wasn't an option, but because no one—*no one*—ever felt worth it.

Until her.

All I've wanted since the moment I laid eyes on her... is her.

And right now, all I can do is hope—pray, even—that she ate enough damn fries to remember this.

Remember me.

Us.

Tomorrow morning, when the fog lifts and reality hits.

Jonah would be proud—me, calling on God right before devouring my bride.

She's laughing, wild and unbothered, as she rips the cheap little veil off her head—the one the chapel threw at us after we stumbled in and said "I do" like drunken teenagers. I barely remember the vows. I just remember her saying yes, and that being the only thing I gave a damn about.

I drag her back to my suite—our suite now, I guess—a penthouse wrapped in floor-to-ceiling glass, the whole city of Vegas blinking back at us like a living, breathing beast.It's the kind of suite that was built for royalty. Or for sinners.

Tonight?

It's for both.

And she's making a damn art piece of the place.

Her black sleek cocktail dress slides off her body first, puddling on the marble tile at the door like a sensual little welcome mat.

Next comes her bra, a whisper of black lace that catches on the corner of a chair before it falls. Her shoes are kicked off halfway to the bed.

Her thong—the final barrier between me and salvation—is tossed carelessly, landing right at the threshold of the bedroom like some final, wicked dare.

She's naked.

Laughing.

Mine.

"Mr. Darcy," she teases, her eyes sparkling, wicked and wild.

"Mrs. Darcy," I growl back.

She grins, sly and sinful, as she pulls me closer by the waistband of my pants. "I think this is where you give me a proper wedding night."

I grin. "Happy wife. Happy life."

She's undoing my pants, my dick aching to break free and before I can say another word, Charlie sinks to her knees in front of me.

The sight of her—bare, flushed, eyes dark with hunger—almost knocks the air from my lungs.

She wraps her hand around my length, stroking me slowly, like she's got all the time in the world.

Then, with a wicked little smile, she leans in and licks the head of my dick, a slow, teasing flick of her tongue that has my hands fisting at my sides.

"Fuck, Charlie," I groan, my head dropping back.

She does it again, savoring the taste of me like she's been craving it, before finally taking me into her mouth.

Warm.

Wet.

Perfect.

"You're so good, Peach. My beautiful wife is so perfect."

She sucks me deep, slow at first, like she's memorizing every inch of me, savoring it.

"That's it, Peach," I murmur, my voice wrecked. "It's okay if you choke. Take your time. Take all of your husband."

Her hands grip my thighs, steadying herself as she sets a lazy, torturous rhythm, bobbing her head, hollowing her cheeks around me.

I thread my fingers through her hair—not to control her, just to anchor myself, because I'm two seconds from losing my mind.

"Charlie," I rasp, barely able to get her name out. "You understand you belong to me now." It's barely a question, but I still expect her to respond.

She nods, her eyes heavy-lidded, and then moans around me.

The sound rips through me like a fucking freight train.

I tighten my grip in her hair as I swell thick in her throat.

The sounds of her moist mouth as she takes me in makes me want to marry her again and again.

"I will end the next man who touches you," I growl, my voice lethal.

She gags a little on my girth, and instead of pulling away, I hold her head there, my thumb brushing her cheek almost tenderly.

"Do you hear that, Charlie?" I whisper, holding her head steady, my dick buried deep at the back of her throat.

"I'm a simple man... but I will end the Earth for you."

She chokes again, her body trembling, tears brimming in her wide, glassy eyes—and I nearly come undone right there.

"Good girl," I groan, bending down to press a kiss to her forehead, breathing her in, grounding myself in the feel of her, the taste of her, the fucking reality of her.

My wife

"I'll take that as a yes."

She moans around me, sending vibrations through my body that make my knees threaten to buckle.

Every slow drag of her mouth, every flick of her tongue, every gasp for air is a promise:

I own you.

You're mine.

And there's not a damn thing you can do about it.

I can't take another second.

I yank her up off the floor, her small body light in my arms, and crush my mouth to hers.

She tastes like sin and surrender. Like everything I'll never deserve but will take anyway.

Without breaking the kiss, I carry her across the suite, the city lights spinning around us.

Vegas blinks and pulses outside the glass, a thousand neon witnesses to what's about to happen.

I slam her back against the window pane, her bare skin pressing to the cool glass, and she gasps into my mouth.

"Look out there, Peach," I rasp against her lips, grinding my dick against her soaked center. "All of it. Every light, every soul out there... doesn't fucking matter. Only you. You are all that matters to me."

She moans, her fingers scrambling for purchase against my shoulders, her legs wrapping tight around my waist.

I grab my length, thick and heavy, and rub it through her slick folds, coating myself in her before lining up at her entrance.

I slide into her in one hard thrust, burying myself to the hilt.

"Oh my—" She cries out, unable to speak coherent words as her head falling back against the glass with a soft thud, and fuck, it's the most beautiful sound I've ever heard.

I pull a nipple into my mouth as I start to move, pounding into her, each thrust driving her body harder against the window.

"All yours, Mr. Darcy."

"Fuck!" That made me thrust harder and the glass shudders with the force of it. But I don't slow down.

I want the city to see.

I want the world to know she's mine. That tonight, she became my wife.

"Xavier—It's deep, baby."

Her nails rake down my back, her mouth open in a silent scream as I fuck her, deep and ruthless, my hand fisted in her hair to hold her steady.

"Every inch of you needs to remember. Mine," I growl against her neck, my body strung tight, seconds away from snapping.

"À jamais à moi." *Always mine.*

Forever my wife.

And when she shatters around me, sobbing my name against the glass, I let go and follow her over the edge, spilling deep inside her, marking her in the only way I know how.

Ours.

Always.

CHAPTER THIRTY TWO

Xavier

Four Weeks Ago

I wake up to a string of text messages from Nathan, his usual bark demanding to know where I am.

I roll over, ignoring the buzzing phone.

Not now.

I'll deal with Nathan—and whatever fresh hell he's dragging with him—later. Right now, I need a minute to breathe. To think. To figure out how the hell I'm supposed to fix the mess I've made.

I step out onto the balcony, phone pressed to my ear, the early morning Vegas air still heavy with heat. Charlie's asleep in the next room—spread out in the middle of the bed like a queen, tangled in the sheets we ruined hours ago.

Jonah's voice booms through the phone. "You *what*, X?"

I pinch the bridge of my nose. "I married her."

Silence. Then a slow, incredulous chuckle

"You dumb son of a—You freaking idiot."

I don't miss the way he changed his wording, seeing as how my mother was no longer with us.

"I thought you said you were gonna ask her out on a date! Married? What were you thinking?" Jonah demands, his voice sharp through the speaker.

"Quite frankly, I wasn't." I pace the length of the balcony, dragging my hand through my hair. "She was high, Jonah. She was drugged. And before you say anything, no—I didn't touch her until after she was *mostly* coherent. Hell, barely touched her even then. I took her to get food, made sure she was okay. Then... it just happened."

"What just happened?" he snaps.

"She proposed marriage!"

There's a beat of stunned silence before Jonah growls, "And your dick made you say yes?"

"That—" I grit my teeth. "—and the fact that it's her. I told you about her, the first damn day I made an ass of myself trying to impress her. I wasn't thinking. I just... I just wanted her."

"But you basically married her unconscious?" Jonah asks, voice laced with disbelief.

"Basically," I mutter, rubbing the back of my neck. "In my defense. It felt like she was sober enough by the time she proposed."

"Felt?" I can hear Jonah's eyebrow raised.

"I know. I'm an idiot. But as soon as she wakes up, I'll tell her everything. Get it annulled. Easy peasy."

"Sure," he says sarcastically. "Now that you've gotten your dick wet, just go ahead and ruin the sanctity of marriage while you're at it. Divorce her the first chance you get."

I roll my eyes, even though he can't see me. "So what, you think I should stay married to her?"

"I think you should give her a choice," he says, voice hardening. "And be man enough to face whatever she decides. Even if that is staying married.

I hesitate, the weight of it settling heavy in my gut. "And if I do want her to stay married to me?"

"Then you better ask yourself one question, Xavier: do you love her? Not want. Not crave. Love her?"

I squeeze my eyes shut, my chest tightening at just the thought of her—her smile, her stubbornness, her fire.

I don't know when it happened. Maybe it was the moment I first saw her at a gala last year. Maybe it was after our time in Greece. Or maybe it was sometime in between. But the answer is as clear as it's ever been.

"Yes," I breathe out. "I'm pretty sure I love her, Lucky."

Jonah lets out a long, heavy sigh, like he's been holding his breath for me. "Then you owe it to her to be honest. Tell her. Give her the choice you never really gave her last night. Because no matter how hot she was for teacher, you know it was due to something else other than you."

I scrub my hands down my face, feeling the weight of my screw-up pile higher. "I know, Pastor Jonah," I mutter, dragging out the nickname.

"Don't call me that unless you're ready to listen," he snaps. "To me and God."

I crack a smile despite everything. "I'm listening to you. I will tell her. First thing when she wakes up."

At least, that's the plan.

And I mean it. I'll wake her up gently, sit her down, tell her what happened, what it means. And maybe—hopefully—she won't hate me for it.

I hang up and slide my phone into my pocket, glancing back through the glass doors.

She's still sleeping. Peaceful.

I sit at the foot of the bed, just watching her for a few minutes. Memorizing her. Bracing myself.

Finally, she stirs.

Charlie blinks up at me, her hair a messy halo around her face. She smiles, sweet and sleepy. "Morning."

I smile back, heart thudding against my ribs. "Morning, Peach."

She stretches, groaning, then looks around the room. "Where are we?"

"Penthouse suite. Still in Vegas."

She frowns, confusion clouding her beautiful face. "Why... why am I here with you?"

The words hit me like a sledgehammer.

She doesn't remember.

"Charlie," I start, voice cracking. "Last night—something happened."

Her brows knit together. "What are you talking about?"

Before I can even gather my thoughts, my phone buzzes again, rattling loud.

I try to ignore it, but the calls keep coming. Nathan's name flashes across the screen, urgent and unrelenting.

I snatch it up and answer immediately. "Nathan, what's going on?"

"You need to get home. Now."

His voice is clipped. No humor. No cushion.

My gut twists. "What's happening?"

"No time to explain. Not on this line. Just trust me. Get to the jet and there will be a file waiting for you. Just...get here. It's bad."

That sick feeling at the bottom of my stomach grows, heavy and cold. My mind flashes back to the night of Autika and Justice's wedding—the same night I got that first cryptic message. And now here we are again. In the middle of what feels like another warning. Another alarm sounding.

"Ok. Got it," I say, already moving.

I end the call and turn back to Charlie.

She's drifted back to sleep.

I want to tell her.

I *have* to tell her.

I try shaking her. "Charlie?"

I kiss her forehead, trying to wake her gently. "Charlesetta. You need to wake up, Peach."

There is a knock at the door of my suite. "Mr. Darcy? Your car is ready, sir."

"Charlie. Wake-up, Peach. Wake up so I can make this right and make you my wife for real."

She doesn't move. She's dead to the world.

And I have to move.

There's no time to unravel this now—not when everything is hanging by a thread back home.

Not when I can't even give her the full truth, the way she deserves to hear it.

Not yet.

I need time to come up with a plan. And if I know anything about Charlie Sinclair, this isn't going to be a quick conversation. This will be a war I'll have to earn my way through.

Still, it guts me that she doesn't remember anything.

Not the vows.

Not the way I made love to her.

Not the way she smiled like I was the only man in the world.

I call down for the hotel's car service, arrange for them to take her wherever she wants to go when she wakes. It's the least I can do. The only thing I can control right now.

And without another word—without explaining the one thing that matters most—I press a kiss to her forehead.

Soft. Lingering. Final.

Then I walk out the door.

Leaving behind my wife.

The only woman I've ever wanted to stay for.

My forever.

CHAPTER THIRTY THREE

Charlie

Present Day

Lucas shifts awkwardly on his feet, his hands fidgeting with the hem of his shirt. I can see him working up the nerve to say something.

I don't even know why we're doing this.

Why Lucas feels the need to open this door now—of all times.

But maybe this is what closure looks like.

Messy. Unplanned. Long overdue.

And maybe it is time.

Time to finally lay the past to rest and close that chapter for good.

But damn, I wish he'd get to the point—because while this has been lingering far too long, I've got no desire to sit in it any longer than I have to.

I'm done with ghosts and half-finished endings.

I want what's ahead. Something real.

Something that feels like mine.

Something that feels like *him*.

Because now, after the way Xavier's been looking after me, touching me like I'm something precious he gets to protect...I almost don't want to do anything that might mess that up. That might make him second-guess what we're building—or whatever the hell this thing is growing between us.

I *hate* this vulnerability shit.

Hate how *deep* it already goes.

And how, for the first time in my life, it feels like I have something to lose.

I lean back against my father's desk and cross my arms. "Lucas, I think I know what you want to say and—"

He cuts me off, voice heavy but rushed. "I guess I just never imagined you with someone like him."

I blink. "A billionaire?"

He smirks, a half-hearted thing. "No. I know your mother too well. That part was expected."

I can't help it—I laugh, a real one, sharp and surprised.

But Lucas isn't laughing. He's looking at me with something closer to confusion...or hurt.

"I mean, if I'm being honest...frank...a white man."

I straighten up immediately, my body locking tight. "Really?"

He shrugs like it's no big deal. "Your family built a proud legacy from slavery. And you dare to—"

"Whoah." I cut him off, stepping closer, my voice nearing something close to dangerous. "Before you finish that sentiment—or dare to say anything else about me tarnishing my family's legacy because of my choices—I'm gonna need you to think real hard about what comes next."

The air crackles between us. People have been trying me left and right this weekend, and I'm not in the mood for another round.

"I didn't mean anything by it," he backtracks quickly, palms up like I'm holding him at gunpoint. "Not like that, Charlie. I just mean that it was unexpected."

I inhale, steadying myself. Then I let the words fly, clear and sharp.

"Lucas. It's true that my family built their brand from slavery. That they purchased their lives and rebuilt it from white slave owners. But they didn't just purchase land and a name, Lucas. They purchased freedom. They voted for it. They bled for it. They built a life that represented it, brick by brick, stone by stone."

I step closer, leveling him with a look that makes him shift on his heels again.

"And my audacity to love and be loved by anyone I choose? That isn't tarnishing the legacy. It's honoring it. In the most beautiful, poetic, and *petty* way possible."

He doesn't say anything. He just stands there, a shadow framed by the doorway. For the first time, the great Lucas Ballentine—my mother's golden boy, the one this town practically built statues for—looks small. Quiet. Almost...fragile.

"I'm sorry," Lucas says, voice rough like it's been sitting in his throat for years.

I nod, giving him a soft, measured smile. "I know," I say quietly. "And I'm sorry, too. *Really* sorry."

The second apology slips out before I can stop it. But it's deserved.

Because the truth is—I didn't just lie to myself. I lied to him, too. Sold him a future I never really believed in. Held onto him like a life raft when I was never planning to stay afloat in the same waters.

And he paid the price for it.

"Yours and my history? I'll always carry it. You were my first. ..*everything*. And for a long time, I thought I owed *us* something more. Thought I was broken because I couldn't mold myself into what everyone expected, couldn't force our story into the perfect love story they all wanted for us."

He shakes his head, his mouth working like he's struggling for words he never learned to say. "No one ever wanted you to be anything but yourself, Charlie."

"I know that now." My voice wobbles, but I hold it steady. "But I needed to figure out who I was before that truth ever meant anything to me."

We sit there a minute longer—two old friends, no longer tangled in what-ifs or could-have-beens, just a quiet acknowledgment of what we were and what we'll never be.

I thank him, honestly, for being my safe place when the world felt too big and I felt too small. I apologize, too—for not telling him sooner about the life we created on prom night. The life I couldn't hold on to.

Lucas looks at me then, really looks—like he's seeing the girl I was and the woman I've become all at once. There's sincerity in his eyes. And something else, too.

Finality.

He grips my hand once more before letting it go. "And maybe," he says, voice strained, "maybe that life wasn't lost, Charlie. Maybe it was setting you free. Releasing you from a future that was never mine to claim."

Emotion rises in me, slow and unexpected, wrapping around my chest like a warm blanket. It's unfamiliar—tender in a way I'm not used to—but in this moment, it feels like exactly what I need. And I let it hold me. Just for a little while.

That moment with Lucas—it was needed.

Beautiful.

Raw.

It's the goodbye we didn't know we were saying back when I left for grad school, but one we say now, fully, finally, with open hearts.

We hug—tight and sincere.

And just as we pull apart, promising to stay friends, the door bursts open.

Xavier.

He fills the space like a storm rolling in off the bayou, his chest heaving, eyes wild, taking in the scene like he's ready to tear the world apart.

But instead, the fucker drops a bomb... we're already married.

CHAPTER THIRTY FOUR

Charlie

I storm across the room, fueled by pure rage, and before I can talk myself out of it, I rear back and punch Xavier Darcy right in his pretty, smug face.

He grunts, staggering back a step, catching his eye with his palm. "Jesus, Peach!"

"What do you mean... *already married?*" I yell, my voice echoing off the wood-paneled walls of my father's study.

Xavier straightens, still rubbing the spot I just lit up, and holds his hands out like he's calming a wild animal—which, honestly, isn't far off right now. "It's not what you think—"

"*It better not be what I think!*" I snap, pacing like a caged beast. "Start talking, Darcy. Fast."

He exhales through his nose, his shoulders stiff. "The night Autika and Justice got married. After you were drugged. After I got you checked out by my private doctor. You... you proposed."

I blink. "*I did what now?*"

He winces, like the memory physically pains him. It could also be the black eye forming.

"You proposed to me, Charlie. And you were...*very* persuasive."

"Oh my God." I slap my hand to my forehead.

"And I may have...accepted."

Lucas, leaning against the desk, lets out a low whistle. "That can't be legal. Hell, the marriage *isn't* legal under those circumstances."

Xavier's head swivels toward Lucas with a murderous glare. "I'm gonna need you to hold your tongue, Lucas fucking Ballentine. This doesn't concern you."

Lucas crosses his arms, standing his ground. "It concerns my best friend's little sister, so yeah—it kinda does."

I whip around, my fury now aimed squarely at Lucas. "And when exactly did you and my brother become *best friends*, Lucas?!"

He shrugs, a cheeky smirk pulling at his lips. "Somewhere between you running off and showing back up a decade later without so much as a damn postcard, *Charlesetta*."

And I thought we'd just called a truce. Bitter ass traitor.

Xavier glares at him before turning back to me. "Peach, focus. Please."

I fold my arms over my chest and glare at him. "So, you're telling me, you married me. While I was high. Out of my mind. Without my consent."

He flinches. "You *did* consent. Repeatedly. Loudly. Enthusiastically. Practically begged me!"

I groan, dragging both hands through my hair. "That's not *legally* consenting, Xavier!"

Lucas pipes up from his seat, looking way too comfortable for my liking. "Yeah, I'm pretty sure marriages where one party is incapacitated are frowned upon in the Sinclair family."

Forget the Sinclair family's opinions. I'm not worried about reputation or some old Southern scandal. I'm worried about safety. About my job. About the former colleagues who still trust me to keep their secrets safe. About the missions I've buried deep enough to avoid dragging anyone else down with me.

My name tied to Xavier Darcy, and then linked back to my father? It won't just cause a stir. It'll light a damn match and blow up everything I've ever worked to protect.

"Does this have anything to do with the firestorm Xavier is under in the media right now? I heard he was under investigation for embezzlement or something?"

Xavier turns a murderous look on him. "Lucas, I'm gonna need you to shut the fuck up."

Lucas throws his hands up in surrender but grins like the devil.

I pace again, my mind spinning. "No wonder that weekend felt...off. Like something huge happened and I couldn't get my head around it. I kept having these flashbacks. You...me...laughing, drinking like we were celebrating something... Oh my God, the veil. The music. '*I Choose You*.'"

Lucas chuckles under his breath. "Every time a Black person dies, it's like the ancestors summon drama. And this..." He gestures around the room like he's hosting a reality show. "This is some premium, top-tier drama!"

I narrow my eyes at him. "You're enjoying this way too much."

He throws his hands up. "Can you blame me? This is better than a front-row seat at a Tyler Perry play. We're one secret baby and a wig snatch away from Madea manifesting out of thin air.."

"*Lucas!*" I bark, shooting him a death glare.

Before Xavier can say anything else, the door swings open and Prince Elijah barrels into the study, out of breath.

"Aunt Charlie! There's some man at the front door with a camera and a microphone! He's asking for you!"

I whip my head toward Xavier, my chest heaving.

He gives me a sheepish, painful-looking smile through his already-swelling black eye.

"So, Peach. That's why I came over here as quickly as I did. Our *marriage* has hit the press."

"You have got to be *fucking kidding me.*"

CHAPTER THIRTY FIVE

Xavier

"P each—"

I follow close behind her, my blood simmering with everything unsaid between us.

"Peach—"

She spins around so fast I nearly run into her.

"Don't you dare fucking call me that right now!"

I hold up my hands. "Fine. Charlesetta." My voice drops. "We do not have the luxury of time on our side, and if you want to keep things safe and in order, we need to move. Now."

I look her dead in the eyes, because she knows exactly what I'm saying. This isn't about some messy family drama anymore. This is about protecting them. Protecting everything she's ever loved. And Lucas doesn't need to know a damn thing about that.

Without another word, she jerks her head toward the back. "Fine. Let's get to the cottage and pack up."

We move quickly, cutting through the kitchen, but we don't get three steps in before Mrs. Sinclair and Big Daddy block our path, concern carved into every line of their faces.

"What's going on?" her mother asks, voice tight.

"We've been getting calls," Big Daddy says.

"People saying there are reporters asking if y'all are married?"

Charlie tries to sidestep them, but the guilt flashes across her face. She stops, goes back, and hugs them both tight. "I promise, I'll explain everything soon. As much as I can."

Mrs. Sinclair kisses her forehead, holding her for an extra beat. Then she looks at me. "Please be safe."

Big Daddy nods, looking at me with those sharp, measuring eyes. I give him the only thing I can right now—a silent vow that I will protect her with everything I've got.

While Charlie is busy reassuring her parents—flashing that fake calm she wears when she's trying not to fall apart—I pull out my phone and fire off a quick text to Hayven. He needs to know what's happening.

Charlie's carrying the weight of it all right now: her family's expectations, the media swarming the gates, and the bomb I just dropped square in the middle of her life. And as sharp as she is—hell, sharper than anyone I've ever met—even she can't see every angle when the walls start closing in.

I saw it that night. The night she was drugged. When the world tilted out from under her and she didn't even know it.

That was the moment I decided: if she ever needed a blindspot, I'd be it.

I'd be the one to see what she couldn't. To move when she couldn't. To protect her when no one else could.

Still, I involve Hayven because he'll know how to move beyond the panic and keep this from blowing up into something none of us can recover from.

Thank heavens for The Fury Alliance.

We slip out the back, but as we near the edge of the property, we spot them—reporters. At the damn gate.

Charlie glares at me, then punches me in the arm, remembering this is all *mostly* my fault. "I still cannot believe you married me! I am married to you! Xavier fucking Darcy!"

"Ouch! Shit!" I hiss back, dodging her blows. "You make it sound like it's the worst thing in the world!"

"When I don't remember it?"

I try not to flinch every time she says it—that she remembers nothing from that night.

Because I remember everything.

Every second. Every word.

And no matter how much I wish I could will it away, erase it from my mind, it's etched into me.

Permanent.

Undeniable.

"It's not exactly the perfect start to a life of 'happily ever afters,' you dick!" She mutters.

"Oh great," I mutter, "the family trait of name-calling doesn't go away just because you're pissed."

Charlie's nostrils flare. "Oh, is the man who takes an unconscious bride getting his feelings hurt?"

I wince like she slapped me. "You know damn well it wasn't like that," I growl, grabbing her hand and dragging her the last few feet to the cottage before any cameras catch us.

Once we're inside, she yanks her hand free, fire in her eyes.

"*You* proposed to me!" I snap, pacing the small living room like a caged animal. "And in my defense, I thought you were sober enough to remember something like that!"

She throws her arms up. "You thought wrong, Xavier! I don't even remember what I had for dinner that night, let alone proposing marriage!"

I stop pacing and face her head-on, breathing hard. "You looked me dead in the eyes, Charlie. You asked me to marry you like you meant it. Like you saw me. And for a man who's spent his whole damn life invisible to people that mattered—" I stop, raking a hand through my hair. "I wanted it to be real. I needed it to be real."

Her anger falters for half a second. I see it. But she locks it down just as fast, crossing her arms over her chest like she's bracing for impact.

"Well, congratulations," she says coldly. "It's real. And it's a disaster."

I must be a lunatic because, standing in this tiny, worn cottage with my heart in my hands, all I can think is—I still wouldn't change a damn thing.

I take a step closer, trying to reason with her. "I tried to reach you, Charlie. For days, weeks before all this blew up. But between my drama that kicked off in Vegas, your grandmother—one catastrophe after another kept getting in the way. I was waiting for the right time. I swear to you."

"You should've tried harder," she snaps, her voice tight with hurt.

"I know," I whisper. "I know I should've, Charlie. But damn it—" I pause, swallowing back everything that's been sitting heavy in my chest. "I love you. And I was selfish. I just... I wanted to hold on to this fantasy a little longer. Pretend I had everything I ever wanted. Even if I didn't deserve it. Even if you didn't know it."

She scoffs like she doesn't believe me.

"I mean it." I take a step closer, lowering my voice. "And if we make it out of this without burning everything to the ground, I want to marry you for real. No secrets. No lies. Just you and me."

She looks at me then—really looks—and for a second, I think I see something soft flash through her eyes.

But then it's gone, replaced with that steel I'm starting to know too well.

"We have a deal and seven days left," she says coldly. "Seven days to figure out who's sabotaging your company before your IPO. After that? We're done. Because once again, Xavier, you've proven you can't be trusted. Why you scare me."

"Peach—" The words hit harder than any punch or kick from her ever could.

She turns, shoving some clothes into a bag, and without looking at me says, "Since this is your mess, you figure out how we're getting out of here without being spotted."

I scrub a hand over my face, letting out a slow breath. "Fine," I mutter. "I know the perfect place we can go to lay low."

CHAPTER THIRTY SIX

Charlie

I've talked my way out of some wild situations before. Close calls. Things that should've ended in disaster. But this? This is a whole new level of screwed.

I'm married.

To Xavier fucking Darcy.

And I don't even remember saying yes. Don't remember proposing, either.

But the way he looked at me when he said why he'd said yes—like it meant something—It makes me wonder what the hell was in those drugs. Because I'm not the marrying type. Or at least I've never thought I was.

Xavier Darcy is everything my mother would love me to end up with—melanin deficiency aside. Which, if we're keeping count, is reason number two thousand three hundred why he and I would never work.

Right?

Now, those fuzzy dreams I kept having—the flashes of white, the heat of his mouth on mine, the sound of my own voice stumbling over vows—I thought they were nothing. Just fragments of a warped fantasy.

They weren't.

They were memories. Real. Jagged. Blurred at the edges but sharp where it counts. The chapel. His hand in mine. The kiss. My dress pooled around my ankles on the hotel floor.

It's all crashing back, piece by horrifying... beautiful piece. And that's the part that scares me most.

With each flicker, one brutal truth settles deeper in my bones: I married the man I swore I'd never touch again and part of me is furious I can't remember it.

Now we've got seven days to figure out how to untangle this mess without setting everything—and everyone—on fire.

How the hell did I let this happen? I'm not reckless. I'm not the girl who wakes up married in Vegas. I'm supposed to be smarter than this.

With everything going on—and reporters settling like vultures on my parents' lawn—I owe them the truth. At least the parts I can safely give.

So, before we leave, while Xavier is figuring out how to get us out of here, I sit my parents down and explain what's happening. Not the full story, but enough to justify why Xavier and I have to leave, and fast.

I tell them about the whirlwind with Xavier, how his business has been compromised, and how we need to lay low to figure out who's behind it. I leave out the parts about my not-so-retired spy life. The part where their lives are in more danger than I can explain without triggering panic.

Mama doesn't take it lightly. Her eyes lock on mine—sharp, steady. "What else, Charlie? What else have you been hiding from us? Why does this feel so dangerous?"

I don't flinch. I can't.

I look her dead in the eye. "I'm sorry," I say apologetically but with an edge.

"I promise, as soon as I'm back in town, we'll have brunch and talk about all the things. Beignets and mimosas at Geneva's. Just you and me."

That cracks her. A small smile breaks through the worry. "You better not be lying about the beignets."

Mama's smile fades just as quickly as it came, replaced with something far more serious.

She tilts her head and narrows her gaze. "Do you remember the stories about the tunnels from the Underground Railroad?"

I nod, unsure where she's going with this. I always thought those stories were just that...stories.

She stands. "I know just how to get y'all out of here without anyone seeing you."

She turns to Xavier. "Have your driver meet you at the corner of Bentley and Premier."

Xavier pulls out his phone and fires off a text without a word. Mama doesn't explain anything else. She just moves, swift and certain, like a woman with a plan she's been saving for the day the world tipped sideways.

We follow her down to the basement. Past old holiday decorations and shelves lined with preserves and family history, she stops at the far wall—a large wooden bookcase that looks like it's never been touched.

She reaches for a dusty family photo album, pulls it from the shelf, and with a soft click, the bookcase shifts. A hidden door swings open.

A hush falls over everything. Even my thoughts pause.

As the weight of it all crashes into me—my accidental marriage, my family's legacy, the promise of a path to love and forgiveness with my mother—Mama pulls us forward, into the past.

Into the shadows of a history that still breathes beneath our feet.

The tunnel stretches out in front of us, dark and narrow, like a secret waiting to be remembered. A relic of the Underground Railroad, it winds beneath our home like a buried lifeline.

The air is cool, thick with memory. The scent of earth and stone clings to the walls, each brick worn smooth by time and desperate hands.

Every step feels sacred. Every echo in this tunnel carries a whisper from the ones who came before us—reminding me that survival isn't just instinct.

It's inheritance.

There's a story my Grandmommy used to tell us whenever we asked why the floorboards creaked extra loud in the front parlor. It wasn't poor construction, she said. It was the sound of history breathing. Beneath that room—beneath our entire home—ran a stretch of preserved tunnels that were once part of the Underground Railroad.

Hidden corridors carved from desperation and hope, smuggled freedom and whispered prayers. For generations, my family has lived over those tunnels, and for just as long, they debated whether to seal them shut and move on from what they represented: fear, flight, trauma.

But Grandmommy wouldn't allow it.

"Pain is part of the story," she said. "And one day, someone will need to tell it. Loud and clear. With light and truth. And when that day comes, these tunnels will still be here. Still speaking."

"The family kept them. Maintained them," Mama says. "And now, all these years later, people come from all over—educators, students, historians—to walk those tunnels."

"Wow. Like a museum?" I ask, stunned.

She sniffles quietly behind me. "Yeah. But not like those plantations that try to romanticize it. This house? We tell the truth here. The hard truth. The kind most folks like to bury or dress up."

"I had no idea, Mama."

She exhales, something tender in her voice. "Just one more thing we need to catch up on."

A chill runs through my veins and tears prick at my eyes as we walk through the damp space.

Emerging from the tunnel, we're met by Xavier's head of security, standing beside a sleek black SUV. Xavier takes our bags and opens the door. Before I step in, I turn back to my mother, wrapping her in a tight embrace.

"I'll explain everything soon," I whisper. "And thank you."

She pulls back from the hug, her hands resting gently on my shoulders, eyes glassy.

"I love you, Charlie," she says.

Charlie.

Not Charlesetta. No *tone.*

Just *Charlie.*

And I don't think I've ever heard her say it like that before.

Inside the SUV, a stylish gentleman greets us with a grin so smooth it should come with a warning label. He looks like he stepped straight out of a Tom Ford campaign—tailored, polished, obnoxiously charming.

"So, is this the Mrs.?" he teases, waggling his eyebrows at me.

"Nathan," Xavier says, sharp. "Be careful. This one bites. And kicks. And she also carries a gun."

Nathan's grin widens. "Noted."

I roll my eyes. "He's exaggerating."

"I have a black eye and bruised balls to prove it," Xavier retorts.

Turning to Nathan, I extend my hand. "My name is Anastasia Sinclair, but everyone calls me Charlie. And yes, I am the *temporary* Mrs."

Nathan chuckles, shaking my hand. "I'm Nathan. And for the record, I warned Xavier against this entire plan."

"You mean marrying me while I was practically unconscious?" I ask, raising an eyebrow.

"Wait, what? No. On the life of my golden doodle, Dolly, I had no idea about *that*. I just told him not to show up at your house unannounced."

I glance at Xavier. "Hmm. I've learned he doesn't listen to reason very well."

"Welcome to my world," Nathan replies with a smirk.

I can feel Xavier stiffen beside me, the tension rolling off him in waves as Nathan and I trade jabs.

But honestly?

I kinda don't care.

I see Hayven's name flash across my screen, and without hesitation, I answer—while Xavier and Nathan keep up their conversation in the background.

I screw up my face, confusion flickering across it. I have no idea how Hayven even knew to reach out, or why. But seeing his name brings a wave of relief. Because if anyone can help, it's him—and the army of elite hackers he keeps on a leash.

"Hayven?" I say, pressing the phone to my ear. "How did you—"

"X reached out. Said you might need backup."

I glance over at Xavier, confused. When the hell did he have time to contact Hayven? And more importantly, how did he even know to reach out to him?

But I don't have time to interrogate the warmth blooming in my chest at the thought of Xavier being this damn thoughtful. Later.

Right now, I need to focus.

"Okay… yes. My parents." My voice lowers, tight with urgency. "I think my identity's been compromised. I need them protected until I can figure out just how deep this mess goes."

Hayven exhales. "We've got you. Now that *you* are involved, things move to a different level. You focus on cleaning up Xavier's disaster—let us handle your family and your security. Nothing's getting past us."

A quiet surge of relief rushes through me. "I appreciate you, Hayven."

"All good. Now throw your phones out the window. Burn them. I've got a satellite phone waiting for you on Xavier's plane."

I blink. "How did you—"

Then I stop.

Right.

I forget sometimes—I'm not just dealing with a friend. Or my boss.

I'm dealing with *The Fury Alliance.* And when you're a friend of *The Fury,* and somebody messes with you, all bets are off.

"Just say thank you, Stasi."

I sigh. "Thank you, Stasi."

Hayven laughs. Then hangs up. Cold. Efficient. Classic.

I turn back to Nathan and Xavier just as Nathan begins going on about something as if he's irritated.

"And by the way," Nathan says casually, scrolling through his phone, "Grant keeps calling and insisting on an emergency meeting with you and Will. I told him it would have to wait."

"Oh my God, I love Grant!" I gush, cutting in without shame.

"Isn't he the nicest?" Nathan replies, grinning.

"Right? Always taking care of people. Like when he flew those attendants home with him after Will and Tim's wedding?"

"I know, right?" Nathan leans in like we're swapping secrets over wine. "Though, I have it on good authority Grant had *other* plans for those two, if you know what I mean?"

He holds my gaze, waiting.

Then I get it.

"Oooh! Let me find out Grant is nasty!"

"Enough!" Xavier snaps, slicing through the laughter like a blade. "We have more important things to worry about than Grant's sexual exploits!"

Then he turns on me like I've personally betrayed him. "And what the hell is up with you being all sunshine and rainbows with Nathan while you threaten to maim me any chance you get?!"

"Nathan hasn't lied to me or tricked me into marrying him, dick-face!"

Xavier groans, exasperated. "When are you gonna get over that already? You act like you didn't agree to marry me."

My head snaps up. "*Excuse* me?"

He gives me that look—smug, mischievous. "Oh, you don't re-member saying yes?"

I blink. Nothing.

"In Greece," he says, leaning forward like he's trying to jog my memory. "At your villa?"

Still nothing.

He sighs like I'm the one being difficult. "You were naked. On the bed. Nipples in hand. I asked you to marry me *right before I*—"

"OKAY!" I shout, cutting him off. "You absolute fucking *freak!*"

Nathan, who's been silently suffering this whole exchange, just blinks. His expression is deadpan. "You did *not* just say that out loud, boss."

Xavier scowls and turns to him. "You're fuckin' fired."

I glance at Nathan, shrugging. "He's an angry elf."

Nathan tries to hold it in. Fails. We both snort, shoulders shaking like we're twelve and just heard the word *butt* in class.

Never mind the fact we're sitting in the middle of my life unraveling and Xavier's whole empire casually combusting in the background.

As we pull up to the airfield, I glance over at Xavier. There's something I haven't asked.

"You said you knew the perfect place to lay low?"

He doesn't look up from his phone. "Yes."

I take his phone and throw it out the window.

"Hey!" He finally says.

"No phones. Hayven's orders."

"You could have waited until I was finished firing off a text."

"Anything you do or say over that line could be compromised so how about you just wait until we get on the plane and take care of business on a secure line."

"Fine. It's a long flight anyway. I'll take care of it while we're in the air."

"Okay? And where is it that we're going?"

"Somewhere safe. You'll see."

I narrow my eyes. "Are you seriously pouting right now?"

"No," he says flatly. "I was ensuring all your favorite foods and snacks were available once we get to where we're headed."

I blink. "How do you know all of my favorite foods and snacks?"

He finally looks at me, borderline offended. "You *are* my wife, aren't you?"

I scoff, rolling my eyes. "You don't know me, Xavier."

Nathan leans in with perfect timing. "Judging by the file he has on you?"

My head snaps toward him.

But Xavier speaks before I can.

"Nathan! Enough—or you're staying here."

"Thought I was fired anyway," Nathan mutters under his breath, then shuts up instantly. So, he knows where we're going. And apparently, he's coming too.

The SUV rolls to a stop at the hangar. Xavier doesn't even wait for the door to open fully before he's out, already moving like the world depends on it.

"Nathan, show Charlie to the plane. I need to speak with the pilot."

Clive, Xavier's head of security, snaps at him for hopping out before the perimeter's been cleared, but Xavier doesn't even flinch.

I've never seen him like this. Focused. Unshakable. Confident—not the arrogant, showy kind—but quiet, grounded, *certain*.

Usually, he's a mess around me. Awkward. Always fumbling for the right words, usually finding the wrong ones instead. But now? Now he's moving like a man who knows exactly what he's doing.

And it's... unsettling.

And comforting.

All at once.

It feels like Xavier Darcy is both everything I've spent my life avoiding—and everything I need.

Like he was made for me.

As I board the plane, greeted by Xavier's staff like I'm already supposed to belong here, I glance back at him—still on the tarmac, commanding the moment.

What would it feel like if I let him in—fully, recklessly?

Then I force myself to shut that thought down.

Because no matter how much he... *we* make sense in moments like this, I have to remind myself—*You can't trust him.*

CHAPTER THIRTY SEVEN

Charlie

S even days until the IPO

After eight hours of silence, snacks, and overthinking, we land just off the coast of the Virgin Islands. The sky is painted in deep shades of blue and gold, and for a moment, the world looks calm—like nothing is falling apart.

During the flight, I got to know Nathan a little better—mostly because the man doesn't believe in secrets or silence. He talks. A lot. And thankfully, he talked about Xavier.

He told me things Xavier would never say out loud. Like how deeply he cares about closing the economic wealth gap—not just in theory, but in action. Quiet donations. Bold investments. Programs designed to outlive him. He also told me how much it actually stings Xavier that the press paints him as some aloof, tortured genius. He acts like he doesn't care, but Nathan says that couldn't be further from the truth.

Nathan's not a blind loyalist, either. He holds Xavier accountable, especially when it comes to me.

"He even mentioned he couldn't dig up much on your past," Nathan says, casually twirling his drink. "He's been trying since he saw you at some gala last year—but he said everything about you seemed... redacted."

I freeze.

Gala?

My mind races.

That means Xavier had a file on me. *Before* Will and Timantha's wedding?

Before everything.

How long has he been watching me?

Why?

As if reading my mind, Nathan shrugs and adds, "I think he's just really shy and thought having as much information on you as possible would help him talk to you."

He gives me a look that's part sympathy, part apology.

"He's weird. But he has a good heart. And mostly good intentio ns... *mostly.*"

I don't care. He's gone too far with me.

When we land, a fresh black SUV is already waiting, gleaming under the island sun. Xavier trails a few steps behind me and Nathan as we head toward the vehicle.

And for the first time in a long time, I feel it—*security.*

Not the kind that hovers with weapons drawn, eyes scanning for threats.

The other kind.

The kind I've spent years providing for others.

Quiet. Steady. Intentional.

It feels... strange to be on the receiving end.

Strange. But not unwelcome.

Clive opens the door, and we slide into the SUV without a word. He takes us through winding coastal roads lined with exotic trees and shadows, the kind of route that feels intentionally designed to erase any sense of where we are or where we've been.

Until finally, we pull up to a private marina.

And that's when I see it.

A vessel—no, a floating empire—anchored like it owns the sea. Towering, sleek, and gleaming under the Caribbean sun.

The name carved across the side in elegant gold script: *Charlotte*.

I don't miss the name's closeness to mine. Charlotte.

I wonder who she is. An old love? A past he never mentions?

This isn't the boat from Timantha's wedding weekend. That one was impressive—polished, high-end, luxurious.

But this?

This could swallow that boat whole and not even burp.

It's massive. A cruise ship dressed up as a private retreat. The infamous "big boat" I've heard about.

And now I'm stepping aboard like I belong here. Like this chaos we're running from somehow ends with me floating in someone else's fantasy.

Xavier's wealth is the quiet kind—anonymous, layered, and clearly built over years of hard work.

He's not the 'diamond-chain sporting, posting his private jet on Instagram' type. No flashy watches or loud declarations.

He collects *spaces,* not things.

Places where the world can't reach him.

Places to disappear.

Places to breathe.

"Just wait until you taste the food on this thing," Nathan says, nudging me down the dock as a line of staff stands at attention. "You'll never go back to land again."

"This is..." I trail off, eyes scanning every impossible detail. I can't even find the words.

"Welcome aboard *The Charlotte,*" a woman says as she hands me a crystal glass filled with deep amber liquid. "Vieux Carré for the Mrs."

My favorite drink.

He *really* did take care of the details.

In an instant my nipples betray me.

I mentally slap them back into submission.

I can handle being cared for. I can.

I just have to keep my walls up and my hormones in check.

I'm a trained liar—I remind myself. If I say something enough, it *has* to become true. Right?

As I step aboard, I feel like I'm walking into a cathedral built by the gods of luxury. Polished teak floors glow beneath my feet. The air smells like jasmine and money. Everything gleams—every surface, every edge—curated down to the stitching. Elegant. Deliberate. Designed to make you forget anything *less* ever existed.

There are a few steps that dip down before you can step up into the boat, and I don't even register the shift—But Xavier is on me in seconds.

His hand finds mine, firm and sure, guiding me down onto the platform where the staff is waiting.

Like it's second nature.

Like he's done it a hundred times.

Like he's the one that's supposed to be catching me.

Just hours ago, I took Xavier's hand as my mother led us through a tunnel carved from desperation—damp brick and darkness, a lifeline for those running toward freedom. A place born out of necessity, not comfort. A place where people didn't dare dream of yachts or champagne—just of *making it out alive. Survival.*

And now, here I am.

Still holding that same hand.

Only this time, there's no desperation in sight.

No shadows creeping behind us. No disruptions pulling at the edges.

Just stillness.

I look up—And all I see is him.

My... *husband.*

It hits me.

This—this feeling of choice, of safety, of forward motion—this is what *they* dreamed for us.

My mama.

Our ancestors.

Maybe not this exact moment.

Maybe not the yacht, or the high end liquor, or the staff in designer linen.

Definitely not taking the hand of a white man as my *lawfully* wedded husband.

But the freedom to stand here.

To *have* this.

To *be* this.

Even if it's complicated.

But the freedom. The *possibility.*

Once I'm safely on the platform, Xavier releases my hand and turns back, heading straight for the security detail that isn't boarding with us.

They speak in low, clipped tones—serious, efficient. It's clear they're staying behind, but whatever exchange happens between them feels like more than just protocol.

It's control.

It's trust being handed off.

"I'm Liora," the woman with the perfect drink says with a smile. "Let me show you around."

She walks us through the main deck, past a lounge with glass walls that open directly to the sea. The furniture is minimal but rich—plush whites, soft greys, everything designed to make you forget the rest of the world exists.

The restaurant comes next. My name is literally printed on the menu. Every one of my favorite dishes—from truffle fries to that obscure Thai curry I only ever order when I'm in D.C.—lined up like it's completely normal to be *seen* like this.

All of my favorite wines. My favorite artists humming in the background.

All those questions Xavier asked to get to know me and the lengths he's gone to understand me—about my favorite music, my favorite color, the way I take my coffee, even the kind of books I curl up with on a rainy day—he wasn't just mindfully inquiring. He was collecting details. Storing them. Studying me like a map he planned to explore.

And now, it's like he turned every answer into a blueprint. One that he's using to build a world around me, piece by intentional piece. Not flashy. Not performative. Just thoughtful. Precise. Quiet in the way love is when it's real. Or so I've heard...read about in my romance novels.

And it hits me—Xavier Darcy really is my book boyfriend. The one I didn't believe actually existed. Not in real life. Not for me.

It's the way he watches me like I'm the only thing that matters. The way he remembers every detail I casually mention and uses it to build something that feels like home. The way he protects without smothering, gives without asking, and somehow manages to show up exactly how I need—without needing to be told.

This boat, this moment, this man... it's not about grand gestures. It's about intention. About being seen, deeply and truly, and realizing maybe the love we read about—the love that feels like it was written just for us—was never fiction after all.

It's almost unsettling how seen I feel. But it's also the most beautiful kind of terrifying.

But as beautiful as it all is, I still can't shake the feeling that there's more.

More he's not saying. More he's holding back. Xavier's reasons for hiding the truth, for keeping secrets, they make a strange kind of sense in this tangled mess we've created. I was juggling a lot. I was guarded. I *am* guarded. And yeah, I know I can be difficult to reach when I'm protecting myself. Maybe he really was just trying to give me space. Maybe he really does mean well.

But meaning well doesn't always protect you.

So as I stand here, wrapped in everything he's built around me, I keep waiting—for something. A sign. A flicker of clarity. Something that tells me it's safe to let him all the way in. That trusting him won't be the thing that breaks me. Because I want to believe in this. In him. In us.

I just don't know if I believe in that kind of safety yet. The kind that doesn't come from plans or backup exits. The kind I can't build myself or control.

Because control has always been my armor—my shield against disappointment, betrayal, heartbreak. But this kind of safety would mean letting go. Letting *him* catch me.

And I don't know what terrifics me more: The possibility that he won't...Or the near-assurance I have that he will.

That he'll show up. Catch me. Love me in all the ways I've never let anyone try. And if he does—if he really is that man—then I'll have no choice but to put the armor down.

And once I do that, there's no going back.

Liora ends the tour at a private suite, complete with a sun-drenched balcony and a view so perfect it looks AI-generated. But what stops me cold is the bed. It's covered in rose petals. A bottle of champagne chills nearby.

It seems Mr. Darcy thinks he's getting lucky.

As I step back onto the main deck, the breeze hits just right, and so does the sight of Xavier standing there—waiting.

Arms crossed. Eyes on me.

Still that strange blend of passion and complete unreadability.

I stop a few feet away. I don't owe him anything, not after what he pulled.

But the words slip out before I can stop them.

"Thank you," I say, quietly. "For the accommodations."

He doesn't gloat. Doesn't even smile.

He just nods. "You're welcome."

And that's somehow worse.

"My security team has emailed you all of the information you should need from our servers," Xavier says, his voice clipped, business-like.

This time, I nod, slipping into the rhythm of it. "Good. I should be able to catch any unusual activity and get you a report first thing. Thank you."

"Thank *you*," he replies, holding my gaze a beat too long.

I clear my throat, pivoting. "Is there Wi-Fi on the boat?"

"Password is..." He hesitates, eyes flicking away for half a second. Embarrassed.

"Georgiapeach0501."

I blink.

May first is my birthday.

I don't say it out loud—but Xavier nods anyway, like he already knows. Like saying the password out loud was a mistake he didn't mean to make.

And for a split second, he looks like he wishes he could take it back.

"How long has it been that?" I ask.

"A little less than a year," he says quietly.

Not long after that gala.

The night he first called me *peach,* stumbling over his words while trying to ask what I was drinking.

Probably the same night he started that damn file on me.

Hell.

The more I learn about this man, the harder it is to hate him.

My thoughtful, calculated, psychotic fucking husband.

CHAPTER THIRTY EIGHT

Xavier

It's evening. Charlie's been locked in for hours, buried in the data from our server breach, completely ignoring me while Nathan plays hype man in the background. I've spent the better part of the day texting Jonah, trying to figure out what the hell to do about this mess. About her.

How to get her back.

Jonah: *Have you tried explaining it to her? Telling her how you feel?*

Me: *I have. It's not working. She won't listen to me.*

Jonah: *Have you prayed about it?*

Not this again.

I start to type something smart, then stop.

Jonah knows better. Normally, he respects the fact that I've distanced myself from church, especially since my mother passed. But lately—with Charlie—he's been pushing. Hard.

It's like he thinks this marriage, however it started, is something sacred. Something that shouldn't be thrown away just because we don't know what to do with it.

And of course, Jonah would feel that way. His parents were married fifty years. His grandparents? Seventy-five. And he's determined to follow in their footsteps with his wife, Hope. Ten years in, and the man still looks at her like she's his entire purpose.

Me, on the other hand, I'm not even sure Charlie wants to be in the same room as me, let alone share my name.

Me: *I will. Later.*

I put my phone down and stare at the screen for a second before finally getting up. It sounds like Charlie has taken a break from working and come out to play.

Outside, music drifts in from the deck. Beyoncé and J. Cole's *Party* hums through the sound system. The volume is low, but the vibe is loud.

Of course Nathan found a reason to party. The man could throw a rave in a panic room.

I step out onto the deck, staying in the shadows as I watch them.

Charlie's barefoot, laughing, spinning, a glass in her hand. Nathan twirls her like they're on some yacht party. She throws her head back, completely free, and for a second, I forget that she's not mine the way I want her to be.

I don't miss the way one of the men on my security detail watches her from across the deck.

I catch his eye and hold it.

Long enough. Hard enough.

Until he looks away.

She doesn't need protection right now.

All she needs right now is me. Even if she doesn't realize it.

Charlie

By the time I make it back to the suite, I'm tipsy, sweaty, sticky, and emotionally fried. I head straight for the bathroom without bothering to turn on a single light.

The shower is a fogged-up cathedral of steam, marble, and eucalyptus-scented bliss. I stand under the hot spray longer than I should, letting the water pound against my skin like it might wash away the last twenty-four hours.

While my hacking software churned through Xavier's servers—combing for anything unusual or incriminating—I kept myself busy doing what I do best: digging. In my line of work, when someone's coming for you this hard, there's usually a reason. A trail of bad decisions. Skeletons buried under boardrooms or behind bank accounts.

But when it came to Xavier, I found nothing. No offshore accounts. No shady shell companies. No burner phones, encrypted chats, or mysterious payments to men with no last names.

Xavier Darcy is—shockingly—clean. And that terrifies me more than any dirty trail ever could. Because I've never met someone like that.

No one except Big Daddy. And he's basically a saint in suspenders.

I towel off, but my mind is still spinning.

Ever since I found out the truth—*that I'm married to him*—pieces of that night have started to drift back to me.

Flashbacks. Heat. Skin. Vows whispered between kisses. Laughter. My voice calling his name.

It was... sexy.

Dangerously sexy.

And seeing him on this damn boat, moving like he owns the sea, all focused and alpha and security-minded—it's doing things to me.

Things I absolutely do not need right now.

Which is exactly why I go for the one thing I *can* have.

I start checking drawers. Calmly at first. Then a little more frantically. My dresser. The nightstand. My suitcase. Even the hidden zipper pocket I stitched into my toiletry bag.

Nothing.

Not in the robe pocket. Not under the bed.

Where the *hell* is it?

The staff unpacked my things earlier, and they *should* have known not to touch *that*. It's not something you mistake for a face roller or a fancy travel toothbrush.

I pause, staring at my suitcase.

I can't ask them.

What am I gonna say?

Excuse me, did you happen to see my rose vibrator while you were organizing my panties?

Absolutely not.

Then—*out of nowhere*—music starts playing over the speaker.

Summer Walker. *Girls Need Love.*

I freeze.

The hell?

I didn't touch the speaker. Didn't hit play on *anything*.

Then that infamous lyric hits the air, soft but clear.

I just need some dick.

"What the *hell* is happening?" I snap, glaring at the ceiling like it's personally responsible.

Someone's playing a twisted joke.

"*XAVIER!*" I shout, storming toward the door.

Then his voice comes through a speaker from the wall in the bedroom—smug and too damn calm.

"You don't need it."

I stop cold.

"What?"

I hope he's not talking about dick because yes the fuck I do but I cannot tell him that!

"Xavier, what are you talking about?"

"You know what I'm talking about."

I whirl around. "The question is *how*, Xavier? How the hell do you know what I was looking for?"

"You don't need it, Peach."

"What kind of sick-asshole hides a vibrator, Xavier?"

"I didn't hide it," he says, too casually. "I borrowed it."

"*You what?!*"

"No vibrators allowed aboard the *Charlotte*. It's a rule."

"A rule you *just* made up today?"

"Maybe."

"Xavier, I'm not playing these games with you."

"Just hear me out, Peach."

"*Stop calling me that.*" I mutter through gritted teeth.

"No." He snaps defiantly. "Now, hear me out."

"I hate you."

"You love me. That's why I piss you off so much."

"*Fuck you, Xavier!*"

"I'm workin' on it, Peach."

I let out a growl, full-body frustration. "What is *your* problem? I'm the one who should be fucking with *you* right now!"

"Trust me. You definitely are."

My eyes scan the room, heart thudding. "Wait—do you have a camera in here too?"

"For security purposes, of course," he says, like it's the most reasonable thing in the world.

Oh my God.

I go still.

I'm naked.

And he saw me.

He saw me digging through drawers—frantic, flustered—on a full-blown mission for my vibrator.

While naked!

Heat floods my face. Humiliation. Fury.

That asshole!

"Peach," he says gently now. Softer. Regret laced in his voice. "I'm sorry. You know how I hate hurting you. Disappointing you."

"You've got a funny way of showing it, Xavier."

"I know. I want to be good for you. Better. But you've gotta hear me out. Trust me."

"I don't trust anyone."

"I've noticed," he says, voice low. "But maybe... you could start with me?"

I let out a sharp huff, practically vibrating with disbelief. "You *can't* be serious. You let me marry you while I was *drugged*, Xavier. And then you lied about it for *weeks!*"

"I really think you ought to get over that now."

I blink. "You've got some *nerve!* My *family* is in danger!"

"And they're being well guarded. Cared for. Nothing's getting past Hayven and his people."

"That's not the point, Xavier! It should have *never* gotten that far to begin with!"

There's a beat. Then, quietly— "You're right."

That stops me.

"I can't say anything else other than... you're right, Peach."

Somehow, him apologizing, soft and *genuine*—it takes the wind right out of me.

I pause, biting back the warmth that rises in my throat.

"I still can't stand you."

"That's fine," he says, and I swear I can *hear* that sexy little smile of his.

Then a beep sounds from the nightstand drawer.

I blink, confused, and open it.

Inside is a sleek, black satellite phone. A Post-it is slapped across the screen in Xavier's handwriting:

Turn dial to Channel 7. Press to speak.

I stare at it.

Of course he's got his own damn private radio frequency. Because why wouldn't he?

I flip the dial and press the button. "What is this? Some Fifty Shades meets secret spy fantasy?"

His voice comes through, deeper now, like he's speaking directly into my ear. "Don't flatter yourself, Peach. If it were my fantasy, you'd be tied up already."

"It's cute that you think you could subdue me long enough to tie me up."

Xavier's voice drops to that gravelly drawl that always makes my knees question their job.

"Oh, come on, *Peach*," he murmurs. "I know exactly how to get you to soften for me. Soft enough to let me tie you up... and take you exactly the way I want."

God, I hate that he knows me like this.

"Not if I tie you up first," I tease.

He moans. "Is that a promise, Peach?"

I hate him. I hate that even from hundreds of feet away, with walls and waves between us, he knows exactly what it would take to make me bend. How to hit the soft spots I pretend I don't have.

Insightful, charming motherfucker.

"Now listen closely. Walk out of the suite and go left. You'll find your first clue waiting under the lifebuoy on the upper deck."

I hesitate.

"Trust me," he says, soft. "Just this once."

My legs move before my brain agrees.

The air outside is cool against my damp skin as I follow his instructions, still wrapped in nothing but a towel and muttering curses under my breath. My hair's damp, legs bare, and I'm barefoot on teak wood, stalking across the deck like a woman on a mission.

I pass two members of the security team stationed near the helm. One does that polite upward nod and immediately looks away. The other stares a second too long before snapping his gaze to the floor like his eyeballs might get fired.

Xavier's voice crackles over the satellite phone, smooth. "Don't worry about security. They've been instructed to leave you alone."

Then his tone sharpens, louder now, like he's speaking into another mic. "And to remember their manners when looking at my wife."

I catch the second guard's eyes again—just for a second—before he turns red and pivots like the deck just got *very* interesting in the opposite direction.

My husband is such a possessive bastard. And I fall in love with him a little more every time I experience this side of him.

Sure enough—just like he said—tucked under the lifebuoy is a black envelope with my name written in that sharp, confident script of his.

Inside the note reads: "No batteries needed. Just bring yourself. —Mr. Darcy."

My brow arches. Oh, so *that's* how we're playing this.

Still barefoot, still wrapped in a towel, I head down the deck, catching my reflection in the polished glass doors as I move—damp hair clinging to my neck, legs out, chest barely secured. If the Coast

Guard showed up, they'd get an eye full if I was forced to raise my hands in surrender.

One of the deckhands nearly walks into a railing trying not to look directly at me.

I keep walking.

The next stop is the outdoor bar. A single champagne flute sits waiting on the marble counter, delicate and chilled, with a thin curl of condensation sliding down the side. Next to it, another card:

"For the nerves. You're going to need it."

"The hell?" I mutter, staring down at the card like it might explain itself.

What does this man have planned?

Whatever it is, I get the sinking feeling that Prosecco's not gonna cut it. I'm gonna need something stronger.

I down the drink in two swallows, feel the chill slide down my throat, and ignore the tremble in my hands.

Xavier's voice crackles back over the line, thick with heat. "Mmm." That low moan of his, lazy and filthy. "The way your tongue touches the top of the glass before you sip. The way your lips curl around the brim. The way your throat works when you swallow…"

He pauses just long enough for the tension to snap taut.

"It's enough to drive me crazy, Peach."

And, I'm wet.

Not from the shower I took.

From *him*. Always him.

I bite down hard on my bottom lip, clutching the now-empty flute like it might anchor me.

"Hurry, Peach," he murmurs. "There's not much time now."

That teasing edge in his voice says *everything*.

Whatever he has planned, it's only just getting started. Then I keep moving.

The note tucked beneath the base of the glass points me toward the library. *Of course* Xavier has a library on this boat. Probably alphabetized. Probably smell-proofed so none of the sea air touches the pages.

I push open the heavy door and step into dark wood and warm leather. It smells like money and restraint.

There, sitting dead center on the reading table, is a first edition of *Pride and Prejudice* with a soft silk ribbon draped over it. A note tucked just inside the front cover reads:

"You must allow me to tell you how ardently I admire and love... the idea of you tying me up."

My breath catches.

I snort. "Mr. Darcy would *never*."

I hear Xavier's voice again. "This one would. And he's waiting for you to punish him."

"Stop messing with me, Xavier."

"Stop acting like you don't get a rise out of this little game, Charlie, and maybe I'll speed past the next clues."

I roll my eyes with mock annoyance but my fingers are already slipping the ribbon off the book.

And he's right. I *do* love this game.

Just like everything else he curated on this damn boat—the food, the amenities, the playlist that somehow knew my moods before I did—this game was made for me. He built a mystery because he knew I couldn't help myself.

He didn't try to lure me with sweet talk or grand gestures this time. No. He fed my need to hunt. To dig. To solve. He gave me a puzzle with his name on it, knowing full well I'd chase the pieces until I found him at the center.

It's brilliant. Infuriating.

Mercy me... this man.

My cheeks are flushed, pulse thudding harder now. I'm equal parts annoyed and turned on—and that's Xavier's favorite combo.

My feet move, carrying me through the corridor and up the narrow stairwell toward the bridge. My towel clings tighter to my body with every step, and I'm still barefoot, leaving little damp footprints across Xavier's painfully pristine floors.

Another security guard spots me and immediately pretends to be fascinated by a wall panel.

I pause at the top of the stairs, the glass doors to the bridge sliding open with a quiet hiss. The space is sleek and spotless, all polished controls and panoramic windows overlooking the open sea.

And there—dead center in the captain's chair—is a small, matte black gift box.

I walk up slowly, heart pounding, towel shifting dangerously with every step.

I open the box.

Inside: a pair of leather cuffs. Not just any cuffs. Soft-lined. Luxurious. Heavy with intent.

Next to them, another card in that same maddening, elegant scrawl:

"Even the captain needs to be reeled in sometimes. Restrained."

Oh my book boyfriend!?

I press the back of my hand to my face, trying to cool the heat radiating through me. My heart's racing now, the kind of thud that fills your ears and your chest and your thoughts.

And I'm almost afraid to see what's next.

Almost.

Because this is... exhilarating.

My skin's still damp, heart pounding, nerves buzzing like live wires under my towel. Every step feels like foreplay. Every clue, a new kind of tease.

His voice slides through the satellite phone again, deep and sinfully slow as I follow the final instruction—down the spiral staircase to the lowest level of the yacht. The private level. Xavier's domain.

"Come find your husband, Charlie," he purrs. "Come make him pay for being such a bad boy."

I swallow hard.

My feet are moving, but everything in me feels like it's humming.

I reach the suite. His door is cracked open, just enough to let a sliver of golden light spill into the hallway. It's warm. Inviting. Dangerous.

Like him.

I push it open with trembling fingers.

I step in slowly.

He's there. Shirtless. Hands behind his back, waiting. Sitting on the edge of the bed, waiting for me.

And next to him, on a table, is an *arsenal*.

Soft ropes. Satin blindfolds. A feather. A paddle. Silk ties coiled neatly like rope in a magician's bag. And beside it all, my missing vibrator—cleaned, placed in a glass case like a trophy.

I stare at it. Then at him.

"Funny. I thought you said no vibrators on *The Charlotte*?"

He shrugs. "I studied it," he says. "Then realized I can do better. We'll toss it overboard tomorrow."

I cross my arms. "So this is what? Your idea of foreplay?"

"No," he says simply. "It's my apology. My surrender."

I furrow my brow. "I don't understand."

"I'm gonna let you take all my power away from me. I'm going to trust you to tie me up, Charlie. To take control. To decide what happens next. You can do whatever you want to me."

I look at the table—at the silk ties, the cuffs, the blindfold laid out with care like an invitation and a confession.

Then I look at him.

At the man I want with every cell in my body... but still don't know if I can have forever.

But the idea of finally punishing him?

Yeah. That I might enjoy.

I pick up the silk tie and let it slide slowly through my fingers. He doesn't flinch. Doesn't move. Just watches me with those intense, unblinking eyes.

"This your idea of gaining my trust back, huh?"

"No," Xavier says. "It's my way of giving you mine."

My fingers curl around the tie. And for the first time in a long time, I smile.

Not sweet.

Not romantic.

Predatory.

The kind of smile I reserve for the moment before I take out a target when they least expect it.

"Good," I whisper. "Because I've got some ideas. Some *plans* for you, Mr. Darcy."

CHAPTER THIRTY NINE

Xavier

The second I hear her footsteps—soft but certain, echoing down that corridor—I feel it.

That shift in the air.

That pull in my chest.

Then the door to my suite inches open, just a sliver of golden light spilling across her bare skin, and I'm gone. *Moved.*

Not just turned on—though Lord knows I am. But *moved.*

By this woman.

By the way she carries herself like she's got something to prove and no time for bullshit.

By the towel barely clinging to her curves, and the fire in her eyes that says she still might kill me for what I did.

And I'd die smilin'.

She's fury wrapped in silk, vengeance in bare feet, and I've never wanted anything more in my damn life.

She steps into the room like a storm I've been beggin' for.

Hair damp. Skin glowing. Wrapped in nothin' but a towel and attitude.

My wife.

And Lord, help me... she's holdin' that silk tie like it's a damn weapon.

I'm sitting at the edge of the bed. My hands stay behind my back, just like I promised. I don't move. Don't speak.

I let her look.

Let her see what I'm offerin'.

Not control.

Not submission.

Trust.

That thing she doesn't give easy—and sure as hell never without a fight.

But tonight, I'm hers. Every inch. Every bruise. Every breath.

She closes the door behind her with a quiet click, and it might as well be a trigger.

My heart pounds. My dick's already heavy. Has been since she yelled my name across the boat, all wild and pissed and lookin' for blood—or a vibrator.

One can never tell with Charlie.

Her eyes trail over the table I set—cuffs, ropes, blindfolds, featherlight things meant to tease, not punish. Because this ain't about pain.

This is about her *touching me* when she's good and ready.

She steps closer, slowly, dragging her fingers along the edge of the table.

"You really think this'll make up for what you did?" she asks, voice sharp as the blade she's been twisting in my gut since I first laid eyes on her.

"No," I say. "But I figured I'd start with lettin' you tie me up and use me like your personal plaything. Since you're the one used to taking prisoners," I say, hinting at her secret past. "Seemed like a decent apology."

She raises a brow. "You sure about that?"

"Peach, I've never been more sure of anything in my life."

For years, control and restraint were my armor. A personal and professional chastity belt that kept me sharp, focused, untouchable. I wielded discipline like a weapon—cutting away distractions, emotions, even desire if it got in the way of building something great.

But somewhere along the way, that restraint? It turned into a kink.

As I planned every inch of this yacht escape—every room, every bottle of wine, every silent security measure—what lit me up wasn't the luxury or the logistics. It was the idea of handing Charlie the one thing I've never given anyone: control.

Because love, real love, is give and take.

Her trust for my power.

My submission for her freedom.

Her smile's wicked now. Dangerous.

She moves toward me, towel slipping just slightly at her thigh.

I ache.

God, I *ache* for this woman.

She circles me slow, dragging the silk across my chest, my neck, like she's deciding where to start. Like she's imagining how I'll look spread out for her—helpless, hard, and beggin'.

"You ever been tied up before, Xavier?" she whispers.

"No, ma'am." I drawl.

"You scared?"

I grin, even as my pulse kicks up. "Only if you stop."

Her eyes roam over me and I can tell she's nervous. Maybe unsure. Her fingers tighten on the silk like she's holding a live wire.

So I do what I do best.

I tease her.

Taunt her into taking control. Taking her power.

"What's wrong, Charlie?" I murmur, eyes locked on hers. "Never had a *willing* prisoner before? Someone who actually *wanted* to be taken?"

She glares, lips twitching. "Shut up. I'm trying to decide what I want to do to you first."

I grin, slow and wicked. "You're a lot quicker when murder's the first response. What's making you hesitate now that I'm nearly naked and at your mercy?"

She doesn't answer. Not with words.

But the gleam in her eye says my fate is sealed—and it's about to be *delicious*.

She hums, pleased, that sound vibrating straight through me. Then she moves in with intention and quiet control.

She instructs me to move to the head of the bed.

And I do.

No hesitation. No questions.

I position myself exactly the way she wants me, with my eyes locked on her like she's the only thing tethering me to this moment. Because she is.

She climbs onto the bed—*my* bed—and straddles my hips, towel slipping from her body like it never stood a chance.

She starts with my wrists. One, then the other. Ties them to the headboard with long strips of silk—tight enough to hold, but not to hurt. Just enough to remind me I've surrendered. That *she's* in charge now.

Then she moves lower, lips brushing against my chest as she snakes the silk around my ankles, spreading me wide. Vulnerable. Open.

My breath comes fast, chest rising and falling as I take her in—naked, flushed, fierce.

And every inhale is laced with the scent of her skin.

I'm tied.

I'm wrecked.

And I've never wanted her more.

Charlie sits across from me like a goddamn goddess of vengeance—legs crossed, spine straight, calm as you please. The towel's long gone. She's bare. Bold. Unbothered.

I'm the one restrained—wrists tied to the headboard with silk, ankles spread and secured. My body's stretched out on the bed, nearly naked, muscles twitching from tension, heat, *need*.

She holds the vibrator like a weapon—deliberate, controlled, lethal in its precision. And even though it's meant for her pleasure, make no mistake... it's aimed at me.

"Since I'm tied up," I murmur, voice rough with want, "I'm gon' let you have your fun with that damn vibrator."

She cocks her head, that wicked little smile pulling at her lips. "As if you have a choice."

My hips tense, helpless as I take her in. "All I need is one hand and my tongue, Peach. I'll make you forget what a rose even *smells* like—let alone how it feels when it's buzzin' between your legs."

She doesn't flinch.

Just lifts the vibrator and presses the button.

Click.

Low hum.

Cruel volume.

Her eyes stay on mine as she lowers it to her skin, parting her thighs like a show she knows I'd sell my soul to watch. To touch.

And all I can do is burn.

Her gaze meets mine—direct, unflinching—as she spreads her legs and presses the toy between them.

"Charlie," I rasp, breath shallow.

"Shhhh," she whispers. "Don't speak." Her voice calm. Commanding. Dangerous in that sweet, sugar-slick way only she can pull off.

I shut my mouth, jaw tight, fists clenching in the ties, erection straining hard against the fabric of my sweat pants—painful, desperate, pulsing.

"I'm gon' sink into you, Charlie," I growl, my voice hungry now. "Countin' the seconds till you climb on top of me, so I can give you my last name the only way that matters—by writin' it all over that sweet, wet pussy."

She moans like she knows every sound she makes is gasoline to the fire burning me alive. Her other hand trails up her stomach, over her breast, pinching her nipple as she rocks her hips, vibrator tucked right against her clit.

I strain against the restraints, hard and leaking, every nerve in my body lit up and begging—aching to be inside her, to taste her, to do *anything* but sit here and take it.

Truth is, I could get out.

Me and a few of the boys did one of those weekend Navy SEAL survival courses in San Diego last year. Thought it'd be fun. Got sunburned, bruised, and half-drowned. But I learned how to escape a knot in under ten seconds.

And the way she tied these? Yeah. I clocked the weak point the second she pulled the silk tight.

But this isn't about escape.

This is her show. Her rules. Her game to play *and win*.

If I break free now, even to touch her—*especially* to touch her—I'll undo every ounce of trust I'm tryin' to build.

So I stay put.

Let my sweet Peach ride the edge, vibrator humming, her body twitching under her own hand.

But I'm gettin' impatient.

Those cries?

Those gasps?

Those soft, ruined moans slipping past her lips?

They *belong* to me.

"Open your eyes, Peach," I growl. "If I can't touch you... then let me see you. Let me see if you come the same for a piece of plastic as you do when it's *me* inside you."

She gasps, body shuddering, legs trembling as she edges closer—so close I can *smell* it in the air. Smell her ache for me.

"I bet you don't," I murmur, teasing through gritted teeth. "Bet it doesn't feel half as good as my tongue there."

Her gaze snaps to mine, heat flaring. "You think you can do better?"

I raise a brow, throat dry, dick pulsing. "One hand and my tongue," I remind her, voice ragged. "That's all it'd take."

My breaths are labored now, and I don't even give a damn how desperate I look. When it comes to Charlie—my *wife*—I *am* a desperate man.

She clicks off the vibrator in one abrupt motion and starts toward the bed, her steps slow, controlled, and deadly.

Then she *crawls* on top of me.

"Fuckin' hell, Peach."

She straddles my waist, body slick with perspiration, skin warm against mine. Then—without warning—she *stands*, knees braced at either side of my shoulders, hands gripping the headboard above me.

And in an instant, her wetness is hovering, glistening, flushed right in front of my mouth.

"You forgot to untie me," I rasp, staring up like a man in prayer.

Her voice is ice and sin. "I never said I was going to."

Then her hand sinks into my hair, rough and possessive, and she *buries* my face between her thighs.

I moan at the first taste—raw, unfiltered, Charlie.

It's like dying of thirst in a desert and finally finding rain. *She's* the rain. My wife. My obsession.

And I am *soaked* in her.

I am completely bound but my mouth's a mess, tongue greedy, lips sealed around the heat of her center. I can't stop. Won't stop. I suck, lick, pull her down harder, let her grind herself against my face like I was made for it—because I *was*.

Her fingers dig into my scalp as she rides my face, chasing her own high. Her moans crack, raw and ruined, and I swear to God I almost come just from the sound of her falling apart on my tongue.

I nip her clit and she jumps, curses, then pushes deeper, and I suck again—harder this time—my tongue flicking over her like it's my only purpose on this earth.

Shamelessly, she grinds into me, which is only making me want to please her more.

I've missed this. Missed *her*.

Missed the taste of her. The way she shakes. The way her thighs quiver when she's close.

I want to rip the restraints clean off, flip her over, smack that ass and fuck her so hard she forgets what she was ever mad about.

But she hasn't released me.

Charlie *hasn't let me go.*

So I stay where I am and apologize the only way I know how—through pleasure. Through *service.* Through devotion at her core.

With my mouth, I say I'm sorry.

With every stroke of my tongue, I swear I'll never lie again.

And with every orgasm I drag from her body—*multiple* orgasms—I promise to keep loving her exactly like this.

CHAPTER FORTY

Xavier

T he next morning is all golden light and strong coffee.

We're gathered around the long teak table on the upper deck, plates full of eggs and tropical fruit none of us can pronounce. Nathan's trying to convince Clive to join him in some kind of post-breakfast rum tasting, while Charlie... Charlie is doing what she does best.

Diggin'.

"So," she says, chewing thoughtfully on a slice of mango, "I found something weird yesterday while going through your background."

I glance up. "Define 'weird.'"

She tilts her head, narrowing her eyes. "Something that suggested you had siblings. Or at least weren't an only child."

My brows pull together. "I don't know what you saw, but... I'm an only child. Always have been. Both my parents are gone."

It's true, as far as I know.

And to be honest?

The idea there might've been a sibling out there—someone who could've helped carry even *a fraction* of the weight I've been hauling around my whole life—It pisses me off.

Because if they *did* exist, and they knew about me, and still chose to do *nothing?*

That's not just neglect. That's not just absence.

That's a special kind of cruel.

And it's the kind of thing I don't know how to forgive. I wouldn't.

She sets her fork down, gently. Like she's easing into something. "Tell me about your mother."

Her voice is soft. Not demanding, but curious. Intentional.

I look down at my plate, pushing around what's left of my eggs. "Her name was Charlotte."

Charlie's eyes meet mine, steady. "Her family called her Charlie. Like me?"

I nod slowly, the corner of my mouth twitching. "She was a beautiful woman. Tall. Long red hair. Looked a lot like Julianne Moore, actually."

My mother was fierce and strong—everything you'd expect from a redhead who'd seen too much and still held her head high.

She didn't just survive—she *fought.* For me. For a life. For dignity in a world that gave her scraps.

I guess that's why I was so smitten with Charlie the second I laid eyes on her.

It wasn't just the way she looked—though God knows that was enough to stop a man cold. It was the *fire*. The way she carried herself like she dared the world to underestimate her.

And somehow, I *knew*.

Knew that Anastasia wasn't her name.

Not really.

That it was something more feisty. Something that carried both her roots and her rebellion. Something with grit. Something with soul.

Charlie.

My Charlie.

And I wish Mama could've met her.

She would've seen it too. That wild, beautiful spirit.

And she would've said, *"That one's gonna wreck you in the best way."*

And she'd be right.

"And she's been gone... how long?"

I stare past her for a moment, letting the answer settle before I say it out loud.

"Years now."

She waits. Doesn't rush me. Doesn't prod. Just sits in the stillness with me, like she understands that silence can be a form of grace.

She can feel it—the weight of what I'm carrying. How every word I try to form scrapes against old wounds I've kept sealed for years. How speaking it out loud doesn't just retell it—it relives it.

And still, she sits with me. Not demanding answers. Just giving me room to breathe. Room to fall apart if I need to.

I sigh, the words dragging out of me. "It's hard to talk about because... I feel like she worked herself to death trying to provide for me. She was smart. Unshakable. And life just kept punching her in the mouth. No breaks. No safety nets. A system that took more than it gave."

I stop, swallowing hard.

"When she died, the doctors said it was natural causes. But I'd watched her suffer. There was nothing natural about it. It was painfully obvious she'd fallen victim to a system that only did the bare minimum for her because she couldn't afford it."

"X, I'm so sorry."

I shake my head, waving her off as I press on. "All she had left was a mountain of medical debt and no life insurance to cover it. Nothing. No legacy, no cushion. Just me—trying to pick up the pieces."

Charlie's gaze softens. And for the first time, I think she really sees it. Why I care so much. Why the life insurance program, the community reinvestment, the charities I support—*all of it*—matters the way it does to me.

She doesn't say anything right away. She doesn't have to.

I feel the shift.

So I take the opening.

I set my juice down and look directly at her.

"Do you think you could ever let go of that silly little thing about me marrying you under duress... and be my wife for real?"

Her brow lifts, but there's a flicker of something softer behind her smirk.

"Xavier, I've never really wanted to be married," she says, trying to keep her voice steady. "I've never had a relationship last longer than a week. And as good as this feels—us, right now—I don't think I'm good for you."

"We might be in a bubble right now, sure," I say. "But I'd take this bubble over a lifetime of anything else without you."

She doesn't look convinced, but I don't let up.

"I never imagined having anything real before you, Charlie. Honestly, I didn't think it was in the cards for me—maybe I didn't even think I deserved it. I was content being alone—hell, I'd practically accepted dying a damn eunuch, never touching another woman again."

She lets out a soft laugh, the corner of her mouth curling. "That's just... *excessive.*"

I shake my head, a wry smile tugging at my mouth. "Then you came along. All fire and edges, impossible to ignore—and suddenly, nothing in my life made sense unless you were in it."

I pause, waiting for her to meet my eyes. "Charlie, we'll survive the real world. Because we're real. And because you're not just good for me—you're *it* for me. Perfect. Just the way you are."

"You make me sound like some sort of addiction or obsession."

I smile and take a sip of my orange juice, trying to cool the fire rising in my chest. "Something like that. I've never lost control the way I do with you. And I hate it just as much as you hate being taken care of."

"I gathered that," she says dryly, probably understanding all too well.

Jonah would be proud of me—pouring my heart out like this without deflecting, without hiding behind sarcasm or strategy.

Hell, I even said a little silent prayer before I dove in.

Not some polished, churchy monologue. Just a quiet, shaky *please* whispered into the silence.

Please let her hear me.

Please let her see I mean it.

Please let her *receive* me.

I don't know if I believe in answered prayers anymore, not the way I was raised to.

But if she reaches for me—if she says yes—maybe I'll start.

She looks at me then—really looks.

There's something in her eyes. Something fragile. Unarmored.

"Xavier?" she says, voice barely above a whisper.

I glance at her, heart already pounding. "Yes, Peach?"

She lets out a slow breath, like she's been holding it for years.

"I think I've missed you my whole life. And that scares the shit out of me."

My chest squeezes but relief washes over me at the same time. I reach for her hand.

"I know, Peach. Me too."

And I do. I know that feeling—the ache of realizing someone you just met feels like someone you've been searching for without knowing it. And in that moment, I wonder if the prayer I mumbled moments ago got answered faster than I deserved.

"You finish with breakfast?" I ask.

She nods.

"Can I show you something?"

She nods again, quiet with a mix of reservation and resolve.

I take her hand—hers, small and warm, sliding so naturally into mine—and lead her toward the steps on the side of the boat.

We climb slowly, the sea breeze brushing against our skin, the soft glow of the early sun painting gold across the water. With every step, the world opens up more. First tier, a lounge deck with sunbeds and a private bar. Second tier, a sleek glass-walled viewing room with telescopes and plush seating. And then—The top.

The third tier.

Up here, it's quiet. Sacred almost. The wind is crisper, the view wide and endless. The kind of view that makes you feel small in the best possible way. A pool stretches across one side, water perfectly still like it's waiting for a reason to ripple. Beyond that, just sky and sea.

Blue, as far as the eye can see.

"This," I say, turning to her, "is why I wanted the boat to have three tiers. I needed to always be able to come up here and see *this.*"

I motion to the horizon. "The water. The sky. All of it. It reminds me of how small I am. How much beauty God gives us—without us ever having to earn it."

She's watching me, that beautiful, unreadable face of hers softening in the light.

"And for the longest time, this... this view was the most beautiful thing I'd ever seen," I continue, my voice dipping. "Until I saw you."

Her eyes widen just slightly, but she doesn't look away.

"I'm almost mad at God, honestly," I say with a dry laugh. "That we grew up in the same city, and somehow never crossed paths until now. All that time, all that pain I was carrying... If I'd had you with me? It all would've been worth it."

She swallows, eyes glassy. Then she says it—soft, but clear.

"It still can be."

Hope. Right there in her voice.

"Does that mean you'll marry me, Charlie? For real?"

She hesitates. I can feel the fear behind her stillness, like she's standing on the edge of something too big to name.

"X, this is all *a lot*. I've never had a relationship last longer than a week, remember?"

I grin, pulling her just a little closer. "How about a marriage that can last a lifetime?"

Before she can argue, I kiss her. Deep. Like it's a prelude to forever.

And then, without letting her go, I rest my forehead against hers and whisper the words:

"I, Xavier... take you, Charlesetta Anastasia Sinclair..."

Her breath hitches.

"To have and to hold. To let me boss around. To cook dinner for—because I'm told she can't cook for shit."

She snorts, half-laughing, half-choked up.

"To protect. To care for. To be everything she never let anyone else be. To let her be free... to become whoever she wants to be. Forever and ever."

I press another kiss to her lips.

"Amen."

And for the first time in my life, I feel like I'm standing in the middle of everything I never dared to pray for.

CHAPTER FORTY ONE

Charlie

I still can't believe I'm married.

Scratch that.

I still can't believe I'm *considering* staying married to this man.

It's not like I have some deep-rooted trauma around marriage. My parents have been together for over forty years. My grandparents—on both sides—had the kind of love stories people write about, still holding hands and finishing each other's sentences decades in.

So no, I've never feared marriage because of what I've seen.

What I've feared is *conversion*.

Being forced to shrink, to shift, to become someone unrecognizable just to make a man comfortable. That's what I was running from. The idea that love required sacrifice of *self*.

But the words Xavier just recited to me?

They weren't chains.

They were permission.

To fall.

To breathe.

To *stay me.*

He said them like an oath and kissed me like a man who meant every syllable.

I'm still dizzy from it.

"Let's get through these next few days and see what happens," I say, trying to steady myself. "But if we do this, I want a *real* wedding. On this boat."

His smile is pure heat. "Be by my side forever, Peach, and I'll give you everything."

I meet his gaze, steady.

"Don't lie to me again," I say quietly. "And I'll give you forever."

I didn't think much of it when I slipped on a bathing suit and threw a big, airy kaftan over it for breakfast.

It was practical. Easy.

We were on a damn yacht, after all.

But now?

Now I'm grateful.

Because the way Xavier is looking at me like I'm the answer to every prayer he's ever prayed—makes my breath catch.

We're alone up here. The sky wide and clear above us, the sea stretching endlessly in every direction. There's nothing but soft breeze, salt air, and the sound of my pulse thudding in my ears.

"I love you, Charlesetta." He says it like a vow. Like a truth he's been holding onto with both hands.

And I freeze.

Not because I don't want to hear it—But because I'm not sure I ever *have*.

Not like this.

Those three words have never wrapped around me like this before.

Not from Lucas. Not even from my father.

But from *him?*

From Xavier Darcy?

It sounds like the lyrics to my favorite song I didn't know existed. A song I didn't know I'd been humming my whole life.

His hands find the tie at my waist first, yanking the kaftan open like he's been waiting all morning.

"I think I love you too," I whisper.

The words slip out before I can stop them, soft and shaky— but real.

His eyes lock onto mine, and I see it—the way his chest rises like he's just been handed air after holding his breath.

And for the first time, I'm not afraid of what love might take from me.

Because with him... it finally feels like it might give something back.

His mouth crashes onto mine—urgent, almost frantic.

He kisses like he's starved. Like it's been years, not hours, since he last tasted me.

I barely have time to catch my breath before the straps of my suit slip off my shoulders, Xavier's hands working with a practiced urgency—fast, sure, but devout, like I'm something rare. Something his.

"Ever been fucked over an ocean view, Charlesetta?" he asks, voice rough velvet in my ear.

"Can't say that I have," I breathe, just as he spins me gently to face the endless stretch of water, positioning me in front of the railing.

The world narrows to this moment. To the hush of waves. To the way his presence cages me in without ever making me feel trapped.

He doesn't touch me right away. He just stands there behind me, soaking in the sight of me—naked, bared, completely his—before his hands finally find me. Slow sweeps down my sides. A possessive squeeze at my hips. A palm between my shoulder blades, guiding me forward until I'm bent for him, arching instinctively.

Then, the sound of his zipper. The tease of his cock as he brushes against my entrance, lazy and deliberate.

His chest presses to my back as he wraps his arms around me, grounding me, holding me. "You're mine, Peach," he whispers, and then he thrusts in—deep and slow—his body fitting into mine like it was always meant to.

A gasp tears from my throat, whipped away by the wind. I grip the railing, head dropping, as he rocks into me again. And again. Each thrust carving the promise deeper: this man doesn't just want me—he worships me.

I cry out, lost to the rhythm. To the way he moves inside me with devotion, like his love lives in every motion. I can feel it—his need, his hunger, his obsession threaded through every stroke.

This man. My husband.

My book boyfriend come to life. My moody, relentless storm. The one who fell first—and hard.

My Mr. Darcy.

And now, standing naked over the sea as he claims me all over again, I realize... I'm falling, too.

Hopelessly. Endlessly. Home.

I'm not even second-guessing. I'm not analyzing or fighting or trying to take control.

I'm simply *his*.

Fully present.

Fully open.

Making love, on *my* terms, to the man who somehow found his way into my soul and became my everything—quietly, completely—without my even knowing it.

Like my heart had already made the decision long before my mind caught up.

And it's beautiful.

Not because it's perfect.

Not because it's planned.

But because now...finally... it's *real*.

And for the first time in my life, that's enough.

A thousand times... Yes.

CHAPTER FORTY TWO

Charlie

W e started the night in Xavier's suite, after spending the entire day on the top deck being pampered like royalty. Massages, fresh fruit, too much wine. And then there was *us*—a full-body kind of surrender that left his suite looking like it had been raided by wild animals.

So, naturally, we migrated to mine.

It feels like one of those mornings that should stretch into lazy kisses and round two. Or Twenty. I've honestly lost count.

Until—*BANG BANG BANG.*

"Boss? Charlie?" Nathan's voice shatters the calm. "There's an urgent call on the satellite phone. His name is Hayven or something and he sounds hot as shit!"

My head lifts from the pillow with a laugh. "*He is!*" I yell back without thinking.

I hate to admit it, but I've become one of *those* cliché women with a gay best friend.

But Nathan gives you no choice *but* to love him and make him your friend.

His energy is relentless. Infectious. He bulldozes through your boundaries with glitter and gossip and somehow manages to make you *thank* him for it.

And now, I get it.

I get why Xavier keeps him close.

Nathan's craziness is the exact kind of noise that keeps a man like Xavier grounded. Reminds him that not everything has to be war plans and silence.

Xavier smacks my ass. Hard.

I yelp, turning to glare at him.

"What? I may be your *wife*, but I will never be *blind!* And Hayven Sally is a fine specimen of a man."

He grins, already pulling on his shirt. "I can make arrangements, you know. If you'd like to be blind to other men."

"And I can cut your dick off," I snap back sweetly with a smile.

"Charlie," he groans. "Again with the homicidal reflexes."

"Xavier," I say, matching his tone, "again with the behavior that drives me to murder!"

We toss on clothes, still bickering as we climb the stairs to the upper deck, but something shifts when we see Nathan's face.

He's not joking. Not even a little.

"All he kept asking was if I was sure you were ok," Nathan says. Fear all over his expression.

My stomach drops.

Is it Xavier's case? More leaks? Did my name get pulled into something we can't untangle?

I don't wait. I grab the satellite phone from Nathan's hand.

"Hayven? What is it?"

"Stasi, thank God," he says, breathless.

The sound of my work name cuts through everything.

It snaps me out of the haze of soft sheets and stolen moments and reminds me exactly where I am—Not in a dream.

Not in some fantasy built on whispered vows and kisses on a yacht.

This is real.

And it's all crashing down on us.

Fast.

"What do you mean, thank God? Hayven, what's going on?"

His voice is tight, like he's holding something back.

"One of your aliases was reported dead. Natasha Britton?"

I freeze.

"What? I don't understand!" My voice is a bit more elevated than it needs to be, considering I'm in mixed company.

Xavier steps toward me, concern etched across his face. "Charlie, what is it?"

I lift my hand, asking for space while I step away, just far enough to have a somewhat private conversation.

"Hayven, all of my aliases have already been retired. I have proof of the burn notices."

Hayven's tone drops. "I know. But it looks like someone's playing a game. Trying to send a message."

"Okay... what kind of message?"

"Best guess? They want to pull Xavier out of hiding. They're sending a message that they know who you are. *Who you were.* And they're planning to use that as leverage. The goal? Force Xavier to back out of the IPO—for good—or they start coming after you. And likely your family."

I clench my jaw. "Fuuuuuuck!" I hiss.

"It's fine," he says. "I got your email with the file on Xavier's family. We've almost got him cornered, Stasi. Does Xavier know?"

He's asking about the suspicious information I found on Xavier's server.

I glance over my shoulder. Xavier's standing with Clive now, trying to look casual but failing. He's tense. Watching me.

"No. He thinks he's an orphan. No siblings, no parents."

Hayven pauses. "Are you going to tell him?"

I swallow hard.

"I will. As soon as there's an opening. I just... need a minute."

"A *minute*? Stasi, you've got *two days.* Tops. Get back to town and we can isolate the bastard, corner him. Xavier won't just get justice—he'll inherit everything. His conglomerate *and* his father's. Get him to The Fury offices so we can end this."

"Shit, Hayven," I whisper. "I'm just not sure Xavier even *wants* that. He's not in this for revenge. He just wants his name cleared. His causes protected."

Hayven exhales on the other end, the sound heavy with frustration and something softer underneath.

"Exactly why he needs the truth. So he can make an *informed* decision. He's owed that."

"I know," I say again, quieter this time. Almost to myself.

Because the truth? Xavier's been through more pain than most people survive. More betrayal than anyone should have to shoulder.

And this, this news that I'm holding onto would crack a man wide open.

Not just the fact that his father is alive—but that he's been *minutes away* all this time. That he was wealthy enough to give Xavier and his mother a life of comfort, ease... dignity.

But instead, he had a family of his own. A public image to protect. And admitting to an affair with the housekeeper? That would've wrecked the narrative. So he did what cowards do—he walked away.

Left them to starve.

To beg.

To *struggle.*

And no little boy deserves that.

No little boy deserves to be left wondering why he wasn't enough.

Boys like that grow into men with invisible wounds—raw, deep, and dangerous. Men who run hot and cold. Men who fight too hard, feel too much, and push everyone away when they need connection most.

I think back to Xavier—his temper, his silence, the way he looks at me like he's starving and terrified of being fed.

And I get it.

I *get* why he's so tortured.

Because all this time, he thought the pain was random.

When really... it was personal.

"I'll tell him."

But what I don't say is this: I don't know if telling him will bring us closer.

Or destroy what we've just begun to build.

But either way—he *deserves* to know.

And I'm running out of time.

I hang up with Hayven, the weight of it all coiled tight in my chest, and walk back toward Xavier.

He's waiting, hands in his pockets, eyes scanning me like he already knows something's wrong. I want to tell him everything—I *almost* do. But I stop myself.

Not yet.

Not the part about his father.

Instead, I give him what I *need to*.

"One of my aliases was compromised," I say, keeping my voice low. "We've got a solid lead on who's sabotaging your IPO, but to wrap this, we need to get back to The Fury offices for the final pieces to fall into place."

His brow furrows. "Is this about that message Hayven mentioned? Someone's targeting you?"

"Yeah," I nod. "It's starting to look personal. And coordinated."

Nathan appears with a tablet in hand. "Oh, and just a heads-up, the media's losing its damn mind. The story's gone national. Apparently, Joe Sinclair's daughter married a reclusive billionaire in the middle of a PR meltdown and *everyone* has an opinion. Most assume you're pregnant."

I let out a sardonic breath. "Joe's daughter married a white man at that," I mutter under my breath.

Xavier turns to me. "What does that have to do with anything?"

I sigh. "There's just... an expectation."

"Like the ones your family's held over you?"

"Yes! Sort of. When your father's tied to progress and civil rights for Black folks, people expect Black love. Black excellence. And Black ass babies. When you don't deliver that image, they talk."

He studies me. "Since when have you ever been afraid of people talking?"

"I'm not," I say quickly. "I don't care what they think about *me*. But my family? They've built something real. Generations of sacrifice and grit, fighting the good fight when no one was watching. And now, a bunch of ignorant people—Black or white—are going to twist this into a scandal. Like love has rules. Like choosing *you* somehow means I'm betraying *them*."

Xavier steps forward, wrapping me in his arms, grounding me. "They can say whatever they want about me. But when it comes to sabotaging you and your family's name because of me, I won't let that happen. Hayven won't let that happen."

I pull back and look up at him. "And because I'm a certified badass, *I* won't let that happen either."

He smiles, pressing his forehead to mine. "I know, Peach. You'll burn the world down for the people you love. Just know you don't have to carry the torch alone, okay?"

We kiss. And for a second, everything feels like it's exactly where it should be.

But then reality pulls me back.

"We've got a problem," I say, straightening. "If we're going to get you to The Fury offices without blowing this entire investigation, we can't risk cameras. You're trending, your face is everywhere. Facial recognition will light you up like a Christmas tree the moment we hit land."

"So what do we do?" he asks.

"We disguise you."

From across the deck, Nathan perks up. "Oooh, did someone say *makeover?*"

I shoot him a look. "How does *disguise* translate to *makeover* in your mind?"

Nathan shrugs. "Are you going to kill my vibe, or let me help save the day in style?"

I shake my head. "I've got this," I say flatly. "Leave it to the professionals."

I turn to Clive. "I need clippers. Scissors. Beard trimmer. And whatever else you can find for a haircut."

Xavier's face drains of color. "Wait—you're going to cut my hair?"

"Yes," I say cheerfully. "*We* are going to cut that beautiful head of hair. It'll grow back. Eventually."

Nathan grins like Christmas came early. "He spends a *thousand* dollars a month on hair. The man was married to his ginger waves long before he married you."

"Nathan!" Xavier snaps.

"What? I'm just saying. You'd pledge allegiance to your hairstylist before the damn flag."

I stifle a laugh. "Okay, boys. Let's get to work, shall we?"

We make our way to the lower deck, one of the larger guest bathrooms where we'll have enough room to move around.

And by the time I'm done, Xavier Darcy will be unrecognizable.

CHAPTER FORTY THREE

Xavier

We're holed up in one of the larger guest bathrooms on the lower deck—white marble, dark wood finishes, and way too elegant for what's about to go down.

Charlie stands behind me, rolling up the sleeves of one of my over-sized shirts like she's about to conduct surgery. Clippers. Scissors. A hand mirror.

I sit on a stool in front of the mirror, legs spread, towel around my neck, my hair thick and full and about to die a very public death.

"Where'd you learn to do this?" I ask, watching her through the mirror as she combs out a section of curls.

She grins, stepping around me with those eyes full of mischief. "I *did* grow up with a brother, you know?"

"I know. I just figured your father would've had him at the local barbershop with the other respectable gentlemen of the community."

Charlie laughs, snipping the side of my hair with clean, confident movements. "He did. But me and Elijah used to play barbershop together. I cut his hair, he cut mine."

I can't help but chuckle. "Your mother must've lost her mind."

"Oh, she did," she says, not even pretending to be sorry. "But that was just me and Eli. We were always in trouble together. He was the big brother, but *I* was definitely the bad influence."

"I'm not surprised," I say, shaking my head, smiling.

"Aye! Watch it," she warns, waving the scissors like a weapon. "I *do* have a sharp object in my hand."

"There she goes again, my homicidal maven," I mutter under my breath.

"And *you love it,*" she tosses back.

I do.

She keeps cutting, steady and careful, and I honestly love how good it feels—how natural, how *close.*

Where I once dodged connection like it was a threat, now I welcome it. Hell, I *prayed* for it when it comes to her.

Damn you, Jonah.

You said love would find me.

I didn't think it'd find me like this.

I watch her in the mirror.

The way she bites her lip in concentration.

The way her fingers graze my skin like she's not just cutting hair—she's learning me.

And I let her.

Every slow pass. Every brush of her wrist.

I let her.

"I also had a lot of practice in the field," she continues, her voice steady as she grabs the clippers. "When you have to disguise yourself at a moment's notice, skills like this become necessary."

There's a quiet pride in her tone, not boastful—just fact.

And somehow, that makes it even hotter.

She's not just good with her hands. She's dangerous with them.

Precise. Unshakable.

And all mine.

Then she turns on the clippers.

The buzz echoes in the bathroom like a siren. My stomach tightens.

I've always loved my hair.

Charlie catches the shift in my face instantly.

"Don't be scared, Mr. Darcy," she murmurs, stepping between my knees. "I've got you."

I look up at her. That face. That fire. That calm.

Trying to buy a moment—prolong whatever this transformation is going to bring—I grab her by the hips and pull her into my lap.

She lets out a soft gasp, but she doesn't resist. She straddles me without hesitation, her hands resting on my shoulders, eyes locked on mine.

"You've got me, Peach?" I ask, voice low.

"If that's what you want," she whispers.

I press my mouth to hers, slow and deep, letting the kiss say everything I don't know how to.

I feel the vibration stop as she powers down the clippers, the sudden quiet humming against my ears like an aftershock.

Then she lets them fall—gently—to the floor, the soft clink barely audible over the sound of our breathing.

And in that silence, it's just us.

Just tension thick in the air... and her straddling me like gravity brought her home.

She melts against me, her body sliding into mine. Her hips rock gently, teasing, testing, and something in me breaks loose.

The kiss grows hotter, hungrier. Urgency unfurls between us like heat in a closed room, thick and consuming.

I should be done. Spent.

My body should be drained of every ounce of moisture, every drop of control.

But just the *heat* of her—her mouth, her skin, her weight in my lap—it reignites something in me.

Like it's the first time all over again.

Like I've never touched her.

Like I've *only* imagined it.

And now that I have her again, I can't stop.

My hands push up under her shirt, palming the smooth skin of her back, feeling her gasp against my mouth.

Clothes fall away fast.

Her fingers tug my T-shirt off, mine find the edge of her panties and slide them over. She's already wet—warm and ready.

The mirror catches everything.

Every angle. Every twitch of muscle. Every stuttering breath.

Her lips parted, swollen from kissing. Her head thrown back in surrender, neck arched, eyes fluttering shut like she's caught between bliss and disbelief.

The curve of her body is poetry in motion—hips rolling slow and deliberate, like she knows exactly what she's doing to me.

Until I can't take it anymore.

I lift her, angling myself at her entrance. My hands grip her hips, holding on like I'll fall apart without her as she lowers herself onto me.

And when she sinks fully onto me, tight and slick and *perfect*, I swear to God—I see stars.

Not figurative ones.

Actual fucking stars—bursting behind my eyes, cracking through every nerve in my body like lightning.

She rocks against me, slow at first, then faster—building a rhythm that drives me straight to the edge.

All I can do is hold on, watch, and *worship*.

She's a vision—flushed, wild, radiant.

The mirror shows every angle, every tremble in her thighs, every flicker of pleasure that crosses her face.

I can't help it.

My hands glide up the smooth curve of her back before I drag my nails down—slow, but hard enough to leave marks. I watch in the mirror as thin red lines bloom across her chocolate skin like proof. *Proof she belongs to me.*

I lean in, my mouth brushing the shell of her ear, my voice nothing but gravel and heat.

"You're taking this dick so good, Peach," I growl. "The way your body gives in, the way you ride me like you own me... Every sway of your spine, every grind of your hips—*this* is what you were made for."

I bend lower, catch one of her nipples between my lips, and bite—not gentle, not soft. I bite like I'm branding her. And when she gasps—sharp and high and breathless—I feel it shoot straight down my toes.

That sound? It's gasoline on the fire.

I grip her waist with both hands, fingers digging into flesh, and lift her just enough to slam back into her—hard. Deep. *Claiming.*

"This is yours, Charlesetta," I grunt, jaw clenched, pace brutal now. "Yours. Every inch. You can push me away, and I'll still come back harder. Deeper. Every time. There is no escaping me."

"Xavier!" she cries out, her voice fractured, her rhythm unraveling beneath my grip.

I press my mouth to her neck, my teeth grazing her skin, my breath hot and heavy against the shell of her ear. She's trembling, every nerve lit and begging for more.

Then I move to her other breast, take the nipple between my lips, and bite—sharp.

She screams. Loud.

No thought for the staff, no care for the world beyond this room. Just us. Just *this*.

I pull back just enough to speak, my voice low, rough.

"When it's me and you like this, what have I instructed you to call me, Peach?"

She's panting now, eyes glazed, her body a mess of heat and surrender.

"I'm sorry," she whispers, voice barely hanging on. "*Mr. Darcy.*"

My lips curl as I drag my tongue over the spot I just bit, soothing the sting.

"That's my good, good girl. You're so pretty when you surrender."

I slow my movements just enough to look at her—*really* look at her.

To see the way her eyes search mine. The way her lips part, breath catching, body offered with no restraint, no hesitation.

My wife.

Laid bare.

Not just her skin. Her soul.

And in that moment—she's not just giving me her body.

She's giving me *everything*.

"I have been a starving man for a very long time, Peach," I murmur against her skin. "But I'm not sure I'll ever get my fill of you."

I kiss the hollow of her throat, slow and reverent. "You ruin me. And somehow, I *want* you to."

Then I move again—slower now, but deeper. Like I'm carving my name inside her with every thrust.

Cursive this time so I touch every spot.

Right now? There's no past. No scandal. No sabotage.

Just me and my wife.

And the kind of love that ruins everything that came before it.

I watch her in the mirror as she works for me.

Then she looks up.

Looks behind her.

Right into the mirror.

And she sees me.

Sees me *watching* her.

Watching the way she slams against my thighs with every stroke.

Watching my hands grip her hips possessively.

Watching how my control—the hunger, the reverence, the obsession—bleeds into her through nothing but my gaze.

It's unfiltered.

It's *us.*

And it's sexy as hell.

Hypnotic.

She picks up the pace, rolling her hips, gripping my shoulders, her body arching like a prayer.

I hold her close, whispering her name like it's the only word I know.

"Touche-toi. *Touch yourself, Peach,*" I command. "I know you like it—taking every ounce of your pleasure from every angle you can."

I feel the shift in her body, the subtle tremble of anticipation just before her hand slides between her thighs.

She moans—soft at first, then deeper—as her fingers find that rhythm only she knows.

She *loves* this.

My Peach loves taking her pleasure into her own hands, knowing I'm right here, buried inside her, feeling every clench, every ripple of heat as she climbs.

And me?

I live for this.

For the way she loses herself while never letting go of me.

And when we come—hard and breathless, together—it's with the kind of intensity that feels like submission and salvation all at once.

Her forehead rests against mine, our breath tangled—hot, uneven.

My hands are still on her hips, her body pressed to mine like we'll fall apart if we separate.

And then—Soft. Barely audible.

Right against my lips.

"I love you."

Three words.

And my heart nearly explodes out of my chest.

Not because I didn't hope for it.

But because hearing it from *her*—after everything we've survived, after everything we've become—it's the most dangerous, beautiful truth I've ever been trusted with.

CHAPTER FORTY FOUR

Charlie

The next morning feels like walking into the final act of a play I didn't audition for—but somehow ended up headlining.

We're headed to shore—Xavier, Nathan, Clive, and me. All business. No wasted words.

The tension rides shotgun with us, thick and electric, stitched into every breath, every glance.

The threats haven't let up. If anything, they've evolved—gotten sharper, more precise. Less like reckless attacks, and more like a scalpel in the hands of someone who *knows* us.

Knows where we're soft. Where it hurts.

We're three days out from Xavier's IPO.

One day from a board vote that could erase him from his own legacy.

And someone is still out there in the shadows, pulling strings, praying for collapse.

But not today.

Not on my watch.

Not with *The Fury* on the case.

When we walk into The Fury offices—hand in hand—I feel the freeze before I even look up.

Everyone stops.

Monitors glow quietly as agents pause mid-keystroke. Conversations cut off mid-sentence. No one moves. No one breathes.

Because I don't *do* this.

I don't walk in smiling.

I don't hold hands.

I don't *bring people here.*

And I *definitely* don't let anyone—especially not co-workers—see this side of me.

But here I am.

Holding hands with Xavier Darcy like we didn't just spend the last week dodging cameras—maybe even bullets—and falling in love right in the middle of the wreckage.

Like we didn't unravel every thread of each other while the world has been trying to burn us down.

I hear it in the silence.

What the hell happened to Anastasia Sinclair?

Kiyah is the first to break the tension.

"Anastasia!" she practically sings, beaming as she strolls over in her signature neon sneakers and a blazer that screams *tech unicorn, but make it runway.*

"We didn't know you were coming in!"

Kiyah is a menace and a marvel. She's all warmth and sunshine until she's not, with a body count that rivals mine and a white chocolate, macadamia nut cookie recipe that could start a religion.

"Hi Kiyah. This is—"

"Oh, girl, I *know* who Xavier Darcy is," she cuts me off. "I've had a whole dossier on him since this circus started."

Xavier extends a hand. "Nice to meet you then, I guess? In a creepy way, since you probably know my blood type."

Kiyah just smiles sweetly, all dimples and innocence—like he's absolutely right, but she'd never admit it out loud.

I smirk. "Thanks for holding it down while I was away. It meant a lot."

"You know Hayven wouldn't have it any other way. Your family's safe, and I may or may not have broken the hand of the reporter who breached the gates. Him and his camera are out of commission indefinitely."

I blink. "Wait—what?"

"Oh! Hayven didn't tell you someone tried to break it?" she asks innocently, just as Hayven strolls up behind us.

"No, I didn't," he says, walking up from behind me. "Didn't want to worry her."

Kiyah shrugs. "Sorry! Anyway, fresh baked cookies in the conference room!" she calls out before vanishing.

"Thanks, Kiyah!" we all say in unison.

Hayven extends a hand to Xavier, welcoming him to The Fury and greeting me as well.

Then we head straight for the Falcon room.

It's Logan Fury's pride and joy—one of the most secure spaces in the building, and definitely the most transparent.

Floor-to-ceiling glass. Black steel. Sharp lines. Smooth concrete. No corners to hide in. No shadows to whisper from.

Logan doesn't believe in secrets. Not among his team. Not in his house.

If you've got something to show, you do it in full light.

He's the only one allowed to keep anything hidden.

We take our seats, and Hayven queues up the wall display. Digital threads fill the screen—images, audio clips, coded message dumps, names and dates and dots connected so tightly, it's a noose.

Hayven starts, cool and direct.

"Lincoln Smith—one of the largest insurance brokers in the country—saw Xavier's business and his mission as a threat. Real life insurance for working families. No traps. No fine print. And that hit his pockets hard."

Images flicker—emails, documents, internal memos.

"He started small. Undermining partnerships. Sabotaging deals. Quiet stuff. Easy to deny."

"But when that didn't work," I step in, "he went nuclear."

Hayven nods. "Leaks. False narratives. Financial disruption. All designed to break Xavier before the IPO could take off."

Xavier leans forward, jaw tight. "How did he even get that close? How did he *know* so much?"

I glance at Hayven. Then back at Xavier.

My heart thuds. This is the moment.

I lean closer to him.

"Because he's your father, Xavier. And he had access to DNA and everything from the time you were born."

Silence.

It swallows the room whole.

Xavier stares at me, eyes wide and haunted.

"How long have you known?"

"Since yesterday. I suspected it before, but Hayven confirmed it when he called."

"And you didn't tell me?"

"I was trying to wait for the right time."

He lets out a bitter laugh, humorless and cracked. "You mean like I waited to tell you we were married? You nearly castrated me for that."

"Xavier—"

"Charlie, my life is *already* on fire. There's *never* going to be a right time to tell me I'm headed for another goddamn bomb!"

"I'm sorry," I whisper.

He stands and starts pacing, hands flexing like he's trying to squeeze the rage out of his fists.

"What does this mean? What do we do now?"

I bring up another screen—mine. My work.

"I've been using his tactics against him. Backtraced every encrypted thread, infiltrated his servers, pulled every corrupt file and deal. It all leads to him. Sabotage, bribery, campaign money, offshore accounts. He's behind it."

Hayven steps in. "And Kiyah found more—embezzlement, judicial bribery, shady real estate flips after Katrina that left vulnerable families in toxic housing. All of it."

Xavier stops pacing. Takes a breath.

Hayven clicks to the final slide on the screen.

"We've got our insurance policy," he says. "We made a deepfake video of Lincoln confessing to key parts of the sabotage, as well as other white collar crimes. It's convincing enough to trigger an internal investigation. And once that starts, the FBI will have grounds to step in and take over. I've already made some calls."

"And this is all... legal?" Xavier asks, eyebrows raised.

Hayven lets out a sharp huff. "Of course not."

I step in, voice calm, clear. "Our goal isn't to prosecute—we're not playing by courtroom rules. We just need to set the right wheels in motion. Expose him. Discredit him. The rest will destroy him."

Hayven turns to Xavier. "Which leaves you."

Xavier stiffens. "What about me?"

"When it hits, and the name Lincoln Smith goes national, so will yours. As his first born son, you'll have claims. Legal, financial, even controlling interest of everything he owns."

"I don't want it," Xavier says without hesitation.

"X," I say gently, "you can't just—"

He turns to me, eyes stormy but steady.

"Charlie, he has nothing I want. Not his power. Not his money. Maybe just a reason—the *why*. But that man left my mother and me with nothing. And I made a way for myself. *Without him.*

He doesn't get to hand me something now and pretend it means he was ever part of my story.

He doesn't get to take false credit for the man I became in spite of him."

The room goes still again.

Then, like a man stepping into fire with his chin up, Xavier looks at Hayven.

"Launch the full-scale attack. Leak what you need. Burn him down. Just leave me out of it as much as you can."

Hayven nods, already moving.

"Where will you be?" I ask.

Xavier buttons his jacket, straightens his collar.

"Now that I've got some answers, I've got a board to face."

And without another word, he walks out.

Head high.

Shoulders square.

Ready to take back what no one thought he'd survive.

CHAPTER FORTY FIVE

Xavier

I've faced betrayal before—investors pulling out last minute, friends folding under pressure, people smiling in my face while sharpening knives behind my back.

But nothing prepares you for *this*.

Finding out the man who tried to destroy your life is the same one who gave it to you?

That kind of truth doesn't land all at once. It leaks in slowly. Quietly. Like smoke under a door.

And now I can't breathe.

Lincoln Smith.

My father.

I can still see his face—clear as day—in the hallway outside Big Daddy's study. That crisp suit. That fake Southern charm. That smile that didn't quite reach his eyes.

He said his name like it was supposed to mean something. And it *did*—but I didn't know why at the time.

All I knew was that the energy shifted the moment he appeared.

Big Daddy didn't even bother to mask it—he looked at that man like he was filth stuck to the bottom of his shoe. And now that I know the truth, it makes perfect sense.

The Smiths have spent decades trying to undermine the Sinclairs, convinced they don't deserve the land they rightfully own. Land their ancestors bled for. Land they refused to sell, no matter the offer.

It's poetic, in the most twisted way, that I ended up in Lincoln Smith's crosshairs—married to the great granddaughter of the very legacy he's spent his life trying to both preserve and erase. The great granddaughter of his demons. And this country's demons.

Perhaps I should feel ashamed. But right now, all I carry is purpose.

Because one day, when we're old—when me and *my wife* are sitting under soft lights, surrounded by family and friends, maybe even grandkids running underfoot—we'll tell the story.

Of how hate brought our families together.

Of how that same hate tried to tear us apart.

But more than anything, we'll tell how love—messy, unexpected, relentless love—brought it all back together again.

And maybe that's what steadies me now, as Charlie and I begin to walk out of The Fury offices.

The air we breathe is heavy—thick with the weight of everything we've just uncovered.

Truths that didn't just shake me. Instead, they *rearranged* me. Tore down everything I thought I understood about where I come from, only to reveal the scar tissue underneath.

But beside me, she walks tall.

Shoulders squared, chin high, fingers brushing mine until they find their place.

Locked.

And for the first time ever, I don't feel like I'm carrying all this alone.

I feel *anchored.*

The sky overhead is that unpredictable gray, the kind that could break into a storm or split open with sun, depending on how you treat it.

We don't speak much. Don't need to.

There's something sacred in the quiet between us right now.

Something heavy and healing at the same time.

Two people bound to history neither of them chose—choosing *each other* anyway.

I grab Charlie's hand and hold it tighter than I need to. Clive is behind us, stoic and silent, like always.

Charlie turns to me. "You're not mad?"

I glance down at her. "No," I say, no hesitation. "You?"

She shakes her head, then lets out a short breath like she's still trying to process it. "No. I think life is funny."

I raise an eyebrow, waiting.

"If I didn't do the work I do," she says, "I probably would've been shocked. About who your father is... what your family meant to mine. I might've even let go of your hand and walked away."

She looks down at our fingers, still locked.

"But I've seen what happens when power is abused in the dark. I've watched good people sell out for control. I've *felt* what that kind of silence does to families."

I watch her as she speaks, her voice low but steady. She's not just talking about *me*.

"But to see how my family survived that? To know it wasn't revenge, or money, or blood that ended it—but *love*?" She shakes her head slightly. "How could I feel anything but grateful?"

She looks up at me.

"Grateful. And completely, hopelessly in love."

"Why grateful?"

"I guess," she pauses to think about it. "I guess because in all of this, despite all of this, we found each other."

"That's all I could ever ask," I say. "Because I feel exactly the same."

She rolls her eyes and I frown. "I can't believe I said that," she mutters. "Who even am I right now?"

Then she adds, deadpan: "Somewhere, the old me is gagging in combat boots."

I laugh—full, chest-deep.

And then she smiles. The real kind.

"Mr. Darcy," she says softly, "I love you."

I run my thumb along the back of her hand, slow, certain.

"I love you too, Peach."

Charlie

Love...It does not dishonor others, it is not self-seeking, it is not easily angered, it keeps no record of wrongs. **I Corinthians 13:5.**

CHAPTER FORTY SIX

Xavier

Major Insurance Tycoon Lincoln Smith Under International Investigation Following Anonymous Tips

New York, NY – Lincoln Smith, the powerful CEO of Smith & Dominion Insurance Group and one of the most influential figures in the global insurance industry, is now at the center of an explosive international investigation, authorities confirmed early this morning.

According to sources inside the FBI and Interpol, a series of co-ordinated, anonymous tips have triggered a sweeping probe into Smith's business dealings, unveiling alleged instances of large-scale embezzlement, judicial bribery, and real estate corruption tied to post-disaster redevelopment efforts. Investigators are also examining offshore financial activities and several suspicious corporate partnerships flagged over the last year.

In a stunning development, a confidential video—allegedly featuring Smith—has surfaced and is being reviewed as possible evidence. Though authenticity has yet to be verified, the contents of the video have already prompted internal audits across several agencies and firms connected to Smith & Dominion.

Both the FBI and Interpol have declined to comment on the identity of the whistleblowers behind the leak. However, multiple sources say the information was so detailed and specific it left "no room for delay" in launching the investigation.

As of now, Smith has not issued a public statement.

Authorities have confirmed this is an ongoing investigation with potential criminal charges pending.

Meanwhile, markets are reacting swiftly, with Smith & Dominion's stock experiencing a sharp decline in early trading.

Xavier Darcy, a rising figure in the same sector and once believed to be a competitor of Smith, has not been formally connected to the investigation.

More updates as this story develops.

End of Release

CHAPTER FORTY SEVEN

Xavier

"She is a *child!*"

I pace the length of my office, jaw clenched so tight it's starting to ache.

It's nearly 10PM, and instead of being where I want to be—curled up with my wife, pretending like the world doesn't exist—I'm stuck on a conference call with two of the most infuriating men I've ever voluntarily gone into business with: Grant and Will.

Buying a soccer team with my buddies was supposed to be the perfect blend of fun and strategy—a boys' club power move with bragging rights.

Instead, it's become a full-time job I never applied for, complete with tantrum-prone talent, boardroom brawls, and a scoreboard that won't stop reminding me this was probably the worst and best idea I've ever had.

Grant groans. "Is this because she's a woman?"

"No, it's because she's *two!*" I shout. "She has no experience, no track record, and no business telling a locker room full of ego-driven, barely house-trained athletes how to do their job!"

Grant has called for an *emergency meeting*—his words, not mine—because he's suddenly decided he no longer wants to own a soccer team.

Says he's had some sort of spiritual awakening, a midlife epiphany where he's convinced he needs to travel the world and "find himself."

Maybe even *find love again.*

I'd probably be sick to my damn stomach if I wasn't currently floating in the afterglow of being completely, helplessly smitten with my wife.

Let the man chase sunsets and soulmates if he wants. Hell, I hope he finds whatever enlightenment he's looking for.

But he doesn't need to make *reckless* choices in the process—like leaving his twenty seven year old daughter to ruin our club just because *she's bored.*

This isn't some hobby—it's a full-blown franchise, one with World Cup ambitions and the pressure to match. And we're not handing it over like it's a startup internship.

I hear Will snort in the background. "Barely house-trained is generous for these guys. You're forgetting the guy who brought a goat to practice because he said it was his emotional support animal."

"Exactly!" I bark. "And we're just supposed to hand over part of this club to someone who's barely older than the players? Grant, I respect your daughter. I like her. I do. But this isn't a lemonade stand. This is *football*."

"It's *soccer*," Will corrects.

"You shut your face, Will."

"I actually don't think it's a terrible idea if we groom her for leadership," Will says, casually. "It could be a good look for us—having a woman in management when so many rights are being ripped from women right now."

"*Not you too, Will*," I snap. "This isn't Blue Ivy and Beyonce. There will be no practice or time to get better. This is real life. You're supposed to be on my side!"

"I'm actually impressed at the Beyonce reference," Will says.

"Hanging out with Charlie and Autika, I know more about pop culture than I ever wanted to."

"Welcome to my world," Will says.

He gets back on topic. "Anyway, I *am* on your side," he says, unfazed. "But more importantly, I'm on the side that makes sense. And in this case, it makes *dollars* and sense."

Grant groans again, something about succession and *letting the next generation lead,* and I swear, if I hear that phrase one more time, I'm selling my stake to Qatar and washing my hands of the entire damn thing.

Then Will suddenly says, "Hold on, Timantha's calling me. I gotta go."

"Oh *great*," I mutter. "Tell her to talk some sense into your thick skull."

"Love you too," Will says, clearly amused.

The line goes dead.

I sigh. Loudly.

"Fine," I say into the phone. "We'll reconvene tomorrow. Early. And if I wake up to another scandal or—God forbid—a goat in the locker room—"

"I actually got them a dog," Grant says, like it's the most normal thing in the world. "He's a rescue. He's been great for team morale."

"I can't believe what I'm hearing," say with frustration. And confusion.

Grant Mills is one of the sharpest men I know—brilliant in the boardroom, ruthless when he needs to be. But for as long as I've known him, he's also been a contradiction: single dad by day, unapologetic playboy by night. A founding member of Atlanta's After Dark Supper Club—which, if we're being honest, serves everything *but* supper. Now he's out here talking about rescuing dogs and finding inner peace?

This is the same man who once left a high-stakes merger meeting early to make it to his daughter's recital... and then got caught getting head at not one, but *multiple* company Christmas parties. I don't know who this soft, self-reflective version of Grant is. But he's not the man I've known the past ten years.

"Believe it. I'm serious about calming down and finding some peace. Rocky's helping. Me and the guys."

"We don't need a team dog, Grant. We need a team therapist like I've been asking you to hire for months."

"Marlow's actually interviewing the final candidates. It's part of my leadership training for her."

I let out a long, exhausted sigh. "I can't even keep talking about this. Because if I do, I'm going to scream at the top of my lungs over the fact that your kid is out here violating HR protocol because you refuse to do your job."

"Sounds like someone needs to go see his wife about some pussy," he jokes.

I hang up. Immediately.

Still in full crisis mode, I scroll through my contacts, land on one of our European partnerships.

Italy.

They've always got some lowkey prodigy stashed on the bench somewhere—some seventeen-year-old wonderkid who eats, sleeps, and dreams formation shifts.

I'm desperate enough to ask if they've got a midfielder with no social life and a valid visa.

We're mid-call, negotiating over a player named Declan Agassi—some scrappy, sharp-footed player who looks like he might be the answer to at least *one* of my many problems—when it happens.

Click.

Everything goes *dark.*

Phone screen black.

Wi-Fi? Gone.

Laptop? Dead.

My smart watch can't even load the weather.

"What the hell..." I murmur, staring at my devices like they personally betrayed me.

I know tech failures.

But this? This is *intentional.*

I rub the back of my neck and sigh again—this time slower, heavier.

Looks like my night just got... redirected.

Charlie

Two months of marriage.

Two weeks since Xavier won the war for his company.

And not just won—*obliterated* the opposition.

Thanks to Logan Fury and his Rolodex of terrifyingly powerful friends, Xavier's name was cleared, his reputation scrubbed clean, and—most importantly—any public connection to Lincoln Smith was erased from existence.

As for me, Hayven worked his magic. Every alias I've ever used was wiped from the web. He even added a block—some digital force field—that ensures no matter who tries to leak information about me, nothing will surface. It's like I never existed outside of my own name.

It *pays* to have The Fury on your side.

And it *hurts* like hell to have them as your enemy.

Once we agreed to give our marriage a real shot, Xavier didn't waste a second. He moved me into his home before I could change my mind—or pack a proper overnight bag.

I expected a penthouse for a man like him. Instead, I got a quiet, sun-drenched estate on the edge of the city. Hidden. Grounded. Peaceful. It's so *him,* it makes me wonder how much of him I still don't know.

And now?

Now we live like a couple who meant to do this.

Like we weren't thrown into a marriage by entanglements and scandals.

He handles affairs for his newly public company by day, and plays executive for the Atlanta Strikers soccer club in the stolen hours between board meetings and press calls.

That team—something he and his friends probably bought on a dare after one too many cocktails—is now a real part of his schedule. And I don't think he realized how *little* time he'd actually have for it.

Or for himself.

And as much as I love working with The Fury—because yes, I still work, even though I don't *need* to—I can see my husband being spread thin.

And we can't have that.

Because the world finally stopped coming for his neck.

Now it's up to me to protect his peace.

It's past 10PM and Xavier's still in his office, pacing, scotch in hand, barking into a phone call with someone in Italy who's either incompetent or suicidal.

He's got his shirt sleeves rolled up, tie loosened, and that permanent frown he wears when someone forgets he came from the streets—long before he ever graced a boardroom.

That look says *don't mistake polish for softness.*

It's the same look that built an empire out of nothing. The same look that says he'll burn the whole thing down before letting anyone take me from him.

And, mercy me, it's part of what I love most about him.

I watch him from the doorway as he paces. I never understood how white men could drink something that tastes like the aftertaste of mud. But he loves it, so I let him have it.

Still. Enough is enough.

He hasn't come up for air in over two hours, and the last thing this man needs tonight is more business drama and bad liquor.

As a hacker, I know how to get him off.

The phone.

And then—*literally.*

I walk past his office like I'm headed to bed, but the second I round the corner, I pull out my tablet, open the encrypted admin panel I embedded into his home server, and begin disabling every signal tower within range.

Cell service? Gone.

Internet? Dead.

Wi-Fi? What Wi-Fi?

I do this on occasion when I want his undivided attention...Or when I want to pay him back for hiding my vibrators.

Yes, *plural.*

He still won't let me use them when he's around. Says my pleasure is his responsibility—almost like it's sacred.

So fine. If he wants all of me, then I'll expect nothing less in return. I'll demand all of him. Every glance. Every breath. Every ounce of attention.

I wait.

It takes him three minutes to come stomping down the hall like a storm cloud in loafers.

"Charlie?" he calls out.

I'm already waiting for him on the balcony, wrapped in a silk robe, a cigar clipped and lit in one hand, two glasses of bourbon—*not scotch*—in the other.

He steps out, blinking at the sudden calm. "Everything's down. Internet. Cell. Even my laptop won't connect to the backup network."

I hand him a glass. "Sounds like the universe is trying to tell you to take a break."

He narrows his eyes. "Would you be the universe in this scenario?"

I take a long sip and raise an eyebrow. "Maybe. But you're here, aren't you?"

He laughs, low and tired. Then sits beside me, stretching his legs out as he takes the cigar from my fingers and leans in for a drag.

This is our ritual now. Nights like this—when the world quiets down—we sit out here, drink, smoke, and talk. Really talk.

Xavier calls it *Truth Hour*. One of his weird ideas to get to know me deeper. No games. No evasions.

Just questions. Any questions.

Tonight, he starts light. "What's your favorite kind of music?"

"R&B and jazz," I answer easily. "Old stuff. Gritty and smooth at the same time."

He nods. "And your favorite singer is India Arie, right?"

"You remembered!" Of course he did.

"You always say her voice feels like home to you. Like truth."

"How many people have you *taken out?* How many bodies do you have?"

I shoot him a look. "Xavier."

"What? I'm talking about spy bodies. Not, like, exes."

I exhale slowly. "Can't say. But let's just say I've been useful in very complicated situations."

He chuckles. "Ever met royalty?"

I smile into my glass. "Let's just say... Meghan Markle is all of us. A timeless treasure who speaks to our collective soul."

He throws his head back laughing, his free hand reaching for mine.

Then, he quiets. Looks at me with that searching gaze of his—the one that doesn't ask questions just to be answered, but to *understand*.

"Were you serious," he asks, his voice softer now, "about what you said to your mom back in New Orleans? About never wanting kids?"

I glance down at our hands, fingers tangled together. It's the first time I've heard him call New Orleans *home* again. That alone makes my chest tighten.

"I never really thought about it," I admit. "Never had the time. Never had the space. But then there was Prince...seeing who he's becoming. It has me thinking.

And now, with *you*..." I pause, searching for the words.

"Perhaps...maybe...Maybe I might want that. Maybe not in the traditional way. But maybe adoption. Family we choose."

His thumb moves slowly over the back of my hand—measured.

"I've been thinking the same," he says quietly. "But before we go there—before we talk about kids or anything like that—I think we need to sit down with your parents. Tell them everything."

I tense.

"Even about Lincoln?"

He nods. "All of it. They deserve the truth. And I need to be able to look them...Big Daddy... in the eye as your husband and be honest."

I exhale. "I don't know how they'll react. That's why I haven't told them yet."

"I get it," he says gently. "But that's my job as your man, Peach. And they love you. I'm sure they'll come around. I'll fire up the jet this weekend."

I smile, relaxing just a little. "I have book club this weekend."

He smirks—because he knows me. Knows I'm stalling just as much as I'm telling the truth.

My relationship with Mama is still fragile.

But it's healing.

Brick by brick. Word by word.

But this kind of news might knock the whole foundation loose.

Mama has always spoken with pride about our lineage—our strength. About how our family rose from slavery, from chains and cotton fields, to become something powerful, something *free*.

But telling her that she'll have to look into the eyes of the bloodline that once *owned* a big part of our town...I don't know how she'll take that.

"Fine," he says, grinning. "We'll go next weekend, then."

"Next weekend," I agree.

And we sit there in the hush of night, our glasses clinking once before silence wraps around us again.

Not empty silence.

The kind that means we're building something real.

One truth at a time.

Then he breaks the silence, voice low and certain, cutting through the weight in the air like sunlight through storm clouds.

"My mama would have loved you."

Just six words. But they land with the force of a thousand.

And I feel it—deep, where the armor doesn't reach.

Not because I needed her approval, but because I know what it means for *him* to say that.

To picture me in the same breath as the woman who raised him. To imagine a world where the two of us could've sat across from each other, shared stories, laughed too loud, maybe even argued a little.

That world doesn't exist.

But hearing him say it makes it feel like it could've.

And somehow, that's enough.

CHAPTER FORTY EIGHT

Xavier

The heat in New Orleans sits on your skin like it has a right to be there—thick and slow, sweet with jasmine and the faint sting of history.

We're back at the Big House. The sun is casting that golden syrup light over the backyard. Spanish moss drips from the old trees like lace curtains. Somewhere, a cicada sings.

It's a Saturday afternoon.

We flew in this morning and have spent most of the day here at the Big House, the weight of memory and history brushing against every step like a breeze you can feel but not explain.

Charlie's been home most of the day with her parents—catching up, unpacking years of distance wrapped in silence. Telling them about the life she built while she was away. The life she was hiding.

Ten years is a long time to be gone, but longer still when you've been carrying the kind of secrets Charlie has.

Meanwhile, I spent the day hanging out with Elijah, Prince, and—surprisingly—Lucas Ballentine.

Yeah, *that* Lucas.

Her ex who I thought I'd have to knock out the first time we met. But instead, we found common ground in the most unexpected way: family.

Turns out, we both care about Charlie.

Just in very, *very* different ways.

And when it was all said and done, Lucas understood what I think he always suspected—he was never meant to be her forever. No matter how much sense it made on paper—the history, the families, the clean lines of compatibility— he never quite understood her *fire*.

Not the way I do.

He saw her shine.

I saw the *heat* that made it.

And while there's still tension between us, it's quieter now. We're learning how to exist in the same space without posturing.

Prince talks enough for all of us, anyway.

But even out there, tossing a football and ribbing each other over bad passes, I could feel it—*something had shifted inside that house.*

Something heavy was being let go.

Whatever happened while I was out with the guys, healing has begun to take root.

Now, Charlie sits beside me on the back porch, legs curled under her, fingers lightly tracing the rim of her glass of sweet tea. Her mother sits on her other side, calm but watchful. Big Daddy's in his chair at the head of the porch like a king on his throne—hat tilted back, a glass of sweet tea sweating on the table beside him.

It's peaceful.

Too peaceful for what I'm about to say.

I clear my throat. My chest feels tight, like it's bracing for the moment I ruin all this warmth.

"There's something we... I... need to tell you," I begin, looking straight at Big Daddy.

His eyes don't flinch. He's listening.

"Lincoln Smith..." I pause.

"Lincoln Smith is my biological father."

The porch goes still.

The breeze dies.

Mrs. Sinclair gasps, her hand flying to Charlie's, squeezing it tight. Her eyes well up, and she looks away, like even the sky shouldn't see her cry.

Charlie doesn't speak. She just lets her mom hold her hand, lets the truth settle between us.

I look down at my hands.

And then I feel it—*shame.*

"I didn't know," I say, my voice low. "I didn't grow up with him. I didn't grow up with anyone. But now, knowing who he is... what his family did to yours... I don't know what to say.

I love your daughter. But I'm not blind to the blood in my veins."

There's a long silence. I don't dare look up.

Then Big Daddy shifts. I feel his presence before I see him, his shadow stretching toward me.

"You listen to me, son," he says, voice like gravel and steel, "and you listen good."

I raise my eyes.

He's looking straight at me. No flinch. No fury. Just *truth*.

"I will not have my daughter's husband sittin' here speaking about their love like it's something dirty. Something to be ashamed of. That woman beside you chose you. And that means you belong here. With us. Not in spite of your past, but because of what you've done with it."

My chest tightens.

"But that Lincoln family? They may have tried to break us. May have left blood in the soil of this town. But *you* didn't."

He steps forward, puts a hand on my shoulder. Firm. Final.

"Lincoln Smith may have played a part in your creation. But I'd like to be a part of your future. As your father."

My throat closes.

I nod.

Because there's nothing else I *can* do.

He pulls me into a hug—rough, warm, grounding.

And right there, in the thick Louisiana air, with Charlie's mother wiping her tears and Charlie watching it all with something like awe in her eyes—I realize something.

For the first time in my life, I don't feel like a man who's come from nothing.

I feel like a man who has *everything*.

A name that means something.

A woman who sees me.

A family that chooses me.

And as I sit here, surrounded by people who once had every reason to turn their backs, but didn't—I say a silent prayer of thanks.

For the pain.

For the detours.

For the love I never saw coming.

For *her*.

CHAPTER FORTY NINE

Charlie

Spending the weekend at The Big House—unpacking more than just bags, but emotions too—has been exactly what my soul needed. Long talks, deeper healing, and witnessing Xavier bond with my brother? Unexpected. Lucas even made an effort to play nice, which felt like a miracle in itself, but I welcomed it all.

Before he had to rush off for an urgent work matter last night, Big Daddy pulled Xavier aside and made him promise he'd bring me home at least once a month—for church and Sunday dinners. Especially after Xavier admitted he hadn't set foot in a sanctuary in years. Big Daddy wasn't having it. "No son of mine is leading my daughter's house or her heart without checking in with God first," he said. Xavier didn't argue, and I didn't even try.

He simply said, "You got it, Big Daddy," before kissing me good-bye and heading back to the airport to catch a quick flight.

Now I'm curled up in my childhood bedroom, no anxiety in my chest, no tension in my bones. Just... full.

Full of joy.

Full of peace.

Full of love.

Until a voice startles me awake.

"Break yo self, bitch!"

The whisper slices through my sleep like a rusty knife.

I bolt upright, instincts kicking in before logic even makes an appearance.

In one smooth, sleep-deprived motion, I grab the Glock from the drawer beside my bed and launch myself across the mattress, taking down the ski-masked intruder with a textbook BJJ sweep.

Whoever it is grunts beneath me as I straddle their chest, gun shoved through the mouth-hole of their ski mask like I'm Angelina Jolie in *Tomb Raider*.

I flick the lamp on with one hand, still aiming with the other—half expecting to see some poor, would-be burglar rethinking every life decision that led them to this exact moment.

That's when I notice the body under me is... fluffy. Fluffy and vaguely familiar.

I yank the mask off and—

"Autika?!" I yell.

She blinks up at me, clearly winded.

"Damn, girl! I thought you were off-duty! Flippin' me over like the damn *Equalizer!*"

She coughs, wheezing slightly. "A bitch came to surprise you, not get rearranged like Ikea furniture."

Before I can begin to process what the hell is going on, the door flies open and in burst *Timantha* and *Geneva,* screaming.

"Surprise! It's your wedding day!"

I blink. Hard.

Xavier said he'd be back early this morning—suited up and ready to take me to church so I could finally meet his elusive, scripture-quoting best friend, Jonah.

So I was definitely *not* expecting my book besties and my childhood ride-or-die to bust into my childhood bedroom at the crack of dawn with enough noise to wake the dead... my mama.

I stare at them all, breathing heavy, still straddling Autika, who hasn't even tried to get up yet.

"Wedding day?" I manage to say, lowering the gun—barely. "What are you talking about?"

Geneva grins like the devil in pink lip gloss. "Xavier might have mentioned you wanted a real wedding. One you could remember? And we thought today might be the best day."

I look around. Tears filling my eyes. "My birthday?"

Timantha nods, hands on her hips like she's been waiting her whole life for this moment. "You said if you ever did this for real, it had to be on your terms. And you said—direct quote—'on a boat.' Well, guess what, bitch? We gettin' back on a boat!"

I gasp. "Wait. *The* boat? *It's here?* In New Orleans?"

Timantha and Geneva start nodding like bobbleheads, barely containing their excitement.

Then Neva jumps in, unable to keep it to herself. "Okay, so when Xavier told us his plan and how he needed the boat docked here to make it happen, Autika decided that sounded like a cruise we needed to be on. So, Xavier flew us to where the boat was docked and let us ride with the crew while they brought the boat here."

"It was basically your bachelorette party without you," Timantha says with a shrug, "but it worked out. Since mine turned into Tika's, you kind of already had two."

I'm sitting there, still in pajamas, barely awake, and completely overwhelmed. "You guys... I can't believe this."

Autika coughs beneath me, her voice strained.

"Can I get up now? You're squishing my bladder. And... my *baby*."

I freeze. Blink again. Then look down at her.

"Wait, what?"

I glance at Timantha, who's beaming like she's been holding in the secret of the century. I look back at Autika, and she nods, her eyes glossing over with tears.

"I'm pregnant, *hoe!*"

A laugh bubbles out of me before I can stop it, and I just collapse—right on top of her, hugging her so tight I hear her squeak.

"I still can't breathe," she wheezes.

"Don't care!" I yell through the tears, squeezing her tighter.

Timantha screams and dives in, landing on top of both of us like we're a human celebration pile.

"Owww!" Autika yelps. "I was *serious* about my bladder! I will pee all over you heffas!"

"We're having a *baby!!!*" We all yell together like we've just won the lottery.

I know I have.

That's when Mama comes storming in, hair wrapped, silk robe swishing behind her, eyes wide.

"What in the good Lord's name is going on in here?" she asks, hands on hips. "Now Xavier said he had something planned with y'all, but he did *not* say you'd be here before the Father, the Son, and the Holy Spirit had time to rise!"

"Mama..." I say, sitting up, eyes full, face soaked. "I'm getting married."

I'm getting married...*Today.*

CHAPTER FIFTY

Xavier

This should feel weirder than it does.

In just a few hours, Charlie and I will stand in front of everyone we love and do the thing for real—vows, rings, "I do's." The wedding she's always dreamed of, on the day she was born. And I'll be standing beside her, wondering how in the hell I ended up worthy of a woman like her.

We're quiet, the four of us. Me, Jonah, Elijah, and Prince.

Standing in the stillness.

Waiting.

I never planned on coming here. Honestly, I didn't think I had it in me.

I haven't stood in front of my mother's grave since the day we buried her over a decade ago. Not once.

At the time, I told myself it was pointless. That talking to a headstone wouldn't change anything. Wouldn't ease the ache.

It felt like walking straight into a storm I'd spent years trying to outrun—and I was already drowning in things I couldn't fix. So I stayed away. For years.

Then Elijah asked me—quietly, without judgment—"When's the last time you went?"

And I didn't have an answer that didn't make me feel the sting of shame.

Then Prince—God, this kid—he looks at me with those big, knowing eyes and says, "I'll go with you if you want. If you're scared."

He said his mom is buried here too. And talking to her still helps him breathe some days.

That's honestly all it took for me. No pressure. No guilt trip. Just an invitation from a boy who knows what it's like to miss someone every single day.

So here I am. Because sometimes healing doesn't come loud. It comes quiet, in moments like this—when you finally stop running.

That's all it took.

Not pressure. Not guilt.

Just the simple, steady kindness of people who want to walk with you through the hard parts.

My family.

We stand here, beneath the weight of the moment, when Jonah breaks the silence.

"Hey, Mrs. Darcy," he says, that Southern drawl thick and soulful. "I told you I'd get your baby boy back home, and look at this here. He's back."

I glance over at him, surprised.

He shrugs. "I stop by sometimes. After church burials. Figured since she always treated me like one of her own, the least I could do was check in on her from time to time."

I swallow hard.

"Thank you," is all I can manage.

When Mama passed, I couldn't even afford a proper headstone. That shame sat with me for years.

So I worked. And worked. And once the money came—once I was able—I didn't just buy her a headstone. I bought the land around it. I wanted her to *own* something. Finally.

She never had that chance in life. But I gave it to her in rest.

"Your son's a pretty cool guy," Prince chimes in. "Even if he does act like a b—"

"Prince," Elijah cuts him off with a warning.

Prince just shrugs. "Sorry. I like him for my Aunt Charlie."

I ruffle his hair. "Thanks, kid."

Then Elijah steps up, clears his throat like he's preparing to speak on behalf of the Sinclair family.

"I think he's scared to admit he's fallen in love with a sistah," Elijah says with a grin. "But I promise you, she's good people. She comes from good stalk. And she loves your boy something fierce."

He pauses, then adds with a smirk, "Even Big Daddy's on board. And you know that's no small feat to make that man like, let alone trust, anyone."

I laugh, a sound I didn't expect to come out of me in this place.

These men are filling in the words I haven't been able to find for myself. Speaking for me when my chest is too tight to do it.

They all became more to me in this moment right here.

"But we want you to know," Elijah says, voice softening, "we've got him now. He's got a home. A *real* family. And we're gonna take good care of him."

They step back, giving me space. Time.

And for the first time in over a decade, I let myself kneel in front of my mother's grave.

"Hey, Mama," I whisper. "I should've come sooner. I didn't understand before... but I get it now. Coming here... being here... it pulls something out of you. Pulls you home."

I glance down, brushing off a fallen petal from her stone.

"You'll be proud to know I've got that now. Home. Family."

I laugh, a little unsteady. "Remember when I was little, and I used to walk past that big white house on the hill on my way to school? I'd come home talking about how one day, I was gonna own a house like that?"

I pause, imagining her warm chuckle, her soft *mmm-hmm* in reply.

She used to tell me folks in houses like that—the grand ones, sitting up high and out of reach—were usually power-hungry, self-important, didn't care about anyone but themselves.

And for a long time, I believed her. In fact, as my wealth grew, I was determined to not become like those men.

But today... I'm sort of proud to tell her I found a man who's different.

"It's called the Big House, Mama," I whisper. "And guess what? The man who owns it—Joe Sinclair—he's got the biggest heart I've ever seen. Cares about everybody. And now? He cares about *me*.

Because I'm in love with his daughter. Her name's Charlesetta. They call her Charlie. Just like your friends used to call you."

I chuckle, breath shaky.

"She's sharp. Bold. Fire in human form. If she weren't Black, I'd swear there was a redhead living inside her."

I pause, my throat tight as I blink away the blur in my eyes.

And I smile—because this part, this moment, this truth—*she* would've loved.

"You'd love her, Mama. And she'd love you.

And today... I'm gonna marry her."

I rub the back of my neck, embarrassed even though I'm alone.

"Well, technically, we're already married—but I'll save that story for another day."

I place my hand on the stone, fingers steady now.

"I just wanted you to know... your boy's doing alright. And Mama—Your son has finally come home."

Charlie

"You may now kiss your bride," Jonah announces, his voice warm, grounded in something bigger than tradition.

Xavier leans in and kisses me. Sweet. Gentle. The kind of kiss that says, *finally*.

Then, of course, Autika yells, "Alright, already!"

The crowd bursts into laughter, and in an instant, the nerves, the past, the weight—it all lifts.

I look around at the sea of faces—our people. Friends from every part of our lives, even colleagues from work, flown in courtesy of Logan Fury himself. Leave it to Logan and Hayven to make a spectacle of something sacred. I'd roll my eyes, but the truth is, I'm grateful.

As I'm scanning the crowd, Jonah makes his way over, grinning like he knows something I don't.

"You know, Anastasia," he says, "I knew it was you."

I squint at him. "What do you mean?"

"Xavier told me about you the first time he met you."

I frown. "On the plane?" Because I don't need the good minister knowing anything about that.

"No," Xavier cuts in quickly, sliding up beside me. "The gala."

I gasp. "What did you say to him? We barely spoke that night."

Jonah smiles, eyes twinkling. "He said he might be smitten for the first time in his life... by a woman with a bob haircut."

Xavier laughs, shaking his head. "Our middle school principal had a bob. She was the one who always paddled me and I hated to see that woman coming. Since then, I have *hated* that damn haircut."

I raise a brow. "Oh really?"

"Until you, Peach." He kisses my cheek. "And I didn't think I'd like your hair longer the way you're wearing it today either, but you're kind of ruining every bias I've ever had."

Part of his obsession with me—besides the obvious—is learning. About me. My culture. My *hair*. He asks questions during our *truth hours* like he's studying for a test he doesn't want to fail. From twist-outs to silk presses, he wants to know it all. And not just know it—make space for it.

It's weird. But it's also deeply, undeniably endearing.

"Thank you," I laugh. "Your short haircut with the goatee is growing on me, too! Very Jon B., Mr. Darcy."

"I'll accept that. Just know I will not be singing or dancing. Leave that side show to Will Huntley."

I laugh, remembering how Will learned how to Chicago Step for Timantha's wedding.

We have truly had some crazy times since finding and falling in love.

When the ladies showed up to surprise me and get me ready for my big day, I had no idea what I was walking into.

I expected ruckus. A lot of squealing. Maybe a mimosa topped off with a gummy.

But what I *didn't* expect?

They had arranged *everything.*

Every detail. Every touch.

Right down to the damn simple peplum dress that made me feel like a little girl.

Apparently, Timantha recruited Hayven to crack my Pinterest password—because of course she did—and together they unearthed a secret stash of wedding dresses I'd quietly saved over the years.

A private little board labeled *"Not That I Want to Get Married or Anything."*

I thought no one would ever see it—those quiet pins and secret boards where I'd let myself daydream.

About getting dressed up.

About being the prissy bride my mother always wanted. But I kept the quiet daydreams alive. Adding dresses and styles whenever I was bored or had a moment alone.

Funny thing is... I never pictured a groom.

Not once.

I think some part of me always assumed I was meant to be alone.

That if loving someone meant dimming my fire, I'd just love *myself*.

And that would be enough.

But standing here now—in this dress I never thought I'd wear, surrounded by people who know every version of me—I realize I never had to dim anything.

Because the right kind of love doesn't shrink you.

It *sees you*. Begs for more. Champions you to be bigger.

And today, as Autika styled my hair, Geneva fluffed the veil, and Timantha zipped me into a dress I never thought I'd wear, it hit me—*hard*.

A wave of gratitude, full and thick in my chest.

For *family*.

For a job that lets me chase my passions without apology.

And for nosy, bossy, up-in-your-business friends who love you enough to dig through your secrets, crack your passwords, and make your quietest dreams come true.

My sisters...they don't wait for you to break down or beg.

They show up.

Uninvited. Unbothered. Unshakable.

And today?

They didn't just show up.

They *showed out.*

Geneva pops up, phone already in hand. "Can I get a selfie with the bride?"

"Of course, girl! Thank you so much for being here."

She snaps the pic, then pauses to look at me, serious now.

"I wouldn't have missed this. And thank you—for letting me be part of it. So many women move on and build new friendships that feel like gated communities. But you've somehow managed to bring all the pieces of you together. Seamlessly."

I laugh. "Not seamlessly. It is taking some adjusting. And I'm not sure everyone will ever have *all* parts of me. But I'm lucky I don't feel like I have to hide anything from the people I love."

Geneva hugs me tight. "I'm glad you figured out we'd love you, all of you, no matter what you brought back home, Charlie."

We turn to the sight of the four men I never imagined sharing air without drama: Will Huntley, Xavier Darcy, Elijah Sinclair, and Lucas Ballentine. All with cigars, laughing like old friends. Jonah joins them, but he's drinking water.

Lucas and I... we got closure in a way most people never do.

I was sure he'd never be able to see me with someone else—*not* him.

Sure he'd carry the break like a scar he'd never let heal. That he'd never forgive me for walking away with his heart still in my hands.

But he's here.

He's whole.

And somehow, he's at peace with this chapter of my life—even if he's not the main character in it.

That's grace and I'll never take it for granted.

I still can't stand his mama, though.

Xavier catches Clive's signal and takes off toward me, that boyish glint in his eye already giving him away.

"Come on, Peach," he says, grabbing my hand. "Your present is here."

I cross my arms and raise a brow. "You already surprised me with a wedding on a super yacht... on my *birthday*. What more could you possibly have up your sleeve?"

He grins—smug, full of mischief. "Everything."

I pretend to protest, but we both know I don't mean it. I *love* this. All of it.

Being seen. Being chosen. Being *spoiled*.

Black women deserve the fairytale. We deserve to be loved loudly, recklessly, all the way through.

So no—I won't feel guilty about having a man who wants to give me the world.

Because I plan on taking every damn piece of it.

We walk hand in hand toward the deck that's been transformed into a stage and dance floor. And there—under golden string lights and the open sky—stand *PJ Morton* and *India Arie*. *Jon Batiste* on piano like it's just another night in New Orleans.

I gasp.

Xavier comes up behind me, slides his arms around my waist, and leans in close—his lips brushing my ear with that familiar mix of charm and trouble.

"Autika said if we were having music, she got to choose... or she'd poison me and hand you everything in the prenup."

I laugh and blow her a kiss. She catches it with flair, then turns to Xavier, eyes narrowed, and drags a finger across her throat while mouthing, *If you hurt her, I will kill you.*

That's Autika.

Dramatic. Over-the-top. But fully committed.

But that's love too.

PJ kicks off *How Deep is Your Love,* and I watch as Big Daddy steps forward, holding out his hand to me. Mama walks straight to Xavier.

And we all dance.

Not just a daughter and a father. Not just a mother and a new son.

Two generations, honoring what love made possible.

As the song fades, Mama gently places her hand on Xavier's shoulder, easing out of his hold as they sway together on the dance floor.

"I need a moment with my baby," she says softly, eyes already shifting toward me.

Before anything can register, Mama pulls me into her arms, and I don't hold back.

I weep—*really* weep—for the first time in my life.

She cradles me like I'm five again and whispers, "I love you, Charlie. I love everything about you."

"Mama," I sniffle through tears. But I can't say anything else.

"I hope you'll come home more often," she continues. "So I can get to know my baby. I want to know you better."

I nod. Because I can't speak. And I embrace her once more.

Xavier appears with a handkerchief in hand. "You got a little snot on your lip, Peach," he murmurs, a smile playing on his lips.

I swat him in the chest, laughing through my tears as I wipe my nose. "Asshole!"

"*Your* asshole."

He tilts his head, giving me a once-over.

"All better?" I ask, lifting my chin, nose angled up like I'm waiting for inspection.

He grins, slow and soft. "Perfect," he says, pressing a kiss to the tip of my nose.

The music shifts, and as PJ Morton's *Home Again* begins to play, something soft and magnetic pulls at my chest. The melody wraps around the room, and the lyrics float through the air like a warm breeze.

Feels so good to be home again...

It's so good to see, my friend.

I hope I get to see you again... soon.

Xavier and I look at each other—no words, just a shared glance—and then we reach for our people. One by one, we gather them onto the dance floor, until the space is filled with laughter, soft smiles, and the kind of warmth that only comes from knowing you're exactly where you belong.

Timantha and Will slide in first, moving like they've done this dance a thousand times. Then Tika and Justice, still in their newly-wed haze. And right behind them, with a bashful grin that's so unlike him, Elijah walks Neva onto the floor.

I arch a brow. "*I knew* something was going on between you two," I whisper-yell as she tugs him closer, boldly guiding his hand to her booty.

Elijah shrugs, unbothered. Neva winks.

Fast, as always.

Even Jonah and his wife, Hope, make their way into the mix—his laugh deep and full, her smile beaming like she's watching a dream unfold in real time.

Xavier leans down, his lips brushing against the shell of my ear, voice low and full of something reverent. "This is our family, Mrs. Darcy."

I turn to face him, hand over his heart. "That's right, Mr. Darcy. *Ours.*"

And then, the first deep chords of *Steady Love* roll over the speakers as India Arie takes the stage.

The crowd erupts.

I laugh. I cry. I *feel.*

Because this—this is what I always wanted.

Even when I didn't know how to say it.

Even when I didn't believe it was possible.

Steady love.

Mine now. Forever.

And I'm never letting it go.

EPILOGUE

Grant

T he airport is buzzing, but in the calm of the Excelsior Airline Executive Lounge, I'm sipping a drink with my best friend these days—my daughter, Marlow.

Will and Grant finally, *begrudgingly*, signed off on my slow exit as one of the owners of the Atlanta Strikers. The deal: I stick around for six more months to train Marlow, show her the ropes, and, most importantly, keep a low profile. No scandals. No antics. No headlines with my name in them—at least not the kind that end in "...seen leaving with two blondes."

Fair enough. I've been... reckless lately. Not just in a "midlife crisis" kind of way, but more like I've been testing how far I can push the line before it snaps. Once Marlow grew up and didn't need me as much, I think I started slipping into this version of myself who thought consequences were for other people.

But let me tell you something: until your grown daughter walks in on you and two *naked, twenty-something* women—women she went to high school with—you don't know real shame. One look. One single, soul-crushing look of disappointment, and I haven't felt much of anything but that since.

So, I made a promise—to myself, to my friends, and to Marlow. I'm going to be better. A better man than the tabloids make me out to be. And honestly? I'm kind of impressing the hell out of myself.

"So you spent two entire days in Vegas and didn't get into any trouble?" Marlow asks, all disbelief and side-eye.

"Yes. Actually, I did. And it wasn't easy."

She rolls her eyes. "It's *Vegas*. No kidding."

One of Marlow's childhood friends got married this weekend. Her dad went full Gatsby—rented out several floors of the Bellagio for the bachelorette blowout and an over-the-top wedding. I haven't been to a wedding in years. Usually I ghost right after the open bar and before the vows. But since our families go way back—holidays, vacations, the whole thing—her father begged me to show up.

So I did. Stayed for the ceremony, skipped the reception. A personal record in maturity these days.

Marlow, on the other hand, looks like life steamrolled her. Two weeks out from her first official day as co-owner of the Strikers, and she's already worn out.

"It wasn't the fact that it's Vegas. I've been here enough times that the lights and glamour don't hit me the way they do some twenty-year-old on spring break."

Marlow frowns. "So what made it hard to stay on your best behavior?"

I glance down at my drink, hesitant to say it out loud. "I met someone," I say, just above a whisper, taking another slow sip.

Her face lights up. "Daddy! That's great! "

I shake my head. "Yeah. It was great... until it wasn't."

Marlow's been on my case for years. Telling me to get back out there, to stop acting like my love life died with her mother. But the truth is, her mother Matty *was* it for me. The only woman I ever saw myself building a life with. The only one I ever wanted around my daughter. So I kept the others at arm's length. Quiet. Temporary. Separate.

But now that Marlow's an adult, I've got no excuse not to go after something real. Something lasting. I just never thought I'd find anyone who lit me up the way Matty did. Until this weekend.

Marlow raises a brow. "What do you mean?"

"While you were out partying with your friends, I wandered into a bar on the Strip. I must've looked pathetic, because this woman came up to me and said I looked like I'd just lost my best friend."

She leans in, curious. "And what did you say?"

"I told her I had. My daughter."

"Aww! Great pickup line—leading with the kid."

"No. She thought you'd died. Instantly sat down to console me."

"Oh. Okay, that's *terrible*."

"Right? Once I cleared that up and explained that you and I have been pretty much joined at the hip lately—and I was just flying solo because you were off doing twenty-something things—she offered to keep me company."

"That's kind of cute."

"And so was she," I say, giving her a pointed look and a waggle of my brows.

I spend the next twenty minutes telling Marlow about Eslin—without ever saying her name. There's no need. I'll never see her again. Even though it felt like we were two people who accidentally collided into something that looked a hell of a lot like fate.

I tell her how this woman—smart, quick-witted, absolutely stunning—talked to me like she'd known me for years. How easy it was. Like breathing. And when we were a couple drinks in, and the music started to blur around the edges of our conversation, I knew I didn't want the night to end. But I also knew I didn't want to cheapen it by asking her up to my suite. So instead, I asked her to take a walk with me.

And we did. All night.

We wandered up the Strip, past the Bellagio fountains—watched them dance in sync with some Celine Dion song that made us laugh until we couldn't breathe. We weaved through drunken bachelor parties, dodged a man in a feather boa passed out on the curb, and waved off an Elvis impersonator who tried to sell us a "Love Me Tender" wedding package.

None of it mattered. The noise, the neon lights, the random flashes of humanity happening all around us—we didn't care. We were lost in the moment, in each other, in whatever the hell that magic was.

At some point, the sky started to shift. The pink edges of sunrise bleeding into the horizon. We stopped for breakfast at some 24-hour spot off the main drag. Sticky menus, bottomless coffee, and a waitress who called me "sugar" every time she refilled my cup.

We'd just started brushing up against personal details—where we lived, where we grew up. She mentioned she was originally from New York but was looking for a change, said she'd been interviewing all over the country, just seeing where life might take her next.

And then she told me.

She was thirty-one years old.

Marlow goes quiet beside me. I see the reaction flash across her face, but she says nothing. She lets me keep talking.

I'm forty-six. Almost seventeen years between us. And yeah, she's grown, mature, no question about that. But the second she said it, something shifted in me.

I couldn't stop thinking about the gap. Not just the years. The life. The fact that she was closer to Marlow's age than mine. And then this ugly thought crept in—*what if the reason I was so drawn to her had less to do with who she was and more to do with what she represented?*

Young. Temporary. Easy to lose.

Everything that's kept me from something real.

Everything I've used to *avoid* something real.

That's not the man I promised Marlow I'd be.

So after the best night of my life, I told her goodbye. No phone number. No last kiss. Just... goodbye.

"Wait," Marlow interrupts, eyebrows lifted. "You didn't even kiss her?"

"No. I told you, I didn't want to cheapen it."

She nods slowly, eyes soft, and I can tell—I've impressed my kid. And that is the best feeling in the damn world. Not disappointing her.

When I finish the story, Marlow doesn't say anything for a moment. Then she reaches over and squeezes my hand.

"That makes me sad," she says quietly. "But also... I'm proud of you. That sounds like a decision a man makes when he's finally trying to do the right thing."

I nod, but I can't bring myself to say anything else.

Because some small, stubborn part of me wonders if I did the right thing. Or if I'll ever feel that again—that spark. The kind that doesn't just light you up. It *changes* you the moment it touches you.

We board the plane a few minutes later. First class, commercial. Marlow's idea. She's been on this whole sustainable living kick and doesn't love the idea of wasting jet fuel just because we *can*.

We take our seats, buckle in. I lean my head back and close my eyes, trying to shut out the thought of her. The way she laughed, the way she touched my arm when she made a joke, the way she looked at me like I was more than some washed-up executive clinging to the edges of his youth.

Ping.

I glance at my phone. New email. From HR.

Subject line: **New Team Therapist – Welcome Aboard**

I groan. I've been dragging my feet on this for weeks. Marlow took over the interviews and the shortlist because I flat-out didn't want to deal with it. Truth is, I think I'm just tired. Tired of the grind. Of the nonstop pressure. Ready to slow down, maybe settle into something that feels more like a life and less like a treadmill.

I've never had the patience for interviews and paperwork. Never cared about résumés or references. So Marlow stepped up—worked with a headhunter, narrowed it down to a shortlist of top-tier therapists and performance coaches. We need someone strong, someone sharp. Someone who can get inside our players' heads and keep them locked in. We've got a real shot at the championship this year, and we need every man operating at full capacity.

Marlow handed off the final list to Will and Xavier last week, and Xavier actually said he was impressed with Marlow's selections.

Looks like HR has made the final decision.

I open the email, scanning it.

Eslin Saunders.

I frown. Weird coincidence. Same first name. Eslin.

And then I see it.

The photo. HR requires a staff headshot for the team roster. Doesn't matter if you're a coach, trainer, or the guy restocking the protein bars—if you work for the Strikers, you're part of the team. Standard policy: get your picture taken, get it framed, and hung in the lobby with the rest of us.

And there she is. That face. That smile. That fucking energy—undeniable, unforgettable—now staring back at me from a crisp team headshot. Her dark hair pulled into a sleek ponytail. The Strikers polo hugging her curves like it was made for her. Confident. Composed. Completely off-limits.

Eslin Saunders.

The woman I walked away from.

The woman I haven't stopped thinking about since.

The woman who, with one night and no last name, managed to rip the floor out from under me.

And now? She's ours. On payroll. Wearing the badge as the new team therapist and performance coach. *And absolutely, without question, forbidden.*

I feel the blood drain from my face. My chest tightens. My heart thuds once, hard, then free-falls.

Fuck.

Shit.

Fuckity fuck.

Fuck.

Coming Fall 2025

Get ready to fall in love with the hottest soccer team headed to the World Cup.

It all kicks off with a multi-POV holiday romcom featuring Grant, Marlow, Eslin, and Declan—where loyalty, love, and lust collide on and off the pitch.

ABOUT THE AUTHOR

Taccara, widely known for her contemporary romance novels and award-winning fiction podcasts, has amassed a devoted following of over 100,000 readers and listeners alongside her husband, Kenyon, using the power of storytelling. A former relationship coach, she now effortlessly weaves lighthearted charm with brooding, complex heroes, crafting romances that delve into the shadowy depths of love while balancing humor and heart in perfect harmony.

Writing as T.L. Martin, award-winning author Taccara Martin immerses readers in the captivating world of dark romance—and occasionally, rom-coms featuring brooding, enigmatic men. While staying true to the witty banter and deep emotional themes her readers love, she weaves in adventure, suspense, and an irresistible touch of spice.

Passionate about portraying healthy relationships, Taccara draws endless inspiration from her own love story. Married to her "forever book boyfriend," Kenyon, she credits the safety and security of their relationship as the wellspring of her creativity and romance-driven narratives.

To learn more about Taccara, explore her award-winning fiction podcasts, or sign up for her mailing list, visit **TLMartinWrites.com**

.

ALSO BY TACCARA (T.L.) MARTIN

Whether you're diving into stories by Taccara Martin or T.L. Martin, the world of *Cinnamon Grove* was designed to bring these characters together in ways that feel interconnected and alive. It's a place where heartfelt, emotional journeys meet lighthearted banter and unexpected connections.

If you're drawn to the emotional depth and complexity of Taccara Martin's stories but also crave the humor and charm of a good rom-com, I encourage you to explore the romantic comedies by T.L. Martin. There's something for everyone in this shared universe, and I can't wait for you to discover all the ways these characters' lives intertwine!

Contemporary Romance by Taccara Martin:
- **Day One,** Love Stories from the Unmasked Podcast, Book

1

- **This Time It's Love,** Love Stories from the Unmasked Podcast, Book 2

- **So Into You,** Love Stories from the Unmasked Podcast, Book 3

- **Become "Us,"** Coming 2026

Rom-Coms with a Dark Romance Edge by T.L. Martin
- **The Black Wife Effect**

- **My Filthy Rich Valentine,** The Black Wife Effect, Book 2

- **The Seven Day Hitch**, The Black Wife Effect, Book 3

Dark Romance by T.L. Martin
- **Fury's Embrace,** Friends of Fury, Book 1

To learn more about Taccara, her fiction podcasts or upcoming projects, visit **TLMartinWrites.com.**

www.ingramcontent.com/pod-product-compliance
Lightning Source LLC
Chambersburg PA
CBHW021844010726
47493CB00005B/1542